ITHACA

CLAIRE NORTH

ITHACA

REDHOOK

Redhook Books/Orbit
Hachette Book Group
1290 Avenue of the Americas
New York, NY 10104
hachettebookgroup.com

First Edition: September 2022
Simultaneously published in Great Britain by Orbit

Redhook is an imprint of Orbit, a division of Hachette Book Group.
The Redhook name and logo are trademarks of Hachette Book Group, Inc.

The publisher is not responsible for websites (or their content)
that are not owned by the publisher.

The Hachette Speakers Bureau provides a wide range of authors for speaking events. To find out more, go to www.hachettespeakersbureau.com or call (866) 376-6591.

Library of Congress Control Number: 2021951532

ISBNs: 9780316422963 (hardcover), 9780316668798 (ebook)

Printed in the United States of America

LSC-C

Printing 1, 2022

Dramatis Personae

>>>

The Family of Odysseus

Penelope – wife of Odysseus, queen of Ithaca
Odysseus – husband of Penelope, king of Ithaca
Telemachus – son of Odysseus and Penelope
Laertes – father of Odysseus
Anticlea – mother of Odysseus

Councillors of Odysseus

Medon – an old, friendly councillor
Aegyptius – an old, less friendly councillor
Peisenor – a former warrior of Odysseus

Suitors of Penelope and their kin

Antinous – son of Eupheithes
Eupheithes – master of the docks, father of Antinous
Eurymachus – son of Polybus
Polybus – master of the granaries, father of Eurymachus
Amphinomous – a warrior of Greece
Andraemon – a veteran of Troy

Minta – comrade and friend of Andraemon
Kenamon – an Egyptian
Nisas – a suitor of low renown

Maids and commoners

Eos – maid of Penelope, comber of hair
Autonoe – maid of Penelope, keeper of the kitchen
Melantho – maid of Penelope, chopper of wood
Melitta – maid of Penelope, scrubber of tunics
Phiobe – maid of Penelope, friendly to all
Leaneira – maid of Penelope, a Trojan
Euracleia – Odysseus' old nursemaid
Dares – a young man of Ithaca

Women of Ithaca

Priene – a warrior from the east
Teodora – an orphan of Ithaca
Anaitis – priestess of Artemis
Ourania – spymaster of Penelope
Semele – an old widow, mother of Mirene
Mirene – Semele's daughter

Mycenaeans

Elektra – daughter of Agamemnon and Clytemnestra
Orestes – son of Agamemnon and Clytemnestra
Clytemnestra – wife of Agamemnon, cousin of Penelope
Agamemnon – conqueror of Troy
Iphgenia – daughter of Agamemnon and Clytemnestra, sacrificed
    to the goddess Artemis
Pylades – sworn brother to Orestes
Iason – a soldier of Mycenae
Aegisthus – Clytemnestra's lover

Spartans

Icarius – father of Penelope
Polycaste – Icarius' wife, adoptive mother of Penelope
Tyndareus – father of Clytemnestra and Helen, brother of Icarius

The gods and assorted divinities

Hera – goddess of mothers and wives
Athena – goddess of wisdom and war
Artemis – goddess of the hunt
Calypso – a nymph

CHAPTER 1

>>

T eodora is not the first to see the raiders, but she is the
first to run.

They come from the north, by the light of the full moon.
They do not burn any lanterns on their decks, but skim across the
ocean like tears down a mirror. There are three ships, carrying
some thirty men apiece, coils of rope set by the prow to bind
their slaves; oars barely tugging the sea as the wind carries them
to shore. They give no cries of war, beat no drums nor blow
trumpets of brass or bone. Their sails are plain and patched, and
had I power over the stars I would have willed them shine a little
brighter, that the heavens might be eclipsed by the darkness of
the ships as they obstructed the horizon. But the stars are not my
domain, nor do I usually pay much attention to the dealings of
little people in their sleepy villages by the sea, save when there is
some great matter afoot that might be turned by a wily hand – or
when my husband has strayed too far from home.

It is therefore without celestial intervention that Teodora, lips
inclining towards those of her may-be lover, thinks she catches
sight of something strange upon the sea. The few fisherwomen
who ride the night are all known to her and their prows are
nothing like the shapes she glimpses in the corner of her eye.

Then Dares – a young fool, certainly more foolish than she – catches her by her chin and pulls her deeper into his embrace, hand fumbling somewhat impertinently for her breast, and she has other things on her mind.

Above the village, a torch gutters upon the cliffs. It has been only briefly raised, a guide in the night to show these raiders where to go. Now its work is done, and the figure who has held it retreats down the hard stone path towards the inland slumber of the isle, feeling no compunction to stay and witness his work. It would be fair of this fellow to think himself unseen, save by his allies – the hour is late and the hot day had faded to a cool, slumbering dark, suitable for vast snoring and dreamless sleep. How little he knows.

In a cave above the shore, a queen in rags and dirt looks out onto the night, the blood still sticky on her hands, and sees the raiders come, but does not think they come for her. So she does not call out to the village below, but cries for her lover, who is dead.

In the east, a king rolls restlessly in the arms of Calypso, who hushes him and says, it is just a dream, my love. Everything beyond these shores is just a dream.

To the south, another fleet with black sails sits becalmed, the rowers asleep beneath the patient sky, while a princess caresses her brother's sweating brow.

And on the beach, Teodora is beginning to suspect that Dares may not be entirely pure in his attentions, and that they should really start talking of marriage if this is the way things are going to go. She pushes him away with both her palms, but he holds her tight. In the brief shuffling of their feet on bony white sand, his eyes turn up and he at last sees the ships, sees their course for this little cove, and with a sluggish wit he declares: "Uh . . . ?"

Dares' mother owns a grove of olive trees, two slaves and a cow. In the eyes of the sages of the island, these things are in fact owned by Dares' father — but he never came home from Troy, and as the years ticked down and Dares grew from whelp to man, even the most pedantic elders stopped labouring the point. One day, shortly after his fifteenth birthday, Dares turned to his mother and mused: "It's a good thing for you I let you hang around," and in that moment her hope died, though he was a monster of her own making. He can fish, not well, dreams of turning pirate, and has not yet tasted hunger in the winter.

Teodora's father was sixteen when he wed her mother; seventeen when he went to Troy. He left behind his bow, being a weapon for cowards, a few pots and a shawl his mother made. Last winter Teodora killed a lynx that was as hungry as her, the knife with which she would otherwise gut fish driven into its snapping jaw, and has few qualms about making snap decisions when death is on the line.

"Raiders!" she shouts, first to Dares, who hasn't yet released her from his embrace, and when he finally does, to the village above and the slumbering night, running towards the low mud of hut and home as if she could catch the echo of her own voice. "Raiders! Raiders are coming!"

It is well known that when a grieving wife looks to the sea for the ship of her husband and glimpses a sail threaded with gold, time will slow its pounding chariot to a crawl, and every minute of the ship's return is an hour pricked out in sweating agony. Yet when pirates come to your shore, it is as if their vessels grow Hermes' wings and leap, leap across the water, now rounding the hard pillars of stone where the crabs scuttle sideways, black-eyed and orange-backed, now driven by the relentless oars prow-first up the soft lip of the sand. Now men leap from the decks of the beaching ships; now they have axes in hand and carry crude shields of battered bronze and animal hide, their faces painted in pigment and ash. Now they charge from the water's edge, not as soldiers do, but as wolves, splitting and circling their prey, howling, teeth bared silver in the moon's gentle light.

Teodora has reached the village before them. Phenera is a place of little square houses set above the thin stream that carves its passage between two cliffs of blackened stone to run giddy into the cove. When it rains too hard in winter, the mud walls slop and flop away, and the roofs are constantly a-mending. Here they dry fish and pick at mussels, tend to goats and gossip about their neighbours. Their shrine is to Poseidon, who protects the thin-hulled boats they push into the bay and who, if I know anything about the old fart, doesn't care a whelp for the meagre offerings of grain and wine they spill upon his altar.

That at least is the picture that Phenera wishes the eye to behold; but look a little closer and you may find trinkets that shine beneath the rough wooden floors, and many a finger that is skilled at more than just fixing a net to catch fish in.

"Raiders! Raiders!" Teodora howls, and slowly a few dusty cloths are pulled back from the crooked doors, a few eyes blink into the shallow dark and shouts begin to rise in alarm. Then voices older and a little more respected sound as other eyes behold the men rushing upon their shores, and hands reach to gather their most precious goods, and like ants from the boiling nest, the people flee.

Too late.

Too late, for so many – too late.

Their only blessing is that these men of snarling lip and beating shield do not want to kill the youngest and the strongest. It is enough to scare them into cowering submission, to beat them and bind them with rope to take to some place to sell. The two slaves kept in Dares' house look upon their new captors with weary eyes, for they have been through all this before, when they were first taken by the bold men of Ithaca. Their wretched despair at finding themselves encircled by blade and shield is a bit of a let-down for their attackers, who expected at the least some abject grovelling, but the whole atmosphere is somewhat redeemed when the masters and mistresses of Phenera wail and weep. They are reduced now to the level of those they had mastered, and their former slaves tut and say just do as we do, just say what we say, you will learn – you will learn.

Teodora stops to gather only one precious thing – the bow she keeps for killing rabbits. Nothing more. She has nothing so precious as her life, and so she runs, runs, runs for the hills, runs like Atalanta reborn, grabbing the branch of the thin-trunked dying tree that juts out from a promontory to pull herself up; climbing over stone and under leaf to the chittering black while below her home starts to burn. She hears footsteps behind her, the drumming of heavy weight upon the scrubby path, glances over her shoulder, sees torchlight and shadow, near stumbles on a treacherous root in her path, and is caught before she can fall. Hands grasp, old eyes stare, blink, a finger to the lips. Teodora is pulled quickly from her path into darkness, into thicket-leaf shadow, where hunkers a woman with hair like autumn clouds, skin like summer sand, an axe in her hand, a hunting knife on her belt. She could with such implements perhaps fight back; perhaps slam her blade into the throat of the man who pursues them, but what use would that be? None, tonight. None at all. So instead they hide, wrapped in each other's eyes, their gazes screaming *quiet, quiet, quiet!* Until at last the footsteps of their pursuer fade away.

The old woman who holds Teodora in safety is called Semele, and she prays to Artemis, who does not deserve her devotions.

In the village below, Dares is less sensible. He was raised on stories of the warrior men of Odysseus, and like all boys has learnt something of the spear and the blade. As the straw rooftops begin to burn, he retrieves his sword from beneath the cot of his mother's house, steps four paces from his smoking door, gripping the hilt with both hands, sees an Illyrian dressed in flame and blood approach, takes up his stance, and actually manages to parry the first blow that comes for him. This surprises everyone, including Dares, and at the next thrust he turns his body and manages to smack his blade down so hard on the end of the short stabbing spear that the wood cracks and splinters. However, his delight at this development doesn't last long, for his killer draws a short sword from his belt, turns in the direction of Dares' next attack, comes under his guard, and splits him clean across the belly.

I will say this for the pirate – he had the courtesy to drive his blade through Dares' heart, rather than simply leave him to die. The boy hadn't earned such a clean death, but neither, I suppose, had he lived long enough to deserve the one that came for him.

CHAPTER 2

>>>

R osy-fingered dawn crawled its way across Ithaca's back
like an awkward lover fumbling at long skirts. The light
of day should have been as crimson as the blood in the sea
below Phenera; it should have circled the island like the sharks.
Look towards the horizon, and even the eyes of the gods strain
a little to see three sails disappearing into the east, with their
stolen cargo of animals, grains and slaves. They will be gone,
long gone, before the ships of Ithaca raise their sails.

Let us speak briefly of Ithaca.

It is a thoroughly backwards, wretched place. The golden
touch of my footstep upon its meagre soil; the caress of my
voice in the ears of its salt-scarred mothers – Ithaca does not
deserve such divine attentions. But then again, its barren
misery leads the other gods to rarely look upon it either, and
so it is a miserable truth that I, Hera, mother of Olympus,
who drove Heracles mad and struck vain royalty into stone –
why here at least I may sometimes work without the censure
of my kin.

Forget the songs of Apollo, or the proud declarations of
haughty Athena. Their poems only glorify themselves. Listen
to my voice: I who have been stripped of honour, of power

and of that fire that should be mine, I who have nothing to lose that the poets have not already taken from me, only I will tell you the truth. I, who part the veil of time, will tell those stories that only the women tell. So follow me to the western isles, to the halls of Odysseus, and listen.

The island of Ithaca guards the watery mouth of Greece like an old cracked tooth, barely a scratch upon the ocean. A stout pair of even human legs might walk it in a day, if they could bear to spend so much time staggering through grubby forest of skulking trees that seem to grow only so far as the laziest necessity for grim survival, or over scrambling rocks of jutting stone that protrude from the earth like the fingers of the dead. Indeed, the island is remarkable only in that some fool thought it an apt locale upon which to attempt to build what the uncouth locals consider a "city" – if a scraggy hillside of crooked houses clinging to the harsh sea may be considered worthy of the name – and above this city, a so-called "palace".

From this termite hall the kings of Ithaca send forth their commands across the western isles, all of which are far more pleasant than this wretched rock. Yet though the people of Hyrie, Paxi, Lefkada, Kephalonia, Kythira and Zakynthos who live beneath Ithaca's dominion may grow olives and grapes upon their shores, may eat rich barley and even rear the occasional cow, all the peoples of this little dominion are as ultimately uncouth as each other, varying only in their flawed pretensions. Neither the great princes of Mycenae or Sparta, Athens or Corinth, nor the poets who travel door to door have much cause to speak of Ithaca and her isles save as the butt of a joke about goats – until recently, that is. Until Odysseus.

Let us therefore to Ithaca go, in that warm late summer when the leaves begin to crinkle and the ocean clouds tumble in too mighty to be bothered by the little land below. It is the morning after full moon, and in the city beneath the palace of Odysseus, some few hours away by bare foot on hard soil, the first prayers are being sung in the temple of Athena. It is a crooked wooden thing, squat as if frightened of being blown apart in the storm, but with some notable pieces of pillaged gold and silver that only rustics would find magnificent. I avoid passing even a place so dull, lest my stepdaughter show her smug, preening face, or worse, whisper to my husband that she saw me afoot in the world of men. Athena is a priggish little madam; let us move by her shrine in haste.

There is a market that runs from the docks all the way to the gates of the palace. Here you may trade timber, stone, hides, goats, sheep, pigs, ducks – even the occasional horse or cow – beads, bronze, brass, amber, silver, tin, rope, clay, flax, dye and pigment, hides of animals both common and rare, fruit, vegetables and of course – fish. So much fish. The western isles, every one of them, stink of fish. When I return to Olympus, I will have to bathe in ambrosia to wash the stench away, before some gossipy little nymph catches the whiff of me.

There are many houses, ranging from the humble homes of the craftsmen who can barely keep a slave to the grander courtyard sprawls of the great men who would rather be across the water in Kephalonia, where the hunting is better and, if you go inland, you might lose the smell of fish for a few minutes to catch instead the whiff of dung – change being a relief of its kind. There are two smiths, who after many years of rivalry finally realised they were better fixing prices together than competing apart. There is a tannery, and a place that was once a brothel but which was forced to take up the weaving and dyeing of clothes when a large part of its clientele set sail for war, and as no ships have returned from Troy carrying victorious Ithacans, they continue weaving and dyeing to this day.

It has been nearly eighteen years since the manhood of Ithaca sailed to Troy, and even the many ships passing through port since that city fell have not been enough for whoring to be better economics than mastery of a nice bit of dye.

Above it all: the palace of Odysseus. It was the palace of Laertes for a while, and I have no doubt the old man wanted it to remain known by that glorious name, his legacy carved into stone – an Argonaut, no less, a man who once sailed, under my banner, to fetch the golden fleece, before that little shit Jason betrayed me. But Laertes grew old before all the men of Greece were summoned to Troy. Thus the son eclipsed the father, new daubs of black and red smeared across the corridors, wide-eyed and ochre-tinged. Odysseus and his bow. Odysseus in battle. Odysseus winning the armour of fallen Achilles. Odysseus with calves of an ox and Atlas's shoulders. In the eighteen years since the king of Ithaca was last sighted on this isle, his somewhat short, unimpressive and far too hairy form has grown in stature and personal hygiene, if only in the poet's eye.

The poets will tell you a lot about the heroes of Troy. Some details they have correct; in others, as with all things, they lie. They lie to please their masters. They lie without knowing what they do, for it is the poet's art to make every ear that hears the ancient songs think they have been sung for them alone, the old made new. Whereas I sing for no creature's pleasure but my own, and can attest that what you think you know of the last heroes of Greece, you do not know at all.

Follow me through the halls of the palace of Odysseus; follow to hear the stories that the men-poets of the greedy kings do not tell.

Even in dawn's thinly mirrored light, the perfect white that bounces in off the sea, the great hall is a shadowed pit of inequity. The stench of men, of spilt wine and chewed bone, of flatulence and bile mingled with sweat – I pause in the door to pinch my nose at it. The maids are about already, trying their best to wash away the stink of last night's feast, to return the plates to the kitchen and burn sweet herbs to clear the fetid air, but their work is interrupted by a few of the men still snoring like pigs beneath the table, hands out-reached to the ashes of the fire as if they had dreamt of ice.

These snoring lullards, these lumpen males are but a handful of suitors who sweep in and out like the tides from Odysseus's door, feasting on his land and pawing at the skirts of his maids. There were twenty of them two years ago; fifty at the last turning of the sun, and now near one hundred men have come to Ithaca, all with one purpose – to win the hand of Odysseus's mourning, lonesome queen.

The painted eyes of Odysseus may watch from the walls, but he is dead – he is dead! the suitors exclaim. It has been eighteen years since he sailed from Ithaca, eight since Troy fell, seven since he was last sighted on the isle of Aeolus – he is drowned, surely he is drowned! No one is that bad a sailor. Come, oh tearful queen, come: it is time to pick a new man. It is time to pick a new king.

I know them all, these would-be princelings, snuggled shoulder to shoulder like sleeping dogs. Antinous, son of Eupheithes, his dark hair waxed and oiled in a glistening hive swept back from his brow, so stiff it stirs neither by rain nor sweat. He wears his father's wealth in his tunic, which is hemmed with crimson purchased from a Cretan man who had no teeth, and in the tapestry of beads and gold slung casually about his neck as if to say, "What, these old things? I found them behind an amphora of wine, as one does – as one does." Antinous was five years old when Odysseus went to war, and stood on the docks and cried and stamped his foot and wanted to know why he couldn't be a soldier. Now Achilles is dead, Ajax and Hector rot in dust, and Antinous asks no more.

Snorting and slumbering next to him, Eurymachus, whose father Polybus avoided going to war by sailing to the western colonies on "urgent business" that took ten urgent years – and whose nursemaid spoiled him rotten and told him he was descended from Heracles. Every little twerp is descended from Heracles these days, it's practically a requirement for entry to polite society. Perhaps it is the tracery of sunlight in Eurymachus's hair that gives the impression of some sordid divinity, but though a young man, his forehead is already climbing and his flaxen mane grows thin. Only his laughable oar-ish height and skinniness distracts from this fact, and he peers down upon the world as if perpetually surprised to find it still turning beneath his flapping feet.

Who else here of note? Amphinomous, son of a king, who was taught that honour is everything and suspects, perhaps, that he is not honourable but doesn't entirely know what to do about the situation. His father was fruitful in sons, gourd-faced boys the lot of them, who rarely quarrelled and who made music like the whines of Cerberus. They are all dead now, three by Trojan hands, save Amphinomous, who will do what he must.

Andraemon, who does not sleep, but watches the maids with one eye open from where he has fallen across his folded arms. Did salt or sand dry his skin so that nails down his back make the sound of bone over leather? Did the harsh sun of Troy bleach his hair to such a burnished hue, does he have to throw discus every morn and every night to maintain such contours about his chest, chin, shoulders, arms – or is he blessed of Ares and Aphrodite, that men might quake and women swoon at his sight?

A little secret: he is not blessed, and arms like his are not casually made.

These are the men of note. We regard them as one might regard a rash – hopeful that it does not spread further – and then move on.

About these slumbering suitors are the other part of this story – the part that the poets do not name, save to lie. The maids of the palace are many in number, for the palace itself is a little industry. No monarch of Ithaca dare rely on favourable winds and rich soils for regular income of grain – instead, the women keep ducks, geese, pigs, goats; they fish in a little cove where only the women go, prise mussels from black stone and tend to groves of olive and fields of barley as mere and tough as the mouths that will eat them; and at night, when the last of the suitors finally are asleep, they lie down and dream the dreams that are all their own. Listen – listen. Let us peek behind fresh-washed faces; let us swim in the soul of a passing maid.

. . . spin the yarn to make the thread an easy job my feet would kill for an easy job . . .

Antinous looked at me last night, I wonder if he thinks . . .

Must tell Melantho must tell her she'll howl she'll scream it'll be hilarious where's Melantho must tell her now!

But here, why listen here, here is a voice that whispers out of tune.

Death to the Greeks, beats the heart of one whose hair falls like clotted blood above her neck, her eyes down to the floor. *Death to all the Greeks.*

Of these maids of Ithaca – these slave women and sold girls, these indentured daughters – so much more of them will I have to say. I am the goddess of queens, wives and women; my tasks may be thankless, but I perform them nonetheless. But alas, events are already in motion that require our attention, and so let us look to the north.

From the hard carved road that winds down the terraced valley into what we will grudgingly call a city, Teodora comes. She has given up running; now each footfall is one at a time, counting the steps, forward without a destination, head first, heels twisting, and people scurry to clear a way before her. She carries a bow without arrows, and an old woman walks at her side. Their arrival will only make things harder, but I never shied from trouble.

By the palace gate, a man called Medon is preparing to do his rounds of the market. He is officially the voice of Ithaca, sent from the palace to proclaim the rulings of Ithaca's king. Ithaca's king has not been home for eighteen years, and he certainly can't proclaim the rulings of some queen, so these days he proclaims very little and just hopes people get the idea and realise what's good for them. Lately his optimism on that latter point is growing thin. With a round, soft belly beneath a round, drooping face, he is one of very few men older than twenty-five on the island, and it is perhaps this novelty that causes Teodora to slow as she approaches him, swaying a little from the rising heat and broken weight of the night, before stopping altogether in front of him, staring long into his eyes as if she might find evidence that all this were just a dream resting in the pupil, and proclaiming simply: "The pirates came."

CHAPTER 3

>>>

In a chamber built to catch the morning light that hangs crooked off the side of the palace like an old dangling wart, three old men, a boy who would be a man and three women are assembled to discover just how bad a day Ithaca is going to have.

Of these, the three men and the boy consider themselves the most pertinent. They stand round a table of yew set with shards of tortoiseshell, and bicker.

One of them we have met – Medon – who has been awake since before the sun rose and is already tired of the day. The other three are called Peisenor, Aegyptius and Telemachus.

Here are some of the things they say:

"Fucking pirates. Fucking pirates! There was a day, you know, there was a day when – fucking pirates!"

"Thank you for that strategic assessment, Peisenor."

"They hit Lefkada a month ago. Full moon, Illyrians – northern barbarians! If it's the same clan then . . ."

"If we still had a fleet . . ."

"We don't."

"We could bring the ships up from Zakynthos . . ."

"And leave the farmers open to attack before harvest?"

"Can I ask a question?"

15

"Not now, Telemachus!"

There are only two kinds of men on Ithaca – those too old or too young to fight when Odysseus sailed to war. (Technically, there is a third category – the cowards, the slaves and that man who could not afford a sword, but who really cares for them? Not the poets; not the gods.) Between these gulfs of age, there is a hollow where the finest of Ithaca's manhood should be. The fathers and would-be fathers of a new generation did not return, so that to see a native man older than thirty but younger than sixty-five is remarkable. There are no husbands for the wives, and more widows than shrines in the western isles.

Let us then consider these men who were too old to go to war and a whelp who had a near miss with a plough in one of his father's more bat-brained schemes when just a babe.

Aegyptius, who might well have served Odysseus at Troy but was such a pain in that king's backside, such a humourless dolt, that the wily general found some other use for him at home that left everyone's dignity intact, and the cramped deck of his ship considerably more motivated. He rises and bends like the willow tree, and his bald head is crowned with a constellation of moles, etched with flowing rivers where bone meets bone beneath the thin skin, baked to leather by the sun. "Perhaps the time has come to consider mercenaries . . . "

"Can't trust a mercenary. They're on your side until they get bored and then they're pillaging the treasure." Peisenor, hairy as the boar, squat as the low hills that bred him. He lost his left hand pillaging for Laertes and cannot hold a shield, and in private laments, laments, laments that he is less than a man and has done everything he possibly can in the last few years to remind the world that he is therefore, absolutely, a warrior and a hero.

"What treasure?" Medon, who feels the ageing process accelerating with every moment he spends in this chamber.

"Excuse me . . . "

"In a moment, Telemachus – look, every other king in Greece came from Troy with plundered riches. They say that when Agamemnon returned, it took five days just to unload his personal treasure – five days. They say Menelaus washes in a golden bath."

"Menelaus has never taken a bath in his life."

"He didn't exactly rush back from war, did he? I heard he and his brother went sailing south, there's Egyptian gold in his haul – I heard that the Cretans are pissed."

"Whereas we have just enough wealth to be plundered, but not enough to defend ourselves."

"Excuse me!"

Telemachus. Eighteen years old, he gets to stand here because he is Odysseus's son – though this is a mixed blessing. His hair is not as majestically golden as his father's (whose hair is in fact a greying brown, but the poets, the poets!), and there is perhaps something of his grandmother naiad in his pallor, a moistness about his freckled features that not even his daily hours of practice with spear and shield can harden into clay. Oh, one day his shoulders will be broad and his thighs will be like the giant's clubs, but for now he is still a boy struggling to grow his first beard, pushing his voice a little deeper than it should go and telling himself to stand up straight nearly as often as he slouches. Athena says he has great potential, and Hermes, whose blood flows through the scions of this house, reports that he just wants to fly down and give Telemachus a big soppy hug. But my brother Hades, who has a more sensible grasp of these things, looks into the mist and murmurs: "Some families never can find north."

Odysseus is a terrible sailor. I do not see any sign his son has inherited a better sense of direction.

"Surely we can train our own men, I mean, we have some men, we have ... "

"That won't work, Telemachus."

"But I . . . "

Telemachus never quite finishes his sentences. When he is introduced to people, it is as "Odysseus's son, Telemachus". His father's name is always put first, and it is as if this quirk of language has infected Telemachus's own voice, so that he can't quite see his way through to the end of any meaningful sentence that might have something of himself in it. His father's fame creates as many problems as it solves, for as the son of a hero Telemachus naturally needs to set sail and be a hero himself, lest his father eclipse him as Odysseus did his own progenitor. However, to set sail, it is most prudent to have an army at your back – much easier to be a hero when there's someone to patch a sheet and do the cooking – and given that Ithaca's warriors have not returned and are, truth be told, all dead save one, this presents something of a logistical challenge.

"There's an obvious answer . . . " muses Aegyptius.

"Here we go," sighs Medon.

"Eurymachus or Antinous . . . "

"A domestic match will bring the wrath of the mainland. What about the suitors from Corinth, or even Thebes? Or what's-his-face from Colchis, he seems nice."

"There's some Egyptian fella waiting outside, can you believe it?" Peisenor has never met an Egyptian before, but is certain he doesn't approve. "Smells nice, though."

"My father isn't dead!" Telemachus has said this so many times, it has become as remarkable to the ears of the listeners as the chittering of the cicada in the field, and so they ignore it.

"No, no, no! An overseas match will bring civil war, the islands won't stand for it, we'd have to send for aid to Mycenae, or worse, to Menelaus, can you imagine Spartan soldiers on Ithaca's soil, it would be . . . "

"Marry the wrong man and Menelaus will come anyway."

"*My father isn't dead!*"

Telemachus has shouted. Telemachus never shouts. Odysseus *never* shouted, except for once when he screamed at his men to take him to the sirens – but then those were exceptional circumstances. No one tuts at the son's breach of protocol, his lack of decorum, but for a moment even the women look up, mute, wide-eyed, watching. Oh – did you forget the women were there too, at this learned assemblage? So too will the poets, when this song is sung.

"My father isn't dead," Telemachus repeats, quieter, calm, fingers gripping the edge of the table, head bowed. "For my mother to remarry is impossible. It is profane."

The older men look away.

After a little while, so do the women, not that their gazes were particularly relevant. They are ornamentations to this scene. If the poets speak of them at all, it will be in much the same breath as a pleasing vase or a nice shield – a sculptural detail, adding a certain flavour to the event. It is perhaps sensing this that the three women have arranged themselves as a picture of modesty. One, Autonoe, chestnut hair and face hard as a dried starfish, brittle and beautiful and not for the gaze of men, busies herself with tuning a lyre. She has been tuning it for nearly half an hour now, and can't quite seem to get it right. Beside her, Eos, shorter and plump around the hips, a grape of a face and freckles across her skin, combs rough yarn into fine threads, brushing it with the same care she applies to her mistress's hair. She can do this with her eyes shut and ears open – always her ears open.

The final woman should perhaps be weaving at the small square loom she is oft seen with in public – but no, this is a private place, for serious business, so instead she sits with hands still in her lap, chin turned up, a little away from the men around the table, listening with an intensity that would frighten Ajax (who was always more scared of women than death), yet with eyes averted so as to not too greatly discombobulate her council with the force of her attention.

She is Penelope, wife of Odysseus, lady of the house, queen of Ithaca and the source, she is assured by a great many men, of nothing but woe and strife. This strikes her as an unfair accusation, but to unravel it now would perhaps take more breath than mortal lungs have to give.

Her skin is unfashionably dark for a Grecian queen, her hair black as the midnight sea – but she will be depicted as blonde, which is more desirable, and the poets will skip over just how baggy are her tired eyes. Though queen, Penelope doesn't sit at the table; it wouldn't be right. But she is still a dutiful wife to a missing king, and though nearly everyone is quite sure that the weighty business of council will pass over her dear little head, it is pleasing to see a woman taking her work seriously.

Penelope listens, hands in her lap, while her council bickers.

"Telemachus, we know you love your father ..."

"There has been no body – there's no body! Odysseus lives, until there is a body he ..."

"... and it's wonderful that he might be alive, truly it is, but the fact remains that the rest of Greece is convinced that he is not and the rest of Greece grows impatient! The western isles need a king ..."

If she is interested in these men discussing her husband, or lack of husband, or prospects for acquiring another husband or whatever it is that is most politically pertinent today, Penelope does not show it. She seems fascinated by the black spirals frescoed onto the very top of the wall, as if she has only just noticed how easily a painted wave may also be a painted cloud, or how the imperfections in an artist's eye gives a thing its character.

At her feet, Autonoe plucks a string – plonk – and it is out of tune.

Eos teases thread from wool, the tips of her fingers barely moving in a busy spider's dance.

Finally Aegyptius says: "Perhaps if we had some of Odysseus's gold . . . "

"What gold?"

Aegyptius's eyes flicker to Penelope, and away. Naturally the wise men of Ithaca run the palace finances and make all large decisions, as men must. Yet the wily mathematics of the Hittites or the peculiar scratching of stylus upon clay or potentates of ash upon papyrus that the foreigners call "writing" have not yet come to Greece's shores, and thus the suspicion lingers – unproven, untested – that there is something more to the fiscal management of Ithaca than these scholars can perceive. Penelope protests her poverty, yet she does keep feeding the suitors, a feast every night, as befits her duty as hostess – how is that?

How indeed? Aegyptius wonders, and so do many who come knocking at Penelope's door. How indeed?

"Why can't we train our own men?" Telemachus is doing his best not to pout, and for a moment the older men shuffle uneasily, unsure whether to waste their time in indulging the question. "We have militias on Lefkada, Kephalonia. Why not Ithaca?"

"It's not like Lefkada's soldiers did them any good," mutters Medon, face like the mudslide. "When the raiders hit them at full moon, half the militia was drunk and the other half away on the furthest end of the isle."

"They were incompetent. We will not be incompetent." Telemachus seems very sure of this, which based on the last eighteen years seems optimistic.

It is Penelope who answers. This is acceptable – she is speaking not as a queen, which would be uncouth – but as a mother. "Even if there were men enough on Ithaca, who would be their leader? You, Telemachus? If you muster from Ithaca a hundred spears, loyal to your name, then who's to say that you won't turn

21

those spears against the suitors and claim your father's crown? Antinous and Eurymachus are both sons of powerful men; Amphinomous and the suitors from further afield can bring in mercenaries from Pylos or Calydon. The moment they perceive you as a threat, leading a band of men, they will set aside their differences, ally against you, and united could easily out-match you. Better to kill you pre-emptively, of course, before it comes to that. Avoid the fuss."

"But this has nothing to do with them. This is the defence of our home."

"Everything is to do with them," she sighs. "Even if it isn't, what matters is that they think it is."

Telemachus, like all mortals and immortals alike, hates being told he is wrong. He loathes it, and for the briefest moment his face scrunches as if he would swallow his own features and spew them up again in bile and blood; but he is not a total dolt, so he just about restrains himself from self-consumption, pauses, considers and blurts: "Fine. We raise soldiers together. Amphinomous understands the way of things. And Eurymachus isn't unreasonable. If they want Ithaca so badly, they'll have to defend it."

"That assumes that one of them isn't behind the attacks."

"Northern devils – Illyrians . . . "

"It is a long way south for Illyrians to raid. Very bold. And Medon is right – how did they manage to hit Lefkada, sail home, resupply and be back in Ithaca by full moon? And why did they attack Phenera, a small village of little note, having sailed all this way? There are implications we must consider."

Indeed there are, but Telemachus is not a boy for implications.

"*I* can defend Ithaca, Mother. *I* am capable."

"Of course you are," she lies, "But until you can raise a hundred men in secret from across the isles and bring them here, or find a way to prevent our guests allying in greater strength than

22

that you can raise against them, I'm afraid we need a nuanced approach."

Telemachus's sigh is audible, and passes without comment. He learnt to sigh from Euracleia, beloved nursemaid of Odysseus, who huffs and puffs and finds nothing to her satisfaction. Of Penelope's many regrets, allowing this habit to embed in her son is high on the list.

In the silence that settles, no one meets anyone else's eye. The maid Autonoe looks for a moment like she might laugh, and manages to turn it into a near-burp, swallowed hard. Finally Medon says: "Have any of the suitors ... mentioned anything pertinent to you?"

"Pertinent?" Penelope's eyelashes are not like those of her cousin, Helen. She is not skilled in fluttering them, but has seen others try, so gives it her best shot now. It is markedly unsuccessful.

"Offers of support, perhaps. Or ... conversations around defence."

"They all say the same thing. They will be the strong man, the brave man, the one to bring peace at last to this kingdom, the king that Ithaca deserves and so on. Details, though – they are weak on details. Details are not a thing to be discussed with a queen."

"The boy's right." Raised eyebrows turn towards Peisenor, who nods grimly across the table as if he were already coated in blood. "*If* we can't afford mercenaries ..." Such a weight in his *if*! Such a turning of his lips around the sound – he too is not entirely sure he knows the source of Penelope's wealth, but unlike the others has not even heard of the concept of accounting. "... then we have no choice. We need a militia to defend Ithaca – to defend the palace and the queen. It's been too long. I'll talk to Antinous and Eurymachus, and their fathers. Amphinomous too. If they agree, the others will fall in line.

23

We'll find someone to lead it that everyone will accept, someone who isn't aligned to either Telemachus or a suitor."

"I want to join," blurts Telemachus, and:

"Absolutely not," retorts Penelope.

"Mother! If our land is threatened, I will defend it!"

"Even if — by some miracle — Antinous and Eurymachus agree to put aside their ambition for more than half a day to raise a militia, who will serve in it? There are no men on Ithaca. There are boys raised without fathers, and old men — forgive my bluntness, Peisenor. The Illyrians may be barbarians, but they are warriors. I will not risk your life ... "

"*My* life!" snaps Telemachus, and again he's raised his voice, his father wouldn't have done that, but ah well, ah well, he was raised by women. "I am a man! I am the head of this household!" He is lucky that he doesn't squeak when he says that. His voice broke a little later than he'd hoped, but it's all right now, he might even grow a beard some time soon. "I am head of this house," he repeats, a little less sure of himself. "And I *will* defend my kingdom."

The council shifts uneasily, and Penelope is silent. There are absolutely things that should be said, matters of deep weight and urgency, but each man now seems lost in his own prophecy, looking to a future in which nothing ends well for a single one of them.

Finally Penelope rises like the swan uncoiling from its rest, and out of courtesy the men take a step back and bow a little — she is after all Odysseus's wife. "Phenera — there were survivors?"

The question takes them aback for a moment, before Peisenor replies. "A few. A girl came to the palace, accompanied by an old woman."

"A girl? I should attend to her."

"She isn't important, she's just ... "

"She is a guest in my palace," Penelope replies, a little harder, a

24

little sharper than perhaps the men expect. "She will be attended to. Eos – Autonoe."

Her maids gather their things and sweep from the room. After a moment, Telemachus nods, and in his most regal fashion strides away, presumably to try and work out how to sharpen a spear.

The old men stay behind, studying their hands, before finally Medon, who always had a decent head for these things, glares at his assembled colleagues and snaps: "I've had sneezes with more guts than you," and follows Penelope out.

CHAPTER 4

>>>

T eodora sits, and does not eat.

Opposite her is an old woman. She is Semele, daughter of Oinene, mother of Myrine. It is not the custom in the
civilised lands of Greece to introduce oneself by one's mother,
but Semele has never lived on any land but Ithaca, and has very
little time for the fashions of more polite places, where the men
are not dead. She is not that old, but years of sun and salt have
given her eyes a perpetual squint, dried out her skin, faded the
colour from her hair, scarred her knuckles and callused her huge
slab-feet as they stride across the broken rocks of this broken
place. She is known to many, for she does not keep her voice
meek and low, nor defer to the wisdom of her betters, nor
worry about finding another husband now her first is almost
certainly – almost guaranteed to be – lost. When pressed on
this latter point, she shrugs and says: "My husband sailed with
Odysseus, and if the queen is going to wait then I may as well
too." Some listeners suspect that she is finding more satisfaction
in this excuse than just a bit of regal loyalty. She is known to the
men as a hunter. Someone on Ithaca has to be. She is known to
the women as something more.

She watches Teodora fail to eat the gruel of barley and

honey that has been put before her, her eyebrows drawn, her jaw tight. Teodora has not spoken since she came to the palace of Odysseus.

"Teodora?"

Teodora looks at the woman with dark grey eyes who stands in the door, and does not know that she looks at a queen. Semele rises, which is a bit of a clue, but it seems too late for Teodora to stand now without being an idiot, so like a different kind of idiot she remains where she's sitting.

"You are Teodora?" Penelope repeats, and she nods in reply.

"I am Penelope. Semele – thank you for bringing her here. Please, sit. You are my guests. You have heard of my house, my ... hospitality. Please. You must stay as long as you desire."

Teodora tries to find words. The only ones that come are the only ones she has left to say: "The raiders came."

"Were they Illyrians?"

"It was dark." This is a repeated mantra, a thing that hides everything – sight, loss, pain. But then again, Teodora was raised to get things done, so she adds with a little frown: "Their shields were round." There is something else important to be added here, something she's missing – but it's gone.

"Where did they come ashore? There is a bay at Phenera, if I recall. Good for rough weather. Sometimes the merchants shelter there if they want to avoid paying the harbourmaster's fees – yes? I won't be angry. I just need to know."

"Yes. Phenera. They came straight for the shore."

"Did you see a signal? Someone to guide them through the shallows?"

Did she? Was there a flash of firelight on the cliffs? She closes her eyes, and in her memory there was, there wasn't, Dares is fumbling at her tunic, Dares is alive, is dead, all these things are becoming one, time flowing like wet clay.

Penelope takes her hand. Teodora nearly snatches her skin away

27

from the cool, unnatural touch. "Do you have family?" Teodora shakes her head. "You must stay here," Penelope murmurs. "You are my guest. Do you understand?" Teodora nods again, stares at the clean fingers twined round her own. She has to stop herself from sniffing them, to see if they smell of flowers. "These are my maids, Eos and Autonoe. They will look after you. Anything you need, just ask."

Another nod; her head is heavy on her neck. Then a question – it feels spontaneous but must have been growing, growing inside her since the prow of the first pirate ship hit Ithaca. "Can you get them back? The Illyrians, they took . . . they took people, they . . . Are you going to get them back?"

"I'm going to try."

"Try?"

"It's going to be difficult. Ithaca isn't rich. Times have been . . . and we don't know where the Illyrians took them. I can ask my contacts to look for them in the slave markets, but . . . it will be hard. Do you understand?"

Teodora can still taste smoke in her mouth. Her teeth are flecked with it. She looks a queen in the eye, and feels the wolf growl. "Then what is the point of you?"

Eos opens her mouth to reply, you ungrateful child, you little . . .

But Penelope hushes her, hand still clasped around Teodora's own. Old Semele watches her from the other side of the table, curious, patient. For a while Penelope considers the question, examines it from every angle, rolls it round her tongue, lets it seep into the very corners of her mind. Then answers.

"That is a very good question. One to which I do not think I have an answer. Semele – a word, if you please."

Semele rises as Penelope does, follows the queen to the door, gives no bow, raises her chin as if she might headbutt any maid who dares interrupt her passage. Penelope glances out into the

28

grey hush of the hall beyond, looks to the left, to the right. The walls of the palace are thin. "Illyrians? Are you sure?"

Semele shakes her head. "They wore the furs and carried the axes, but they had short swords too, Greek weapons. I could not hear their language. Besides, Phenera? They sail straight past Hyrie, straight past Lefkada and go to Phenera?"

"It is ... troubling," muses Penelope. "I thought we had more time to prepare. Have you spoken to the others?"

A little nod, sharp and brisk, as with all things Semele does. "We meet in the groves above the temple of Artemis. More come every week, but without a leader ... "

"I'm working on that. Keep spreading the word, quietly of course, but with haste. The men are talking of raising a militia."

If she were on her own farm, Semele would spit. Being in a palace, she just about catches the saliva in her mouth before it can fly. "Boys and old men?"

Penelope waves the idea away, as if bothered by a wasp. "It is foolish – disruptive. But I may not be able to prevent them. This girl, Teodora – she has a bow. Can she use it?"

"I don't know. Girl was smart – she ran rather than fight."

"Talk to her. See if you can use her."

Semele nods once, and slips back into the room where Teodora stares at images only she can see, at her life, at damnation, and again, as one who has seen the mists of Hades and drunk the forgetful waters of the grey river, at nothing at all.

CHAPTER 5

>>

Long-eared Medon is waiting in the shade by the door to the animal pens when Penelope emerges. Some people can nonchalantly lean against a narrow wall, casual as a cat, as though to say – oh, is it me you were looking for, lucky you? Medon cannot. He is graceful as a fart, which perhaps is what Odysseus liked about him. He is sixty-eight years old, but when the muster was called for the war, Odysseus looked at this spherical fellow with a face like a fig, and pronounced, "Good Medon, you are already a man weighed by time!" and if Medon felt a little exasperation at this description, he felt far more relief at being spared the voyage to Troy, and has ever since shrewdly been anywhere between four to nine years older than truth, depending on who's asking. He wears his robe slung loose across one shoulder, as if his clothes, as well as he, are perpetually sinking down, down, down, and it is unclear to observers whether that is laziness or a careful affectation to enhance his aura of shrivelled wisdom. Perhaps both – perhaps over time one became the other. His white hair is in fast retreat from both his forehead and his crown, racing towards an invisible battle-line across the top of his skull where some defiant walls tuft up like ruined battlements; he is missing the little finger from his left hand, which he says was

30

lost in war and was in fact infected with the scratch of a thorn when he was just a boy.

Now he detaches himself as Penelope approaches the pens of bleating sheep for the slaughter, Eos and Autonoe at her side, and blurts: "Girl all right?"

Penelope glances at the old man as she draws level with him, then nods once, lips tight. Odysseus's palace has been built haphazard over many years, from its first construction as merely a sturdy hall of timber and mud in which the people could shelter from a storm and the violence of their neighbours, to a hall with a kitchen and a well, to a hall with a kitchen and a raised set of pallets upstairs that the rats and the cockroaches might struggle to reach. Then were added cellars of dried fish and wine, carved out into the curve of the hill that rises from the town itself; hidden treasuries, the fullness or otherwise of which are a matter of some dispute; rooms for guests, dormitories for slaves, latrines out of the wind, courtyards, olive trees, rooms built around the olive trees, fresh troughs for washing, a forge for beating metal, walls and gardens of vegetables and herbs both bitter and medicinal. To Penelope's relief, many of her suitors refuse to stay in it, but instead lodge further in the town. They say it is to avoid being too great a burden; the maids whisper it is because a guilty man fears tight corridors and dark corners more than a worthy one.

Medon also dislikes halls where one cannot always know who is listening, which is why he lingers in the outdoor spaces where it is harder for a public ear to hear private discourse. Thus he falls into step at Penelope's side as if yes, why yes, he would love nothing more than to chat with her while inspecting the stinking mouths of ewes – what a perfect opportunity to talk about meaningless nothing! "So. First Lefkada, now Phenera."

Penelope raises an eyebrow. She practised arching it most magnificently for hours in front of the dusty bronze mirror in an attempt to mimic her cousin Clytemnestra, wife of

Agamemnon, who really nailed imperial hauteur in a way that evaded the Ithacan queen. It is one of very few of Clytemnestra's magnificent qualities that Penelope successfully emulates.

"You have something to say that could not be said in council?" she asks, as they move through the fly-buzzing, sheep-stinking hum of the yard, Autonoe and Eos busying themselves at a polite distance about the feeding trough.

"Two raids in as many months, and no messenger sent to the palace? Pirates only raid to force you to pay them off. Theirs is a bold negotiating position."

"And what," sighs Penelope, "do you think these pirates might want to barter for?" What is there to buy on Ithaca, save fish or the hand of a widowed queen?

"You haven't been approached?"

"I am avoiding being in any situation where I could be. As soon as I am forced to tell these raiders – whoever they are – no to whatever their demands might be, they will have no reason to hold back. There will be no corner of my kingdom that will not be subject to their whims. Better, in a way, that we are *not* negotiating, if their ignorance breeds restraint."

"You consider their current actions 'restrained'? An attack on Ithaca itself? What if they had come for the palace?"

Her lips grow thin, and she does not answer, turning her face towards the sky as if surprised that she cannot see the sun in the framed square of this little butcher's yard. The bleating of a sheep grows loud, and then is sharply silenced by knife slicing through skin and bone.

Medon draws a little nearer, almost so close he could lay a hand upon her arm – closer than any men dare go. It is perhaps his blithe obliviousness to her existence as a woman, let alone a sexual being, that permits him this intimacy. It is almost as if he sees her as a friend more than a woman. I envy her that, sometimes. It is not apt for a god to envy a mortal; it usually ends badly. "Do you believe Peisenor can defend Ithaca with his militia?"

"I do not." The words are harder than she meant, and for a moment another question hovers on the tip of her tongue, never to be expressed. Does her son think it can be done? Will her son risk dying for a thing that cannot be saved? She shakes herself a little, opens her eyes fully, seems almost surprised to find Medon still standing there. "There are ... other options I am investigating."

"What other options?" When she does not answer, he puffs his cheeks, raises his hands. "Conspire if you must, I know I can't stop you. But when I last checked, even you did not know how to sweet-talk a pirate."

"I have a new suitor to greet," she announces, a breezy turning-away, a hard end to this line of enquiry. "He's Egyptian."

"How very novel."

"Isn't it just? I imagine he is interested in the amber that sails through my harbours."

"That's not a metaphor, is it?"

Despite herself, a flicker of a smile passes across Penelope's lips, but it is gone as soon as it is born. "First, welcome an Egyptian," she muses. "And then I think I should take a little ride."

CHAPTER 6

>>>

O nce upon a time, there were three queens in Greece. One
was chaste and pure, one a temptress whore, one a murderous hag. That is the how the poets sing it.

All three came from Sparta, and shared some of the same
mortal blood. One was the daughter of a naiad. This creature
of sea and pearl, seeing Icarius, prince of Sparta and brother to
the king, bathing one day by the mouth of the river, exclaimed,
"Hey, prince, get a load of this!" or words to that effect, and he,
with very little forethought, absolutely did. When nine months
later she slipped out of the stream behind the palace and presented him with their daughter, he politely accepted the wailing
bundle from the naiad's already departing form, took her to a
cliff and serenely threw her to her death. A flock of helpful ducks,
who understood that naiads might not want to raise their own
children but would certainly be insulted if one was left to die,
carried Penelope to safety, and getting the quacking message at
last, Icarius took her home to his mortal wife with a jaunty cry
of "Dearest one, the gods have blessed us with this fortunate yet
mysterious infant! What luck, what!"

Polycaste, wife of Icarius, had a choice to make then, and how
strange was her reply. For on the day her husband tried to kill this

34

infant child, Polycaste took her into her arms and said instead: "She shall be loved," and meant it with all her heart, and all her rather sensible head too.

This act of mercy – this compassion – is as baffling to the gods as to mortal men. I do not dwell upon what that says about us, who are worshipped by all.

Thus came Penelope, some-day queen of Ithaca, into the world.

The other two of our Grecian queens were daughters of my husband-brother Zeus.

Around the same time Icarius was sporting with a naiad, Zeus, king of kings, mightiest of the gods, became smitten with a foolish mortal called Leda. She was married to Tyndareus, king of Sparta – but she will not be remembered as a queen, merely a vessel for another's seed. Sacred marriage vows are for wives, not husbands, so down Zeus descended in the form of a swan.

He does this a lot. He will appear as an injured animal – sometimes a bird, sometimes a bull – limp towards a tender maid, who exclaims, "You poor dear, let me shelter you!" and then poof! Just when you least expected it, that delicate, innocent creature you nurtured upon your bosom has transformed into the naked form of your brother, hand between your thighs, lips upon your throat.

"I knew you wanted me," he breathes. "I knew you loved me all this time." You cry out, no, no – please, no – but it is no good. Your protestations just prove to him how ignorant you are, how little you understand your potential, all that you can be, once you are his. And when he is done, he lays his head upon your breast and coos like the soft creature he feigned being – love me, love me, love me, he seems to whine – oh, how harsh it is that you of all women could not love me. This thing I do – why, now you know how much I need you to love me.

Then he bids you stroke his head, and you try to breathe

without making a sound, until at last he transforms into a creature of the sky and flies away again. This is my husband-brother, greatest of the Olympians, paragon amongst men, whom I know best of all.

Well then, down Zeus comes in the guise of a swan, and "Oh look, what a lovely thing," exclaims Leda, and wouldn't you know it, that long feathered neck wasn't a metaphor after all, and the next thing you know, Leda is laying eggs. Actual eggs from between her spread white legs. These eggs eventually hatch, producing Castor and Pollux, the whining little twerps, and Helen and Clytemnestra.

Let us deal with Helen first. She is accounted the most beautiful woman in the world by blighted mortals who would be struck blind by true celestial radiance. Beauty is a whim, it changes as easily as the tide. I was once considered the most beautiful, until familiarity bred tedium.

She is also acknowledged as the daughter of a king – not even a Spartan prince is going to make too much of a fuss when the suspected source of your wife's pregnancy can smite you with a thunderbolt for slacking off on childcare. And even if she were not considered fetching in a mortal kind of way, there's nothing like being a half-celestial half-princess-of-Sparta to really make your mark politically.

So she grew from babe to child – was for a while kidnapped by Theseus in a whole escapade so baffling in its twists and turns that I cannot even be bothered to contemplate it – and finally, being returned unsullied to her father's court, came of a marriageable age. This presented as much of a challenge as it did an opportunity, for her should-have-been father, Tyndareus, was at his wits' end as to which of the great princes he should appease and which incense by giving away Helen's hand in marriage; when a hundred heavily armed men who won't take no for an answer compete for a prize only one can win, poor conversation at the dinner table is the least of your worries. Then along comes Odysseus, a no one prince from a nowhere island on the western edge of the civilised world. "I hear Helen's cousin, Penelope, is a rather lovely sort," quoth he. "Let me wed Penelope, and I will give you a ruse that will settle all your worries."

Tyndareus turned his gaze from the hordes of suitors in his hall to a shadowed corner where sat young Penelope, daughter of Icarius. "I don't know," he mused. "She may not be a Helen, but she is still a princess of Sparta. She should at least wed someone who doesn't smell of fish."

But Odysseus was never one to propose a scheme unless he was certain everyone else would go along with it. "I can bring us peace," he murmured. "Brotherhood amongst all the Greeks. Surely your brother's child is a fair bargain?"

So it was settled, and at Odysseus's suggestion, all the princes of Greece swore an oath that whoever should marry Helen, the others would come to his aid. And who would not? For each man there seemed certain that *he* would be chosen, *he* was the greatest of all men. This is the kind of heroic logical fallacy that makes even icy Athena howl in fury. So they swore; so it was done, and so in the end Tyndareus chose Menelaus, as he was always going to, and everyone agreed it was a disgrace, a terrible disappointment, but too late — too late! They were bound by their oaths; Odysseus himself swore it upon the altar of Zeus on his wedding day.

When the poets talk about the schemes of cunning Odysseus, they tend to gloss over how that particular plan went so catastrophically wrong for such a clever, clever prince. For lo, Helen fled — or was taken, depending on who you ask — to Troy with that little wart Paris, and now Menelaus and his big brother Agamemnon send their messengers to all the little kings of Greece from east to west. "Oh ho ho!" they exclaim. "We are going to war against our enemies in the east, against King Priam and all his wretched sons, and by a lovely twist of fate, all of you – every single one – swore to fight by our side, to defend the husband of Helen! Here's a funny thing, here's a how-to-do for the ages!"

Agamemnon had always wanted Priam's riches. They say Helen gifted them to him through her treachery, setting the spark to the flame of battle – but it was Odysseus's cunning that made war possible on such a grand scale. Best not to dwell on that, the poets say; let's focus on all the business with the Cyclops and Scylla, proper manly stuff, tied to a mast and straining against his bonds with tricep-bulging fervour at the song of the sirens – why yes please – rather than that first, monumental, city-razing, god-shaking little miscalculation.

And where is Odysseus now? Ah yes, he is fumbling up Calypso's skirts on the island of Ogygia, all the while protesting that he loves his wife, he loves his wife and he would be free of this nymph's paradise of sexual delight. My displeasure is an ill wind that brings goosebumps to a lover's arms, but even Calypso, who should know the touch of a goddess's ire, is so confident in her catch that all she does is pause in their copulation to close the shutters that banged open by the bedroom door. I'll have her – just you wait and see, I'll have her.

At that fatal feast of Tyndareus where Helen was betrothed to Menelaus, where Penelope was given to Odysseus as the prize of his cunning, there was one other notable event. For it was here that Helen's sister, Clytemnestra, caught the eye of greedy Agamemnon, the greatest of the Greeks, king of Mycenae, ever hungry for more. She was already wed, but Agamemnon always fancied himself a Zeus amongst men. He could not turn himself into a swan or a bull, but when he drove the sword himself through Clytemnestra's former husband and ripped the bloodied clothes from her back, the end result was much the same. And when his business was done, he let go of her throat and pulled himself from between her thighs and whispered: "Now you know how much I love you."

Then he put his head upon her breast, and she did not breathe.

And she did not breathe.

And she did not breathe.

Until at last he rose and left her alone again.

That is how there came to be three queens in Greece, voices uttering prayers that no poet-prince, husband-king nor king-above will ever hear.

CHAPTER 7

》》》

H is name is Kenamon.
His name is actually significantly longer than Kenamon, but he finds the barbarian Greeks are so poor at pronunciation that it's easiest for their uncivilised heads to just say his name is Kenamon of Memphis and leave it at that.

His ship landed in Ithaca some two days since, and he has been fed – he already tires of lentils and fish – treated with the utmost courtesy and utterly failed to gain an audience with Queen Penelope. He tells himself he is not frustrated by this.

He considers Horus to be something of a personal protector, and if I could be bothered, I might have sat beside him and laughed and said Horus, *Horus*? That interloping little twerp wouldn't dare set foot one step beyond the head of the Nile. Now Isis – that's a woman with a bit of pluck, that's someone who gets things done, she and I once played tavli for the soul of a manticore and both cheated so much it was practically fair!

His head was shaved when he departed, but months of travel and the turning of the sea has permitted a ragged growth that he is not sure how to tame. His skin is the sunset desert, his hands are large, suggesting perhaps a little competence with the sword he has politely left in his cockroach-crawling room. His

40

eyebrows are bushy black, his eyes are wide, flecked with amber and grey. He wears a long linen tunic and a collar of coloured faience and a bracelet of jasper, amethyst and carnelian threaded with gold. He sits in the largest yard, between the palace gates and the great hall. He has found a thin sliver of shade beneath a columned walkway where the wall lizards scuttle, as mottled brown as their surroundings, and now he watches the last of last night's suitors drag themselves into the open air. They are hung-over, as always, and will need to spend the daylight hours recovering their stamina to resume another night of gorging and drinking and pawing at the skirts of the maids. This is the terrible burden of their lives, they lament. They would be warriors; they would be kings! It is a tragedy befallen upon their youths that they are having to waste their days in chasing some aged old bat, some withered so-called "queen" of Ithaca rather than raiding, pillaging and slaving as true men should.

Andraemon, he of the lovely arms, says: "I heard pirates. Comes to something when Ithaca can't even defend itself."

Antinous, dark-haired son of Eupheithes, growls: "Fucking mercenaries. She's got the money, why doesn't she just hire her own?"

Amphinomous, royal child who would be a soldier, tuts: "It's more complicated than that, and you know it."

Eurymachus, long-limbed son of Polybus, opines: "I had a thought about this – what if . . . "

Antinous blurts: "No one cares what you think, Eurymachus," and no one does.

The suitors do not pay Kenamon much attention as they pass. Many foreigners come to Ithaca, most seeking supplies before sailing for Corinth or Patrae. Only the gold about his wrist might briefly draw their muddy eyes.

He waits.

Pray to me, I whisper in his ear. *Pray to Hera, for whom the women once cut the throats of lions and burnt the flesh of men. Horus will not hear you now; Horus does not care. Pray to me and perhaps you need not drown in blood in the great hall, when all is done.*

Kenamon does not hear me, and I do not labour the point.

When the maid approaches he leaps to his feet like the eager pup finally allowed to chew on a bone. She looks at him with only mild interest to see a foreigner, and in her heart beats a rhythm he cannot hear: *death to all the Greeks.*

He is led to a hall through the tangle of crooked passages and rough-hewn stairs. It is a small, cool place, blessed by gentle breezes from the sea but sheltered from the storm. In it is a throne. It is not much to look at. Odysseus judged it suitable to have a high wooden seat of some impressive design, just to make it clear that he was a king; but he was careful to keep it smaller than anything Menelaus or Agamemnon might sit on. Odysseus is modest – when modesty is a weapon.

Penelope does not sit on the throne. That would be absurd. Her cousin Clytemnestra ostentatiously held court from her husband's throne while Agamemnon was away, and it was a source of much gossip and endless, distracting debate, which, Penelope cannot help but feel, probably made matters of governance harder. Instead, she sits on a chair a little bit below and to the side of her husband's throne. Near enough that it is clear this is a thing she is guarding; far enough away that she does not claim ownership. In the secret hours of the night, she and Eos spent some significant time precisely studying its position, while men slumbered.

The women have returned to their traditional poses for this audience. Autonoe plucks a few notes from her lyre for Kenamon's entry. Penelope inspects the thread Eos has prised from her basket of washed wool. Eos combs the knotted curls. It's always lovely to welcome a new suitor with a ladylike scene; so nice to make a good impression.

42

Kenamon, as he stands awkwardly before them, is unsure how near to approach, how far to remain. His gifts have been presented, and they are significantly better than Penelope expected, though she makes no sign of this. She likes that he's trying to get the etiquette right. Penelope always appreciates a bit of effort.

"Noble queen . . ." A bow – a really nice bow, proper, bending at the hip, he'll get over that soon enough, they all do. ". . . it is an honour to stand in your hall."

"We are gratified by your presence, sir," Penelope replies, eyes running to the gold at his wrist, the jewels at his throat, the colour of his eyes. He is not a boy, as most of her suitors are. Memphis is not yet a land of widows. "Many men have come to my husband's palace looking for some favour, but you have come further than most. Truly we are blessed."

"I have only been here a few days, and already Ithaca feels like home."

Autonoe strums a note, a little loud, slightly out of tune. Penelope's smile does not falter, though there is something about her eyes that men might fear. To everyone's surprise, Kenamon sees it and, licking his lips, tries again. "By which I mean . . . the hospitality, the graciousness of your palace and your people – it is as if I were surrounded by my own kin."

Better, Egyptian. Better. Spill wine before my altar and I'll teach you exactly what to say to win a Grecian heart. Your pharaohs simply erase the history of those they dislike, drowning inky words in silence; our living poets are far more dangerous, for they know how to make a monster from a man long after he is dead.

"Anything we may provide, anything you desire, and if it is in my meagre power it shall be so," intones Penelope, a gracious gesture of her hand encompassing hall, palace, island, sky and sea.

"My lady, that is most kind. But there is only one thing I could ever truly desire."

"Ah. Of course."

Kenamon curls his tongue into the roof of his mouth. If he is honest, he has already taken a dislike to Ithaca. The people are rude, the weather is drab, the food is poor, the company boorish and this whole business a fool's errand. But his brother sent him, and on his brother's goodwill he depends, and so . . .

"I am a stranger to this place. I am unfamiliar with your customs. In my land when a man seeks a woman . . . "

"In your land, I am sure men do not seek other men's wives, no?"

The strings beneath Autonoe's fingers twang, taut and dissonant. Penelope's smile is as thin as the knife she hides beneath the folds of her robe, tucked at her back across the curve of her spine. Kenamon catches his breath, and for a moment I nearly lose interest in him, just another suitor, another ode to her white bosom, the prowess of the ox, strength of the lion and so on.

Then he says: "My lady – do you seek a husband?"

Autonoe's fingers freeze on the lyre. Even Eos pauses in her casual ministrations. None of the women can remember this question ever having been asked in all the dozens – hundreds – of men who have come through this door. It is so strange that Penelope has to repeat it to herself, stagger through the enquiry as if she is learning his language, or there was something in his accent that has made the whole thing unintelligible. "Do I . . . seek a husband? That is . . . such a curious thought. My husband is Odysseus. No body has been found. Therefore he lives. I am married to him and that vow is unbreakable. I do not, therefore, seek a husband."

"I see." Kenamon bows a little, wonders what he will tell his brother when he gets home. These Greeks, he'll say, they're all mad – quite mad.

"However," she continues, "I am informed by everyone of note that I am mistaken. That in the years since Troy fell, my

44

husband must be dead. That it is becoming inconvenient for him *not* to be dead. When Agamemnon was at war, Mycenae was ruled by my cousin Clytemnestra, and there seemed less question as to her . . . capability. But then her husband still lived, a promise of retribution should anyone cross either him or his wife. Though the soldiers of Mycenae were somewhat delayed in returning, there was no doubt that they would – fathers and husbands, capable of holding a spear against the city's enemies. You will observe that we have a shortage of both on Ithaca. Currently my husband's reputation keeps the worst of the raiders away, just in case he comes back and is unimpressed to discover his so-called allies have been pillaging his lands in his absence. Illyrians – barbarians from the north who do not understand our ways – sometimes strike, but never other Greeks. Not yet. Odysseus's name is powerful, you see. The poets sing of him in the same breath as Achilles and Neoptolemus. But with every month that he does not return, that power wanes. The fear his name inspires wanes. And so there must be someone new who our enemies – and our less consistent friends – can fear. Clearly they will not fear me – I am just a woman. And my son, Telemachus, does not have loyal veterans and trained soldiers to draw upon. So a husband is required, though it is impossible that I marry. Does that answer your question?"

Quite, quite mad, he'll tell his brother. Maybe the sea, the size of the horizon does something to the mind. But he must at least try, for a few months if no more – he must make it look like he's given it his best shot. And so: "They say your husband was wise. Would he not see the necessity of you marrying again – to protect your kingdom, your son?"

"They do say that, don't they? Truly it must be a great man who could contemplate taking his place."

Kenamon takes his time to consider this. Penelope does not mind. The silence of men is a novel experience, and she is prepared to thoroughly enjoy it. At last: "My brother trades in silver and amber from the north. He must do business with the merchants in your port, who control the northern seaways. He is an extremely vain and foolish man, but I am one of nine and my fortunes in my homeland have not been ... excessive. I am instructed to tell you that should you wed me, the ships of the south will no longer trade with your rivals; that any Greek who wants gold, copper, the grains of the Nile or incense of the east will have to do homage at your feet. I am also instructed to make some matter of my military service – which I have performed – without in any way seeming to undermine or compare with the feats of your famed, lost husband."

Autonoe's mouth is agape. Even Eos is flushed with surprise. Penelope does as she often does when she fears that her features are going to lapse into some un-queenly state, and gazes upwards in a pious pose. This is a trick she learnt from Odysseus's mother, Anticlea, who had a lot of advice for her daughter-in-law on hiding one's true face behind a solid bit of prayer – or a cup of wine. Nevertheless, Kenamon shifts in his place, before blurting: "Did I say too much, my lady? If I have caused offence, I apologise."

"Not at all. No offence. It is ... refreshing to hear a man lay out his position so clearly. A great many who come to my hall waste my time, first with speeches dedicated to my beauty, then with speeches dedicated to theirs. The actual business of how many soldiers they can bring to defend my isles and which of their rivals they will slaughter first often evades them. But they are boys – one must remember."

"Are rivals often slaughtered here?" he enquires politely.

"Oh heavens, no. The duty of a host and the behaviour of a guest are sacred! For blood to be spilt under that covenant would be unforgivable. But one day someone will crack, and stab their brother in the back. I think it will be Antinous, or maybe Eurymachus – one of them will either end up dead or do some killing. Then it will be a bloodbath, unstoppable, profane to gods and men."

"You seem sanguine on that subject."

"It is a likely outcome. We have all learnt lessons from my cousin Helen – there will be no more oaths of brotherhood sworn between noble men, should I choose one of them. Rather, the disappointed shall band together to kill the fortunate, and when he is dead, those allies will turn to bitterest foes and slaughter each other until there is but one king left standing upon the ruins of my kingdom – the bloodiest, or the most cowardly, whichever has the gods' favour that day."

"That does not seem like a desirable outcome. What happens if you do not marry, may I ask?"

"Oh, at some point someone will make an attempt on my life and that of my son. Once we are gone, the only legitimacy will be strength; if they quickly and effectively kill the other suitors before they can arm, they may secure the throne for themselves, albeit through a sea of blood. But most likely Menelaus will take the opportunity to invade from Sparta and annex the western islands in the chaos. He's always had an eye for opportunity."

"I see." Kenamon has the seriousness of a child who has just discovered that one day the baby crocodile he loves will grow into a hungry beast. Perhaps the Greeks are not all mad – or at least, no more mad than any creature that has tasted blood and ash on a hungry night. "I will admit, my lady, that you are not offering as many potent reasons for this match as I had expected – not of course that such a burden should be yours, for your virtues are clear to all who have eyes to see."

She clicks her tongue in the roof of her mouth, nods at nothing much. "Well, as you have so fairly laid out your position on this matter to me, I should say for my part that my mother bore children until she was thirty-six; I have excellent teeth and a

47

solid head for household matters, and am considered adequately good-looking for my age."

To her surprise – to her astonishment – Kenamon laughs.

She has not heard the laughter of a man for . . .

. . . for so long.

She has heard the boys who would be men cajoling and slobbering over her maids. She has heard them roar at a drunken jest, leer in cruelty and puff themselves up at matters they do not understand. She has seen Medon smile a little smile as if to say, "Were I a younger man, I would find this amusing," and once she was told that Peisenor laughed so hard at a fart joke that everyone feared he would die, breathless and wheezing on the floor. She has not personally seen him merry, and sometimes, in weary moments, tries to imagine it, and fails.

But now Kenamon laughs, and it is utterly astonishing. He puts his hands on his hips and rocks forward, rocks backwards, and when he catches a moment exclaims: "Those are excellent reasons for any man, my lady! Excellent indeed!"

Autonoe is smiling, beaming, her eyes sparkling with life. Of all her maids, Autonoe was always the one most prone to mirth. Euracleia, old nursemaid to Odysseus, tried to beat it out of her, but Autonoe saw how much her happiness distressed her tormentor, so grew brighter and wilder and full of light, a defiant, petulant roar of ecstasy that should have had her sold to the whores, until Penelope said: "I like her," and no one challenged the whims of the queen. Even sombre Eos, whose father sold her for a barren ewe when she was but four years old, has something in her eye that may be, if not delight, then at least fascination. Eos learnt many years ago not to let even the slightest spark shine in her features, save in the quietest hour of the night, but this – well, this – this is something strange and new to her indeed.

Penelope smiles too. The feeling is strange upon her lips. She does not weep herself to sleep every night – she's a practical woman, with things to do. But neither do people go out of their way to entertain her. She is a delicate clay pot that must be passed with the greatest of care from one sombre servant to another, lest the slightest whisper crack her ashen glaze. For people to laugh in her presence is considered rude; she is, after all, a widow pining. And so, though she remembers being merry once, there has not been that in her life that has provoked much mirth. Until, that is, now.

She smiles and rises, which silences the Egyptian, to whom she holds out her hand.

Foolish stranger – he does not know what danger this motion pertains, for he takes it and bows again. He is not sure whether it is a custom for a man to touch a woman in this land, let alone whether he should press his lips against her fingertips. He is the first man whose skin has brushed hers in more years that she can remember. It will linger in her heart, so vividly that she will eventually crush it, reject it, stamp it out for fear of longing for impossible things.

"Sir," she says finally, pulling away – a moment, just a moment, ended. "Let me be clear. If I show you any special favour during the feast, you will be murdered in your sleep. The bond between host and guest is sanctified by the gods – but you are not one of us, and my suitors grow restless."

"I can protect myself, my lady."

"I'm sure you can. But if you are not murdered, if I show you any favour, *I* may be murdered in my sleep. Or my son. Safety depends on balance – any action I take, whether to say yes or no to any man, risks tipping this balance into bloody war. Do you understand?"

"I believe I do."

"Good. Then understand that while you are welcome here, I will not walk with you, I will not share food with you, I will not discuss the lands of Egypt or the places between here and

49

there, or the languages you speak and the wonders you have seen. Sometimes you may chance to speak to me, and I will reply as a hostess must. For your part, you may remain here as long as you desire. And when you depart, I will bid you farewell, and of course, there will be sorrow to see an honoured guest depart. I regret that it must be this way."

The poets will not sing the name of Kenamon of Memphis. He does not sit easy in the tales they would tell.

The audience is over. Later, as he walks by the sea at midnight, he will think of all the witty things he should have said, the clever little remarks and charming epithets that did not in fact spring to mind when they would have been most needful. To his surprise, he finds he would have said them to make her smile, rather than because he has much in way of a worthwhile cause to advance.

For now, he simply says: "Thank you, my lady."

"Welcome to Ithaca," she replies.

CHAPTER 8

>>

L et us push Helios's chariot through the heavens; let us bid the sun turn a little upon the land.

Here – come with me – come see.

In a temple tucked deep in a forested grove, a woman with blood on her hands and blisters between her toes falls down before a priestess who smells of pine and crimson leaves, and says: "Sanctuary."

Across the still waters of the south, men are pulling at oars until the wind will blow, their ebony sails limp against the mast. I glance down to the waters of Poseidon, but dare not whisper my brother's name, dare not speak to him of these black ships and the island to which they go.

Odysseus cries out at the touch of Calypso's lips.

Menelaus holds Helen down by the back of her neck, face turned to the wall. When he is done, their daughter Hermione finds her mother on the floor, half shrouded in her shredded gown, still staring at that wall. Hermione will contemplate her a while, then turn and walk away.

And in the afternoon sun, Penelope, Eos and Autonoe ride to Phenera.

There are three men with them, all armed, all soldiers who

fought in Troy. None are from Ithaca. Penelope acquired them over several years from Sparta and Messene, men vouched for by people she trusts to have a sensible head on their shoulders. It is a source of frustration to her that of all the soldiers in her watch, there are so few she can be certain of, if and when the dice should fall.

The women wear veils when they leave the palace. Eos and Autonoe are not obligated to do so, but consider it good form to share in their mistress's modesty. Penelope's veil is the grey of the young goose, and occasionally doubles up for protective garb when she is tending to the honey bees in the herb garden. She wears it also when she deigns to attend the evening feast, sitting aloof from the men who dine at her fire.

She wears it as they ride to Phenera, and is grateful that it hides her eyes.

The carrion that circle the village now mark its ashes more than smoke, yet as the women draw near, they find that the crows only have a few feasts – those foolish enough to fight, or old enough to be not worth selling. The flies don't mind. They will enjoy a pool of blood in almost any setting. Someone has closed Dares' eyes, but that does not stop the bloated insects that burrow through his swelling flesh. Most of the livestock are gone. A few well-fed sheep will fetch almost as much in some markets as a human of less than premium stock. Sheep breed more reliably. Every house has been gutted, floors ripped up and torches thrown into the bottom of the well – whoever ransacked this place was looking for hidden riches, buried by nervous hands.

There are others, from other villages, come ostensibly to mourn, and perhaps more sensibly to pick over the remains. A single fishing boat drifts, empty, out in the bay, washed away from the shore. Three young men are preparing to compete for who can swim to it first and claim the prize. There are few children on Ithaca younger than seventeen, and of those there are, many were fathered by men who were simply passing through. Such things only lend themselves to boisterousness.

There are priests too, come to give the rites. It is an awkward affair. There are few inhabitants left alive, and none of means to pay for mourners to tear their hair and rub the ashes of the burnt-out place upon their faces. There will be no tombs carved from stone, or hollow plots of earth adorned with the dead's worldly goods. Penelope whispers in Autonoe's ear to send for some women to have a good wail. There are many skilled mourners on Ithaca – it's almost as popular as fish.

Amongst the priests come to show an interest, there are several noble men from Athena's temple, who discovering that they had no stomach for war devoted themselves instead to the worship of its goddess and thus avoided sailing to Troy. It is a hypocrisy I remind Athena of whenever I get the chance. There are some priestesses too, in which job there has been a certain influx of eligible ladies who found themselves without marriage prospects.

One is out of place – a priestess of Artemis, who is more usually seen pouring oil on the head of the newborn child than singing sad songs for the departed. Her name is Anaitis. Like most people on Ithaca, she has a secret. Unlike most people on Ithaca, she is not used to having secrets, and is already going a little mad with it.

Penelope walks through the ruins of Phenera with her maids. The ground is dusty and disturbed by footprints, by the dragged lines of feet kicking at the earth, by the scars fingers leave when they claw at sand and rock while some unseen figure hauls their owner by the neck towards the sea. Here, someone swung a sword a little too hard, and it missed its target altogether and struck the wall behind it, cracking mud and bronze alike. On the beach, the marks of where the raider's ships were pushed up onto land are still visible, gouges in the earth filling with salt and small scuttling crabs. To the north, the sand curls away to harder turf, black rocks and round grey stones, a rising cliff to which the scrubby trees cling, spindle-branched and dark-leafed, nature as stubborn as the people of the isle. There are hollows in the cave, half hidden behind fallen fingertips of rock and walls of vine. Some are natural. Some were natural, and were expanded upon by people, chipping away down the centuries for purposes sometimes vulgar and occasionally profane.

A little knot of women has gathered on the stone beneath the cliffs, dragging at something in the water. There are woven baskets upon their backs, empty, and a few have tied ropes around their waists. These women, whose husbands never returned, who are as stubborn as the stone, have come to climb up to the caves where, it's rumoured, the smugglers of Phenera kept their treasure. They will be sorely disappointed by what they find.

As Penelope approaches, they move away, eyes down. She nods and pretends not to notice their scavengers' tools. Instead, her eyes turn towards the object in the shallow pools between the ebony rocks that the women were trying to haul onto firmer land. The tide has washed away most of the blood, though there is a high-water mark of thin crimson against the tendrilled green slime and indigo weeds. The body has started to bloat, but the inflation of his tunic around his torso hides, for now, the worst of it. His hair floats like foam about his head. He always was proud of his hair, lovely bouncy curls with a hint of copper in them.

The women drag his body in, pull him onto dry stone by flesh that slips and sloughs beneath their fingers like the loose skin of an onion, roll him over. Little darting fish that sweep in and out of the rock pools with the tide have been nibbling at his face and chest, sucking at flaking skin and grey eyes, a feast for the translucent wrigglers of the shore.

Penelope asks: "Does anyone know him?" and someone

replies, "Yes," instinctively, because she is honest, and then immediately regrets it, because now a queen is looking at her and was she here to loot what little remained of Phenera's illicit goods, why yes, she absolutely most definitely was. Still, too late now.

"His name is Hyllas. He's a merchant."

"He looks ... my age." It is not seemly for a queen to discuss her age, but when there are so few men on the island to compare to, sometimes even a lady has to reference herself. "Is he Ithacan?"

"No. He's from Argos, but he sails north and west. Trades amber, tin with the barbarians, bronze and wine with the Mycenaeans."

"I'm surprised I don't know him."

An awkward shrug. It's not polite to speak ill of the dead.

Eos kneels down over the body to whisper a prayer, and looks more closely at the corpse. Of the two maids, she is by far the more pragmatic about death. Blood, tissue, fluid, pus; someone has to make these things their business, and a good maid knows how to make herself useful. She tilts his neck up, sees a little wound between throat and jaw; tugs his shirt to see if there are more wounds hidden beneath, does not find any, frowns, glances up at waiting Penelope.

Penelope is not thrilled to kneel on damp stone beside a bloating corpse that stinks of liquid eruptions, whose very flesh looks as if, when squeezed, it might ooze out its own organs – but they are here for business. She arranges herself in what she hopes looks like the best deportment of queenly thoughtfulness, hands clasped near her bosom, a little invocation to Hades for kindness and a speedy voyage to the Elysian fields audible for others to hear. Autonoe shoos the women back, asks them to fetch some cloth to wrap the body in, to give the queen space for her prayers. If Eos is calm no matter what, Autonoe has mastered the art of selective hysteria, of falling about and weeping at the most pertinent of moments.

The scavengers back away a little as Autonoe permits her lower lip to tremble and a sigh of "Such sorrow" to mingle with the sea breeze. There was a time when Eos and Autonoe hated each other, ice and fire combined. The years have taught them to value the merit the other brings, and so now Eos half smiles at her fellow maid, then turns her attention back to the corpse on the beach.

This Hyllas – he is not young. Old enough to perhaps have sailed supplies to Troy, to have grown rich on plundered gold to pay for grain to fatten Agamemnon's troops. Neither is he a stooped elder. There was good slavery to be had out of him yet. The tips of his fingers are hardened by oar and sail, but his belly was full and he ate well before he died.

"The wound, below his chin," murmurs Eos, as Penelope mutters a few more half-thought prayers to mingle with Autonoe's more pronounced declamations of piety.

Penelope leans in, closer to the body. Her fingers rest briefly against his chest, and she swears she can feel salt water gush from the tiny holes fish have gnawed in his slippery flesh, and knows it's her imagination, and pulls her hand back anyway. There is no spear through Hyllas's heart. There is no great tear of sword across his belly, no curve to his skull where it was caved in by a hammer. She follows Eos's gaze to the single wound that is visible on the body. It is no wider than her thumb, puncturing windpipe and spine both as it was driven through. There is a slight red round-ness around its entry, in the shape of the hilt of the blade – too small to be a sword, a knife for gutting fish perhaps, double-edged and deadly. Eos eases back a wet fold of cloth from Hyllas's legs. The skin is pocked with a hundred tiny red spots, the rubbings of salt and sea, but no cuts or bruises. She feels across his belly, and stops. There is an object tied there, hidden, wrapped in leather.

Penelope says: "Oh help me, Autonoe, I grow faint."

Autonoe at once kneels by Penelope's side, holding her left hand in hers, and though this is a profoundly pious scene of feminine weakness, it is also now a huddle of curved back and womanly distress that hides what Eos does next from all onlookers.

She slips a blade from her gown. Water has made the leather cord resilient, but Eos was long the palace butcher, before she was maid to the queen. It snaps beneath her knife, and in a tight knot of shrouded sorrow and pious distress, they unfold the little packet contained within.

Inside is a ring, heavy, a single onyx set in its heart, the curve dotted like leopard spots. Penelope takes it from Eos's hand, holding it close to her body, away from the eyes of the watching women. Says, not quite believing what's in her voice: "I know this ring."

Eos looks at Autonoe; Autonoe looks at Eos. Men think that Autonoe is the optimist of the two, but they are mistaken – she is simply more willing to laugh at the darkness. No one laughs now.

Then there is a priest, an old man of Athena, a busybody gossip, approaching with a tut and a cry of "Ladies, please! What is this . . . Oh!"

Together they rise, Penelope's fist tight around the ring, a polite smile on Eos's face. "We were saying prayers and thinking on all those who are lost," Penelope intones. "Such a dreadful thing."

In the evening light, the mourners come.

They are professionals, from the village round the other side of the hill, wearing their most raggedy robes – no point tearing a perfectly decent gown if they aren't being paid properly – and at Autonoe's request they form a circle and set about rending their hair, clawing at their skin and generally making an absolute racket. The few men stop their business to show their respect. The local women gather to offer a polite moan of their own, just to show willing, though most of these ladies spent their tears many moons ago.

In the shadow of the setting sun, Penelope and Eos stand a little apart. Penelope murmurs: "Is anyone watching us?"

Eos shakes her head. The mourners are really quite the scene; it's what they're paid to be.

"Let's go look at these caves."

It is not dignified for a queen to climb jagged rocks up to a smuggler's cave. Athena would tut; Aphrodite would exclaim, "Her poor nails!" and feign a swoon. Perhaps only Artemis, goddess of the hunt, would give a single short, sharp nod of approval. But it can be hard to tell with that one whether she approves because she appreciates the labour of the mortals, or whether she just likes scandalising her more civilised sisters with her crude and uncouth views.

Nevertheless, to the mouth of the cave Penelope and Eos climb, while Autonoe stays below and whenever the wailing starts to lack or waver sets up a really good howl of bosom-rending despair, to keep any potential onlookers occupied. "Oh, good priest," she shrieks, flinging herself at the feet of the hypocrite of Athena when his eye starts to drift, "Whatever shall we women do?"

Autonoe will never admit it to man or woman until the day she dies, never give them the dignity or satisfaction, but sometimes there are days when even she enjoys her work.

The climb to the caves is not as hard as it at first appears — many hands have grasped at the black stone, many feet worn smooth the thinnest pathway of wiggling rock, invisible until you know to look for it and then at once immediately apparent as a thing of human creation. Up this Penelope and Eos slip in busy silence, hems tucked into belts, knees knocking on stone, until they reach the first mouth carved in stone.

The caverns of Phenera have been picked clean. There is still the odd sign of things that have been – spilt wine and broken dust of clay, goose feathers and goat droppings, bone dice dropped by a drunken sailor waiting for the tide to turn. What the pirates didn't find and take for themselves, the women of Ithaca have. Penelope kicks at dust, which billows and settles soft as sunset.

"Strange," she murmurs. "I am not meant to know that smugglers skulk in the caves here; my council has no idea. So how did Illyrians know where to look?"

Eos shakes her head, without an answer. There is nothing here, and as they move to the next hollow, they find more of the same nothing, more of the same ransacked emptiness where secrets should have been. They are about to turn back when another place – barely more than an overhang of stone hollowed out by the sea, hardly shelter from sun and storm – catches Penelope's eye. There is soot across the roof of this dome of rock, and signs of a meagre fire beneath it. Eos kneels over the ashes, finds them cold, but the wind and the sea have not yet knocked away the shape of the hearth that was kindled here, nor the whorl of disturbed sand where a sleeper lay, curled against the chill west wind.

"Another body?"

Penelope jumps, and feels immediately like a fool, but composes herself to turn slowly to see the speaker. She is unfashionably short and unreasonably stocky, thin hair dragged back from a high forehead. She wears no obvious sign of her priesthood, but is known to the islanders, and the women especially, who find that the blessing of the huntress comes in handy when times are hard.

"Anaitis," murmurs Penelope, half nodding to the priestess as she approaches. "I didn't expect to see you here."

"Have you found another?"

"No – no. Just ash. What brings the servant of Artemis here?"

"There were many people in Phenera who honoured the huntress," Anaitis replies – always wise to give your patroness a plug, particularly one as whimsical as Artemis. "I heard rumours of an attack in Lefkada, and they say ... "

"I know what they say," Penelope snaps, a little harder than perhaps she intended. Anaitis raises her eyebrows; she is not used to people talking over her, but for a queen she supposes she can grudgingly make an exception. Everyone knows Penelope is mourning, and probably therefore hysterical, poor dear. "My apologies," Penelope adds, a little quieter, a little shake of her head, a smile without feeling. "It seems that Ithaca this day is nothing but stories. But yes. Lefkada was attacked last full moon. I didn't think the Illyrians would be so bold as to come all the way to Ithaca itself."

"*Is* this Illyrians?" asks Anaitis, looking up towards the crimson sky beyond the jaws of stone as if Artemis might send a falcon as a sign to answer her enquiry. Artemis will not. She is far too busy bathing naked in a dappled forest brook to give a damn about such things.

On the edge of the shore, the mourners are really getting into their thing, very impressive, really good lungs on some of them, excellent show. Autonoe pulls at her hair – careful not to actually tug free any fibres, but really going for a dishevelled, rent-apart look that she knows will be rather fetching with the evening light at her back. Penelope eyes Anaitis carefully, sees a face weathered by sun, hands used to skinning and the touch of sacred fire. "Is there a reason to think it isn't?"

A shrug. "I thought the only thing more profitable than actually taking slaves was to send to a queen and tell her that you would. Easier to be paid not to attack than to actually go through with it. Less dangerous. Less time being seasick and all that."

"What you are describing is the behaviour of our brave Greek warriors. The Illyrians are too barbaric for such manly nuance."

"Gold is gold. Besides, the bodies I've seen were stabbed. Like so." She mimes stabbing – Anaitis has stabbed a lot of things in her time, it's just the way of things. "Illyrians use sicas, slashing weapons, like so." Another thrust of her hands, turning an imaginary blade – oh, if Anaitis has been born a man, she would have revelled in it, she would have dared Hector to the fight without waiting for all that nonsense about dead lovers and teenage sulks. Athena likes a good bit of poetic drama before a duel, a nice speech about mutual manly respect, but Artemis is a creature of the wolf and the forest. She likes to gets to the point.

Anaitis shakes herself, as if from a dream, and looks not quite at Penelope – she has never been comfortable with eye contact, was forced by the priestesses to learn how to stare towards another eyeball as if she were engaging in something human within it. This has sometimes been disconcerting to people, but at least, Anaitis reasons, she is trying to fit in with their expectations. "Two attacks in two full moons. There will be more blood soon," she says. Then, as easy if she were discussing the price of pottery: "Semele came by the temple with a girl – Teodora. I'm sure the others will welcome her, but when the pirates come . . . "

"I am working on a solution, Anaitis."

"Pirates are not rabbits, queen." For a moment she hesitates, as if she might say something else. Here it is, then, here is her secret, the thing she wants to scream to the whole island. If she were not sworn by the sisterhood of her bond, she would – she would howl it to the moon. But though she does not understand much about people, Anaitis understands everything about oaths. So, as quick and simple as if she were a child playing with another: "Huntress's blessing on you!"

She turns, and darts away.

CHAPTER 9

>>

Night falls in Ithaca, beneath the greedy waning moon. Ithaca is at its best in the dark, when the drab indoors of hard stone and split timber becomes at last a refuge, a place of murmured safety, a clasped hand that holds whispers and darting eyes. It was the sound of secrets and the glance of hidden faces in the scoured night that drew me here in the first place, though not for that did I remain. My husband rarely glances down from Olympus these days, spills his hours in nymphs and wine, but were he to ever bother to look towards the west, this is a darkness where I can hide even my celestial light. Lady of secrets; lady of intrigue, whispering in the shadows where no men go. I feel it now, the old thrill, the taste of the ancient power that has been so long forbidden to me. I was a queen of women once, before my husband bound me with chains and made me a queen of wives.

In the lamplight, Peisenor and Aegyptius, councillors of Odysseus, sit with the old men outside the great hall, the sound of laughter and music drifting on the air. There was a time when the fathers of Ithaca revelled in such delights, but their sons have been missing for eight years, and that is in its way worse than a death.

Peisenor says: "We need a hundred spears. Not for Telemachus. Not for me. For Ithaca."

The old men, masters of the harbour and the field, of the olive grove and the merchant ship, look uneasily at each other. Polybus, father of Eurymachus, is the first to speak. "You've got men in other islands. Bring them here." The father's golden hair is but a few lingering strands draped across his skull like a broken net, but the son's height came from the father, and the father refuses to bend.

"And who will guard the port at Hyrie or the groves of Kephalonia?" chides gloomy Eupheithes, father of Antinous. "We have few enough men to protect our most valuable land, let alone Ithaca." This is not an agreement with Peisenor, of course. It is merely a disagreement with Polybus. That is the way of things between these two, who were once the very best of friends – until they grew ambitious for their children.

"Until now, no one thought anyone would attempt to raid in Ithaca," Peisenor cuts in, before the two men can start hissing at each other like warring snakes. "Lefkada was a disaster, but predictable. Phenera showed that pirates are willing to strike even here, in the heart of Odysseus's own land. What if they had attempted to kidnap the queen?"

"And who will lead this militia? Not you. Not Odysseus's man."

"Who else, if not me?" growls Peisenor. "I don't see any of you taking charge."

Eupheithes shifts in his long, fading robe. There is a streak of beetle red around the hem, fantastically expensive, a gift – he says – from old Nestor before the famous king died, to thank Eupheithes for all his labours. Antinous did not learn many lessons from his father, save this: if you make enough people believe you are important, one day it may actually be true. There was a time when Eupheithes was close to the household of Odysseus, a loyal friend of Laertes and all his kin. But that was before his

63

boys went to war and never came back, leaving him two daughters and Antinous. He wants to be proud of the son he has, and sometimes he forgets that and despairs. "Penelope has treasure. Pay the raiders off."

"What treasure?" scowls Peisenor. "The sacked gold of Troy? The fruits of her husband's labours? Every animal raised on her land, every pot of wine or sack of grain goes to one purpose and one only – feeding *your* sons every night. Do you see gold on her? Do you see jewels in her hair?"

Eupheithes' lips chew at the air in his mouth, as if tasting the texture of it. "It is true that our land is in danger," he muses. "Foreigners threaten all of us. It is disgusting that Penelope tolerates them at her court. A show of native strength could be of use."

"And who will defend us against your men, Eupheithes, if you arm?" snaps Polybus. "Will your boys defend the shipyard if it is attacked, or will you stand idly and let it burn so that those you do not like are ruined?"

"This is bigger than the docks ... " begins Aegyptius.

"And are we to believe that Polybus would risk any of his tribe to protect the granaries, if the Illyrians come inland?" retorts Eupheithes. "Or will he order them to stand by while all that I have is burnt to the ground?"

The assembly dissolves at this point into furious squabbling, accusation and insult. I glance quickly into the nearby shadows, into the hot places of the earth beneath their feet, for Eris, lady of discord, wondering if she has stolen into this little assembly – but no, this is entirely, absolutely the stupidity of man without the interference of gods. It is fascinating in its detail and pettiness.

"I will lead ... " begins Aegyptius.

"What, a man who can be bought?" hoots Polybus, and again:

"A man without experience?" grumbles Peisenor, and of course:

"A man who is sworn to Telemachus?" snarls Eupheithes.

And again, they go to it.

"Joint command," Peisenor blurts finally. "A council of some of the wisest of Ithaca."

"That won't work, that will be . . . "

"Aegyptius, Polybus and Eupheithes in command, bringing twenty men each . . . "

"Twenty? Impossible!"

"Fifteen . . . "

"Do you think I have fifteen men to spare?"

"Perhaps ten – that will be thirty spears. And we will provide ten spears from the household of Odysseus – that will be forty. Telemachus wants to serve . . . " Another scoff of laughter from nearly all assembled. ". . . and he will bring a further five or six spears with him, hardly enough, I am sure you will agree, to be troublesome to your troop of thirty. I will also speak to Amphinomous. He has a strong arm and his presence may deter Telemachus from . . . youthful spirits."

There is a general shuffling of sandals. No one particularly likes Amphinomous. He is not merely the chief of all the suitors who have come from that fabled and unhealthy land of "not Ithaca", he is also unpleasantly friendly and honest. When asked "What will you do if you are king?" his first answer is "Attempt to heal the sorry division that has come upon the good men of the western isles," and to everyone's amazement, he appears to mean it. This would make him a fool, of course, nearly equal to Eurymachus for inanity, were it not that Amphinomous also once killed three men who had attempted to steal a goat from a woman in the market, using nothing more than a butcher's blade and a broken table leg. Such qualities of morality and capability do not sit easily with the old men of the isles.

"I agree." Aegyptius is the first to rise, the matter settled.

Eupheithes is the next to signal his assent, if only to get in there before Polybus can. "Ten spears each, and a joint command. No one can dispute that when the four of us stand together, we speak for all of Ithaca. Not just Odysseus's son."

At the walls of Troy, the Achaeans followed Agamemnon, but the Myrmidons followed only Achilles. Didn't that turn out well?

Peisenor manages to hold back a sigh. It is already going badly, but he can see no other way. So he stands, looks into the eyes of the men whose sons would be king, and thus a very foolish accord is struck.

CHAPTER 10

>>

T he moon rises. In less than thirteen days, she will be shrouded, her face hidden from the sky. Thirteen days after that, she will be full again, and you do not need a goddess of great potency and wisdom to tell you, to assure you, that yes – oh yes – the pirates will come again. Their presence will be too small to stir Ares from his brooding; the flash of a blade will barely rouse Athena from her scrutiny of Odysseus where he lies slumbering on Ogygia. But for the island of Ithaca, it will be a bloody day indeed.

Yet for now, in the great hall of the palace, the feast is under way, as it always must be. The suitors have come, no swords on their hips and daggers in their smiles. It was a law established early in the house of Penelope that all who ate at her table should be unarmed; she is disgusted that the rules of civility have been strained so far that such a proclamation should be necessary.

Away from the sound of music and the roar of men, Penelope holds a ring in her hand that should not be on this island, and looks out to sea, and thinks she sees sails on the horizon, beneath the fat light of the waning moon.

"Peisenor will get his militia," Eos says, as she lays out a clean robe on the bed. "He is certain of it."

"Boys with spears," Penelope replies. "Led by men whose only interest is protecting their crops while their neighbours' land burns."

"What does good mother Semele say?"

"She says we are not ready. I've kept the suitors waiting; we should descend."

A half-bow, a little nod. The ring in Penelope's hand is nearly the same temperature as her skin, dull and heavy as she clutches it tight between her fingers.

Below, in the feasting hall, thick with the bodies of men, the warmth of breath, the snapping of bones and grinding of teeth, two maids move Penelope's loom into place, so that the suitors may watch her work upon it in her shadowed corner. She is weaving a funeral shroud for her father-in-law, Laertes. When it is finished, then she will marry a man – so she says.

As political devices go, this has presented thus far two major problems. Firstly, Laertes is very much alive and well on his pig farm in the hills, and less than amused at the topic of his expected and inevitable demise being such a popular theme in island gossip. Secondly, if anything has been learnt about Penelope over the many, many, *many* months in which she has been attempting to loom what should be a fairly simple piece of cloth, it is that she is a truly abysmal weaver.

Kenamon of Memphis sits a little apart from the other suitors as the maids bring in wine, meat, lentils, chickpeas, beans, fish – more fish – bread to hold between your fingers to sweep up the grease in the cracked crimson bowl. He has not yet been welcomed into any one clique of amorous men. The local contingent from Ithaca are suspicious of foreigners, men from across the sea who would try to rule their sacred hereditary lands. The men from further afield, the suitors of Colchis and Pylos, Sparta and Argos, are perhaps more willing to accept an Egyptian into their number, once they have shunned him long enough for him to understand that he doesn't stand a chance in this bloody race to the throne, and is merely tolerated for being quaint, harmless.

One of the palace's dogs – an ancient, yellow-eyed, shaggy grey beast that once knew how to hunt, and now merely sniffs at the tails of nimble-footed rats – shambles up to Kenamon and presses its snout against his calf. It is not a creature much appreciated by the suitors, but Eumaios the swineherd still rubs its belly, and whenever Telemachus pulls his head out of his arse long enough to pay attention, the dog is beloved of Odysseus's son, who seeing it pawing at a suitor's side, now approaches.

"Argos likes you, friend." Telemachus calls everyone in the hall "friend". He finds that saying the names of the suitors themselves makes him want to retch with disgust and shame, so instead he has spent some time cultivating a word that he can speak with acid but the men hear with flowers.

Kenamon scratches behind the dog's long, loose ears. "I like him." A silence, a place where names should have been. First the host, then the guest – that is the way of things.

"Telemachus," the son grudgingly concedes.

"Ah – the son of Odysseus!" Telemachus has also learnt to turn a flinch into a smile. There is something similar, you see, in the narrowing of the eyes. But then a strange thing happens, for Kenamon rises, and bows a little, and there is almost respect in his voice. "It is an honour to meet you. They say that Odysseus's fame eclipsed that of even his own father. By that reckoning, I can only wonder at all that you are, and all that you shall achieve, and am honoured to tell people that I have met Telemachus of Ithaca."

"Do ... do you mock me, sir?"

"I swear I do not. Please forgive me, I am unfamiliar with your customs. If there is some way I have caused offence, I must know."

Everyone and everything causes Telemachus offence. It's just a habit he's got into. This foreigner, however, is just foreign enough that for a moment Telemachus is disarmed. "No," he stutters at last. "No offence. Please – you are welcome here. Eat, drink, whatever you want. No guest of my father's will be treated badly while I hold a place in this house."

This sentence causes some translation issues for Kenamon. There are implications – questions of father, possession, of status and who precisely is doing what and to whom. But for now, he nods, and smiles, and raises his cup to the son of Odysseus – barely sips it, the night will be long, he thinks – and says: "You honour me; you honour us all."

Telemachus manages to nod instead of scowl, and turns away.

When Penelope comes down to the hall, the men bang their fists on the table, a concussive cacophony. There was a time when this was a mark of respect, a greeting to their host. Now it has become a thunder, an assault, a jeer that Penelope ignores as if it were the southern breeze tickling the end of her nose.

The maids serve meat.

There are nearly forty women in the household of Odysseus, of varying degree. Some are from Ithaca, the daughters of widows who could not feed their sons so turned to their daughters and said, "Melantho, this is for the good of your brothers," as the slavers came. Many are not, and find their lives on Ithaca of mixed estate. True, the western isles are drab and harsh, smell of fish, and the palace feasts have nothing on the preening grandeur of Agamemnon or Menelaus's courts. On the other hand, Penelope has not personally butchered another man to ravish his wife, kidnapped a child to make her a bride, defiled the corpses of her enemies, bashed the brains out of an infant babe or been sired of a lineage of incest or cannibals. These omissions make her something of an anomaly amongst the monarchs of Greece, and indeed the gods of Olympus themselves.

Some of the maids we already know. Laughing Autonoe, whom Hagius of Dulichium once tried to grapple upon the kitchen floor, he losing an eye in the process. Quiet Eos – if her demeanour were not already off-putting, she sits too close to the feet of Penelope, and even the most reckless of the suitors sense that the mistress would be displeased were harm to befall the maid. But there are others – so many others – moving now through the hall.

Euracleia the nursemaid, muddy-eyed and serpent-tongued, hovers in the door. Technically she is not required in this place, for the feast is Autonoe's domain. Technically she has no duties at all, is free to go whenever she wishes, but she hangs around like an old smell, and scowls at the younger maids, and coos at Telemachus, and tuts about how things were better in the good old days. If queen Anticlea had not with her dying breath bade her daughter-in-law "do right" by Euracleia, and if Telemachus was not so quick to leap to her defence, Penelope would have had the stooping old bag shipped to some house in Hyrie, a decent stretch of water between herself and Euracleia's lashing tongue.

"Your hair is filthy!" she barks at a maid. Or, sniffing the sweet aromas drifting from the kitchen: "What a terrible smell! Call yourself cooks?"

She is nearly knocked aside as Phiobe scuttles in with more wine for the men, darting beneath Euracleia's folded arms with a little "Oh sorry yes there hello excuse me yes!" Small and quick as the agile fox, Phiobe's mother served in the house of Odysseus before her, and shielded her daughter so much from the world beyond its walls that she was almost fifteen before she touched herself in her private places, and seventeen before she tumbled giggling into the arms of the blacksmith's boy. The boy is gone now, but there are many young men come to Penelope's palace to woo a queen, and Phiobe is not starved of choice when it comes to picking a handsome protector with nice teeth.

It is necessary to understand that the maids are sexual beings too.

Melantho, sold by her mother so her brothers might thrive. When the first suitors came to Ithaca, she tasted a few, fascinated by these strange males in the women's world. Since then she has learnt that the sweetest taste is safety, and so from some minor no-hope nobody sitting far from the fire, she has made herself available to a little lordling, a would-be kingly, a could-be master of all he surveys, and now is most often seen bent over the table of Eurymachus, the curve of her breast a little closer to his nose than is strictly necessary. He is a merely adequate lover. The promises he makes, though – they are nectar indeed.

"Sweet Melantho," croons one, "you have the most beautiful eyes."

Or, "Phiobe! I have not seen those beads on your wrist before – did some lover give them to you?"

Or perhaps: "Will I see you later?"

"You're drunk."

"I have barely touched my wine. Try me, and I will prove any test."

"People are watching."

"But no one sees. Will I meet you later?"

"Perhaps. If you mind your manners."

A man's hand slips from where it brushed the calf of a maid beneath the serving table. There are those who say that Penelope should keep a house as chaste and pure as herself. Old Euracleia spits and mutters that it is a disgrace, an absolute disgrace! Telemachus, bless him, doesn't really understand the way of these things yet, but when he finally does, he will splutter outrage and amazement, indignant scorn at the impiety of these women! The women, of course, are the impious ones – not the men. My husband Zeus has made this point very clear, and mortals do learn from their gods.

See here too – there is one maid who works with the others, hair the colour of clotted blood, eyes pressed to the floor. Her name is Leaneira, and in her heart and in her eyes beats a drumbeat that has pulsed against her flesh since the day she was torn from Troy: *death to all the Greeks.* We will have much more to say of her before our tale is done.

Leaneira, Phiobe and Melantho, Eos and Autonoe – these women with a dozen others serve the feast. When the suitors first came to Ithaca, the maids were as icy as their queen, numb and nearly mute. But that was over a year ago, and these men – these men! They thought it would be so easy to worm their way into Penelope's bed, and when it was not, what were they to do?

What would any warm-blooded creature do?

Apart from it all, Penelope sits weaving, Eos at her side, guarding her as Argos once guarded his old master Odysseus.

Andraemon, he of the lovely arms and furrowed brow, his father some distant potentate in the east, his discus throw unmatched amongst the suitors, his voice deep and dark as the iris of his eye, approaches the loom. "May I speak to the lady of the house?"

At his back, Antinous and his assembled table of Ithacan boys – boys who know they will never be king but think perhaps Antinous has a shot – jeer and laugh at Andraemon's audacity. Eos, guardian of the step, considers Andraemon for a moment, then leans down to whisper in Penelope's ear. Penelope whispers back. Eos steps aside: he may approach.

"My lady ... " This is the beginning of another speech, another declaration of love or piety, or perhaps, if we're lucky, another round of gift-offering. Penelope loves gifts. They help pay for the wine. ". . . I hear you have pirate problems."

Penelope is a very bad weaver. Her fingers pause for a moment over the loom. At Andraemon's back, Antinous tries to make a joke, a stab of mirth at his rival, but it is drowned out by a roar from Eurymachus's table. Eurymachus probably doesn't have a hope of the crown, but his father, Polybus, has enough men in his debt that those who follow him don't have the luxury of discernment.

"The raiders will be taken care of," Penelope replies at last. "Peisenor is raising troops."

"I heard. I am sure they will be very brave."

Some of them probably will be brave. Ajax was brave; Patroclus was brave; Hector was brave. Odysseus, when he hung by an olive branch above the gaping whirlpool that swallows ships whole, begged and gibbered for the mercy of the gods, and he's not doing so badly for himself, all things considered.

"I hope you are enjoying the feast, Andraemon," Penelope muses, plucking at a thread as if it might sing. "You do not want for anything?"

"The seas are full of dangerous men, my lady. Soldiers from Troy who do not feel they received their due. I know some of them. I know how they think, what they want."

"How they think ... what they want ..." she repeats. "Tell me: do you think they will ever get what they want? Do you think they will ever be satisfied while someone else has more than they?"

"I could act on your behalf, if you wish. Speak to some who, like me, know what it is to fight. I have many brothers from Troy." His hand rises instinctively to a stone he wears upon a leather thong around his neck. It is no bigger than his thumb, a thing polished by sand and touch, with a hollow in the middle through which it may be threaded. It is the kind of gift you might give to a child in lieu of any finer present, save that Andraemon, whenever people enquire about it – and they do – can speak fluently on its history and discourse as thus: this is a piece of stone from the city of Troy. I carried it with me when we left – not gold, nor slaves, for it was not considered fit

74

that one of my station take such rewards. I should wait upon the generosity of my master. My master was not generous, but this stone – still I carry it, to remember.

What the nature of those memories is, he does not further explain. He finds that silence on this topic lends the hearer the power of imagination, which is usually far richer than the truth.

Penelope sees him tangle his fingers round the stone now, and smiles thinly beneath her veil, imbuing a slight simper to her voice. "That would be so kind, but I cannot possibly ask it of a guest."

"Nevertheless – for Ithaca."

"Your generosity astounds me. But do not trouble yourself. Ithaca can defend itself."

"If you say so. But it is my concern, my lady, that these attacks will not stop without someone . . . more familiar with how men think taking action. I hope you are not offended by this, it is just how I see the thing."

"I am not offended at all. And I believe I see your meaning perfectly. Thank you, Andraemon. I appreciate your clarity."

He is dismissed, a little too soon for his taste, but even if he would happily stand before Penelope and give her a good hard slap until she got the point, such a violation would be unthinkable. So he must smile, and bow, and step away, and take his frustration out someplace else, where only the gods may see.

Penelope does not watch him go. Instead she murmurs: "Do we have someone following him?"

Eos nods, spinning twine around her fingertips. Penelope has made a row of thread too tight. Ah well, such a shame, she'll have to peel it back a little bit at a time, pinching and tugging the loom into order.

Now councillor Medon approaches, but he is old, and thus basically irrelevant in the eyes of the suitors. He stands easily by Penelope's chair, contemplating the room. "Andraemon?" he enquires.

"He offers me his martial experience."

"How nice."

"His timing is notable."

"Does he negotiate?"

"Not yet. Not that we are yet in a suitable position to reply if he did. It might be coincidence." Medon scowls at the very idea, and Penelope smiles, adds: "Antinous son of Eupheithes offers me all the grain of Elis."

"Highly valuable."

"Eurymachus son of Polybus offers me a merchant fleet capable of controlling the amber trade from the northern ports all the way to the mouth of the Nile."

"A sound investment. And the Egyptian?"

"Ah, the Egyptian. He has nice hair."

Medon stifles a laugh, but though he is smiling, his voice is sombre, leaking from the corner of his mouth. "The shroud is going slowly, I see."

"It's hard to focus when one is so preoccupied with womanly feeling. There's a man killed in Phenera – Hyllas. Not one of us. It might be in the council's interest to find out more about him."

"Might it so?"

"If a woman were to advise."

Medon bows, the deepest bow of anyone in the room. He remembers when Penelope first came to Ithaca, little more than a girl huddled at the back of Odysseus's boat. He has seen her grow, and one day wishes he would be able to express something of meaning to her on this theme; but the words are tangled on his lips, it is never quite his place to say it. "I will make some enquiries. I think your son wants your attention?"

Telemachus has been eyeing them across the room, and now draws near. He does not like to be seen too often near his mother. He is a man now, not a boy; it doesn't do to hide behind his mother's gown. But there are matters that must be discussed and it is good for the hall to see his presence, his reassurance, the protection he offers the women of his house. Medon bows again as he approaches, and slips away.

"What did Andraemon want?"

Penelope smiles at her son, thin as the crescent moon. "To help, in his fashion. I hear Peisenor has struck a deal to raise a militia."

"Yes. I intend to serve."

"No – that won't do."

"Mother, I . . . "

"I will not risk your life on some . . . glorious effort."

He stiffens, stand up straight, and there is something of his father, there's a tilt of the chin that had Odysseus staring into the eyes of Hermes himself and demanding: hey, you in the funny shoes, what do you think you're playing at?

"What effort is worth a man's time," he snaps, "if not a glorious one?"

He turns away before she can answer. She would only have attempted to dissuade him with common sense.

"Telemachus!" coos Antinous. "Telemachus! Did your mummy tell you to go to your room again?"

A snarl of fury, a flash of rage – Odysseus has a terrible temper too, but he has learnt to turn his fire into ice, the precision of the archer rather than the fury of the axe. Telemachus isn't there yet, which is why he rounds on Antinous and barks, "I don't need to wait for my father to return, Antinous. By blood and by might I am king of these isles, and it is only in honour of your father's name and by the laws of the gods that I permit *you* to feast at *my* table!"

Antinous is on his feet in an instant, his boys rising behind him. Others rise too. The musicians drift to a casual halt – they have played this tune before. Kenamon watches from his corner of the hall. "Do you hear?" hisses Antinous. "Do you hear the bards say your name? Do you hear the people proclaim it in the streets? No. Neither do I. Go hide behind a woman, boy. Go beg your mummy to protect you. When I'm king, I'll make sure you're safe."

Penelope rises too. There are rules, as a host. She cannot harm her guests, nor can they harm her – but who is to say what really happened, when daggers are drawn between those who share a meal at her hearth? Only the poets, and they can be bought.

"Antinous," murmurs Amphinomous, quiet, steady, eyes fixed on Telemachus's face even as he addresses his fellow suitor. He has perhaps half a dozen allies at his back, all from lands as distant as he. Antinous puffs his chest towards the son of Odysseus. Eurymachus is counting the men in the room. There may not be swords, but there are knives for cutting flesh; there are stools to be thrown, tables a man might smash a skull against. Every suitor now looks to his neighbour, pondering who to the left, who to the right is enemy, ally, or a coward who will flee.

Telemachus's fist grows tight at his side. Antinous is stupid, drunk. His lips roll in, then push out, and with a little popping of air, he blows Telemachus a fat, womanly kiss.

Telemachus sways as if punched. Amphinomous's hand closes around the knife on the table. I bid the air freeze, time slow like the turning of the sea before the whirlpool opens, like the breath of the ocean at the changing of the tide. Come, see with me the unfolding of all things; know the world as a goddess might.

In Delphi, a prophetess shrieks, clawing at her skin as the golden statue above her hearth begins to weep salt tears. On Ogygia, Calypso bites her lip to swallow the sound of ecstasy – Odysseus has grown moody recently with her delighted cries, though even in his moods he comes back to her, hand pressed over her lips as he does his business. And by the misty banks of the Styx, Cassandra, cursed to know all and be believed by none, tuts and wags her finger at the endless mist and whispers: *told you so*. Now that she is dead, throat cut by a vengeful queen, she is letting herself express these things a little bit more.

The lives of mortals are a flicker of sparks, but now let us pause and catch at one, see how it may burn away to ash. See how time unravels from this moment, a future possibility waiting to be born. The Furies are preening their feathers within their halls of molten stone, the blind owl shrieks in the dark, and so: neither Antinous nor Telemachus will strike, for they realise the death that will be guaranteed them both if they do, the first one to break the sacred compacts of hospitality. Yet neither can they retreat, unmanly and unmanned, and so ... and so ... ah yes, here it is – it will fall to a suitor by the name of Nisas, stupid Nisas, teeth-rotting Nisas, to smash a pot across Telemachus's skull. He will do this not because he has thought about the consequences – Nisas does not think – but because he wishes to impress Antinous, wishes to really show how loyal he is to a could-be king. So grinning, leering, mouth split in a simpleton's grin, he will rise from his seat, swing with all his might from his hips, rain down ceramic shards against Telemachus's head and in doing so spill the blood that will become a river.

This glancing blow will not kill the son of Odysseus – his family are renowned for their thick skulls – but in that instant Penelope's peace will shatter too, and the only strength that will matter is that of the warrior, of the man. Telemachus will spin on the spot, eyes shot with fury, and hurl Nisas to the ground, the suitor's legs kicking uselessly at the air as he is knocked onto his back. With one hand around his throat, Telemachus will squeeze and squeeze until the boy's eyes bulge and his tongue flaps, and before Amphinomous can pull the prince away, the light will fade from Nisas's eyes, the first corpse of this bloodbath. Then one of Amphinomous's men will shove one of Antinous's a little too hard in the cluster of manliness that has formed around this murderous scene, and he will shove back, and in the general fray that breaks out, one of Eurymachus's men will draw the little blade he has kept hidden about his garb in rank defiance of the laws of guests. This fellow will see the chaos, hear the roaring of voices and the cries of "Treachery, treachery, murder!" and seize the opportunity to drive the blade into Antinous's ribs while he thinks no one is looking – though by now all the gods will be staring down from Olympus – throwing the knife aside the moment the pallid suitor falls, as if that could hide his sin.

Thus, Antinous will die along with seven others that night, and nine more of their injuries later. Penelope will flee, Telemachus be dragged at last to safety, still screaming foulest murder as once his father did before the sirens. Peisenor will barge in and attempt to bring order to the scene; he will die when shoved too hard aside, head cracking on stone. Two maids also will die, having been seized and ravished by those suitors who, their oaths broken and war unleashed, have no better way to prove their meagre, limp manliness than to express their power upon the unwilling.

I half close my eyes at the prophecy now unfolding, but see, see – we must not be afraid, you and I, to see the future in its full.

When Antinous's corpse is brought before Eupheithes, the old man will weep and proclaim a love for his son that he never expressed while the boy lived. Love is vengeance, of course. Even the poets understand that. Knowing this, Eurymachus and his father Polybus will not wait seven days for Eupheithes to grieve, but will strike on the night of the fourth day of mourning, slaying all in Eupheithes' house while the soul of Antinous still awaits the boatman of Hades on the waters of the Styx. They will then march to the palace to seize the throne and Penelope too, but she – ah, she will have fled. She will have run to a little bay where is hidden a certain speedy vessel that can be rowed by six strong men – or six hearty women – and raced across the thin waters to Kephalonia, to take refuge amongst the most honourable of that isle.

Telemachus will not flee. He will defend his palace, hurling his spear from atop the shuttered gates, and both he and Eurymachus will be dead of their wounds before the moon is dark, and Menelaus will be on his way from Sparta beneath sails of crimson, rubbing his hands together – don't you worry, little ones, Uncle Menelaus will sort things out. Uncle Menelaus will see you right.

So will fall the house of Odysseus. Unless ...

I reach into the secret part of myself, the hidden power that I keep veiled from my husband's jealous eyes. It will cost me – oh, it will risk all should I be seen, but perhaps something small, too minor to catch the eyes of Olympus, a convenient cobra attack maybe, I could pull off one of those, it's not my most subtle or nuanced of moves, but when the need arises ...

Antinous's bloated kiss hangs in the air between him and Telemachus. The son of Odysseus stands ready to strike. Stupid Nisas prepares to rise from his place.

And then – a thing I had not seen – the prophecy changes. For in that moment when all was to be unleashed, blood and fury and sacrilege in the feasting hall, Kenamon steps forward, clears his throat and says in that strange accented way of his: "Forgive me, I am unfamiliar with the way of things here. Are we rising to drink to Odysseus?"

I stare incredulous at the Egyptian, and so perhaps does everyone else. Kenamon, you gorgeous little mortal, if I could squeeze your beautiful face; if the touch of my fingers wasn't instant death to your naked flesh, I'd be all over you, yes I would.

Then I hear it.

A sound on the edge of even my celestial perception, a thing beyond the comprehension of little mortal brains. I catch it on the verge of its departure, and there it is – there it is – the beating of white feathered wings.

And I look again at the Egyptian, and I see the tiny traceries of another god's touch upon him, the subtlest nudge of divinity, fading from his skin.

Well bollocks.

Damn damn damn triple-cursed Titan-chewing damnation!

No time to deal with it now.

Telemachus hangs for a moment poised between his own overwhelming pubescent idiocy and a tiny modicum of common sense. Kenamon smiles uneasily, and adds: "Or perhaps we are drinking to Agamemnon? I heard your king of kings was ever an ally of the house of Odysseus?"

The future hangs upon the edge of a blade. Here at least I have a certain subtle knack, and so I lay a hand upon Telemachus's shoulder and murmur, *Don't be a sardine-brained pillock, boy.*

"Of course," he declares, and as he does so, the prophecy changes, the blood washed from the walls, the corpses living and laughing again – at least for now. For now. Telemachus raises a cup that is hastily pushed into his hand by Autonoe. "To the greatest of the Greeks, hero of Troy – my father. And to the great king Agamemnon too, ally of Ithaca, dearest friend of my family, long may he bring peace and justice to our lands!"

No one will not drink to Agamemnon. Sobriety is not wise. Even Antinous steps back to raise his cup, and that moment buys Telemachus a chance to exhale, to step away.

There will be a reckoning, some other time.

Not today.

Even Penelope sips a cup of wine, and inclines it, so I think, perhaps a little towards the Egyptian as he regains his seat.

CHAPTER 11

>>>

The moon turns, fading into darkness.

I fly through the night on wings of shadow, seeking that other god, that other Olympian presence whose breath mingled in the air of the palace feast; but she is long gone, vanished no doubt to her gaudy temples in the east, or to wheedle once more at Zeus's feet. Did she see me? Does she know what I do here? I must be careful; I must work with the utmost subtlety upon the hearts of men.

And so the moon turns.

In the highest part of Ithaca lives Laertes, father to Odysseus.

When Penelope was eighteen years old, still bulging with the weight of Telemachus in her belly, Odysseus sat down with his father and said: "Look. You don't want to be king and I do. You're rude, you're lazy, and frankly you smell. I would like us to handle this civilly, so – what will it take?"

Laertes, who by the time did indeed smell terribly, worse when he exhaled, considered his price. "Eight slaves, an olive grove, three – no, four pigs, two cows, two goats, two horses, a donkey, first pick of the best wine, and once a year you hold a big party for me in which everyone has to bow and grovel and scrape and call me 'Wise King Laertes'."

"On Kephalonia?" suggested his son optimistically. "You can have a bigger farm on Kephalonia, maybe that nice one by the . . . "

"On Ithaca," his father replied. "So my grandson doesn't have an excuse not to visit."

Odysseus managed not to roll his eyes, and all things considered, counted himself lucky to have got the old man to bow out of the kinging business so easily.

In his early years, Telemachus visited his grandfather eagerly. Laertes was, after all, an Argonaut, a hero of Greece, a child of Hermes, and was willing to impart the kind of manly wisdom that his mother and grandmother clearly misunderstood, as so: "What a woman wants is to be protected. A man must demonstrate his strength, his lion-like aggression, his power, so that she can see he is the guardian she needs!"

Telemachus has never seen a lion, but he gets the general idea.

Once a year, as promised, Penelope threw a big celebration in her father-in-law's honour, and he oiled and shaved and turned up looking very smug indeed as people crowded round to say how generally wonderful he was. Even old Eupheithes and Polybus seemed to lay aside their bitter hatreds long enough to do a bit of "so good to see you, you should come and dine!" at Laertes' untrimmed feet.

When his grandmother Anticlea died, Telemachus wept salt tears over her grave, and Laertes descended from his farm and put a hand on his grandson's shoulder and said: "None of that nonsense! You're a man, not some simpering little girl!"

Anticlea had always told Telemachus that his father was a hero. She had never had much to say about his grandfather – her husband – and Telemachus had never bothered to enquire why she kept herself away from him, in the palace. "Oh, just to help your mother out" was the closest she ever came to an answer. Whether Penelope needed help was unclear.

"What was Father like?"

Telemachus has asked this question of so many people in so many ways, and never quite found a satisfactory answer. To Anticlea, her son was the bravest, boldest, cleverest man in all Greece. To Euracleia, the old nursemaid, Odysseus was a coo-cooey little wonder, yes yes he was, yes he *wassss*, wasn't he, and Telemachus is a coo-cooey little wonder too, look at your little cheeksy-weeksy, yes you are, yes you *aaarrre*.

To Penelope, his father was a Good Man. Very little more was forthcoming, which confused Telemachus deeply.

But then: "What was Father like?" he asked Laertes, and to his surprise, the old man ceased chewing the mush of seeds round and round his gummy lips, spat a gobbet of husks towards the fire and looked up towards the soot-stained ceiling before finally proclaiming:

"Boy knew he was smart, knew how to play it. Not too smart that people think you're a threat, not too dumb that people don't know you're useful. No room for double-guessing or getting worked up about might-be or could-be or is-it, though. Smart makes its choice and sticks with it. Takes work. He put the work in."

There is something here, Telemachus suspects, something in his grandfather's voice that, a bit like his mother's distracted explanations, he is missing. It takes him years to find it, but one day, when he was seventeen, he finally managed to put his finger on the question that had evaded him for so long.

"Grandfather," he said, sitting by Laertes' fire. "Is my father good?"

Laertes jerked in his chair, as if punched, and for a moment Telemachus feared his grandfather would die too soon, too soon, before his mother had finished weaving his funeral shroud, and the war that was waiting just on the lip of Ithaca's horizon would break free at last with the death of Odysseus's father. Then he heard a crow-like cawing, a hacking of phlegmy breath, an expiration like the wind through a skeleton, and with a start realised his grandfather was laughing. He laughed at the question until his laughter broke down into sputum-flecked hacking, but even then, his eyes rolled with amusement and his hands shook as he patted his grandson on the head.

"Bless you, boy," he cackled. "What a thing to ask!"

And so the moon turns.

CHAPTER 12

>>

In the palace, feasting. Feasting! Feasting! It is as though nothing happened, as though the deaths of all these men were not a sneeze away, *more wine!* You girl – bring us wine!

"Amphinomous, you're such a bore!"

"Eurymachus, if you keep playing like this, you won't have a tunic on your back – no, no, I'm happy to take your gold, of course I am, shall we roll again?"

"So, Egyptian. What is this 'writing' you describe?"

"No Telemachus tonight? Run away, has he?"

"Telemachus is visiting his grandfather, paying his respects."

"Of course he is, scuttled back to the old man!"

The men laugh, and Penelope slips another knot into her loom.

Another night, another feast: it is late when Penelope returns to her room.

"Ourania and Semele are upstairs," whispers Eos, as the first of the suitors start to snore, faces stained with blood and meat. "With a foreign woman."

"Thank you," murmurs Penelope, creaking her fingers, weary from the motion of weft and weave. A little nod, a little turning of her head this way and that to ease out the stiffness. "Good night, honoured guests," she murmurs to the stinking hall of feasting men. None stir at her departure, save two, who watch her through half-lidded, sober eyes.

Only one lamp burns in Penelope's bedroom. It frames three women more in shadow than in light.

"Hello, your majesty," says the first. Her grey hair is woven into a plait at her back, her hooked hands rest easy in her lap. Her eyes are lazuli, and she has a chin like the prow of a trireme. Her name is Ourania, and somewhat unusually, her name is known beyond the shores of Ithaca, though no poet will ever do her homage. In ports along the coast there are many who say: "Ah yes, I know Ourania," or "Good grief, another cousin of Ourania!" for she has over a great many years extended her business into every corner of trade, and can pronounce on the quality of wool as easy as the price of timber. None of this she does for herself, of course. She does it for her husband, or perhaps her father – maybe her son. Quite what man she serves changes on a regular basis, but only rarely do people whisper the truth: she does it for Penelope.

At her side stands Semele, the daughter of mothers, the mother of daughters, an old farmer who dares to define herself by something other than a man. She is dressed now in the same garb with which she rescued Teodora, always with a muddy hem and a hunting knife at her side, the same in shrouded thicket as royal bedroom. Her arms are folded across her chest, face like the dry wood she chops every day for the stove. Ourania smells of sweet marjoram, rubbed into ageing wrists. Semele smells of sweat and smoke. These two – the merchant and the farmer – are something of a council for the Ithacan queen, as perhaps Aegyptius, Medon and Peisenor fancy themselves unto missing Odysseus. They go where a mourning queen may not, Ourania's messengers scattered across the western seas, Semele's sisters and friends in every farm and village throughout the ragged land. By disposition they should not be friends, and they did try to dislike each other for a while, but neither could keep the effort up.

These two women are not infrequent visitors to the women's places of the palace. The third is a stranger.

Let us consider this last creature, sprawled loose-limbed in Penelope's favourite chair. She has washed the worst of the mud from her face and the caked dirt from her long, ragged nails, but that is about all the concession she will make to being in a queen's most intimate chambers. There is a world in which she once had charming dimples, a smile that made her whole face change like the breaking waves of the ocean. That world burnt, eight years ago. Her sooty hair is roughly cut to a crown around her skull, which in many places marks her out as shamed, though the only person who thinks she should feel that way is herself. Her eyes are low, the colour of summer dust after rain. She is small for her people, and compensated for her size by biting the ear off a boy who mocked her when she was seven and he was nine; and again by gouging out the eyes of one who tried to touch her inappropriately when she was fourteen, for which sin she was only somewhat severely punished, all things considered. She wears a rough tunic of faded hide and trousers that stop just above her knees in a style that would be scandalous if anyone dared attach scandal to one who carries so many bladed things about her person. Her shoes are laced so high and tight up her calf that it would take a robber some twenty minutes to get each one off, should they attempt to loot her corpse on the battlefield. She has nearly a dozen scars, ranging from light training knocks across her hands to the two gashes on her right arm, one below her elbow and one above, where an attacker's blade slipped past her guard. There is also a scar down her back that should have killed her, but Apollo remembered he was a god of medicine that day, which is unusual for the prancing little squirt.

Her name is Priene. She sprawls by the open window, and

though she is not of my people, tonight she may be of service to me and mine.

Penelope — tired and disturbed by events she does not yet feel she can control — blinks a smile into her eyes for wily Ourania, nods greetings to rough-fingered Semele, and finally turns a much less convincing smile onto her lips for Priene. "Ourania, Semele. I apologise; I have kept you waiting far too long. I trust you have been appropriately looked after?"

"Your maids have been very attentive, as always. Ah — and is this the famous loom?" Ourania rises as the wooden frame is brought in by Autonoe and Leaneira, ready for another night away from the sight of men. "Laertes' shroud will be ... intricate, I'm sure."

Ourania once was a slave in the palace. When the man who should have protected the quality of the grain grew lax, she took the task upon herself with unfashionable efficiency. Freedom only increased the efficacy of her work, though there is not a single poet in all of Greece who would dare breathe of such an outcome.

Now on this moonless night in Ithaca, Penelope detaches the last pin that holds back her veil, glances at the chair that should really be hers, thinks twice before challenging the armed woman in it for possession, and slumps down instead at the end of her bed.

"What word from abroad?" she asks at last.

"Many different words, depending on who you ask. There are rumours of trouble in Mycenae. Some business with Agamemnon and his wife."

"There's always business with Agamemnon and Clytemnestra — they were never happier than when apart."

"I have a cousin ... " Ourania has a lot of cousins across the Aegean Sea, some more related than others, "who says that when Agamemnon stepped off his ship, the first thing he did was put his Trojan concubines in his wife's old chambers."

"And where did Clytemnestra put her lover, I wonder?"

"I am sure somewhere safe. She had a lot of fun wielding power while her husband was off pillaging his way around the southern seas. She issued edicts, passed laws, punished her enemies . . ."

"That is what a queen is meant to do, you know."

"Ah – of course. Silly of me to forget."

Penelope's lips thin. She rolls back onto her bent elbows, creaking her neck back and side to side, eyes half closed beneath the bower of the olive tree from which the room itself, and the bed on which she rests, was hewn. "Peisenor is raising a militia of men."

For the first time, there is a little sound from the woman Priene. It is a snort of contempt. It is not a subtle snort. It is not a little womanly attempt to swallow some compromising laughter. It is a proper, pig-snuffling, snot-swirling mucus mush of amusement at someone else's expense. Penelope pushes herself up a little higher, eyes the woman with one brow raised. "Priene, yes? Your name is . . . Priene?"

Priene shrugs. She lost interest in her name many years ago.

"If I were to tell you that an army of boys, raised without fathers, are arming themselves right now in the last tatters of armour and spear we have left on these islands to fight Illyrians by the midnight sea, what would you say?" Another snort, this one only slightly less extreme than the first because Priene had blown so much of her bile in her initial response to the whole laughable situation. "My son is going to be one of them. He is very keen to be a hero."

"Only soldiers have their throats cut by Illyrians," Priene replies. "To be a hero, you have to be killed by a hero."

"I have tried to explain this to him, but in recent years . . ." Penelope lets out a sigh. There are things here she, who prides herself on a certain clarity, has not said out loud even to the dusty shadow of her face in the bronze mirror. "I have a problem, Priene. Ourania thinks you might be able to help me. My isles are being attacked by men who dress themselves as Illyrians but kill like Greeks. They attacked Lefkada two months ago, then Phenera, on Ithaca itself. They come when there is moonlight on the water. They come too soon for Illyrians to have sailed home and returned in the time since last they came. They come at just the right time to put pressure on me to marry someone who might be able to protect my shore. They attacked a settlement whose chief occupation and business is smuggling. An Ithacan would know that, of course, or someone who has been residing a while on my island. But an Illyrian? Would an Illyrian really know what secrets Phenera held? This is my problem."

"You have a lot of problems, queen."

Penelope nearly laughs, hands pressing briefly to her eyes. She is tired; so very tired. "Yes. Yes, I do. My son is going to join a militia commanded by at least two men who want to kill him, one who doesn't care and one who can't hold a shield. He is going to sulk around the coast looking for pirates, and when they come, they are going to kill him. My lands will burn, my subjects will be taken as slaves, and even the danger – the very slim danger – that my husband is alive will no longer keep the men who say I should marry at bay. Either I take a husband capable of raising troops and winning a civil war, or I let the western isles fall into chaos, at which point Menelaus will be only too happy to sweep in as our heroic and lingering saviour. None of these options are acceptable. So I need to kill some pirates."

Priene shrugs. "You're a queen. That's your job."

"No. My job is to pine for my husband and get out of my son's way."

"Then your island will burn."

"Do you know how Ithaca has survived these last eighteen years?" Priene doesn't know; Priene doesn't care. "Who brings in the firewood? Who keeps the wolves at bay? Who hunts the wild boar, sets traps in the forest, builds walls when the storm has battered from the west? Who was left, when my husband took the men to Troy, to do all this?"

Priene doesn't answer, but neither does her face ripple with her accustomed contempt. Her eyes flicker to Semele, cracked as driftwood by Ourania's side, then away again. Priene is so, so far from home, from those far-off lands where once Penthesilea rallied her warrior women from atop the fanged chariot. She can never go back. "Hunters aren't soldiers," she says at last. "You don't skin a Greek like you do a rabbit."

"No. But we live on an island of wolves, not rabbits," muses Penelope. "I was asked by a woman – little more than a girl, really – what the point of my being queen is. I make no public declaration, rarely show my face, keep myself modestly away from the voices of men. And yet I am the queen, and I will defend my kingdom. Do you understand me, Priene?"

Priene sucks in her lips, puffs them out, tucks her knees in, then stretches, then curls around that old scar in her back, winces, and finally, at last, sits up straight. "I don't work for Greeks."

"Then why are you here?"

"Sometimes Greeks pay me to kill Greeks."

"Priene, I rather think I'm offering precisely that. They tell me that in your tribe the women fight like men. That your queen ... "

"Don't say her name!" Her voice is loud enough that in the hall outside the maids stir, eyes meeting, should they go in? Should they call for help? Their instructions were clear, but Penelope likes a bit of initiative when death is on the line.

Ourania is stone, a barely breathing thing. Semele has a knife on her belt, but her folded arms do not twitch. Penelope lets out a careful breath. "I apologise. I heard she was brave, honourable and wise. But I need an army that will fight without honour. In the east, your people are feared. In the west, if it is known that Ithaca is defended by widows and the daughters of men who never came home, every mercenary from here to the court of Minos will come to our shores. My son can have his armour and his heroics if he absolutely must. But I need to win. The women are already gathering. They meet in the forest above the temple of Artemis, but they are, as you say, hunters, not warriors. I need them to be both. Will you help me?"

In the east, in the tribe of Priene's people, there is a goddess clad in golden flames, keeper of the sacred hearth. I saw her once, blazing fire on the still waters of the river, while around her the men dressed themselves in women's garb to kneel down and offer bloody sacrifice to her name. There were lesser gods at her back, Papaios and Thagimasidas, Api and Oitosyros, all come to offer her homage, but she – she stood above them all, catching the dawn of the valley in her crimson hand. I hid my face from her sight, and fled back to Olympus before she might catch sight of me and see in my eyes my envy and my despair.

Priene's queen is dead, and she has sworn to recognise no other. But in this moment, she surprises herself by finding that she is considering the problem as laid before her, lips drawn and fingers still by her side. Finally she rises, nods once to Penelope, nods a little deeper to Ourania, to Semele, thinks she sees perhaps something familiar in the old huntress's eyes. "In two days," she barks, "you'll have my answer."

Then, as she is not comfortable, perhaps, with the roar of voices below or the press of the maids' ears to the door, she goes to the window, and climbs out through it as if it were the most natural and civilised thing in the world.

CHAPTER 13

>>

L et us consider a boy who is most definitely not a man.
Telemachus.

Every dawn he retreats to this place, away from the palace, on a grubby path that smells of pig shit. The farm technically is his – or at least, his father's; the distinction is a little vague. It is guarded by Eumaios, swineherd to Odysseus, a man sold as a child, bought into slavery and never quite freed because it was never given unto him to consider the faintest concept of freedom, nor given unto his masters to consider it even at all.

There are pigs snoozing in the house. There is still the last grey of night hanging like a cobweb on the day. There is a javelin, a sword, a shield, a spear. There is a man made of straw propped up by a wall. Sometimes there is his father's bow, stolen from the armoury, which he has panted and sweated and strained at as he tries to string the thrice-damned thing, but to no success. Now he steals it less frequently, and when he does, it is a badge of shame.

Telemachus is a boy, but absolutely aspires to manhood – of course he does. Every boy on Ithaca, when he turns twelve, is convinced that he is Achilles reborn. Of course, if he had not died at Troy, Achilles would just have been a whiny little

95

mummy's boy who dressed himself as a girl to avoid being called to service; but there's nothing like a really good war, a decent massacre or two, to get the poets' attention.

It has occurred to Telemachus, in one of his shrewder moments – and in fairness to the boy, he has some – that he will need to either participate in, or possibly engineer, a truly spectacular war for the ages if he is to be remembered. A proper genocide, maybe punctuated by a volcano or earthquake, at least fifty thousand nameless dead, and a half-dozen proper heroes too.

He may one day be a good enough man to realise that this is a terrible metric for valour. Right now, being as he is merely a squirt with a spear, his moral compass fluctuates.

He trains with sword and javelin on straw men. Sometimes a few soldiers – ancient Ithacans too old to lift a shield even when Odysseus sailed, or those half-dozen trusted men who liked fish enough to settle on this isle – train with him. He is reasonably competent. He has a few friends, boys of his own age. They became his friends in awe of his father's name, but it is nice to see that most have stuck around in personal loyalty to Telemachus, who, if slightly dull company, is at least faithful to his companions. He thinks, if he called on all his allies on Ithaca, Kephalonia, Zakynthos and the half-dozen lesser isles that sprinkle his father's domain, he can muster eighty spears.

He stabs a straw man, who does not resist.

Eighty spears.

It would be enough to kill the suitors. Especially if he took them by surprise. Locked the armoury door, attacked them when they were drunk. It would be enough. Raising that many men in secret would be hard, but if he was clever, like his father; if he was wise . . .

Thwack – he buries a blade in a straw neck, which bleeds a little hay but otherwise does not object.

Sometimes, when duty forces him to look Antinous in the eye, he plays a game of imagining precisely how he'll kill this suitor, only a sniff older than him, who would be his stepfather. He finds the exercise allows him to maintain eye contact, politely, as if he were not calculating the best angle to slip a blade up between his ribs.

Thwack – he twists the sword in a straw gut. He once heard an old soldier say that fighting clean was for fools. First you survive. Then you make up the story of how.

A voice says, "Um, excuse me, I think . . . Oh."

He turns, sword up, ready to fight, ready to kill, someone has intruded on his sanctuary and he is . . .

But the man who stands behind him isn't armed. He smiles, a little embarrassed, raises his hands placatingly, says: "Apologies. I heard the sound of weapons and I thought . . . but I did not mean to disturb your peace."

"Egyptian," huffs Telemachus, lowering his blade, a flush of shame rising unbidden, as it always does, to his rosy cheeks. "I mean . . . Kenamon, yes? Why are you here?"

"I was walking. I have been trying to explore every path I can find from the palace, to learn something of this island. As I said, I heard the sound of a sword striking, unmistakable, and I thought . . . But this is clearly some private place. My apologies. I'll leave."

The door of the little house creaks open an inch, letting out the smell of pig. Eumaios has one eye to the crack, not quite bold enough to step out, not quite sly enough to stay hidden within. Odysseus's swineherd was always more loyal than he was wise. Kenamon turns to leave, his cloak swung across a shoulder in a manner, Telemachus notes, that might make it easy to reach and draw a blade should he need to – interesting that, that's something a man would do – and as he goes, Telemachus calls out after him.

"Please, you are not disturbing me. Please." He puts his sword down, though quite why the gesture is needful, he doesn't really know, and steps a little away from the smell of pig. "I owe you . . . thanks . . . for last night."

The boy is ashamed, so, so ashamed he wants to curl up and cry at the memory of it, but Telemachus will be a man, and men are honest, and face up to their fears, and acknowledge other men when they are worthy.

"I am new here." Kenamon smiles. "I thought perhaps I misunderstood the custom of the feast."

Telemachus draws level with the Egyptian, noting now everything about his stance, his poise. Knees soft, ready to spring; feet planted, somehow both solid and light – how does he do that? "It shames us when a stranger is more courteous than even some of the Greeks. But perhaps we need strangers to remind us of the value of the things we take for granted?"

"I find that a man does not appreciate what he has in his home until he is far from it."

Telemachus is chewing his bottom lip, and forces himself to stop immediately, to lock a smile in place. "If you are exploring the paths of this island, perhaps I can show you some of the more pleasing places? Very few suitors leave the confines of the town, but there are waterfalls and streams, high hills with excellent vistas that you may find ease the pain of being so far from your homeland."

"I would appreciate that very much, but I do not want to impose."

"It is no imposition. You are my guest; I am your host. Please – walk with me."

They walk for a while in silence, climbing towards the sound of a running stream, a bowl of hollowed stone, the trees keeping down the heat of the rising day. Sometimes Kenamon asks what do you call this, or that, or what is the sound of this particular bird that sings in a silver branch? And Telemachus answers as best he can, and warns that there are wild animals, and Kenamon asks: "Who hunts them, when the men are gone?"

And it occurs to Telemachus that there can only really be one answer to that question, but he himself has never bothered to ask it until now.

And it occurs to Telemachus that Kenamon might be around his father's age, or perhaps a couple of years younger. He has seen men of that age before, of course, but he has almost never wandered into the morning forest with one.

They push through a grove of pine-needle trees to the top of the waterfall, which rushes down loud enough to drown out speech, and Kenamon laughs and hollers over the roar that he has never seen such a thing, and that in Egypt the only water that makes such sounds are the great rapids of the furthest south, where the land fractures into a thousand floating islands of impassable green.

Then they climb a little further, up above the trees to the sun-bleached white stones that crown the highest hill, and look down to the sea, the sun glistening and glaring off its mirrored waters, and Telemachus asks the one thing he's been dying to: "Were you a soldier?"

"I was, yes."

"You fought in battles?"

"Not battles like your great battles of Troy, if that's what you mean. But I fought in bloody skirmishes in the south, in night fights and crimson mud."

"I am to fight in a battle soon," muses Telemachus. "To defend what is mine."

"Against whom? Not the suitors, I hope?"

He shakes his head, though of course yes, yes, one day: yes. "There are raiders, attacking our land. I have joined the militia."

"Ah, that is good. Can you fight?" The question is a joke, but the tight collapse of Telemachus's face withers even Kenamon's easy smile. The Egyptian swallows, reaches out, stops himself before putting a hand on the younger man's arm, turns away to the sky, then back to the sea. Thinks he is going to say something, and says instead: "What are those?"

Telemachus follows his gaze, down to the floating horizon.

There are three black sails on the water, coming out of the east.

He rises at once from his perch on the top of his – his father's – his – *this* kingdom, and blurts, "I have to go," and runs towards the palace and the sea.

CHAPTER 14

>>>

Penelope is counting sheep with Leaneira when the call comes. She has spent a lot of her life counting livestock of some manner or other. Without the regular supply of slaves and plunder that kings provide, she has been forced to invest her energies into such unfashionable exploits as agriculture, manufacturing and trade. No one takes such things seriously, of course, but then if no one takes it seriously, neither does anyone truly have a sensible grasp of the profits that might be available to a wily queen with an eye for a nice hoof.

"My queen!" It is Phiobe who arrives, breathless, from the port. Very few of Penelope's maids address her as "my queen" unless there is an awkward public occasion that needs a little enlivening, or the matter is too serious to draw respectful breath. "Black sails!"

"How many ships?" Penelope asks, turning away at once from her counting. And in the same breath: "Leaneira, my veil."

Leaneira scurries inside to fetch all the necessaries of widowly modesty, as Phiobe gasps: "Three, from the east, rowing hard."

"Fetch Eos, then send Autonoe to gather my council and what men we have. Where is my son?"

"I, uh ... " Phiobe doesn't know, and is too breathless to

conjure some excuse. Penelope dismisses the question with a waft of her hand.

"Send to Semele, warn her; then Ourania, tell her to prepare my boat. Go!"

Phiobe scurries away as Leaneira returns, veil in hand. "Black sails?" she murmurs, as her mistress adjusts the flow of fabric across her brow.

"Never good," Penelope replies. "And three ships are more than you'd send to simply spread bad news."

"Could it be your husband?"

Penelope's answer sticks for a moment in her throat. How strange, she muses, that it had not even occurred to her that the answer might be yes. But no, a shaking of her head. "He would not come back to Ithaca under sails of black. News of him ... perhaps. People will speculate. But if that is so, we need to be the first to meet it, and try to salvage what we can. Come – we must not let Polybus or Eupheithes beat us to the messenger."

Polybus and Eupheithes are already at the docks when Penelope arrives. Their sons, Eurymachus and Antinous, are dragged from their beds and told to make themselves presentable. Next is Andraemon, with his servant, dark-eyed Minta, huddled in a low cloak against the sea-breeze salt; then Amphinomous and a dozen more suitors. Telemachus appears at a breathless trot, realises this is how he appears, and slows down, trying to turn his gallop into something more akin to a stately walk as he enters the growing throng.

Penelope arrives flanked by six of her maids and six of her more loyal guards, Medon in tow to show some semblance of masculine authority. If she cannot make a prompt entrance, she may as well at least make a grand one. All her maids wear veils, a token of pre-emptive respect to whatever grim message the approaching black sails portend.

102

Everyone is there before the ships, of course. The result is fantastically tedious. The port of Ithaca is busy at the worst of times, and there is a great deal of "left a bit – right a bit – watch the oars!" about the jutting, crooked quays. Manoeuvring three fine ships with ebony sails into the small harbour is so dull that old Polybus, who tires easily, calls for a chair, and not to be outdone, so does Eupheithes, leaving only Penelope and her entourage standing with anything much in the way of dignity.

The women are grateful for their veils. They can let their faces lapse into expressions of utmost boredom, without the pressure to maintain the sombre frowns of deep import that Telemachus and the men are currently aching in, or the polite smiles of welcome that may become needed in the next few moments. In a small way, Penelope is also grateful for the time it takes to secure the ships, for it gives her a chance to consider a dozen scenarios that might be about to play out. Only one of those concerns her husband – that these ships have come to inform her of his final, confirmed death. She hopes they haven't brought a body. A body will force her to spend many hours in public weeping over what will almost certainly be a pretty grotesque thing, especially if he drowned. The needful display of grief will rob her of valuable time that must be spent acting in privacy, and haste.

Somewhere less than an hour's walk away, in a little curve of the isle where sand meets sea, Ourania and her maids are preparing a ship of some dozen oars to carry Penelope and her son to safety. Penelope does not know if she'll need it, and this is not the first time the alarm has been sounded, but it is best to be prepared for the very worst.

When the first great ship of black is moored, no one disembarks.

This is frustrating for two reasons. Firstly, it forces the waiting crowds to wait a little more, those looks of profound import really starting to grate in the unveiled faces of the men. Secondly, there is an implication – a not entirely thrilling implication – that on one of the other ships are dignitaries considered important enough that their accomplices must politely wait on deck for said dignitaries to disembark. That makes this whole affair more significant. The best-case scenario will be some lesser king, sent to add weight to a declaration from Menelaus or Agamemnon. Perhaps Peisistratus, son of Nestor – or Nestor himself. The old man might just consider turning up in person if Odysseus was dead; he has that sense of pomp. If it's Nestor, that might be useful; no one will start a civil war with the revered old man, beloved ally of Odysseus, by Penelope's side, and it probably wouldn't occur to him to attempt to annex Ithaca straight away. She might have to marry Telemachus off to one of Nestor's daughters – Epicaste seems nice, likes a bit of poetry – but that is a small price to pay for holding the isles.

And then look again, and there are motifs upon the prow of the ship – something of the bull and something of the lion – that don't seem to be Nestor's style. And there upon the shields of the men standing on the deck of the largest ship, she has seen that design before, when men of Mycenae came to take her husband to war. Oh Penelope, she's got this sick, sinking feeling in her belly . . .

The largest ship is tied off to the wooden jetty, a horn is sounded, a flat, farting blast through white bone rimmed with bronze. A few soldiers disembark first to flank their precious cargo. Penelope sees two figures step into the circle of their men, one dressed in statesmen's robes rustled by the sea, the other in a crude grey tunic, ash upon her brow. They approach at a pace so sombre, so depressingly slow that even the sternest of onlookers in the crowd feel their bladders clench with the need to get on with it, *get on with it!*

Penelope is the first to recognise them, the first to step forward and greet them. She bobs lower than is strictly required, as she is queen of this island, but it is a good habit for a mourning monarch of a minor nation to get a solid dose of meekness in early. The approaching men stop; the two figures in their midst step forward to greet her.

"Noble Orestes, gentle Elektra – honoured children of Agamemnon," she says, the words coming out flat and low as her mind runs through possibilities, none of them good. "Of all the Greeks, you are most welcome to Ithaca."

I can compose a list of the ten least welcome faces of all the isles that Penelope might have welcomed to her shore, and it is my omnipotent, infallible pronouncement that Orestes and Elektra take ninth and sixth places respectively. This is not about to be altered by their words or deeds, for lo: Elektra has drawn ashes from the crown of her head to the bottom of her chin with two fingers, bathed her nails in soot, scraped ashes into her hair. She must have had a little fire going on the ship – superbly dangerous – in order to keep the look so fresh, Penelope muses. Or perhaps she carries a box of charcoal with her – that would be more sensible – powdered with a little beeswax to serve as fixative. If Penelope was going to spend her days on the high seas being blasted by salt water, she'd definitely want to adulterate her burnt offerings with something to keep them in place.

Orestes hasn't quite gone for the same look, but then it would be undignified for a man to be quite so sentimental as his sister is. Instead, hand upon the pommel of his sword – his father's sword? – he intones in a voice barely more living than Penelope's own: "Thank you, noble wife of Odysseus. But we are children of Agamemnon no more. Our father is dead."

CHAPTER 15

>>>

This is how Agamemnon, greatest of all the Greeks, mightiest king in east and west, conqueror of Troy, lord of Mycenae, died.

"Fucking whore, fucking whore, come here, you little bitch, you slut, you ... come *here*! When I catch you, I'll ... "

One of the disadvantages of a well-appointed palace of white marble and gold trim is that your words may echo mightily through its halls. Slaves turn their faces away; courtiers scuttle into the shadows as the king passes. But even in the great court of Mycenae, sooner or later there is nowhere left to run.

Afterwards, when he had caught his wife by the neck and made his feelings clear to her, she washed, and beholding her hair pulled back wet around her face, he said: "You look like a fucking ... "

The rest of the sentence was cut short by the blade that his wife drove through his windpipe and the back of his neck. He stood there a moment, his weight supported by the upward thrust of her arms still clinging to the blade that had silenced him. Then his bulk, fattened on offal and bloated on crimson wine, became too much for her to support, and she let go the blade and he fell bleeding to the earth.

Of course, when the poets tell it, they either add a certain artistic flare – he was in the bath; he was being caressed by his wife's sensuous touch at the moment of oddly sexualised betrayal; he was cut down by Clytemnestra's lover, since men are so much more reliable at this sort of thing; he was surveying the riches he'd plundered from Troy, and a few other places besides. If his drunkenness is mentioned, it is as a thing that put him into a meek stupor, since if we accept for even a moment that a woman – a *woman!* – could kill the conqueror of Troy, butcher of Priam and all his kin, then absolutely, but of course, Agamemnon had to be a little drunk. A lamb-like intoxication, gentle and subdued, rather than the raging spittler he actually was.

I watched his death from above, as did many of the gods. Even my husband Zeus, who always had a soft spot for rambunctious men, simply tutted and turned his head away. Though Agamemnon was once beloved and blessed, there was now not one god left on Olympus who didn't feel this whole thing had got a bit much. So no miracles came, no signs were seen, no mercies cast. Just his wife's knife through his throat, and a body half undressed, floppy on the floor.

In the palace of Odysseus, Pylades, sworn brother and servant of Orestes, tells it somewhat differently, while the ashen children of Agamemnon sit in the place of honour and listen. Even the suitors are subdued and silent as the Mycenaean relates his tale of a tyrant queen gone mad with lust and power. Of the treachery of women, of betrayal and grotesque barbarity by savage Clytemnestra – a plague on treacherous women! he howls.

In Mycenae, in Pheneus, in Olympia itself, this declaration has produced nothing but shouts of acclamation, of roaring praise. A plague on treacherous women, treacherous women!

In Ithaca, there is absolute silence. Even the most foolish of the suitors are keeping their mouths shut, minds racing.

Penelope sits a little apart from her great guests, hidden behind her veil, which barely flutters with the disturbance of breath.

All the men queue to cast their libations on the fire. They were not forewarned of this matter, so will have to rush home later to find proper sacrifices that they can be seen publicly to burn upon the sacred altar. But even in death Penelope is a good host, and has ordered that every man be given a fistful of grain and a cup of wine from the palace stores, discreetly passed around by the maids as Pylades made his speech so that not a man who rises may be unprepared to show their devotion to the great murdered king.

Even Kenamon, whose customs are not of this place, does as he sees the others do, and pours his libations before the feet of ashen Elektra, stone-faced Orestes, children of the slain monarch, and mutters some brief words of prayer, though he does not know what god might care for the heart of such a man as Agamemnon.

There will be no feasting that night, nor for seven nights to come, and Penelope, for her part, is both relieved and concerned by this turn of events. Seven nights' respite will be a blessed thing for her household, but then again, where will the suitors go, what will they do, if she is not there to watch them?

Orestes says some few words – words of vengeance and blood.

Elektra says nothing, but holds his hand when he returns to his chair, squeezes it so tight Penelope thinks she can see the blood pushed from his fingertips, leaving just pale flesh, cold, though Orestes, if he notices, doesn't seem to care.

The children of Agamemnon are given the finest rooms in the palace. Not Odysseus's room, of course – that would be sacrilege – but the quarters of old Laertes himself, and his dead wife, Anticlea. It is perhaps apt that the first woman to sleep in the mother's dusty bed be the daughter of a dead king.

Penelope catches Telemachus by the arm as he passes by her

in the hall. "Stay close to Orestes," she breathes, but he pulls his arm free.

"I don't need telling what to do, Mother."

"He will be the most powerful man in Greece now that his father is dead. You need his support."

"He is my cousin. I don't need … women's tricks …" Telemachus stumbles over the words, trying to catch those that convey the full scale of his contempt for this back-corridor bartering. "We share blood and honour."

"Right now that boy's mother just killed his father. His father killed his sister. His uncle hungers for the Mycenaean throne. In Athena's name, think before you speak."

Telemachus turns, and though he is forced to walk away from the direction he actually wanted to go in, it is the only direction he can walk to make a point of turning his back on his mother as he strides down the hall.

Later, once she's gone, he sneaks back the way he's come, so as not to ruin the effect.

Eos stands by Penelope's side in her room of olive wood and cold sheets, and follows her gaze down to the sea.

"What now?" she asks simply.

"Hum?"

"What should we do now?"

"I don't know."

"Do you need the ship? Should we flee?"

"Not yet. Maybe. Not yet. I need to think. This changes everything. Fear of Agamemnon was the only thing holding the princes of Greece in line. Unless Orestes can secure the throne, the only king capable of keeping the peace is Menelaus, and he is …"

What of Menelaus? He is hearing news of his brother's death, one leg slung across the armrest of his golden throne, one hand dallying in the soft hair of his wife, Helen, as she crouches at his feet. He nods at nothing much as word is delivered, and pulls in his bottom lip, and does not cry, and does not frown, and does not laugh out loud, and says only when it's done: "And where is young Orestes now?" Thus does the news come to Sparta.

On Ithaca, Eos turns her gaze to the ground. "Did you think it was Odysseus, when you saw the sails?"

"It was a possibility."

"Did you hope?"

"Hope?" The word is strange on Penelope's tongue, a curious notion. "That my husband was dead?"

"Or that he was living?"

Stranger and stranger! Of all the possibilities she had considered, what to do if Odysseus was alive had not been one of them. The revelation is briefly funny, briefly sad, but this strange dance of emotion lasts only a moment, and the frown around her brow will make her old before her time. "No. I did not hope."

A gentle knock on the door: Autonoe, her veil pulled back only briefly while she is in this private place. All the maids who are seen in public will be veiled for seven days, or if there are not enough veils to go around, they will draw ashes across their brows, with a little something extra in it so they don't have to waste too much time constantly refreshing the pious look. "The lady Elektra asks to speak with you," she murmurs, voice heavy with warning. No sorrow is there for the death of a king, merely for all that must follow.

CHAPTER 16

>>>

There is only one lamp burning in Elektra's room – the room that used to belong to Odysseus's mother. It throws hard dancing shadows up one wall, lets the darkness of Hades creep in deep around the edges. Odysseus met the ghost of his mother on the shores of the Styx nearly five years ago. She sucked the blood from his fingertips, hollow eyes seeing only the scarlet liquor he offered her, until at last, a little nourished, her flailing tongue grew back into the hollow of her skull and she pronounced on matters of grief and the dead.

Penelope doesn't know this, of course, and all those who travelled with Odysseus to the land of the lost are now shallow ghosts themselves, wandering through fields of blackened wheat; but in this place, tonight, she thinks she feels the kiss of the departed upon her neck, and wonders if it is her husband.

Elektra still wears her ashes. There is a commitment there that Penelope both dislikes and is forced to respect. The daughter of Agamemnon is a few years older than Telemachus, yet still unmarried, waiting, she always said, for her father to choose a man and give her his blessing. Though she shares some blood with Helen, there will be no murals to her beauty painted on the walls of any palace. Her father's hawk nose and her mother's stubborn chin combine to give her a profile like folded metal. Her hair is stiff curls, too tight to be fashionable, too thick to be controlled. Her eyes are huge in her face, but whereas the poets say in her brother there is a charming sincerity about his moon-gaze, in Elektra the movement of her head is the turn of the hawk, hunting, absorbing light as if every soul were but a quivering rabbit in her sight. Her father had those eyes, but had learnt to turn his head slow, the lion who is deciding whether he will consume you, or if the blood in his belly is enough for now, himself too fatted and slow to strike.

Elektra is sticks and skin, draped in grey. As a child, she wore armbands of gold, given to her by her mother, who would hold her so tight she thought she would break from squeezing, and whisper in her ear: "You will live, my daughter. You will live and no one will ever harm you."

Elektra was five when her sister, Iphigenia, was sacrificed on the altar of Artemis by her father's bloody hand. She doesn't remember much about her sister; only the occasional flash of pain.

"Lady Elektra," Penelope says, as she seats herself opposite the young woman in the shadowed room. Elektra has brought two maids, as ashen as she, who now flit away at a limp twist of the woman's skinny hand. It is hard to know how to address this slim, hunched creature. She is not a queen, but technically, now her brother Orestes is all but enthroned in Mycenae, she is the sister to the greatest monarch in all of Greece. And yet, what are sisters without husbands, in these times?

"Penelope – may I call you Penelope? We are cousins, are we not?"

Penelope smiles, nods. "Elektra. I trust you have everything you need? May I bring you more light?"

"No, thank you. This is sufficient. Your hospitality has been sufficient."

Ithaca is nothing if not sufficient. It's practically the island's motto.

"All of Greece grieves for your loss." This is a nice, easy statement for royal figures to make. It spreads out the burden for floods of tears and rending of hair to lots of different people, and thus protects your fine coiffure from immediate danger of dismemberment.

"I know. My father was beloved."

Agamemnon, butcher of Troy, who led the greatest men of Greece to their deaths in a ten-year war over an absent queen. The poets certainly love him, and when bones are dust and the dust has blown into the sea before the crumbled ashes of Troy, on that day indeed the poets' love will be the only love that matters. Penelope does not have the words to answer this.

A silence settles. In this silence there should be more small talk. Penelope, for all her wits, is not very good at small talk. Being permitted to grieve profoundly for an absent husband has been something of a social blessing these last eighteen years, an acceptable shroud for quiet. But in this darkened room, there are certain rituals that must be followed, certain patterns of behaviour that now Penelope tries to dredge from her over-busy thoughts.

She opens her mouth to begin with some passing remark – the quality of the bull that will be sacrificed in Agamemnon's name, or some anecdote perhaps in which her husband told her wonderful things about this great king, when they were young together. All of Odysseus's stories were about him when he was young. Penelope only knew him before he had time to grow old.

Then Elektra says: "You want to know why we've come."

Well thank ye gods, Penelope thinks, and out loud she replies: "Any child of Agamemnon is always ... "

"You want to know why we've come to Ithaca," Elektra

cuts in – terribly rude! Yet a rudeness that is in this place welcome, refreshing, blessed. "We could have sent messengers. Many people – great kings – are hearing the news from some paltry slave. Even my uncle, Menelaus, is hearing it only from a favoured cup-bearer. You want to know why my brother and I have come all this way to Ithaca, to an island that is ... " Her nose wrinkles for a moment, trying to seek out a word that is accurate without being an outright insult. "... so far from Mycenae's interests."

"The question had crossed my mind, yes."

A little nod. Elektra's mother loved flattery, she loved a good wit. A fine poet stood before her once and dazzled her with his games, his verbal dance; he was no warrior, he was no mighty king, but Clytemnestra took him in her arms and he was ...

... anyway. Enough of what he was. Elektra has sworn not to think of such things ever again. She has rejected not merely her mother's blood, but all qualities of Clytemnestra that could have possibly been transmitted with it. A fondness for music. A love of fresh, warm bread. Long hair worn high in a braid across a woman's brow. The colour yellow. A delight in words. All these must die with the woman who killed her father.

"Clytemnestra." Even saying the word makes Elektra shift uneasily, despising it upon her tongue, but there is a job to be done, and she will do it. "After she murdered our father, she fled. My brother killed her lover, but she got away. It is ... unmanly ... unacceptable ... an insult before the gods that my father's killer breathes. Do you understand?"

"I think I do. But that does not explain why you have come to Ithaca."

"Doesn't it?"

A flash of something in Elektra's eyes, there it is again, the lion, the hawk, she may tell herself that her strength came from her father but her mother looked like that too when the men started gossiping behind her back, when they whispered that a woman should not rule as a man.

It would be kind now for Elektra to speak her mind, to lay it out fully. But she is not kind. She has sworn never to be kind ever again.

Instead Penelope moves uncomfortably in her chair, and tries to find a way with words that is not a confession, is not a threat. "Very well. If we are speaking so directly to each other, as perhaps cousins should ... Orestes cannot be king until he has killed his mother," she proclaims. "No Greek will follow a man who is too weak to kill a woman. Strong men with greedy hearts will look upon Agamemnon's empty throne. Menelaus, your uncle, for one. A warrior of Troy. So Orestes must move quickly to revenge his father's murder and end his mother's life. Why then come to Ithaca? Why waste time with this isle?" She looks again to Elektra, waiting for her cousin to say out loud the words that should be said, but Elektra does not. Her silence is illuminating. Her silence tells Penelope a great many things she does not like about this woman of Mycenae. "You have come to kill Clytemnestra."

Even the lion would take a breath before answering. Elektra does not. "Yes."

"You believe she is in my husband's kingdom?"

"We do."

"Why?"

"I have intelligence that she is fleeing west. Ithaca is the gateway to the western seas. If she wishes to escape, she must take ship from your port. We have followed her here; we do not think we are far behind."

"I am not without eyes in my own kingdom. I would know if my cousin were here."

"Would you, cousin? And what would you do then?"

Careful — so careful now — Penelope reaches for her words

115

"Had she come to me as a queen, I would have honoured her. Now I know that she is a killer, I would happily see her burn." This is a lie. I rest my hand upon the Ithacan queen's shoulder, give it a gentle squeeze. Almighty Zeus, if he looks down from Olympus tonight, is perhaps watching young Telemachus as he fawns at Orestes' door. He is watching the men of Mycenae prowl around their boats; he is watching the flicker of something in the corner of Menelaus's eye as he hears the news of his brother's demise. My husband is not watching this room, these women. Tonight any divinity that comes upon them shines from me.

"Well then," muses Elektra at last. "Well. My mother is cunning. She knows how to hide."

"I can send word, order every ship searched, every . . . "

"Yes. Do that. Close the harbours."

"We are not a land of riches. It is not merely tin and amber that passes through the port. It is grain for my people, feed for their animals."

"Then you need to find her quickly, yes?"

Penelope catches a breath, swallows it down, turns her head towards the thin, flickering light, then back to Elektra. "My husband was an ally to your father. The western isles are at your service, as always."

Elektra smiles, and it is the smile of the skinless skull that laughs at jokes only Hades enjoys. She half bows her head, and Penelope rises. The shadowed maids draw back even further into the dark, as if to say: who, us? We were never here.

Then, with Penelope's hand upon the door, Elektra says: "You played with my mother as a child, did you not? Both of you growing up in Sparta."

Once upon a time there were three queens playing together in the fields of Sparta, children running barefoot in the sun. Where are they now? Penelope's eyes are fixed on some distant place. "Clytemnestra pulled my hair, and Helen said I walked like a duck."

"She ruled Mycenae, as you now rule in your husband's place."

"Yes," mused Penelope. "She did. Yet I am certain that tomorrow morning, Orestes will go and speak to my council – loyal men who love Odysseus – and discuss these heavy matters with my son, and when they are done, they will send to me and say that they wish the harbours closed and the islands searched. And what queen – or king – would not comply with such sage council?"

Elektra barely knows her cousin Penelope, but she thinks she sees something of her mother in her, and wants to love her, wants to hate her, wants to ask her blessing and spit in her face. Elektra has not been held by another's arms for eleven years, when she last pushed her mother away and screamed: "I am *NOT* Iphigenia!" and ran from the room and was never loved by her mother again. Elektra once kissed a slave boy behind the blacksmith's workshop and his hands went into her private places and she wept and wanted more then shoved him away and ran from the smell of metal and flame and later had him sold so his eyes could no longer burn her face, and has never looked at another man since.

My expert opinion, as a goddess who knows about these sort of things: Elektra is a very confused young woman.

So she says: "It is as you say, cousin. It is as you say," and does not sleep all night, except for when she does, but that is not what the poets will say.

CHAPTER 17

⟫⟫⟫⟫⟫⟫⟫⟫⟫⟫⟫⟫⟫⟫⟫⟫⟫⟫⟫⟫⟫⟫⟫⟫⟫⟫⟫⟫⟫⟫⟫⟫⟫⟫⟫⟫⟫

I thaca sleeps, and as it sleeps, it dreams.

Telemachus, of thrusting spears and broken shields, of the cry of battle and sunshine on the armour of valiant men. He will train every hour of the day and some of the night to serve his country, to be a hero as his father was – is – was. Yet in his dream he thrusts his spear towards some bloody enemy and it seems to slow and stick in the air, become too heavy for his arm, while all around him nimble daggers strike, and so in slumbering, he dies.

Athena on occasion sends him better dreams, but while the father lives, she is often neglectful of the son.

Elektra, of peeping through her mother's door and seeing a woman cry out in ecstasy, a poet's lips between her legs. She had not imagined that women could experience ecstasy. When she questioned her teachers on the matter, she was told it was obscene, and the priestess of Aphrodite was sent for, who explained in one really rather remarkable afternoon where babies came from, how Elektra would bleed with the turning of the moon, how women's pleasure was given only to serve the pleasure of their husbands. The conversation did not cover what happened when men snatched women from their husbands' side to pleasure themselves, because really, why go into trifling little details?

It has been two moons since Elektra's father was slain. Elektra has not bled in all that time. She wonders if she will ever bleed again.

Orestes dreams of three shadows standing before the door, and thinks he hears the wild laughter of the Furies, and knows that his life is an unravelling thing.

The maids dream too – even those who the poets will not name.

Eos – of one day being as Ourania is, a lady of shadowed power and secrets. She will manipulate men to her whim, her might will be whispered of across the seas, and yet no one will know her name. She thinks that is the greatest power of all, and smiles to think of all the men who would give up their lives to be remembered by the poets, when she would rather live, live, live in wonder, and be forgotten immediately upon the end of a long and happy life. She is not there yet, of course. But she knows how to make herself invaluable, and for a slave that is a kind of power – perhaps the only kind she will ever have.

Autonoe – of an endless black forest from which she can never escape. She tries to laugh and tries to smile, to conquer the dark with merriment as she has conquered all things, to drive back the nightmares with her defiance, but the nightmares do not leave her.

Leaneira – of running with her sister to the temple of Apollo, little feet on dusty paths, little hands reaching up to figures of gold, back before the city burnt. But even in this unsullied memory, the fires come. They creep into her childhood, they fill her youth with blood and smoke, they hollow out the skulls of her murdered brothers and her mother, screaming upon the floor. The fires of Troy take away even her past, even her dreams, until there is nothing but burning left.

In a house that smells of jasmine and fish, Priene dreams too.

She dreams of Penthesilea, her warrior queen, and the day the messengers came from Troy, summoning their allies to the fight. She dreams of the day she saw Achilles, too far off, dancing – such a dance, bronze and sunlight and a flow of flesh. He fought as the women do, not with brute force but cunning and speed. He did not wait to see if his strength was greater than his opponent, but sprang to the side of an overbalanced spear to nick the pulsing vein of a foolish, staggering brute. He resisted the slash of a heavy sword only long enough to let its momentum carry him around and away, a slip of the blade under guard and through the cracks in gleaming armour. But Penthesilea held him at bay – moved as he moved, refused the offer of an easy trap when he presented it, kept her distance when his long arm snapped across the bleeding air, sought tendon and joint, wrist and fingers, taking whatever prey she could get before moving in for the kill.

In her dreams, Priene is running, running towards Penthesilea, running to aid her queen. For all that the lady of the east was a woman without compare, a creature of the land of wolf and bear, she too had been infected by the poet's disease, for in this one battle against Achilles she had proclaimed: *I shall fight him alone.* Stark madness. Absurd rejection of their warrior ways, for they had been pack sisters since they first shared mare's milk beneath the silver sky. And yet: *my name shall be sung as the killer of Achilles,* she said. And thus, by the hands of the poets as much as by the sword of Achilles, the lady died.

Priene dreams of horses galloping across the great plains, and of mosquitoes over the river, and of how when she breathed, the wound down her back would open and close like the lips of a panting fish, and then she wakes and reaches for her blades, which are never far away, and finding them close and comforting, falls down to sleep and dream again.

There was a night by the walls of Troy when Athena entered

the dreams of Odysseus and said – I paraphrase barely – *goodness, what a nice horse.*

There was a night in Sparta when Aphrodite slipped her fingers into the cup of Paris, smearing his lips red, and murmured: *his wife's got a nice bum, hasn't she?*

I do not often enter the dreams of mortals, for my husband fears that I might implant in them some picture of myself, some touch of my mouth upon their sleepy lips, some obscene intimacy shared beneath a starry sky. Even the most flattering monuments to my glory depict me as slightly chubby, double-chinned, a mother who let herself go a bit. No one wants a visit from squelchy old Hera in the secret hours of the night. But tonight I look down at Priene, sleeping warrior from the east, and I remember how her goddess looked as she raised her hands above the great river that flows down to the sea, how her eyes blazed and her tongue flicked at parted lips, and with a surreptitious glance over my shoulder to check that no one is peeking through the scudding clouds tonight, I slip into Priene's dreams.

"Behold me, daughter," I whisper, voice of running water, hair of dancing flame. "Teach my women to fight."

It has been so long since Priene dreamt of her gods. She thought they had forsaken her, and reaches out now with shaking hands and cries out in her native tongue, *Mother, Mother, Tabiti, Mother.* I do not stay to answer. Even though we are far from her land, the lady of the east might be displeased to spot even one as magnificent as myself hijacking her prayers.

"Teach my women to fight," I breathe, as night dissolves into day.

CHAPTER 18

>>>

On the second day of mourning, the boys of Ithaca assemble.

Yes, there is great wailing and scattering of libations for Agamemnon. Yes, there will be no feasting in the halls of Odysseus tonight. But still the moon is turning, why she is turning – she has grown thin and dark as though she too wailed for the tyrant Agamemnon, and now she fattens again, her silver light kissing the sea, and just this once the people of the western isles look towards her growing smile and resent it, for with the moon, the pirates come.

In the shadow of the palace walls, Peisenor trains boys who had no fathers in the art of war.

It is a sorry sight.

It is not that these boys are particularly lacking in will or talent. Many – especially those closest to Telemachus – volunteer willingly, sensing glory in the chance to defend their homeland. Some practised with a sword when they were young, but without anyone particularly dedicated to their training, put it aside after a few swishes of metal cutting air, having performed the needed act of seeming really very valiant indeed without the learning of the skill of killing. Many are the cast-off whelps that Polybus and

Eupheithes will not miss if they die. The youngest is fourteen, and can barely lift his shield.

"All right!" growls Peisenor. "Let's try this again!"

Others watch. The four commanders of this little band – Aegyptius, Peisenor, Polybus and Eupheithes, look on as this gaggle of barely-youths bat swords at each other, and sometimes strike brave poses that waver as they overbalance beneath their weapons' weight, and generally do their best to look merry at this futile dance.

Neither Antinous nor Eurymachus are members of this troop. Their fathers will not risk their lives. Amphinomous has said he will lend his aid, but he has no need of training. He will come when called, so he says. So he says.

Another suitor watches as Peisenor drills his men. Kenamon of Memphis catches himself shaking his head, and manages to stop the motion, knowing if seen it would be considered terribly bad taste.

By the council table of yew and shell, old Medon spits the husk of seeds from between his teeth, chews the squelching innards slowly, and mouth full finally says:

"Well then we're buggered, aren't we?"

When he addresses the full council of learned peers, Medon is somewhat more circumspect in his language. When it is only his queen he speaks to, who after all has things to do and places to be, he feels more at liberty to get to the bloody point.

"That's not how I would have put it," Penelope replies.

"What else is it? Clytemnestra on Ithaca? If it's true, we're halfway up the Styx and sinking."

"Not if we find her and give her to her children." Medon would like to swear a little more, but even Penelope has her limits, so he settles for a fluently obscene flash of eyebrow and curl of lip. Penelope sighs. She has been sighing a lot these days.

She should not entirely blame Euracleia the nursemaid for her son's habit in that regard. "What else would you have me do? If Orestes does not find her, his position in Mycenae becomes untenable. His uncle will step in – Menelaus king of both Sparta and Mycenae, can you imagine! A tyrant who makes his brother look like a beacon of restraint. And if he decides that we have harboured a murderous queen, he won't need any better excuse to invade. Menelaus has always looked on the western ports with jealous eyes. No – we either have to find Clytemnestra or find some way to prove to Elektra that she's no longer on these shores."

"You mean Orestes?"

"What?"

"You said convince Elektra. You mean Orestes."

"Yes, yes, of course I do," she tuts, with a wave of a hand. Medon sucks in his breath, long and slow, displaying beneath his furled-back top lip a loose set of yellow buck teeth, tinted with honey. "What?" she snaps. "Just say it."

"Why Ithaca? If Clytemnestra is here, why? She could have fled south, to Crete, or north into barbarian lands. Why Ithaca?"

"You think she'd come to me for help?"

Medon shrugs. Someone will think it. Someone probably has. He may as well do his scholarly duty and think it also, just to keep on top of these things.

Penelope's sigh is on the edge of becoming a growl. "We may share some blood, but we were hardly family, let alone friends. You know what she said when Odysseus married me? 'Penelope-duck, getting her feet wet at last with the son of a goose.'"

"But you are a queen."

"Hera be praised, am I? I hadn't noticed."

"Two queens in Greece, both their husbands lost . . . "

"But no one went clamouring for Clytemnestra's hand while her husband was away – don't you think that strange?"

"Perhaps because that hand was so far up a poet's arse it's a wonder he could speak without the fingers showing."

"That is frankly disgusting."

Another shrug, Medon is an everyman doing his best to be useful. "Everyone knew it. Perhaps the only bastard who didn't was Agamemnon. Imagine the surprise he must have had when he found out."

"Imagine the surprise Clytemnestra must have had when he got back. She ran that country for years – ten years of sending supplies across the sea for his endless campaign, seven more keeping the peace as bored, angry veterans drifted back home and started raiding again while her husband was off pillaging the southern seas. And then one day it's Agamemnon sauntering up to the door with a cry of 'Hello, sweetheart, here's my treasure and my concubines, find them a room.'"

Clytemnestra slit the throat of Cassandra, princess of Troy, on her way out of the palace. Cassandra didn't resist. After the first year of being pulled by the hair into Agamemnon's bed, hand at her throat, tongue wet, she had learnt that screaming changed nothing. After the second year, even he believed that her silence was a kind of consent, and imagined all kind of stories in which she valued his power over her. By the time Clytemnestra killed her, seven years later, Cassandra had given up on speech altogether, knowing no one would believe her, and no one would care. Thus died the prophetess of Troy, plaything of gods and men.

"Closing the ports hits us hard," muses Medon, into the silence of dull contemplation. "We are nothing if not a trading people."

"Have you already dispatched word to the north?"

"The messenger sails with the afternoon tide."

"I wonder if they should go by Zakynthos first."

"Why?" Medon's eyes are tight with suspicion. "The wind is not in their favour; it will only delay their mission."

"But there are regular ships to the western colonies from Zakynthos, and besides, if she were in the north, we surely would have heard?"

Medon's eyes are slits narrowed against an unkind sun. For a moment he wonders whom he should trust – the girl he knew or the queen who now stands before him. He chooses. He repents. "Very well. They will sail south first. Perhaps we'll be lucky. Perhaps Clytemnestra isn't on Ithaca at all," he breathes, in the voice of one who has never believed a thing less. Penelope has learnt how to hide her face from the gaze of men, but Medon knows her silence, so looks up, sharp, and says: "What? What is it?"

"I found a ring. In Phenera."

"What were you doing in Phenera?"

"Being queenly! Any king would have gone and made some heroic speech about vengeance and blood – that sort of thing. I should do that. I should be ... There was a body beneath the cliffs, a man called Hyllas, a smuggler. Do you believe the Illyrians are raiding our shores?"

"No. Do you?"

Penelope purses her lips, head on one side, sizing up this man whom she has known nearly her whole adult life, whom she trusts, and yet whom she can never trust until the last dice of this dance have fallen, as she will never trust any man again. "No. I think they're Greeks, dressed in barbarian clothes. I think one of the suitors is paying them, forcing my hand. Wed or be damned. A bold move. Reckless but bold." There is a kind of admiration there. Hector admired Achilles too, until the end.

"Do you know which one?"

"I have my suspicions. But whoever these pirates are, whoever has sent them against us, raiders take slaves, not corpses. This Hyllas – he wasn't stabbed in the heart or slashed across the chest. There was a single knife wound here." She touches the top of her throat where it meets her jaw, such a strange place for touch, a jolt of feeling that surprises her. "A small blade, the kind of thing . . . "

. . . the kind of thing a queen might hide about her person; one who is scared of being defiled, and is not sure that the Furies will answer her when she calls. It is not wise to express such a thing, even before a man as worthy as Medon.

"How close must you be, I wonder, to kill a man like that?" She rises, measuring the distance between herself and Medon. The old councillor shuffles away a little step, doesn't notice he does it. "Either you see the death coming and have nowhere to go, back against the wall, powerless and frozen like the hare before the wolf – or you are so close to it that you don't even notice the blade, confident until the moment you find you cannot breathe for the metal in your neck."

"I had no idea you knew so much about death," Medon mutters, and is briefly disconcerted to realise that this woman who was once a child-queen in the court of Odysseus has been shaped by forces he doesn't fully understand.

"I know very little about killing," she replies with a shrug. "That is the men's business. But it is the women who come to dress and wail at the corpses when the killing is done, no?"

Medon's wife died from a growth within her chest, black and swollen. When living, she did not let him pull back the cloth that bound this aching sorrow, and in death the women carried her to the burial ground. He licks his lips, turns his mind away. "You mentioned a ring."

"Ah yes – hidden on Hyllas's body. Gold, stamped with a royal seal. Agamemnon's seal."

"A smuggler had this?"

"A dead smuggler. That's the part that worries me the most. A living smuggler might be, for example, paid for his services with this weighty ring, which would hopefully be to smuggle my cousin as far away from Ithaca as bird can fly. A dead smuggler, however – a dead smuggler still carrying a very recognisable ring that he hasn't yet had time to cast into more malleable shape – he has not had time to fulfil his duties."

"You think Clytemnestra gave it to him?"

"It is possible, to buy her passage. But if he is dead and still on Ithaca, that does raise the question of whether passage was bought at all."

They lapse into wretched silence, considering this thing. Finally, staring at nothing so much as his own nightmares, Medon grunts: "This militia is a terrible idea."

"I agree."

"You know he only has forty boys? Aegyptius will try to send out patrols, Polybus will want to defend the harbour, Eupheithes will order them to guard the granaries – by the time they actually hear word of a raid and muster, it'll either be too late or too few of them will have shown up to make the difference."

"I know." Voice soft as the butterfly wing, loose as cobweb, Penelope stares into a future, and is so tired of looking. "I'm relying on their incompetence to keep my son alive."

"You know he'll be fine. He's Odysseus's . . . "

"If you dare tell me he's Odysseus's son as if that's some sacred charm, I will scream," she answers, clear as the ringing of the hollow drum. "I will wail and rend my hair, the whole thing. So help me, Hera, I will do it."

Sweetheart, I whisper, I'm here for it. Many is the time my husband has returned from his frolics and I've turned on the waterworks, rent my garments, flung myself upon the ground and sworn that I shall die, scratched at my eyes, drawn blood from my celestial skin and beaten my fists against his chest. It doesn't change his behaviour long-term, but at least I get to embarrass him some tiny, tiny fraction of the way he humiliates, demeans, dishonours and diswomans me. So you do the wailing; I'll bring the olives.

128

Perhaps Medon hears some sliver of my voice upon the air, the touch of my breath goosebumped along his skin, because he has the grace to avert his eyes and take his time before finally raising them to say: "What are you going to do?"

"About what?" she sighs. "The pirates? My cousin? Elektra and Orestes? My son?"

"All of them. I was thinking . . . All of them."

"Medon . . ."

"It's been eight years since Troy. I know it'll be a disaster, I know, but if marrying one of them is less of a disaster than the alternative . . ."

"A little civil war, some light carnage now to put off something worse later?"

"Well, frankly, yes. Say you marry Antinous, yes, you'll have war with Eurymachus, but at least the granaries will be secure, and once he's on the throne . . ."

"And what if Eurymachus wins?"

"All right, Andraemon. He'll be a terrible king, but at least he brings military experience and connections, which will allow you to . . ."

"Amphinomous will never tolerate Andraemon on the throne, and Amphinomous is bright enough to have allies on Kephalonia . . ."

"Penelope!" He's raised his voice. He hasn't done that since she was eighteen and threw a pot at Euracleia for stealing Telemachus from his crib. *Who's a little hero, yes, you're a little hero, coo-cooey-coo*, whispered the old nursemaid, as Penelope's son gripped her thumb with sub-Herculean strength. "Your majesty," he corrects himself. "There is going to be war no matter what. You cannot prevent it. Choose someone now, while Orestes is on the island; use this moment to your advantage. All you're doing is putting off the inevitable."

"That's not what I'm doing."

"Penelope – your majesty . . . "

"It's not. Medon – it's not. I am not putting off the inevitable. I know that I'm going to have to marry again. I do."

"You're waiting for your husband."

"What? No. I mean . . . Yes, of course, it plays on my mind."

"You still love him?"

Penelope has learnt how to hide her face from the gaze of men, but sometimes even she is astonished. "What?"

"I mean, given the tears, the grief, the . . . "

"The incredibly useful, incredibly helpful tears and grief."

"So you *don't* . . . ?" he tries, squeezing the words between his lips like an infected blister.

"We married when I was sixteen. He was nice, it was nice, I was very pleased it was him instead of . . . practically anyone else. I remember looking round my father's court at the men of Greece and thinking 'Well, praise Hera – that could have gone worse.' Is that love?"

Penelope, a girl not yet become a woman, lay in her husband's arms beneath the stars and felt . . . so many things. She was a young woman discovering her body, herself, the person she wanted to be, and she wanted so much to love. She pressed her nose into his chest and he held her close, her arms cold and face warm from the warmth of him, and she thought, perhaps yes, perhaps this is love, and her mind was full of fantasies of what that might mean.

The poets rarely speak of love beyond a moment of enrapture, a moment of betrayal. Heracles, slaughtering his wife and child in a fever dream. They blame me for his insanity, but though I pluck at the hearts of men, I do not make them. Wondrous Medea, scorned and scornful; Atalanta, sworn to chastity lest her strength be torn from her; Ariadne, her loose body tossed between gods and men. No songs are sung of a life lived quietly, of a man and a woman growing old in contentment.

Can one love, wondered Penelope on that first and final voyage to Ithaca, without being a hero?

And yet she remembered also how Menelaus caught Helen by the chin, gazed into her eyes and said: *You are mine*, and how her cousin smiled and simpered and turned it all into a game, and was afraid. It is good to belong to a man, Helen said after Menelaus had grunted and pawed his way inside of her. It is good to know that I need not worry for anything. Perhaps Helen imagined that if she said it, she would believe it – but clearly she had not quite worked this trick well enough before Paris came.

Penelope, sixteen years old, left her father's court behind to marry a man she had known for three weeks, and as she stood upon the prow of the ship that carried her to Ithaca, she closed her eyes and repeated: I will love, I will love, I will love. She will find her place and her contentment, and she will call it love. Love is more than a queen might hope for, but the least a woman might do.

Now it occurs to her – not for the first time – that she has been a grieving, lonely woman for significantly more time than she was ever a happily married wife, sharing her husband's bed. She has spent more time frowning at the mention of his name, putting on a countenance of profoundest sorrow to please those who look upon her, than she has smiling at his presence. That when she says his name, it is to perform some political act rather than because she hears her husband there.

I will love, I will love, I will love, whispers Penelope to the shadows of the day.

She is not sure who, but one day, perhaps, she will love again.

"If it is not love, then what are you waiting for, may I ask?"

Medon, speaking. He once loved his wife, but love is not something appropriate for a man of his stature to discuss.

"What?"

131

"If you are not waiting for Odysseus to return, and if you must marry, then why wait? There will be war no matter what. What does waiting achieve?"

"War no matter what – I do not like inevitabilities."

"You think there is some way to prevent it?"

Penelope's lips thin, and for a moment she considers mentioning a warrior from the east, a woman with blades in her eyes as well as her hands. She does not. If Medon does not speak of love, it is not apt that Penelope speak of war. "Maybe not. But I owe it to my people – to my husband's legacy – to try."

"For how long? How long are you going to weave Laertes' funeral shroud?"

"As long as I can."

"Forgive my bluntness, but this doesn't sound like something you do for Ithaca. It sounds like something you do for yourself."

"For ... *myself*?" Penelope's voice is a slap across the face, a rise of stifled fury. "You think I let a hundred slobbering men dribble over my body and my land every single night *for myself*? You think I tolerate their endless slander, their relentless talk and insult, demeaning myself every day, *for myself*? I do it for my people, and I do it for my son!" Now Penelope covers her mouth, lest the sound of her voice raised has disturbed the listening ears of the palace. Both she and Medon stand in silence a moment, attention turned to the scurry of fleeing footsteps or the stifled laughter through a half-closed door. There is nothing. The gulls are quarrelling over the intestines of a rotting fish; there are bones boiling in the kitchen pots.

Finally Medon says: "You cannot protect Telemachus for ever."

She slumps. "I know."

"He has to find his own way."

"If he had his own way, the moment he turned sixteen he would have rallied whatever loyal servants of my husband he could find and claimed Ithaca for himself. Can you imagine it? An untested boy-king on the throne; we would have been overrun by invaders in a week."

"Orestes isn't much older, and he will be king in Mycenae."

"Will he? Then why isn't he already? Ah yes, I remember – first he has to kill his mother, prove that he has the mettle to rule. Killing your own mother as a test of kingly authority – there's a notion I'd rather Telemachus didn't take to heart."

"He'd never ... You can't imagine he would!"

"What would you do if I took a lover?"

"Retire immediately somewhere far away."

"Why?"

Medon doesn't answer, and she smiles, nods, sometimes thinks she might cry, can't remember the last time she didn't cry on demand to make a point but let real tears flow. "The second I take a lover, I am dishonoured as Odysseus's wife. The claim to Ithaca that comes through marrying me will be dissolved by my impiety and I will be nothing but a burden to Telemachus. In the best-case scenario he will have to banish me to some far-off temple to rub ashes into my hair and repent. In the worst-case scenario, to prove that he *isn't* his mother's son, he'll have to do as Orestes – show he's his own man, his father's son, worthy of defending Odysseus's honour and his throne."

"He never would."

"Wouldn't he? I sometimes wonder. I have not always been ... It is hard, when you love a child, to know how to protect them."

Medon is quiet a while, then folds his arms, protecting himself against the blows to come. "Fine," he blurts. "Marry Amphinomous. He's just as well prepared as the rest of them for a war, he won't treat you too badly, and he probably won't kill Telemachus on the spot. You negotiate exile for your son in exchange for your hand – you can call it a quest! Amphinomous can send Telemachus on a very heroic quest to find something valiant – Achilles' shield or the tail of a sphinx or something – and that will buy the pair of you enough time to fight this war and settle things down, and when Telemachus returns he'll either be enough of a hero to kill Amphinomous and claim his own – without needing to kill you because of the sanctity of marriage and the validation of having done his quest ... thing – or he'll be enough of a grown-up to settle down and not cause too much trouble. Either way, everyone wins."

"Or my son dies on a meaningless quest."

"Or your son dies on a meaningless quest," Medon agrees, a single, sharp nod of the head. "Where he has a far lower chance of dying than if he stays in Ithaca where Antinous or Andraemon can slit his throat as he lies sleeping. How say you? You, Amphinomous, all the gold in Ithaca and every spear you can muster, at the altar, day after tomorrow?"

So close is Medon to sealing this bargain as though he were buying fish that he has to stop himself from spitting and holding out his hand. Penelope stares at this mercantile wrangler for a moment, not sure what to believe of his firm-set brow and jutting chin, before at last she laughs. She laughs, and after a moment he laughs too, and it fixes nothing, and neither can remember the last time they laughed together, or perhaps at all, and for a little while, I laugh with them, for where else should I find my merriment but in the lives of others?

When the laughter subsides, they sit a moment in hiccuping calm, until at last Medon clears his throat and says: "So what now?"

"I can't stop Peisenor training his militia, and the price for the raiders to stay away is almost certainly beyond my means to pay. There is something I'm considering instead, but it is ..." She hums her way in search of a word, fingers plucking at the air.

"Profane?" suggests Medon helpfully. "Reckless?"

"Something of both, yes. As for Clytemnestra ... we must find her. I have some notion of where to look."

"Orestes' presence could be useful to you. No one is going to start a war while Agamemnon's children are on your island."

"Perhaps. But every minute that Orestes is not ruling in Mycenae is another in which his uncle might decide it's his turn. Perhaps my son could attend Orestes' investiture? That would get him off Ithaca for a few months, might be good for him ..."

"Safer than a quest, give him time to really know his cousin ..."

"Precisely. Perhaps he'll get seasick and consider that adventure enough."

"I have always admired your maternal ambition."

Penelope opens her mouth to say something rude, to snap, to make the kind of noises that as a child she was beaten for uttering in the open air, but a knock at the door catches her breath. Autonoe eases it back, shuffles forward, whispers in Penelope's ear. "Ah," mutters Penelope. "I see. Medon, forgive me. I find myself overcome with womanly weakness and must retire."

"I have always admired the exquisite timing of your weaknesses, my lady."

"I am glad someone appreciates it."

He half bows, smiling again, and for a moment she is happy too, and marvels at the strangeness of the feeling. Then the door closes, and she is in the tight corridor, looking left, looking right, always looking for eyes that see, before she follows Autonoe upstairs, moving as fast as a queen may dare.

"She came through the palace? People saw her?" she whispers.

"No, she climbed in through the window."

"What, my window?"

"Yes."

"So much for my domestic security."

"I've sent for Semele and Ourania."

"All right then, let's ..."

Autonoe pushes back the bedroom door. Priene sits in

Penelope's favourite chair, in Penelope's most intimate quarters, as if she has grown there like the olive tree. Her expression is as sunken as her posture, as though she had slid down, down, down like mud from the storm-soaked hill, too weary to hold herself up against falling rain. She doesn't rise when Penelope enters, doesn't show obeisance to a foreign queen. Instead she raises her chin a little, waits for Autonoe to leave, then barks: "I want to be paid really, really well. They say you have gold hidden in the caves."

Penelope takes a moment to fold her hands before her belly, stand up a little straighter. When she haggles over the price of grain, she finds her most useful attribute is her willingness to take her time, hiding her desperation behind a slowness that sometimes verges on the soporific. "We will have to discuss in further depth what 'really well' means," she replies. "Do I take it you accept the basic principle of my offer?"

Priene unfolds a limb at a time. Andraemon might recognise something of the warrior in this, in a woman who is in no hurry to expend a drop more energy than she must, until it is the killing time. Priene would recognise certain things in Andraemon too, and seeing them she would bare her teeth. "No heavy spears – not like the men use. No bronze plate. We use bows, arrows, traps, twin blades, fire."

"I agree."

"No one questions me. Not you. Not anyone. What I say, we do – yes?"

"So long as what you say is for the defence of my isles – yes. You will have complete authority. But if you spread sedition or attempt to turn my people against me, I think you should understand – I have been queen in Ithaca far longer than I have been Odysseus's wife. My women know me for the value I hold, and I will hear of it."

Priene smiles, the curling of the wolf.

"There is one other thing," Penelope muses, a little distant, as sometimes she had seen her father be when he pronounced judgement upon innocent men. "If word spreads of this . . . enterprise of ours, if people find out who is really defending Ithaca, it will make my domain a target for every mercenary in Greece. We are not like your people. Our men do not believe that women can fight. Secrecy is tantamount. Do you understand?"

Priene shrugs. "So long as your women don't tell."

"No, that's not it." Penelope meets Priene's eyes, forces her to hold her gaze. "When women fight, no man can be left alive. No man can live to tell what they see. No mercy. No quarter. Ourania says you want to kill Greeks. It is one of the reasons I asked her to find you."

"Queen of Ithaca." Priene's smile is the same smile she wore the day she bested the strongest man in her tribe, and she remembers the power of it now. "You will find no better butcher than me."

CHAPTER 19

⟫⟫⟫

T he men still needed food, of course.

There is no music at the feast, and Penelope does not weave Laertes' shroud.

The tables sit in hush, and what wine the maids serve is poured in offering to dead Agamemnon and his stiff-backed, stiff-eyed son.

I sit in a corner, and find the whole affair fantastically boring. Where is Eris, goddess of discord, when I need her? Where are the fights, the schemes, the knives in the back? By my name, I miss Medea's filthy jokes, and that thing Thalia can do with a bendy stick.

Then again . . . Leaneira approaches the shadowed chair where Penelope sits, bends down and whispers in her ear.

"Andraemon would like to speak to you."

"I'm afraid I am in mourning for Agamemnon."

"I have told him as much."

"I am sorry that you must tell him again."

"He is persistent."

"So are you on his behalf, yes?"

Leaneira nods, without a smile, and turns away. Andraemon

watches her from the corner of his eye, and she does not meet his gaze.

Telemachus sits both next to and a little below his cousin Orestes and attempts to make manly conversation.

"So, um ... your father must have been ... I mean, of course your father was ... but, um ... so you were in Athens?"

Orestes answers only with his eyes, mouth too tired to shape words.

"Yes, he was," Elektra replies, leaning past her brother, hand on his knee. "After our mother sullied herself, bringing dishonour upon us, my brother felt he had no choice but to flee to Athens to continue his training as a warrior, and a king, until such time as he could join our father and wreak vengeance."

"Um, yes, of course, I mean, yes, that makes ... of course."

"I stayed in Mycenae. Someone had to bear witness to our mother's profanities. Our father wept when I told him. He was violent. He held me by the throat, here, just here." Elektra touches the base of her neck with two fingers. It is so thin he can see each ridge of her windpipe like the steps of a ladder down to the bridge of her collarbone. "He threw me to the floor and said if I was lying he would slit my throat on the very stone where he sacrificed Iphigenia. He was a man of absolute power."

Orestes will be a man of absolute power one day. If I flicked my little finger at the side of his head, would he roll over, knees still locked in place, expression without change, a statue swatted by the touch of a god? Is there blood in him? Helloooo? Orestes? Anybody home?

Elektra smiles again, sorrow and wry darkness in the painted corners of her eyes. "I saw Odysseus once, when I was young," she muses. "He helped my father steady his hand when he drove the knife into Iphigenia's chest."

It occurs to Telemachus that this means Elektra has seen

his father more recently than he, not that this is much of an achievement.

It also occurs to Telemachus that Elektra is, in a strange way, the most sexual woman he has ever seen, and yet oddly, and at the same time, about as attractive as a nosebleed. He is a young man who finds this dichotomy very confusing, though perhaps in time he will learn.

He changes the subject, and being an Ithacan, talks about a topic on which he has greater insight.

"So, um . . . do you like fish?"

And then a change in the air – a certain turning of the quality of the evening light. My heart is ice, my cheeks are fire, I am aware of her presence the moment she enters the room, my eyes snapping from the princeling to the door. She is disguised, of all things, as a beggar, and has overdone the smell to the point of repugnance. Her lower lip is curled and drooling, and if I ruffled her hair, I think a sparrow might erupt from within it. I nearly rise from my place and shout, "Stepdaughter, you will clean up and pull yourself together right this minute or I so swear I will tan your rosy hide!" but this is Ithaca. Her temple, meagre and pointless though it is, is greater than mine. It is I who should not be at this feast, not her.

She knows it, of course; sees me in an instant. I scowl, but do not bend before her gaze, rather holding myself up a little stiffer, a little taller. She moves slowly, so slowly, hobbling from place to place to beg a scrap of meat, a handful of grain. Antinous tells her to get out, to leave, a stinking, hobbling cripple no less, get gone, get gone! Eurymachus smiles and simpers and says oh yes, oh yes, of course, oh yes, and gives her nothing from his plate. Amphinomous gives her a scrap of bread dipped in gruel, Andraemon pretends she isn't there, Kenamon stops and actually tries to engage her in conversation, tell me about you, tell me how you came to be in this place, it's fascinating, and she indulges him for nearly a minute before she gets bored of his curiosity and hobbles on. When she draws near Penelope, the queen orders that the beggar be seated by the fire and given drink and food as is the palace's custom, and Elektra remarks that it is apt that one so near to death should visit a feast for the dead, because there is nothing in this life right now that Elektra won't make about her father.

And so finally she sits beside me in the honoured place by the hearth, adjusts her walking stick, makes a show of sucking on a sliver of greasy bone, fingers sticky and a little too dirtless beneath her tattered gown, before at last, driven to near insanity by her rudeness and hauteur, I bark: "What in the name of Hades do you think you're playing at?! You look utterly ridiculous, you can't just . . . I mean, your hair! And what is that smell, is that . . . "

"Pig shit," Athena replies, the lightness of her celestial voice audible only to my ears. "I find it creates the most authentic disguise if one smears it carefully into one's wrists and the nape of one's neck."

I recoil, eyes boggling, and catch myself half a breath away from blurting: I'll tell your father, I will, I'll have words with him, he won't stand for this, just you wait, just you . . .

But Athena simply smiles, as if she can already hear the words I might say, as if she knows all of this already, and knows its outcome, smug little cow, little madam, always flaunting her so-called wisdom, her so-called intellect, it's just . . . she makes me . . . by my name, I loathe her!

"And you are . . . ?" she asks at last.

"A merchant of Argos," I snap, running my ringed fingers through my carefully oiled hair. "Although they see me only in the corner of their eye, and forget at once upon turning away. Unlike some, I don't need to make an entrance."

"A merchant of Argos," she repeats flatly. "Lapis-lazuli?

Crimson leather boots? Gold plates around your belt?" Her scorn is matched only by how hard she is trying not to laugh.

"At least I am perfumed with the scent of sense-lulling ambrosia rather than the faeces of swine!" I hiss. "At least when people barely see me, what they barely see is pleasing to their dull mortal eyes, rather than ... *this!*" I gesture furiously up and down her ragged form, but she just grins teeth of enchanted yellow with which she tears another mouthful of bread. I turn my face away in disgust, batting the image from in front of my eyes like a whining mosquito.

For a moment this is all there is between us: her mouthing and my disdain. But there is a reason she has come to this hall tonight, I think, and I will not give her the pleasure of making her enquiries easy.

Athena speaks with her mouth full, eyes sweeping the room, when her curiosity finally overwhelms her pride. "I sensed your presence this last moon upon this isle, but didn't think you would stoop so low as to walk amongst mortals. There was a fight – or there would have been a fight – between the suitors. I solved it, of course; but you were there. Why have you come to Ithaca, schemer?"

"And where should I be, goddess of war? Up on Olympus wheedling with Zeus to send your Odysseus a favourable wind? Or are you done debasing yourself for a man?"

"You speak of him as if he were my pet – yet *you* are in his palace. What might your husband-king make of that?"

"By dawn I'll be in Crete drinking the blood they offer me from a golden bowl, don't you worry, stepdaughter," I snap. "But sometimes it befits even the greatest to remember the more ... meagre of her subjects. Such quaint worshippers you have here on Ithaca. What they lack in offerings, manners, riches, culture and grace, they make up for with a fascination for fish – and some slight dedication to your name."

"There is a difference between us, stepmother," she replies with the smile of the shark. "I earn worship through learning and deeds. To the farmer I give the olive tree; to the warrior I give a shield. Whereas you seem to merely ... *expect* devotion, without that action that merits it. Do you wonder why, this being so, no meat is burnt in your name on Ithaca?"

No meat is burnt in my name because there is very little meat on Ithaca to burn. Spinsters and widows keep their prayers quiet, to themselves. "You have been too long watching Odysseus. You forget that Ithaca is an island of women. The men may pray to you, may spill blood in your honour, but the mothers call my name when their waters break."

Athena blinks at me, wide-eyed as the owl that is her messenger. It is not often that you see the goddess of wisdom confused, but when she is, it is as though some part of her mind has hit a wall that she simply cannot comprehend, as if for any matter to exist beyond her scope to fathom it, it cannot exist at all. Then slowly, a word at a time, as if unpacking some great incomprehensible matter: "Who gives a shit about the mothers?"

My husband swallowed Athena's mother whole to try and prevent his daughter's birth, but she crawled out of his skull anyway, sticky with his brain fluids and clad in blood. Zeus, for reasons that evade me, took to the girl at once, and for her part Athena hasn't mentioned the whole maternal cannibalism business once, just to keep matters civil.

If I were to eat Athena, I'd want her served on a bed of dates. Legs slow-cooked, belly fried fast in oil. The thought sometimes amuses me, but on reflection, she'd probably give me indigestion.

"Who ... gives a shit about the mothers?" Athena repeats, trying out the words for size and finding them satisfactory. "The poets don't sing about ... about childbirth. The poets don't care whether a mother's milk flows easy or slow. The only mother worth naming is the one who welcomes her warrior child home! The only songs they remember, the only songs that are sung in the palaces of kings, are of the men who make something of themselves! The warriors and the heroes who die fighting to make a name! Who the fuck cares about the fucking *mothers*?!"

"I've touched a nerve," I suggest politely, enjoying the crimson flush rising up her neck.

When she is at her most enraged, her cheeks puff in and out like a fish. She got that from my husband, only he also has a thing where the wriggling little vein on the side of his neck snaps and writhes like a suffocating eel.

"Why are you here, old mother?" she barks at last. "Your husband would suspect you of great indiscretion were he to find you skulking here."

In Olympus, if she dared address me in that way, I'd turn to Zeus and shrill, "Are you going to let her talk to me like that?!" and to Poseidon, who despises her perhaps even more than me, and weep and say, "Why do all my kin forsake me?" and they'd shuffle their feet and look a bit awkward and tell Athena it wasn't well done at all, and for a few weeks she'd sulk round the eastern isles dressed as a shepherd until everything cooled off, and a few nymphs would rub my feet and fan my face until I got bored of their incessant nattering. These days, that would be a win.

But tonight, on Ithaca, there are only mortals, and they do not comprehend the words of the gods. "Perhaps I am watching the family of Odysseus. Perhaps someone should."

Athena's lips curl in distaste. "I *protect* the family of Odysseus. I am his protector."

"His – not theirs. Have you looked at this hall? What precisely is the nature of the protection you offer? Muttering in some Egyptian's ear? Stomach cramps for a suitor who dined on too much boar?"

"Their time will come. Odysseus will return."

144

"Oh, Odysseus will return! Well that's all right then. I'm so glad to hear you've got it handled."

"I could speak to Zeus of your indiscretions," she growls.

I lean all the way in, and there is a hint of it in me still, a hint of the fire that only comes from the prayers of the bleeding women who beg that their child does not die. "And I to my brother Poseidon, who loves me almost as much as he despises my husband, and though we would be punished for it, we could raise the seas and drown little Odysseus, feed his bones to the jellyfish. I would take the punishment, to spite you."

Athena is a goddess of war and wisdom. I have seen her raise her spear with sorrow in her eye, as though to say "Ah well, ah well – I tried to show you mercy, but you are too foolish to live," and when the moment comes, there is no stopping her, no redemption or hope of escape. At least with blazing Ares, you can pray that his heart may melt after it has blazed.

For a moment we balance together, she and I. We could rage – oh, we could shatter the stone walls of this isle right now with our matched divinities – but then who would see? The eyes of Olympus would turn to Ithaca, and though I would surely be punished for having dared to act as a goddess should, having dabbled in the affairs of men – of *men*, my husband would say, of actual *men* instead of mere mothers! – Athena's state would hardly be better. Though she has sworn herself a virgin, at night I see her peeking down to Calypso's island, tip of her tongue flicking at the parted cherries of her lips, while Odysseus groans in the nymph's pearly bed. If some man-god saw her gaze, what might he say? What ravishment might Zeus proclaim if he realised his child was a sexual being after all?

For a moment I forget how much I hate her smug, preening face, and want to whisper in her ear, *let me send someone to your bed*. If not a man, then take a woman. The gods can't imagine that we could take sexual pleasure when a man is not there to please us. It isn't breaking the rules, it's merely . . . living a little. Here. Do you not feel something just here? Do you not deserve to feel a little something more? Demeter and Artemis, even boring old Hestia, know something of what I speak. We have done things when the moon is veiled, cried out an ecstasy whose sound, if the men in our lives could hear, might make even Zeus question his own vaunted prowess. You could too, Athena, if you forgot for a moment to think like a man.

I think I see it in her eyes – the calculation of all that stands between us. Of that which stands above us – the eyes of men, watching our every move – for all at once she sits back, turns her face a little away, chin up, as if there were nothing disordered here, nor in the world. "I see Agamemnon's children have come," she muses, cool as the sea.

"So they have."

"Looking for their mother, no doubt."

"No doubt."

"It is a terrible crime for a son to kill his mother – and also a crime for the son not to avenge his father. I wonder how Orestes will reconcile these two."

I shrug. I couldn't give a damn whether he reconciles them or not.

"You loved Clytemnestra, I recall. She acted like Zeus himself. Made decrees. Passed judgement. Strode through the palace while all bowed and scraped before her. Took lovers, who dedicated themselves to her pleasure as well as their own. How often did she pray to you that her husband might not return? Some of the breeze that blew Agamemnon from his shores did not come, I think, from Poseidon's trident. Does your brother of the sea know you have dabbled with the north wind? Does your husband?" I say nothing, but she has the courtesy at least not to smile. "You know Clytemnestra must die. Orestes will be king; a great man. That is how it will be."

"You have a soft spot for needy young men, don't you? Do you think Orestes will thank the gods for commanding him to kill his mother? Do you think the crown will sit easy on that thick skull of his when it's done?"

"His name will be sung by the poets, and I will be at his side." Her eyes dart to the boy by Orestes' feet, and there is a shimmer of something there I do not like. "Telemachus too."

"Perhaps, just this once, our interests align. I am no enemy to Odysseus."

"But you are friend to Clytemnestra."

"I am a friend to all queens – Penelope too."

"Penelope? Penelope isn't ..." Athena glances towards the woman sitting in silence in the furthest corner of the room. Perhaps I've said too much; there is an unaccustomed stillness in Athena's face, as if she were seeing Odysseus's wife for the very first time, a twitch of something unexpected on the end of her nose. She rises, and there is a looseness in her beggar's disguise, a glowing of something celestial in her aura that makes even the discontented suitors glance her way, gazes sliding upwards as if their eyes were blind but their hearts could see a little piece of Olympus.

Then she is gone in a billow of gold, and I hastily lay a certain charm upon the druggy eyes that witnessed it, that they might not be struck instantly blind by my stepdaughter's passage, and forget they had seen the glimpse of a goddess.

Typical bloody Athena, always getting others to clean up after her. She could be a problem, before all this is done.

CHAPTER 20

>>

There is a valley near the temple of Artemis, buried within the scraggy forest where only the wild creatures go. A stream runs from it to the sea, oftentimes vanishing into the rocks itself so its source is hard to trace. It is sheltered from the wind by high walls of ragged stone, though the sound of a voice raised in anger may travel all the way from its highest point to the island's edge. It is to this place, in the darkest hour, that the women go.

Semele has led them here, her word whispered out across the isle by Ourania and her helpful cousins. To the forgotten ones; to the unmarried daughters of dead fathers, to the widows of lost husbands, she has sent her message. Come, says Semele, as the women assemble. Do not be afraid, for there is something here you can do.

Tonight Teodora, child of burnt Phenera, comes too, risen from her rough cot in the shacks that rim the shrouded temple, her bow on her back. Teodora has no home, no family, no man. She follows the women through the night.

She follows by muted lamp and glorious starlight to the deepest part of the island, to where the forest grows black and you can no longer smell salt on the air. She follows to where the bears might growl or the wolves might howl, to a grove picked out in firelight, where the women wait. Some she thinks she knows: Semele and her children; the wives who say he is but missing, only missing; the mothers who stand stiff-armed and stubborn-chinned away from feeling and grief, just getting on. On Ithaca that's what you do – you just get on. Tonight there are forty women assembled. Tomorrow there will be more.

In the centre of them all stands another woman, dressed in scraps of torn animal and belts of knives. She turns to assess this ragtag could-be army of the forsaken and the lost, takes in their weapons of wood-chopper's axe, fisherman's knife, farmer's sickle and hunter's bow. She does not seem to disapprove.

"All right," says Priene. "Which of you can kill a wolf?"

In the thin dawn light, I think I hear an owl screech. Athena is about – oh, she is about this place, working her business – but like me, she wishes to be unseen. It would not do for Zeus to imagine we goddesses dabble too much in the affairs of men.

The light bounces silvered off the mirrored sea, and high in the palace of Odysseus a man dribbles his fingers down the spine of the maid who lies beside him and whispers: you shall be free. You shall be free. You shall be free.

Other men have tried to take her to their beds, promising her nothing, assuming that they owned her body as well as her labours. She kicked and screamed and bit, and all but one relented. He is the first man who has held her and said: you shall be free.

You shall be free.

She thinks he is lying, is almost entirely sure of it, and yet the sentiment is the greatest aphrodisiac.

You shall be free.

In the rising light of day, Telemachus dons his armour and runs through the hills of Ithaca.

Running in full armour is something he knows the Myrmidons used to do, those famed warriors of Achilles. They would pull on their plumed helmets, and with shield and spear run up the mountain and through the lapping edge of the sea. At noon they would stop only long enough to fight, wounding each other most gravely so that they might learn a tolerance of pain, then they would run on until at last, in the evening, exhausted with their manly labours, they would feast on wine and women, who swooned at the prowess of these men, because there is nothing quite like sex with a man who's been out jogging for twelve hours to really set the mood.

This is how Telemachus understands the Myrmidon way, and is in nearly all points profoundly mistaken. He is now capable of jogging a good twenty-five minutes in full armour before collapsing into a semi-fugue state of exhaustion, head pounding and limbs of lead, manly as a dandelion. If he knew his father – if his father had been here to teach him the way of the warrior, as fathers must – Odysseus would have sat next to him and said: "In Athena's name, boy, what are you doing? You never train to run into a battle, only from it! Have I told you about the tactical genius that is the three-minute sprint?"

No one else can explain this to Telemachus except his father. From other men it would be cowardice, unbelievable. From Odysseus it is sage parental wisdom. Telemachus has all sorts of funny ideas about parental wisdom. My old man ate me as soon as I was born; our fathers aren't all they're cracked up to be.

And yet . . .

. . . approach the top of the hill behind Eumaios's farm, gasping for breath, and there is already another there, someone else who enjoys a brisk constitutional first thing in the morning. Kenamon sits, chin turned up and head towards the south, as if he might smell his home carried in the light of the golden rising sun. Does he have his Penelope, waiting somewhere at the end of the Nile? Will he turn this rock white with salt tears, and defy the gods to return across a vengeful sea? Perhaps – but the poets do not care.

Telemachus slows, feeling at once a sense of outrage that his privacy has been broken by the intrusion of this stranger into his kingdom, his morning and his training, and yet also a curiosity. Like his mother, he is not sure he knows what it is to see a grown man on the island, at least one who is not hung-over or bartering for fish, and there is such stillness in Kenamon's face that he thinks perhaps the suitor is at prayer, and it does not do to interrupt a man in communion with the gods, even foreign gods who do not listen to voices thrown up so far from home.

(Is that true? A beating of the wings of the falcon, a shape blotted out against the sun – Horus, if that's you and you haven't brought some proper offerings, I will do you, cheeky little shit, you get back here right now!)

(Maybe it was just a falcon . . .)

Then Kenamon opens his eyes, sees Telemachus, rises, bows. "Prince of Ithaca – good morning."

Telemachus gestures – please, it is nothing. He enjoys making the gesture. It is very regal. His mother sometimes does it, but with a gentler, woman's sign as though to say "Why, you honour me, but truly, I am not worth your respect." Telemachus hates it when his mother does that, and has sworn that when he dismisses people, it will be in a proper, kingly way.

"I see you have found your favourite place," he says, lowering himself to the grass beside the Egyptian.

"Indeed. Thank you for showing it to me. It is . . . both liberating and imprisoning," says Kenamon, "to be bounded by so much water," and Telemachus is kicking himself, because that's precisely what he should have said, that's the kind of insightful bit of pith Odysseus's son should have come out with. Instead, he sits there dumb, too wrapped up in his own internal monologue to really engage with the things the Egyptian says, until finally Kenamon asks: "How is the training?"

"What?" Telemachus, dripping sweat, full armour on a hill; now is not the time to forget why he runs in the morning, but for a moment it seems perhaps he has. "Oh, the militia, it's . . . it will be good, I think. We are all training hard. I come here in the morning, before Peisenor gathers us, because . . . well . . . "

"You are the son of the king," Kenamon offers to Telemachus's fading quiet. "It is your duty to be the strongest, the bravest, to defend your fellow men, yes?"

When the poets speak of Achilles, they do not mention a couple of things. They skim over how much time he spent weeping into Patroclus's chest hair, and just how snotty all the tears were. They are a little hazy on how squishy the Myrmidons got when singing songs together about brotherly love, and the difference between a manly slap on the thigh and a caress of your neighbour's leg. And they utterly fail to mention how much time Achilles spent being really rather clumsy with a sword, or that time he accidentally hit himself in the head with his own spear while he was twirling it dramatically like the wings of the sycamore, because it's just not fashionable to have to *work* at being a hero. Heroism, if you believe the bards, is an innate quality gifted at birth, and the idea that prior to your manly adventures there is a fifteen-year training period replete with pulled muscles and using the baby bow just doesn't fit the valiant milieu.

Telemachus understands what it is to be a hero from the bards, rather than his father. They will insist that Odysseus, by the age of thirteen, was wrestling wild boars unarmed while outwitting Hermes and composing epic verse with a nautical theme. Whereas I, for whom time is but a mist to be parted as the clouds, could have informed him that the best of Odysseus's teenage verse went like this:

I saw a goat in the morning
It stood upon a hill
I went to catch it
But it ran away
Like a crab

It is of course useful to Penelope that the bards sing the more thrilling version of Odysseus's life. She even secretly sometimes pays them to add a verse or two that goes "Te-dum-te-dum and when he returns te-dum-te-dum he will slaughter all who have sullied his home te-dum-te-dum oh mighty mighty Odysseus."

Regrettably, Telemachus is unaware of his mother's subterfuge, and instead old Euracleia regales him with stories of how, aged two, Odysseus was already killing snakes with his teeth, and how by the age of five he spoke three languages and had a dream about an eagle – a sure sign of greatness.

Telemachus has not once dreamt about an eagle, though Apollo knows he tries.

Now he sits next to a stranger from a far-off land, and he has this terrible feeling that unlike all the other heroes of old, unlike that shit Heracles and those blessed by gods and poets, he, Telemachus, son of Odysseus, really needs to put the work in if he is to survive. Not for him some unnatural gift of speed, the dance of the sword or the easy way with words. Not for him the luxury of some Olympian quest – find a fleece, kill your mother – to establish his credentials. Instead, pirates and hard fighting by a bloody shore, schemes at midnight and the drunken mockery of men who would be his father. And if he is to survive, he must get up every morning and run until he can run no more, and train every night and acknowledge – how this grates against him! – acknowledge when he makes a mistake.

Here it is, then: the moment of crisis.

I check the heavens to make sure Athena isn't watching, but if she is, she's hiding it well.

I sit beside Telemachus, a goddess to his left, a stranger to his right, and take his hand in mine.

This is it, boy, I whisper in his ear. *This is your chance to not be an absolute bloody moron.*

In his heart, the poets sing of mighty deeds. There is a place where his father should have been, but it was filled with women and the stories of other men, creating an image of his father that would never have been real, could never have been human.

Are you a hero, Telemachus?

I press my lips into his ear and ask the other question. *Are you a man?*

Kenamon says: "... I mean, I like fish as much as the next man, and you do some lovely things with it, of course, but where I come from, there isn't so much fish, the diet, you see, it takes a bit of getting used to and I find that ... "

Telemachus blurts: "Will you teach me?"

Kenamon turns and says: "What?"

"Will you teach me? How to fight? You said you were a soldier, and Peisenor is ... he is not so very ... and my father did not have a chance to show me how to use his bow."

His lips tremble as if he were a child caught standing over the broken pot. May one be a man and be vulnerable? May a man ask for help, may a man beg another man for assistance? And yet Odysseus does pray to Athena, does fall down and weep, and how she thrills for her name upon his breath.

"The militia ... " Kenamon mutters. "I thought Peisenor ... "

"He teaches us to stand in lines with a spear. If I were in an army, fighting the Trojans before their walls, it would make sense. But we are to fight raiders, Illyrian pirates. They will not stand in a line. They will not fight ... honourably. And when the fires are lit and we are called, I do not think ... I cannot be sure . . . I am not sure how many will actually come. If Odysseus's son dies unremarked, in the dead of night, I think perhaps . . . I think that is easiest for everyone." This is as close to an honest truth as Telemachus has ever dared let himself think, let alone say out loud. It cannot last for long. "When my father returns, there will be blood. He will slaughter all the suitors. There will be war. It will be necessary to cleanse Ithaca."

Kenamon's lips are tight, his eyebrow drawn. He knows the meaning of "cleanse" but is not sure he understands it here. There is something in the language of this place that his learning misses.

"Those who ally with me," Telemachus continues, "will live. But it is dangerous. Every day that my father does not return, I am in greater danger. Danger from men who do not fight with . . . honour. I have to survive until my father gets back. Peisenor teaches me what he can, but it is . . . You were a soldier. You can . . . teach me."

Kenamon is silent a moment, and though his mind is not so clear to me, I think I catch a glimpse of it. For a moment he is a suitor, looking at the boy who could, if he is not careful, turn on him in a moment and slit his throat. Will Telemachus do it? Neither of them knows.

And then Kenamon is just a man again, who remembers the day his nephew was born, and how he loved to play with toy swords while the insects chittered in the evening light, and he sees how young Telemachus is, and for a moment he feels old.

"All right," he says at last. "Prince of Ithaca, I will teach you how to fight."

They clasp hands around each other's forearms, squeeze tight. This is a bond of men, and the next night, Telemachus will dream of falcons, which isn't quite an eagle, but is definitely getting there.

*

In the first light of day, as her son matches blades with a stranger from a far-off land, Penelope stands on the cliff above Phenera, veiled, Eos at her side.

"Right," she says at last. "If you were my cousin, where would you go next?"

CHAPTER 21

>>

P enelope prowls the cliffs above Phenera.

This is not unusual. Standing upon a cliff staring mournfully out to sea is a fashionable pastime for Odysseus's wife. It strikes all the right notes of chaste togetherness that are expected and required, while also giving her a chance to get away from the relentless stench of the suitors in the palace. If she is seen, people will remark: there goes Penelope, there goes our grieving queen, let us not disturb her for she is clearly mourning now so that later she may seem as ice. Aw, bless her broken heart, isn't it a marvellous thing to see a woman who keeps her feelings only to herself and the deep dark sea?

Usually she chooses a cliff fairly near the town, in case of emergency, but the presence of Orestes and Elektra in her second-best beds provides a certain respite from the threat of immediate violence, a brief flurry of anxious peace, and so she can go further afield.

She has not seen her son for days, but this thought has not yet really occurred to her in all its rich fullness and potential. When it does, she will feel a tightening in her throat, a nausea in her chest, a churning in her belly as she concludes, once again, that she is a terrible mother.

Right now, standing on a cliff looking chaste also gives her the opportunity to walk on, near or around said cliff, preferably with the wind whipping at her garments in a manner that embodies both the wild storm of her grieving heart and, simultaneously, a woman standing strong against the harsh elements, stiffened in her fidelity and courage.

She sometimes catches herself wondering whether Clytemnestra might not have benefited from living nearer the sea. In the rich comfort of Mycenae, blessed with gentle breezes and the luscious bounty of the juicy harvest from a fertile land, it must have proven much more challenging to strike the correct notes of pious pining required of a queen. Perhaps if she'd had greater opportunity to give the impression of some solid humility and a bit of virtuous self-neglect, Clytemnestra might not have had to flee from the impaled corpse of her dead lover, her son howling fury, fury, vengeance and fury at her back.

Perfumed Ourania, trader in all things that may be bought and sold – but secrets most of all – stands a little way off from Penelope, Eos at her side. It is acceptable for women to bear witness to things like this – they add a certain gravitas to the occasion. Finally, with none but the three women and the wind to catch her voice, Eos says: "Andraemon was demanding to see you again last night."

"Was he."

"Antinous quarrelled with Amphinomous. Antinous says that since his father is paying for the militia, it is as though he himself serves in its ranks, and thus he does not need to go to war. Amphinomous laughed and said Antinous was always a coward, and the two nearly came to blows."

"Where are they now?"

"Antinous sulks in his father's house. Amphinomous trains with the spear."

"Someone should warn Amphinomous not to get too good at that. It would be a pity if he became a target for midnight knives too soon."

"He often looks fondly at Melitta. I'll have her whisper in his ear."

"Do that. And where are Elektra and her brother?"

"Orestes prays."

"No, I mean where is he ... Wait, seriously?" Penelope stops in her pacing long enough to stare at her sombre maid. "All the time?"

"All the time. I have Phiobe attending him day and night and she reports that he eats almost nothing, drinks nothing but water, and prays constantly to Zeus. He seems ... very pious."

"That's one way of putting it. And Elektra?"

"She also prays, but in the much more traditional way of things. She has found a nice spot in the shade by your favourite bathing pool."

"The stone above the hollow where the water falls?"

"Exactly that."

"She has excellent taste in scenery. Go on."

"There she bathes, enough that one might consider it ritual, then rubs dirt into her face, then bathes again. Leaneira and Autonoe attend her, but whenever visitors arrive she is quick to adorn herself in mud and put on a distracted, mournful manner. And the second they are gone, she stops and talks earnestly with that man of hers, Pylades, and sends out orders and receives reports. Then in the evening, she returns to the palace, re-adorns herself with ash, goes into her brother's room, stays there until the feast is called, then follows him as the nursemaid might follow the child down to the feast."

"Do you think Orestes knows that his sister is in charge?"

"Autonoe is not entirely sure how much Orestes knows or cares of anything. He is preoccupied."

"The imminent murder of one's mother might do that for a man. Is he . . . reliable?"

"I suppose that would depend on how you mean. He hasn't been rude, or tried any business with the women, if he even inclines that way. He says thank you and has asked Autonoe her name, sincerely she thinks, at least four times."

"How is he getting on with Telemachus?"

"He hasn't asked your son his name more than twice already."

Penelope sighs. "And Elektra? Does she seem . . . interested in my son?"

"She smiles at him, and sometimes holds his hand, and says how grateful her brother is for all Telemachus's help, and what a loyal ally Ithaca has always been to her father. But Telemachus is so busy trying to talk to Orestes that I'm not sure he would notice the sister's attention even if there was much there to see."

It takes all of Penelope's will not to roll her eyes. "I'll talk to him about that. How goes the search for Clytemnestra?"

"The Mycenaeans do not know the island. They are growing . . . rude. Yesterday they searched Semele's farm and were rough with her and her girls, stole some grain, the women said. Nearly found the weapons too."

"Send my apologies and a gift to Semele. How well do you know Phenera, Eos? Ourania?"

"There are flowers that grow nearby that, when crushed, release a pleasing smell," muses Eos, in the manner of a poet. Then, somewhat more practically: "Also we have sometimes had to buy goods from the people of Phenera that they smuggled past our ports, when winter was hard."

"If you were fleeing this place in the night, where would you go?"

"There are some fisherwomen in the bay beyond," offers Ourania, eyes not leaving Penelope's face. "And the palace is not far."

"What else?"

"Caves, but they take some knowing. The temple of Artemis, old Eumaios's hut, though he is hardly welcoming to guests."

Penelope nods at nothing much, eyes turning back to the sea. "We have to get the Mycenaeans off Ithaca." Her fingers roll round a golden ring bearing a seal that should not be seen on this island. She has known Eos since they were girls together, a princess and a slave dragged to Ithaca; Ourania held her hand as she screamed when Telemachus was born, yet even now she hesitates. Then she shakes her head, holds out her hand to Ourania, the ring in its palm. "I need you to take this."

Ourania lifts it slowly, turns it this way and that. She is a little slow to understand; then she is not, and fear blooms across her usually serene face. "Is this ... Where did you find this?"

"On the body of a smuggler, dead in Phenera."

"Is it ... hers?"

"I think so. My cousin never did understand the value of all the beautiful things she had. Arguably she had too many to really appreciate them all."

"What do you want done with it?"

"Take it far from here."

"Wouldn't it be easier to throw it in the sea?"

"I need it to come back."

"Really? Why – when?"

"As soon as you can. It needs to go north, to Hyrie. I dispatched a messenger some few days since to spread word of my cousin throughout the western isles and order the ports closed. I dispatched him ... slowly. If you are quick, you should reach Lefkada before him. No one but us can know of this business. I cannot afford to have Orestes be ... insecure at this time. Who knows what the suitors will do if Mycenae withdraws its protection from the house of Odysseus."

"I'll get it done. Is there anything else?"

"Yes. Our little boat, in case of emergency. Who knows of its existence?"

"Myself, Eos, Autonoe . . . "

Penelope nods, half listening, eyes towards the sky as if seeking an auspicious sign. "The time may have come for a few others to be let in on the secret."

Ourania grips the ring tight, eyebrows high. "What precisely did you have in mind?"

CHAPTER 22

>>>

There is a temple up a dusty winding path in a small valley in the heart of Ithaca, framed by low grubby trees that cling to the rocks of this isle like twisted hair of the armpit. It has a different quality of shabbiness from the greater shrine for Athena, some two hours' walk away down a narrow track. Certainly, less royal wealth has been spent on it. Less plundered loot has been dedicated to its honour, and fewer people with fat bellies and bloated minds come to bow and scrape at its dirty doorstep. Yet look a little closer, and its rough wooden walls and swept-dry floor speak of a certain dedication, though the subject of its worship wouldn't notice or care.

The smell of dark green needles hangs on the air about this place, and the whiff of fresh leather drying in the sun too. White wild flowers grow among the stones that recline against its western portions, as if the temple were pulled from the ground itself rather than built by mortal hands, and there are garlands of climbing ivy and withering vines set above the door. I am circumspect about approaching, even though the child it honours is nothing compared to me, and rarely bothers to show her face for anything but the most outrageous of sacrileges. Too many family spats have begun over disrespecting a shrine, and I will

163

say this for Artemis – she can hold a fantastic grudge. That at least is something we have in common.

There are a number of women sworn to the service of the huntress, but only one interests us now, for we have met her before. Anaitis, who stood on the bloody shore at Phenera and knew which way an Illyrian sword might cut. The priestess returns now from the forest with a pair of dead rabbits at her hip, satisfied with her labours, and is astonished to find that of all the many – usually shabby – worshippers who come to her door, today Penelope herself is kneeling before the shrine. This has attracted some attention; worshippers who come as much for the gossip and the occasional shared taste of honey from the temple hives are now displaying a sudden piety to be near the praying queen. Gathered too are a number of the youngest of the priesthood, trying their best not to fidget or look too amazed at the presence of royalty, their unruly hair hastily pushed back from their faces, their grubby nails hidden in their palms.

Anaitis sees all this, but Anaitis is not like the other women of Ithaca. She is not, she has been assured, much like anyone anywhere. She does not have patience for people who do not say what they mean. She does not understand why one might say, "Why, Hestia! I love what you've done with your hair!" when what one actually means is "Oh not that old bore Hestia – Hestia, don't tell that story about the barley farmer again, we've all heard it, it wasn't amusing the first time – oh no, she's off, someone pass me wine, *strong* wine." In that sense she has much in common with my beloved son, my Hephaestus, who has been so often mocked by my ignorant siblings that now when he shuffles resentfully into the room to gaze upon the Olympians, he can hardly be bothered to open his mouth to say "good morning" or "good afternoon", knowing that whatever answer emerges will ultimately bore him.

In Anaitis, priestess of Artemis, I recognise something of my boy, and for that she will receive more courtesy from me than perhaps she deserves.

This is why, seeing a queen kneeling before Artemis's altar, she doesn't rush in with a bow and a priestly bit of grovelling, inclining swiftly towards conversations about repairing the roof or a nicer pit round back to piss in. Instead, rabbits still bleeding down her thigh, she walks up to the queen, nods once towards the crudely whittled figure on the altar that might be a woman but bears no resemblance to a goddess, and says: "What are you doing here?" Penelope raises her head slowly. This gives Anaitis time to reconsider her position and add: "Your majesty."

"Shouldn't a queen show piety to all the gods?"

"I thought Athena was your patron."

"Athena is my husband's patron," she replies with the faintest, emptiest of smiles. "My position is more fluid."

Anaitis doesn't like the word "fluid". She's heard people use it and then laugh in a manner that makes her profoundly uncomfortable. Nor is she entirely sure that a woman should pick and choose the centre of their devotion as easily as the wind changes. Certainly you might make offerings to Poseidon before setting sail, then pray to Demeter before scattering seeds to the wind – but long-term Anaitis was always taught it is best to pick a patron and stick to it, on the basis that the celestial intervention of one really loyal deity who's got your best interests at heart will always make a greater impression than a spontaneous prayer to Ares now that the going has got tough.

In this regard, as with so many others, I would say that Anaitis is right; many a half-mumbling slave could learn something from the priestess's solid commitment. Yet who should a queen dedicate herself to, being the head of a whole land? Does she not pray also for the blacksmith and the tanner, the whore and the shepherd too? Which deity is most appropriate when it takes the blessing of us all to keep a kingdom together?

Pray to me, the queen of queens, I whisper, soft as the skin of the newly flayed hind. *I will teach you to flatter them all into submission.*

A chill wind blows, tumbling the leaves about the temple door, and I hastily retreat, straining to hear from across the threshold lest Artemis catch a sense of my presence upon her sacred ground.

Anaitis is not sure how to argue with royalty. She shifts her weight from foot to foot. She has a feeling that things that should be obvious and easy are, with this queen, not. She manages to drop her voice to a whisper, to the barest pad of the fox through the winter wood. "I saw a woman of the east in the forest above the temple last night, leading the women who come here. She said she will not pray to Greek gods, but that any good hunter would understand the business she was on. Do the men know? I heard talk of a militia."

"No. They do not. Why – are you reconsidering your offer of shelter to the women in the grove?"

"No. Artemis would be pleased. Athena too, I think."

Athena will be incensed when she finds out, though I am not yet sure whether it is because she is so hung up on the antics of her heroic little men, or because she didn't think of it first. Either way, it will be an absolute stinker of a row, but to me, on this, she will yield. If she ever wants her Odysseus to come home – if she wants Odysseus to have a home to come home to – she will yield.

"If the women are called to fight, will you join them? You clearly have a good eye and a strong arm."

"Perhaps," muses Anaitis. "Will they kill the suitors?"

"Ah – no. At least, not yet."

"Why not?"

"Because if we kill the suitors, it will provoke an invasion from the mainland. A woman should not butcher the men in her palace, let alone with an army of women at her back. It would be entirely unacceptable and justify even our oldest allies – even Nestor – coming in to sever my head. Or getting my son to do it for them, which would be the correct move if he hoped to survive the onslaught of his fellow would-be kings."

"But . . . if Odysseus returns? Will he not kill these men?"

"Perhaps."

"And would that not also spark an invasion?"

"Perhaps not. He is a king. Killing a hundred unarmed men is a kingly thing to do."

"I see." Anaitis does not. She understands, of course, that this is society and how society works. She is smart; she has learnt these lessons. What she doesn't understand is why, being the way it is, society is so insufferably stupid, run by flaming idiots. On that point again, we are inclined to agree. "I think I understand why you come to pray to the huntress, rather than the virgin warrior," she adds, squatting down a little more comfortably beside Penelope.

"You've seen the Mycenaeans, I take it?"

Anaitis scowls. "They came here yesterday. They were rude."

"They did not dishonour the shrine? Did not enter the sacred place?"

"No – even they would not stoop so far. Artemis held the whole Greek army at bay until Agamemnon sacrificed his eldest daughter to appease her wrath," she adds, brightening at the thought. "They would not risk angering her again."

"*Daddy!* Daddy Daddy Daddy Daddy they killed my sacred stag Daddy Daddy Daddy Daddy!" whined Artemis in my husband's ear. Those weren't quite her words, of course, but if you were to translate the fevered shrill of indignation she brought to Olympus when Agamemnon slaughtered one of her blessed bloody deer, that's basically what you would have heard. "Daddy Daddy Daddy Daddy *Daddy Daddy DADDY!*"

"Fine!" my husband snapped. "You can have your damn human sacrifice!"

Always the trouble with Zeus, never stopping to think things through. Menelaus held Clytemnestra by the neck to stop her clawing her husband's eyes out as Agamemnon drove the knife into Iphigenia's chest. None of the other gods watched – not even Artemis. Hermes went to tell her when it was done and she said, "Oh, really?" and lo, the winds turned towards Troy. Only Hades and myself stood by to witness the child on the altar, while Clytemnestra screamed and Elektra, too young to see so much blood, cried without understanding. Iphigenia was nine years old. The poets pretend she was older, wise beyond her years. Wise enough to agree to die. That way the heroes of Greece didn't have to hold her down by wrists so skinny they kept slipping through the soldiers' grasp as the knife cracked her bones.

"Well look now really, you let Artemis have Agamemnon's daughter so why not give me Odysseus's crew?!" pouted Helios when Odysseus's men slaughtered his sacred cattle, and well yes, why not really? My husband let a father kill his own child for a deer hunted in error, so giving Helios, always an awkward relative, the lives of the last men of Ithaca seemed only fair. This is the kind of shoddy precedent that gets set when the king of the gods is too busy peering down some mortal's gown to do a proper bit of ruling.

"Artemis is truly a great goddess," Penelope concedes, as perhaps she too contemplates precisely how flexible is the term of greatness. "A protector of women."

Anaitis shifts her weight back and forth a little, and does not look at Penelope. "Well. A protector of women. Yes."

"And her temple is a sanctuary that the men will not disturb."

"They would be slaughtered by the goddess," replies Anaitis primly, and she may in fact be correct. Athena loves it when a hunky warrior clad in bronze kneels before her inner sanctum, and when a man violated a woman upon her altar, it was the woman whose hair she turned to snakes in retribution for this sacrilege. So much for the wisdom of Athena. Artemis, however – Artemis is far less infatuated with the qualities of men. "Do you ... require sanctuary?"

"No. Not yet."

"But you ... might?"

"I hope it will not come to that. I have allies on Kephalonia who, if things should become ... challenging, I trust will give me aid."

"I heard the ports were closed."

"There are other ways to reach Kephalonia than through the harbours. This isle is full of coves and hidden places where one might keep a little ship, fast and with oars and sail, that a woman might use. The people of Phenera understood that."

Anaitis nods, and, having nothing good to say, says nothing. Penelope half closes her eyes again, offering up some meagre devotion – barely enough to stir the sanctified air of this little place. I watch her prayers like dust in sunlight, before she rises, clasps hands briefly with Anaitis, looks for a moment as if she might bow, then turns and walks briskly away from this shrine of leaf and pine.

Eos stands outside, waiting.

"Did it go well?" she asks in a hush, but Penelope silences her with a brief finger to her lips, until they are beneath the curl of the wood that shrouds the valley, and none but the gods might hear them.

"Very well indeed," she says at last. "If we are lucky, half the island will know about our boat by sundown."

CHAPTER 23

>>

An evening encounter in a corridor. Elektra still wears grey. Penelope wears her veil. She has done well at avoiding her cousin from Mycenae thus far, choosing instead to dedicate her attentions to Orestes. But Elektra has learnt the corridors of this palace – found even the armoury where they have hidden Odysseus's bow – studied the patterns of its inhabitants.

"If she's anything like her mother, she'll seize the armoury and have us at spear-point if she doesn't get what she wants," warns Eos.

"If she's anything like her mother, she'll leave the armoury untouched and slaughter us all in our sleep with a butcher's knife," corrects Autonoe, peeling back the thick skin of a fig with a juicy smile.

Now Elektra stands before Penelope, each guarded at their back by veiled maids. At her side, Orestes is squeezed in by his man Pylades, as if they could not quite work out whether to walk in front of or behind the women, and ended up shoved in between. The corridor is too tight for this awkward formation, and it falls to Penelope to force her voice into a manner some-where between soft and serious. "How goes the search for your mother, good cousin?" she enquires.

And: "Not well," snaps Elektra, before immediately replacing her grimace with a smile and adding, sweet as nectar, "Not well. We shall have to start searching the sacred places, or maybe even the palace."

"You can of course search the palace – of course! But sacred places? Would that not anger the gods?"

At Elektra's side, Orestes nods. He knows all about angering the gods; his family is famous for it. Elektra knows too that her family is cursed, but being cursed considers that the worst of the damage is already done, so to Hades with it. What more can the gods bestow?

Sweet pea, I whisper in her ear, *you haven't seen anything yet.*

"Perhaps more men," Elektra muses. "Perhaps we could ask my uncle to send help from Sparta, some of his soldiers to help secure the isles."

"What a marvellous idea," Penelope chirrups. "I can send to Nestor in Pylos too, and all the kings of Greece. I am sure everyone of good heart and noble spirit has an interest in this affair."

Elektra's smile is thin as the dagger her mother drove into her father's heart, sharp as the blade that slew her sister. She nods once at Penelope, who stands aside to let her by.

At night – a desultory feast.

Orestes does not eat, unless Elektra feeds him. She holds up a plate before him, picks up meat in a finger of bread, bids him eat, good brother, eat, and dumbly he consumes whatever she presents him.

Two Mycenaean men stand at his back, watching the room as if perhaps Clytemnestra has disguised herself as a suitor, is here already, seeking to win Penelope's hand.

The poets sing a few songs of Agamemnon, of his greatness, his might, his infinite strength. One begins a song that mentions in a verse how Agamemnon's father killed his brother and fed his brother's sons to him in a stew, making him in fact the second member of that particular family who served a relative's flesh at a feast – but judging the crowd, the bard hastily skims over that part of the ditty.

The maids move about the room, serving in silence to the hunkered mass of men.

The poets do not sing of women.

Oh once – once they called my name, they raised the figure of blessed mother goddess, womb full and breasts heaving to the heavens, they dug their fingers into the earth and cried Mother, Mother, Mother! But one day my brother Zeus grew weary of his toils in the matter of the mortal and the divine. He saw what others had and wanted more, more for himself – though he was already accounted great, the thunderer and the bringer of lightning from the sky. He did not see it that way. The bounty that others had was diminishing to him. The honours others received, he felt as an insult bestowed upon his greatness. And as to be great amongst equals was to be meagre and ordinary in his eye, he raised himself up – and having fewer heights to rise to than already being the father of the gods, this of necessity required that he put others down.

The poets do not sing of the women, and the women sing only at funerals, or away from the ears of men.

But when the feast is done and the air is black, while the poets sleep and the thunderer snores beneath golden skies, I shall sing, and you shall hear. Come with me; let us wander through the hearts of the silent maids while the men of Ithaca and Mycenae snore in drunken splendour.

Eos was thirteen when Odysseus gave her as a wedding gift to the young Penelope. For a while, Penelope was aloof and hard, doing her very best to be a queen. But Eos held her hand and Ourania her feet when Penelope screamed and Telemachus was born, and when a woman has spent that much time staring into another woman's dilated vagina, you can either shut that other woman out for ever and pretend it never happened, or you can get over yourself and admit to a bond that runs deeper than blood.

Eos has sworn she will never have a child. Consequently, Athena-like, she has sworn never to have a man either, but unlike my stepdaughter finds plenty of other ways to entertain herself in the cool winter nights.

Autonoe had served in many houses before Penelope bought her, and been accounted an acquired taste. There was defiance in her eyes, a sharpness to her tongue that led to many a beating. Though it was commanded by the law of all civilised places that no man might touch his property without consent, in the manner of enforcement these laws were always lax, and if her former masters had hoped to implant their seed in her belly, the only thing that grew from their assaults was vengeance, vengeance and fury, vengeance.

"What do you want?" Penelope asked the day after Autonoe nearly scratched a man's eyes out in a moment of rage and defiance, and Autonoe was astonished at the question, had never conceived it might be asked, had no idea how to answer it.

"Power," she retorted at last. "Power like the power you have."

"How will you get it?"

"Perhaps a man will marry me?"

"Is that your plan?"

Autonoe hesitated. In truth, the only thing stranger to her than being asked what she desired was being invited to consider how she might achieve it. Then Penelope said:

"Take it from a queen – the greatest power we women can own is that we take in secret."

That was when I knew I loved Penelope. Of all the queens in Greece, I had not thought I could love one who seemed so meek and who bowed so deep to the inclinations of men. I was wrong.

Melantho didn't mind being sold to Penelope. At least in the palace of Odysseus she gets decent meals, two days off out of every eight, clothes that don't itch too badly, and her own bed. Besides, she too has smelt the stink of power, and though she does not know it, cannot comprehend it, a hunger has been hollowed out in her belly that must one day be filled.

Phiobe was born a slave, prays to Aphrodite at night, enjoys the touch of men who have put the work in, and one day will realise that she should pray to me instead. Aphrodite is a goddess for the young, and those who have not yet lost.

Euracleia was Odysseus's nurse when he was born, beloved of Anticlea. When Penelope came to Ithaca, Euracleia fussed with her hair and said, "Don't you worry about a thing, Auntie Euracleia has got all this sorted!" and would feed Telemachus sweet cakes when his mother had forbidden him, and let him lick honey from the bowl, and pinch his cheeks and say things like, "Don't you listen to your mummy when she shouts, you're special!" until finally Penelope stormed into Anticlea's room and shrieked: "I want that woman gone!"

Then her mother-in-law just looked up slowly from her bed and blinked a few times at the youthful queen and sighed at last: "You're being hysterical, dear. You should have a little lie-down."

When Anticlea died, Euracleia pulled out her hair. Or rather, she pulled out a few clumps, but it was hard work and slow going, so she crudely cut the rest of it when no one was looking, which achieved much the same effect. Three days later, Eos came to her and said: "Penelope says you have been so loyal, and given so much. She feels that the time has come for you to hand off some of your duties to younger maids, that you might enjoy the richness of your age."

Euracleia shouted and snarled and called Penelope all manner of vile things to her face, things that were she not the nursemaid of Odysseus would have got her sold to a pig farm in a minute. Penelope smiled and let her rant her bosom out, and when it was done said simply: "Well. I trust we have settled that," and so Euracleia was done. She still haunts the palace, muttering and condemning every speck of dust, every whispered word, but no one pays her much attention any more. She wonders how she missed Penelope becoming a woman, instead of a girl. She feels Penelope must have done something very tricksy indeed to pull that off when no one was looking.

Leaneira was dragged from the ashes of Troy by the hair.

She does not speak of her dreams, not even to the man who swears he loves her.

"You know I will never hurt you," he said, the night she finally yielded to his embrace. "You know you can say no whenever you want."

Leaneira has not said no for such a long time. It has not been an option given to her. She tries it now, to see what it's like, whispers it, then says it a little louder, and as promised, he stopped. A man, no less, a warrior, and he stopped when she asked. She wept, and he held her, and the next night she did not say no again.

"When I am king in Ithaca," he said, "you will be free."

There are a number of suitors who have whispered this to the maids. It hasn't occurred to dark-eyed Antinous, who just assumes his animal charms will be enough to seduce any creature on two legs, and feels conspired against that this is not the case. But Eurymachus has tried it, stumbling, awkward over the words, and Melantho at least seems to put up with it. Even Amphinomous gave it a shot, but he couldn't really get any conviction into it, so fell back on a few trinkets and a story about shooting stars.

But he – Leaneira's lover – he said it in a way that felt true, real and whole. He was not a boy, but a man, wise and shrewd. He held her close and said: "You will be free, though it will break my heart to have to lie with your mistress instead of you," and she turned her eyes to the growing moon and didn't reply, which he took to be a sign of her affection, and he held her a little closer to the warmth of his chest.

Now Leaneira waits by the palace gates, wrapped in a midnight shawl, and as Eos returns from her conference with Ourania, lady of spies, Leaneira approaches her and murmurs in her ear: "Andraemon. He wants to speak to Penelope – and in private."

Eos slows, only a little, then puts her hand on Leaneira's arm and murmurs: "Not here."

They sit by the well. No man draws his own water in the palace of Odysseus. The stones are cool, moist, green moss clinging to their darkest edge. Eos sits with her knees angled towards Leaneira on the edge of the dark lip, hands in her lap, ready to reach out and comfort as she has seen Ourania do when the old woman wants something done. "How long since you were set to watch Andraemon, Leaneira?"

Eos learnt from Ourania that it was best, when asking questions, to already know the answers. Leaneira knows this too. She learnt fast, when the Greeks made her a slave. "Nine moons."

"And how long since he took you to his bed?"

Leaneira watched the Greeks take turns with the women of Troy, and it seemed to her that they did not do it for pleasure or lust or enjoyment of women's flesh. They did it because all of it – all the war, all the rage and hurt and loss and pain – had been for nothing. For what? For a single night of flame and a few kings taking the spoils? When the sun rose over the ashes of her city, the soldiers of Greece were still hurt, still bloody, still lost, only now there were no stories left, no poets to tell them that they were heroes. So instead they became beasts, performing sacrilege upon the living and the dead, for their fathers had taught them no other way to be a man than to howl at the crimson sun.

She had not thought she would look at a man ever again after that day. To smile would dishonour her sister, violate her mother, their bones still unburied in the ashes of Troy. And yet now she sits by the well with the woman who would be Penelope's favourite spy, who smiles as though tender and says: "Andraemon is handsome, is he not?"

"Three moons. I have ... consorted with him ... for three moons."

"You are not ...?"

A quick shake of her head. This is the question that only the women ask. "No. I am careful. I count the days from when I bleed. He ... understands."

"Do you enjoy his company?"

"He is not unkind. He is different from the others. The others are boys. He is a man." Eos waits, hands folded in her lap. Leaneira lets out a breath, long and slow. "He wants to speak to Penelope. He is insistent. He says only he can protect Ithaca from these pirate raids. He offers to bring seventy mercenaries over from Patrae. But Penelope won't meet him."

"Why do you think that is?"

"She cannot show favour to any one suitor."

"Yes, of course. But more than that. You have heard of these raids on our shores? Lefkada, Phenera? Pirates do not raid just to take slaves. They raid to be paid not to raid again."

"Andraemon wouldn't do that. He is a good man."

"Do you believe that?"

"I do." She believes. She does not. The hearts of mortals are fickle things, fluttering their way to death with the irregular beat of the butterfly's wings.

"I don't." Eos rises quickly, like the skinny heron unfolding from the riverbed. "I think he's just like all the others."

177

What do you know of men? Leaneira wants to cry. What do you know of the things men do, when their stories are broken? What do you know of who they are, when every word that has been poured in their ears – hero, warrior, conqueror, king – is shown to be a lie? You in your palace of shadows and secrets, what do you know?

She does not. She is not like Eos, safe in her mistress's favour, or Autonoe, who was lucky enough to learn to laugh. Instead she stands as Eos does, and facing her says: "You asked me to grow … close to Andraemon. To learn his secrets. To be your eyes. I am telling you what I have seen."

"And has he not said the same thing to you that every other man in the palace has said to every other maid? 'Help me, and when I am king you will be rewarded. You will be free.' Has he enquired after gossip, whispered suggestions in your ear, asked you to spy on Penelope?"

"Of course he has. That man who does less is a fool."

Eos sighs, lets out a tired breath. "What do you want?" she asks at last. "If Penelope shows him any favour, the others will see him as a threat."

"She has met men in secret before. And that woman climbs in through her window."

"You did not see her – *you did not see her!*" Eos rages like her mistress does – in cold, sharp bursts that vanish as quickly as they appeared. Clytemnestra does much the same – you queens of Greece are not as different from each other as you think.

For a moment the two women regard each other in the evening light, and it is Eos, not Leaneira, who relents.

"I will speak to Penelope," she says.

CHAPTER 24

>>>

T elemachus is training to be a man.

In the morning he trains with the Egyptian behind Eumaios's farm. In the afternoon he trains with Peisenor and his band of boys and brats. The squirts of old man Eupheithes, father of Antinous, all band together at one end of the yard, and the infants of raging Polybus, father of Eurymachus, at the other. Telemachus and his gaggle of youthful followers do their best to be friends to all, but no one responds to their polite overtures. Amphinomous and Aegyptius swing from one end of the group to the other trying to nudge and cajole a little cooperation, but in the evening, when the militia departs in sweat and oil, the fathers whisper unto their men: don't you listen to that Peisenor or that Aegyptius or whoever! Listen only to me. You serve *me*, not Ithaca.

Telemachus finds himself looking towards the moon. She grows fat, and he is not so dumb that he cannot count the days until she is full again. Perhaps this time the Illyrians will not come. Perhaps Lefkada and Phenera were just unlucky.

"Meet your enemy's eyes. Let them see your intent," intones Peisenor to the boys staggering beneath their shields. "They will lose the battle there, in your gaze; in that moment they are already crushed. Roar like the lion! The business with the sword is just finishing the job."

Did Achilles roar like the lion? Probably, Telemachus decides. His eyes were like the eyes of Ares, which smite just by looking. (The eyes of Ares do not, in fact, do this. They are numb from looking too long on the world and seeing only danger. That was a quality Achilles eventually shared with the god of war, and then he died.)

Across the isle, Mycenaean men – veterans of Troy – beat against the doors of every hut and every workshop. "Open up, in the name of Agamemnon!" they roar. They are not yet roaring for Orestes. Telemachus watches them, marvels at how grubby is their armour, how dented their shields and yet how much greater these scars seem to make them.

And yet: "Move your feet! Get behind the strike!" barks Kenamon of Memphis, and Telemachus obeys. "If you can't reach my throat with your blade, the least you can do is cut off my fingers!"

Kenamon has a very different approach to warfare than Peisenor.

Were Telemachus the son of Ajax or Menelaus, he might ignore Kenamon's teaching altogether and choose instead to settle on Peisenor's more valiant learning. But he remembers that he is Odysseus's son – Odysseus who liked to shoot with bow and arrow from a safe distance, who concocted nonsense with horses and secret designs, and who always managed to make it to the battle lines just sluggishly enough to be three or four men back from the sharp end of the brawl. "Sorry, sorry I'm late, chariot got bogged down again, useless thing!"

Remembering this, in the afternoon Telemachus roars for Peisenor, roars to show that he is a warrior, but in the morning, before his more formal training, he aims a solid kick at Kenamon's exposed knee, misses, and instead wallops him in the nuts.

"Oh I am so sorry, I am ... oh I am just so!" he babbles, but secretly is rather impressed at the overall effect.

And in the night, though the official period of mourning is over, the suitors are subdued before the glare of Elektra on her high stool, and the moon waxes, and Clytemnestra is not found.

One night when the moon is nearly full, Andraemon grabs Leaneira by the arm.

"What in Hades' name are you playing at?" he snarls. "She hasn't even *looked* at me. You said you could get her to talk! You said you could ... "

Leaneira is confused. She pulls her arm away, rubbing it. She has been grabbed and punched and pulled before, of course. The physical shock is nothing. But this is a man who has sworn himself to her, and now his eyes are red in the firelight and the suitors wait behind half-open doors and the air is sticky and cool in the corridors of the palace.

"She'll see you. She will see you soon."

He just shakes his head, and turns away. Disappointed, not angry. Saddened by her failure; he had thought so much of her before.

In the heavens, the moon grows full.

There is a boat, hidden in a cove known only to a few women of Ithaca.

At least, it *was* known only to a few – Ourania, Eos, Autonoe, a few trusted of Penelope's house.

Then it was known to Anaitis, the priestess of Artemis, who whispered it to a novice in absolute secrecy, who murmured it to her sister who immediately told her mother who told her cousin who told a friend who – would you know it – sells fish, and actually, within a very short amount of time ...

It is a dangerous slither down to the water's edge, by rope

ladder slung from the edge of the cliff. But if you make it down to the shore, there are black rocks you can pick your way across, carefully, reaching out sometimes to balance by fingertips on salt-crusted beards of hanging weed and slippery slime. This place is too small to be of much interest to all but the lowest-end of smugglers, and too difficult to get to for the fisherwomen to bother with. Sometimes children come crabbing here, and you can get good fat mussels from the wave-smashed rock face around the corner of the bay if you are willing to risk the climb.

The boat is Ourania's boat. It can carry ten people, six of whom can row, and has a patched triangular sail. It is kept stocked with dried meat and clear water, and even when the wind is against you is strong enough to carry its passengers the little distance between Ithaca and Kephalonia, where one might find, for example, willing allies or a place to hide. Usually Ourania keeps it in plain sight, and her women go out fishing and fetch a reasonable catch. Sometimes it is kept beached at the end of a path hidden by the high green shrubs that cling stubbornly to the spiny hills of Ithaca like a Fury's fingers, ready to carry away an anxious queen in search of hasty respite.

Tonight it is in this cove, fully loaded and prepared for such an emergency, a darker skew of darkness in the night.

A woman, swathed in filthy robes, approaches the cliff edge. She hates how she smells. She hates the thorns that prick at her legs. She hates the taste of fish and the smell of salt. She hates the darkness and the broken path, and above all else, she hates this damn island. This pestilential cursed place, she despises it. If she could have gone any other way, she would have, but all the western ships must stop at Ithaca.

She carries a stolen lamp, and for a moment fumbles by its meagre glow in the dark, looking for the rolled rope ladder above the cliff. When she finds it, she cannot quite believe that this is the thing she is meant to descend by, walks further to the left, then further to the right, finds no other means of going down, kicks it out over the fall, hears the slow slurping of the sea below, its bellowing up and its sucking down into a stony deep, pauses to reconsider her choices, shields the flame of her lamp as the wind plucks at it.

A logistical problem: how to descend while keeping her light alive. She sits on the edge of the cliff, eases one toe out, immediately pulls it back. This is not the way. She tries rolling onto her belly, legs kicking out over air, feeling for the rope, snarls at the night: "How in the name of all that ... What even is ... This is the most stupid ... *I hate this cursed damned island I hate ...* "

A cracking of brittle gorse to her left catches the words in her mouth. She leaps up, raising her torch high like a weapon, feeling for the little blade on her belt. She has kept that at least, and she knows she will use it.

Semele stands in the shadows, her daughter Mirene by her side. The old woman coughs politely, leaning on her axe. Mirene, child by a long-dead, never-known father, peers past her, politely curious, clutching a shepherd's staff, eyebrows drawn in a frown as if trying to puzzle out the mystery of this woman who cannot use a ladder. Then another woman, and another, and three more again emerge from the darkness. One has her bow drawn – Teodora of the broken town of Phenera amongst them, an arrow notched, something upon her face that was not there when she merely hunted rabbits.

For a moment the women stand there, contemplating each other in the high thumping of the western wind. Then the woman in rags lowers her torch, spits, raises her eyes and mutters: "Well damn."

CHAPTER 25

>>

T hey meet at Semele's farm.

It is, like so much of Ithaca, a modest affair, yet its modesty belies a certain truth. The women of the house have been forced to lay aside their womanly dignities and take up enterprising ideas in matters of craft, labour and industry. Thus two freed slaves live on some small plot a few minutes' walk from the door who have an absolute genius for smelting tin and lead, and at the other end of the farm a former hand, crippled when he tripped while ploughing, has in his convalescent days had several interesting thoughts about the use of manure.

The woman in rags sits on a low stool by the fire. Her hair has grown unkempt, but she still makes some effort to pile it high upon her head, and to arrange a few dark brown curls in loose tresses around her pinched face. They say she hatched from an egg, and there is something in the swanny length of her neck, the creamy pallor of her skin, the flash of her amber eyes as her gaze flashes this way and that to mark her as a daughter of Leda. Not for her a make-up of lead white and an evening bath of honey – she has no need for such things. She has her father's jutting chin and her mother's full, tight lips, but her hands – I will say her hands are most beautiful, most perfect, eight delicate fingers and two long thumbs that seem to curl across the slope of her legs like resting banners before a war, the nails strong and clean, the skin near glowing from years of oil and shade.

There is a knife on Semele's belt. It is a fine, slim thing – not a farmer's tool. She pulled it from the woman's gown while the other screamed and kicked and bit, but now the ragged woman sits there calmly, as if nothing had happened; as if this were the simplest thing in the world. She waits, and does not grace her guards with conversation, but sits back, tall and steady. I have waited many a time in that manner, ready to spin upon my husband and exclaim my proud defence: "But baby Heracles strangled the snakes so why are you shouting at me anyway?" After pride there is always yielding, of course – a breaking-down and a sobbing and pawing at the hem of his gown – but you have to take time to get there, let the man feel like he's worn you down and you have truly learnt the error of your ways.

She has mastered the first – the proud retort, the flash of fury in the corner of her eye, and there was a time when Agamemnon, who was also that way inclined, found it incredibly alluring. But neither she nor he ever mastered the second part of the process, and thus their marriage faltered, to say the least.

When Penelope arrives, she is bleary-eyed from being woken, swathed in a farmer's cloak, a little breathless. She stands in the doorway, framed in stars eclipsed by scudding cloud, while the low mist drifts in around her ankles. For a moment the women regard each other, before Semele, who has been awake a long day and a long night now, snaps: "Well? Is it her?"

"Yes," Penelope replies. "That is Clytemnestra."

"Hello, little duck," says Clytemnestra.

"Hello, cousin," Penelope murmurs, looking around for another stool. For a moment none of the women understand; then Mirene realises and scurries to offer hers to the queen, who smiles and takes the proffered chair while the daughter of Semele stands, arms folded, uncertain what to make of so much royalty by their hearth. "I think you have gorse in your hair."

"I *hate* this island!" Clytemnestra splutters, fumbling in the crown of curls above her scalp to tug at her tangles. "You, girl!" An imperious gesture to Mirene, who has clearly been judged malleable. "Help me!"

Mirene glances to Penelope, who gently shakes her head. "Eos, would you be so kind?"

Eos steps from the doorway, sets down her lamp, approaches the fumbling queen of Mycenae and begins carefully to part her locks. "Eos has a talent for even the rudest of hair," explains Penelope, her eyes glistening in the firelight. "Amongst many other gifts. Semele and her daughter may be your hosts, but you are their guest and should deport yourself in accordance with that custom."

"I thought guests were sacred on Ithaca."

"They are. That is why Eos is helping with your hair."

Clytemnestra gives a single loud, hard bark, again not unlike the squawk of the swan they say birthed her. "Took you long enough to find me, Penelope-duck."

"You should be glad it is me and not your daughter."

"Elektra? She's here? Of course she is. Can't leave things alone, can she."

"And your son."

Clytemnestra stiffens, hands clenching tight before, a habit, an instinct of calm, relaxing again. The smile is locked on her face. It is the poisoned smile that finds amusement only in acid, and the discomfort it brings to all who see its venomous lips. Agamemnon found that smile enthralling, for a while. He who had conquered all of Greece thought he could conquer it too, a final victory that for so long had evaded him, and he was wrong.

"Orestes? How is he?" she murmurs, as if it were the lightest question in the world.

"He prays a lot."

"He is a good boy."

"He's here to kill you."

"Of course he is. He has always understood his duty."

"You don't seem particularly upset by this."

"Orestes could never upset me. He's doing what has to be done." Penelope raises an eyebrow at this, and Eos's fingers pause in their careful unpicking of Clytemnestra's hair. The Mycenaean queen shifts a little in her seat, then barks: "How did you find me, little duck?"

"Please don't call me that. I am the queen of the western isles."

"Oh duckling," pouts Clytemnestra, "your husband is dead, your son is without an army and you are . . . what? Desperately courting my boy for his goodwill and fortune? Maybe trying to match Elektra and Telemachus? Take it from me – she will swallow him whole and shit out his bones."

"You're her mother."

A snort of disdain; clearly Penelope understands nothing of the relationship between a mother and a daughter.

"I found a body by the shore – a man called Hyllas," Penelope says, just about keeping her voice from snapping with imperial distaste.

"Did you now."

Semele passes Penelope the little knife taken from Clytemnestra's belt. Penelope turns it between her fingers, observes the tip of the blade, the tiny guard that might leave a bloody ring where it drove into a man's neck. Returns it to the old farmer, shakes her head a little, finds a strange fascination with the ground beneath her feet, talks distantly, as a general might speak of dead soldiers on some far-off field. "Orestes and Elektra brought men to my island. It's been really rather novel, having a large troop of males stomping around. They have searched every farm and village. They are going to search my palace. It is disgraceful, of course – but the kind of disgraceful that, as you say, a queen of small, scattered lands must tolerate. That they could not find you left three possibilities. That you were hidden in the wilderness – hardly likely, given everything I know of you. That you had escaped this isle; or that you were in temple sanctuary. I am in the process of attempting to convince my cousins that it is the former."

"Elektra won't believe you."

"I am working on persuading her."

Clytemnestra's lips curl, something that might almost be an acknowledgement, a flash of respect, but she is so unfamiliar with the expression that she cannot hold it for more than an instant before her poison smile returns to its familiar place.

Does Penelope see it? Perhaps. But like her husband, she knows when to talk as though there were no audience, to weave a tale as though it were some intimate thing, a secret shared. "The night Hyllas died, Phenera was attacked. But he was not killed by Illyrians – although I don't think anyone was killed by Illyrians that night."

"No." Clytemnestra flicks the word out like dirt from her nails. "I watched from the cliffs. They were Greeks, dressed in Illyrian plumes." She sees her cousin's eyebrows rise, and shrugs. "Since my husband beat so much of Greece into sub-mission, many Greek soldiers have sailed as though they were from barbarian tribes, crudely disguising themselves to make it appear that they still honour Mycenae's peace. It is a child's tactic, easily seen through if one has spent as much time as I have receiving actual Illyrian ambassadors and actual Illyrian gifts to one's court."

Here it is; here is the reason Odysseus chose Penelope above all the other women in Sparta. Not just for the convenience of the match and the minor boost of prestige it brought him; not just because she was said to be a naiad's daughter, blessed with a little magic in her blood. Here it is – here is the moment her cousins laugh and point and sing: "Penelope-duck, Penelope-duck!" and the young Penelope, whose father threw her over a cliff when she was just a babe, and whom the seas saved from drowning through the somewhat inelegant means of a concave of valiant ducks, here she sits while the girls laugh and sing and pull at her hair, and it is as if she were in another world, another place where no jibe or barb can touch her, without pain or anger upon her brow. In the end, the bullies grew bored of singing at stone, and Odysseus sat by her side and said: "It is futile to mock the ocean, is it not?" and she looked up, and though she was silent, there was that in the corner of her mouth that seemed to agree.

Now Clytemnestra, a daughter of Zeus, sits in a shabby farmhouse in Ithaca, and speaks to Penelope again as they were wont to do when children; and it is as if the water gazes back, swallowing every thrown pebble without a ripple.

"You killed Hyllas, that night in Phenera," sighs Penelope. "My theory is that you paid him to smuggle you from Mycenae to Ithaca, and the plan was to continue the journey from Ithaca to the west. But somewhere in the voyage he either raised his price beyond your willingness to pay, or he discovered who you were and realised how much more he could get for betraying you, yes?"

"Smugglers are greedy," replies Clytemnestra with a shrug. "Hyllas was only averagely greedy, and averagely stupid. He threatened me, spoke to me as if I were some ... some fleeing Trojan! He was going to betray me. I had no choice."

"He did not think you were a threat. You were able to get close; close enough to smell his breath. You drove your blade – the blade now on Semele's hip – through his throat." Clytemnestra does not deny it. She is perhaps proud of it, as I am proud of her. "However with Hyllas dead you had no easy way off Ithaca, and his body would soon be discovered. Here, though,

189

you were fortunate. The not-Illyrians came, and you were able to dump his body amongst the dead, just another corpse."

"Do you know why the raiders targeted that scummy little village?" Clytemnestra asks suddenly, leaning forward into the firelight. "Would you like to know?"

"Phenera was a smuggler's haven – profitable yet undefended."

"Any queen should know that. But do you know how the *pirates* knew it? I do. I can tell you, if you ask me nicely. I was not the only one who watched the village burn."

Penelope's lips thin. "You killed Hyllas, left his body, and the raiders came. That much is clear. But you had already paid him for part of the journey, to take you as far as Ithaca. You gave him jewellery, gold, stamped with the seal of Agamemnon. A ring – a unique piece."

"You found them?"

"I did."

"Where?"

"On Hyllas's corpse."

"Hah! I always knew you were a crow rather than a duck! King and queen of Ithaca – scavengers, picking at other people's plates, the pair of you."

"I am the queen who might yet save your life, cousin."

"Barely a queen. Does anyone actually bow when you pass? Does anyone praise your name? I know what it is to rule."

"You knew once. Now you're just a murderer. When Orestes finds you, you will be a corpse."

"He's a good boy," she snaps. And again, a little quieter, "He's a good boy."

When Agamemnon met Clytemnestra for the very first time, he'd just run her husband through. Their baby child screamed from the next room, a boy so fresh to the world that Clytemnestra still bore the pain of his birthing upon her flesh. She grabbed the dagger from Agamemnon's belt and tried to drive it through his heart, but he caught her wrist and held her tight while his men went into the room where the baby lay, and then the baby cried no more. There was such hatred in Clytemnestra's eyes, which never left his face – it was an intoxicant unlike any the tyrant had seen before.

I'll have that, he thought as her gaze burrowed through him. I'll break that.

Agamemnon always enjoyed breaking things. He gave her the dagger as a wedding present, and she accepted it without a word.

"I was a little stumped as to how to lure you out after you killed Hyllas," Penelope confesses, as the eastern dawn pricks the horizon grey. "Though Ithaca is a small island, it is full of places to hide. You were not in the wilderness – you are too soft. Nor the villages, nor Kephalonia – either my people or Mycenae would have found you by now. Seeking sanctuary in a temple seemed the most likely – the only place the Mycenaeans wouldn't tear apart. The only place I would not violate either. Not the temple of Athena – again, I would have heard. Too many men of power assemble there, too many eyes watch from its confines. Where then? Artemis's altar perhaps – far from the towns, a sanctuary for women, for all that goddess has a less than favourable relationship with your tribe. It was near enough, and the priestesses would protect you if you came to them in need. They could not protect you if you left, of course, but you were hardly getting off Ithaca while Elektra's men were prowling my island. I remember you as the epitome of impatience, rude and flustered. Hiding must have been torment."

"I have learnt patience, cousin."

"But not enough," Penelope replies, sharper than she meant. "Given it was almost certain you were at the temple, the question was how to drag you from it. It is generally suspected on Ithaca that should things with the suitors not work out, I will be forced to flee to my allies in the isles. To this end, I keep a

191

boat, secret but always prepared. It was a simple matter to raise this with Anaitis in her shrine. The people of Ithaca do love to gossip, and Anaitis ... well, I imagine she was thrilled to see you gone without violating her sacred oath of protection. And so, here you are."

"Here I am," Clytemnestra agrees. "Which makes me your poison now, does it not?"

Penelope shifts in her chair, leans forward, fingers tangling together, leans back; for a moment forgets, it seems, how to be a queen. Eos runs her fingers through a loosened knot of Clytemnestra's hair. I play with the ends, rub the Mycenaean queen's back, whisper: *I am here.* Glare at Penelope, add a little louder – yet not so loud that mortals might be struck down by my hidden presence – *here I am.* Penelope may be a queen, a supplicant in my dominion, but Clytemnestra was the only daughter of Sparta who dared to sit on her husband's throne.

"Why did you come to Ithaca, cousin?" Penelope breathes.

"Not for you, little duck," Clytemnestra retorts, sharp and high. "I had no choice. Your miserable islands are in my way, would that Poseidon sinks them."

"Did you think of asking me for help?"

"Absolutely not."

"Why not?"

She snorts. It is not a pleasing, pretty sound, but then Clytemnestra has never felt the need to please any creature other than herself. That too was something Agamemnon found fascinating, until he did not. "Because I know all about you, little duck, moping and whining for Odysseus. Oh poor me, oh my miserable life, what will the men say? You are no queen. You are just some widow, legitimising with your simper whatever the men of Odysseus's household decree. You don't have the spine to help me."

Penelope sighs, shakes her head. "Do you see any men here?"

Clytemnestra glances at her captors, and seems for a moment to finally see them for their sex. There is a flicker of something – could it even be doubt? – across her brow, which she hides in an instant, flapping Eos away from her side, sitting up straighter in her chair. "From what I can tell, there are only two kinds of men in Ithaca. Old men cowering in their corners, and boys queuing to get between your legs."

"That is an excellent assessment of the manhood of Ithaca," Penelope concedes. "Since you can see that so clearly, I am surprised you cannot see the consequences. Elektra has ordered the ports closed. I could give you my boat, but it will only carry you as far as Kephalonia, where Mycenaean men are prowling the shore, and great rewards have been offered for your head. They will catch you, and kill you. Your son will spill your blood on my soil. So you will remain here, a guest of Semele and of me, until I have secured the removal of your children from my isles."

"Remove? How?"

"Clearly by waiting impotently for some old man to do something. That is all I am good for, no?"

Clytemnestra was born from the same cluth of eggs from which Helen hatched. Her brothers shine bright in the firmament. Very little surprises her, and yet perhaps now she reconsiders a number of assumptions she has made. She has not had to reconsider anything much, her whole life. "Elektra will never give up."

"She is a lot like you."

"She is nothing like me!" Penelope puts her head on one side, watching the Mycenaean queen recompose herself, before quieter Clytemnestra adds: "That girl always took after her father."

"Daddy is a hero and you're just a stupid whore!" screamed Elektra, eleven years old, slamming the door in her mother's face. Clytemnestra can't remember why her daughter slammed the door, but assumed it was just a phase she was going through.

"Father is a hero and you're just ... just ... just a woman!" snapped Telemachus, twelve years old, storming away from Penelope as she tried to get him to ... something. Learn basic horticulture. Study law and precedent. Something useful for a king, no doubt. Something that wasn't being a hero before the walls of Troy. She thought it was a phase too.

Two queens sit now in silence, and wonder: is there a limit to what a mother can give? We gods applaud those who give all, all, more than all and more than could ever be enough. Any woman who gives merely all she has to give, and then has no more left in her, we condemn to Tartarus's burning fields, and simply say: it is for the children.

It occurs to Penelope that she does not know if she *likes* her son. She loves him, of course, and will stand before spears to save his life. But does she like him? She is not sure there is enough of the man who will be Telemachus for her to know.

Clytemnestra does not like Elektra. She saw her daughter peeking round the door of her rooms one night when Aegisthus was about his work, but she did not cry out stop, stop, my love, stop. She had never known what it was to be worshipped by a man, to experience her own pleasure, her own ecstasy, until Aegisthus. Later she told herself it was for the best that her daughter *should* see, that Elektra should know that women too can cry out in delight at the touch of a man; that a man can choose to think of a woman's pleasure as well as his own. She thought perhaps Elektra would understand then, and be happy for her mother, but it seemed that after that day Elektra loathed Clytemnestra more than ever before, more even than the day they stood by the altar on which Iphigenia died.

"Daddy had to kill Iphigenia," Elektra proclaimed, one drunken night when the feast was ending. "He did it for the Greeks and for the gods. You should not have tried to interfere!"

Both Penelope and Clytemnestra told their children that their fathers were heroes, when they were still young and asking where their fathers were. It seemed a kindness. It seemed the right thing to do.

"I suppose I have no choice but to rely on your ... discretion," Clytemnestra muses, as the two queens sit in the huddled shadow of the fire. "That must make you happy."

"It does not. Yet I will be discreet."

"I saw torches in the forest above the temple a few nights ago; and now there are women wearing swords on your island. Are you ... *conspiring*, little duck?"

"When one has neither gold, soldiers, name nor honour, what else is a woman to do?"

Clytemnestra nods. She had gold, soldiers and name – not exactly honour, but the first three would do. Now she has rags and dirt in her hair, and her name – why, she is not sure what her name is now.

For a moment the two women sit in silence, Clytemnestra straight as a column of the temple of Zeus, Penelope hunching a little, her curiosity showing through her ridged demeanour. Finally Clytemnestra snaps: "Spit it out, duck! Don't just sit there staring!"

"Why did you do it?" Penelope breathes. "Why did you kill Agamemnon?"

Clytemnestra's eyes widen in rage, in despair, and in her heart she cries Aegisthus, Aegisthus, and feels his tongue still against the warm curl of her neck. Her voice, when she speaks, is the burning of ice, not of fire. "Why ... did I kill him? The man who killed my daughter? Who killed my son? Who came back from his war with whores to put in my bed? The murderer, the monster of Greece, the ... You should *thank* me. All of Greece thanks me! You should be on your knees kissing my feet, you should be ... *Why did I kill him?*"

Penelope's brow crinkles for a moment, confused rather than

wounded by Clytemnestra's words. "No," she murmurs at last. "Not that. I mean . . . why did you kill him like *that*?"

Clytemnestra freezes like the snake poised to strike, then curls back into herself, smaller now, a woman, not a queen. And of course, there is more. For yes, yes, all this true, this legacy of blood and murder, but still – Clytemnestra bowed and simpered and said, "Oh loving husband, welcome home!" when Agamemnon reached the docks. She threw herself at his knees and proclaimed, "My hero! My love! Oh greatest of kings!" and there were petals strewn before his feet and he was carried upon a chair of gold to his palace while Clytemnestra very publicly, and with only a little aid of onion, wept joyfully at his return.

Only later, when his back was turned, did she let the scowl twist at her face, the fury hammer in her heart. Then Aegisthus drew out of the shadows and held her tight and whispered, "Not yet, my love. Not yet. We must be careful. We must be wise. Do not strike. Not yet."

Aegisthus, who was himself the son of a king, the slain uncle of Agamemnon, a man with as much right to rule in Mycenae as any other. Yet he had been reduced to a poet, down to a man who had to pleasure women to get on in life, the lowest of the low. He held her as she shook with fury, as her skin crawled with Agamemnon's touch, and whispered: wait, my love. Wait. You are so brave, you are so strong. No one else in all Greece could do this, but you can.

She had feared Agamemnon might immediately demand to have her, his hand pressed against her face to turn her head to the side so he need not look at her as he did his business. But no – he was too glutted with wine and the adoration of the men of the city to bother with his wife, and so she stood behind him and smiled and said, "Whatever you wish, my love," and put his Trojan slaves in the second finest room in the palace and wondered if he crushed their faces away when he did them too, if their necks ached from bending.

Wait, wait, Aegisthus whispered, and so she would wait. Wait until the time was right, for poison, or the ague, for some subtle chance to take her revenge that would let her play the grieving widow. But then one night, as she was drifting off to sleep, Agamemnon burst through her door and roared: "What the fuck have you been doing, woman?"

She crawled from her slumber as he descended upon her, striking her once across the face – and she knew to fall immediately, she knew he liked to hit women when they were standing. "What the fuck is this? You banished people? You banished my *friends*?"

"I enacted the law, I banished enemies of Mycenae, I ruled as you bade me do . . . "

He hit her again, even though she was down, and then she feared – truly feared. "You do not rule!" he screamed, spittle in her eyes, blood flowing from her nose. "I am king! *I am king!* You are just some . . . some *thing*! You do not give commands! You do not exile my friends! You do not speak to men or merchants or generals or council or any man *unless I say*!"

And here it is, here it comes.

Someone has whispered in his ear, murmured: "Agamemnon, about your wife . . . "

Someone told him that when he was away, she sat in his chair, spoke with his voice, and those who questioned at first were quickly silenced. She was a woman, and she ruled like a king, and now – here it is, it was always going to be this – he picks her up and throws her upon the bed, and though she screams and claws and tries to dig her fingers into his eyes, he is still stronger than she. He has always been stronger than she.

And when he's done, he lies breathless upon the sticky sheets, his point made the best way he knows how

Aegisthus sends a message from outside the palace: *I am coming, I am coming, I will gather men and we will take back what is ours . . .*

But he does not come.

Agamemnon calls back his banished friends, the thieves and liars who had robbed his court blind while he was gone, the flatterers and tongue-licking scoundrels who whispered honey as they defied the law. He strips Clytemnestra naked before them, says: "Beg for their forgiveness," and when she does not beg, when she does not bend, he throws her upon his knee and beats her until she bleeds, and still Aegisthus does not come.

And then, one night, when he has pushed her head towards the wall and dragged her legs apart – *whore, fucking slut, fucking whore, I'm the king, I'm the king, I'm the king!* – one night when his business is done, he lies there, sweating wine and offal, and she rises to wash herself, to scrub him from her, and sees the knife that she sometimes uses for cutting fruit lying still in its silver bowl. That blade that was her wedding gift.

And stops cleaning herself, since she will only have to wash again.

And takes the dagger.

"You look like a fucking . . ." he says, but the sentence will never be finished.

She does the deed.

Not for her son, dead in Tantalus's court.

Not for her daughter, slaughtered upon Artemis's altar.

She does it that night, reckless and rash, for herself.

None other.

I love you, I whisper, as the blood runs down her arms.

I love you, I proclaim, as Aegisthus is summoned from his lair to stare, horrified, at the corpse. "What have you done?" he breathes, and she has no answer.

I love you, I murmur, as she flees into the night. *You are beloved of the queen of the gods. You set yourself free, you fly like the moon through the night, you are justice, you are vengeance, you are the righteous blade in the dark! You are my Clytemnestra.*

A few days later, Orestes threw the spear that ended Aegisthus's life. He was the first man her son ever killed.

I love you, I breathe, as Clytemnestra sits still and silent in the Ithacan night. *I am here.* I slip my fingers into hers, then reach out again and catch Penelope's hands in my own, binding them to me, each to each in that quiet place. *My queens,* I breathe, as the sun pricks the eastern horizon. *Do not be afraid.*

Outside, an owl calls into the fading night, and I feel for an instant the presence of another, carried away on the beating of feathered wings.

CHAPTER 26

≫≫≫≫≫≫≫≫≫≫≫≫≫≫≫≫≫≫≫≫≫≫≫≫≫≫≫≫

In the darkness beyond Semele's farm, Priene waits. Teodora of Phenera is by her side, bow across her back. Ourania, spymaster of the queen, stands a little off with one of her maids. There are others too – peer deeper into the darkness and there they are, the widows, the orphan girls, the unmarried maids and ragged fisherwomen. The queen called and they answered, and now as Penelope approaches with Eos at her back, they wait in silence in the dark.

Penelope takes Ourania's hands, whispers in her ear. The old woman nods, gestures to her women to leave; their work here is done. There will be more work soon.

Then the queen approaches Priene. The warrior does not bow. She shows no deference to woman nor man. Penelope stops a few paces away, considers Priene by the low light of the lanterns, regards the gathered darkness about them, the eyes half hidden in shadow. Says at last, loud enough that all might hear: "Priene. Captain."

Priene has not been called "captain" before. In her tribe there was no need of these titles. Everyone understood their duty, their place; it did not have to be spelled out by stories, imposed by the strong upon the weak. But this is Greece, where these words have a power all of their own. "Queen," she replies, not sure if this is the correct form of address, and not caring much either. Then: "So it is Agamemnon's wife."

Penelope glances towards the sky, to the setting moon, the line of grey upon the horizon, then gestures a little to one side, that the two might walk together in quieter speech. "Yes. It's her."

"Did she do it? Did she kill him?" Priene cannot quite keep the thrill of admiration out of her voice. "Was he in the bath, naked, like they say? Did she drink his blood? Did she eat his manly ... "

"I have not made those specific enquiries. How goes the training? It will be full moon soon." A shrug – this is evident, and therefore not worth commenting on. "The raiders come with the full moon," Penelope adds, watching the thin light play upon Priene's face, hunting for a sign in its motion. "Will the women be ready?"

Priene only considers the question long enough to kick a little stone that was in her path. "No."

Penelope catches herself, holds back the sharp breath she would have released, wants to argue, remembers not to. She is patient. She reminds herself of this all the time. To be patient is to feel burning rage, impotent fury, to rage and rock against the injustice of the world and yet – and yet – to hold one's tongue. That is what she has come to understand of patience, though no one else seems to comprehend the heat of it in her chest. So instead she says: "Very well. I will leave you to your business. Good day to you."

"Queen," blurts Priene, before Penelope can depart. "This Clytemnestra."

"What of her?"

Priene draws up a little straighter, and touches two fingers of her right hand to her heart. "I will pray for blessings and fortune upon her."

Priene has not prayed for a very long time. *Pray to me, pray to me!* I whisper in her ear, as the women depart. *Pray to me, my fierce one, pray to Hera!*

Priene does not hear. Her heart is closed to all but the lady of the east who bathes in the fire of the morning dawn.

In the morning, Anaitis stands at the palace gates, feet splayed like the roots of the ash.

"A priestess of Artemis, how wonderful," shrills Autonoe. "Please, do come inside."

Anaitis glowers at the woman, at the palace, at the very town around her as if suspecting it of all being a trap, then finally, reluctantly, crosses the threshold. She does not drink the wine she is offered, nor sit in the chair proffered, but stands, a trunk of a woman with arms folded, for nearly an hour as groggy, hung-over suitors pull themselves past her, until finally Penelope appears.

"Good priestess," intones the queen, "We are honoured by your visit."

"No you're not," replies Anaitis. "That's not what people are like."

"Please – let us talk in private."

They talk, somewhat awkwardly, before the little household shrine of Hestia, where only the women bother to pray. My sister is too much of a dull old maid to care if another goddess's priestess stands before her shrine as if she owns it, but if it had been *my* image before which this servant of Artemis spoke, I should have sent warts.

"Well? Where is she?" hisses Anaitis.

"If by 'she' you refer to my cousin, she is perfectly safe."

A snort, an intake of breath, but Anaitis is not sure what to make of this unexpected information, had not prepared suitable words other than perhaps a drawling "But *is* she though?!"

which, now she is actually standing here, seems a little juvenile. Penelope sighs, smiles, resists the urge to pat the other woman on the back. "Leaving aside my ... complicated feelings about the fact you have been hiding the single most valuable woman in all of Greece in your temple, and my equally rich and nuanced sentiment over how willing you were to tell her about my boat ... "

"Which you told me about!" Anaitis nearly squeaks, before glancing to her shadow to see that no others have heard her shrill. "You *wanted* me to tell her! You wanted me to get her off the island!"

Penelope waits a beat for the priestess's ire to diminish, then smiles and nods again. "I do of course want Clytemnestra gone. But she is *not* a daughter of naiads. Her sailing skills extend to comments about the oiled shoulders of the nearest handsome rowers. This outcome is the least bad currently available."

"She is under *my* protection. She claimed sanctuary."

"She *was* under your protection. When she left the temple grounds, she was under no one's protection but her own. Now she is under mine."

"Artemis will be ... "

"Artemis bid Agamemnon kill her daughter. However the gods move in our lives, good sister, let us not imagine they move for any whims save their own."

If I were Apollo, master of stories and weaver of ballads, I might end my tale right here on that most pithy of points. Alas, he is busy stringing his lyre in Delos while nubile boys with unbroken voices attend to his, shall we say, musical inclinations, and so I shall let the story roll on even though I doubt a wiser, more appropriate point shall e'er be made.

Anaitis flusters and puffs her cheeks, and if she is entirely honest, doesn't know how she feels about this entire situation. Finally: "I want to see her."

"No."

"Why not?"

"Because I do not want all of Ithaca to know where Clytemnestra is."

"I would never . . ."

"Yet you understand why I do not take the risk."

Anaitis definitely feels something – perhaps it is indignation? – at this, but again, she is never entirely sure until she has had a chance to sit down and think about things what sentiment guides her most strongly at any given hour. So instead she says, nose turned up, eyes away: "I can keep your secrets, queen. You know I can."

"I know it. I am grateful."

"It will be full moon soon."

"I am aware."

"Will the women fight when the pirates come?"

"No."

"Why not?"

"They are not ready, and even if they were, I am not sure where the Illyrians will strike."

"Oh." Anaitis's enthusiasm is as fickle as her mistress – they have that in common too. "Then what can we do?"

"I have given this some thought. The priests of the temple of Athena sometimes honour the full moon with a sacrifice – I myself have often attended to pray for my husband. It seems to me that the temple of Artemis might also wish to celebrate. Perhaps some sort of . . . midnight festivities? Some sacred feast to coincide with the full moon? Song, dance, honey cakes for the children, that type of thing? The kind of devotional that might encourage the people of the coast to move a little inland, away from the gentle waters of the sea."

Anaitis's eyes brighten. "The temple of Athena is of course well provided for. Everyone who passes through the harbour stops to

do homage to Odysseus's famous patron. Whereas Artemis ...
we are deeper within the woods, fewer people come ..."

"I will ensure you are properly provisioned."

"... the roof has been leaking too, the storms last winter ..."

Penelope is too tired to barter, too weary to roll her eyes.
"I will send carpenters to attend to the roof, and carts with
offerings."

"The goddess does love a midnight dance," Anaitis concludes
with a single satisfied nod, which quickly dissolves again to a
frown. "And this other matter? The ... the woman who did not
take a boat?"

"For now, she is safe, I swear."

"For now?"

"I am working on it." Penelope sighs. "I know it is ... I know
that I am asking for your trust. But I am trying my best to resolve
all these things."

It seems to Anaitis that the world is full of people trying their
best, and that rarely means anything. Yet perhaps trying their
best is all she can really ask. Anaitis knows that she has been
used, and is not greatly offended by it. Using her is the reasonable
thing to do, and she has no time for people who cannot respect
reason. "I am sure the goddess will be thrilled by our devotions,"
she muses.

Penelope nods, smiles. "We do what we can to honour
the divine."

CHAPTER 27

>>

In the clouded night, I squint down from the heavens and I think I see . . .

. . . yes, look again, and there she is.

Athena sits and hoots like an absolute bloody idiot, an owl upon the blackened branch of an ancient withered tree. Hoot bloody hoot she goes, blinking reflective darkness, as if I wouldn't see her, as if I can't always see through her pitiful disguises.

Hoot bloody hoot, and I let her hoot a while on the tree above the palace, because though I resent it, Ithaca *is* more her domain than mine, and one must save one's battles for when one is certain one can win.

Hoot hoot, she says, and no – wait. Look again. Beneath the scudding sky I could almost miss it, but she is doing more than hunting mice tonight.

Athena calls into the midnight mist that rises from the choppy sea, and the mist answers. It weaves itself into the dreams of old Eupheithes, father of miserable Antinous, who would see his son king of the western isles and now finds himself standing naked and ashamed while Polybus, Aegyptius and all the crowd of ancient men point and laugh and pelt him with the dung of pigs. How did it come to this, he wonders, as he twists and contorts in

206

shame, hiding his shrivelled form from their spite, that old men who were sometimes servants of Laertes, sometimes fellows in arms and friendship, have turned against one another?

Athena calls into the midnight mist, and at her command it slips into the nostrils of Amphinomous, a soldier who became no more than a suitor to a widowed woman, who dreams of spears and blood and the dance of death, and falls, falls, falls beneath the sword of a golden-haired hero whose face he cannot see, only to rise and fall, fall, fall again.

Athena calls into the midnight mist, and her dreams touch all the suitors of the palace, nightmares of blood and terror and vengeance long overdue. And her dreams touch sleeping Orestes, but a touch is not enough to break through the bonds of anguish that have already wrapped themselves around his slumber, she'll need a battering ram to drive away the image of his mother's face as she turns from his bloody mind.

And her dreams touch the old warrior Peisenor, for whom she has a soft spot, and for one night only he believes that his militia of scraggly boys can win. And her dreams touch Kenamon of Memphis, who really has no idea what to make of this violent intrusion upon his sleeping hours, given that this is the first time a goddess of Greece has sent him visions.

Her dreams do not touch the women of the palace.

Hoot hoot, goes the owl, hoot hoot, and it does not occur to my stepdaughter that the women of Ithaca are worth a little trifling with.

I could laugh, spit in her face, clamp my thumb and index finger over that stupid beak of hers and shout *hoot bloody hoot* into those blinking yellow eyes. Later, perhaps. Not yet.

Then I glimpse another dream she has sent, nearly miss it, tiny and black as char. This dream is not carried on the mist at all, but is dispatched in the nibbling of a thin-winged fly that hatched from a pool of standing water beneath the window of

Telemachus. It crawls up between his sheets, whining shrill and high, sniffing the hot exhalation of his breath, before at last it latches on to the soft pulse in his neck and, with a thrust, digs its proboscis into the sweet lava of his crimson blood.

And as it feasts, he dreams, and he cries out in his slumber and I do not know what dream she has sent him, I cannot see it. I could drop down from Olympus and pluck the insect from his throat, squeeze out the mirage she has twined in it, but she would know, she would see, and she would fly to my husband and say, "Oh mighty father, does it not bother you that your wife is interfering with the minds of mortals?"

And then my husband would say: "No, not Hera, absolutely not!" and within a day I would be summoned to his side and told that he has a feast he wants me to prepare or some prophecy that needs shaping or some utter nonsense, some blistering farce to keep me from the realm of men, while he watches me over the tip of his nose and wonders whether I – I – have been unfaithful.

That would be how that story goes, as it has gone so many times before. I am, after all, the goddess of wives, and it is the wife's duty to remain at home.

So I let Athena send her dream to Odysseus's son, and I have no idea what he dreams, only that he wakes sweating and panting for breath, and tonight my ignorance terrifies me.

And so the moon hides her light behind the clouds, but for those of us who part the sky with the brushing of our fingertips, she grows.

And then:

The day before full moon, on an overcast afternoon of scudding sky the size of which one may only find over Poseidon's changing waters, a sailor is dragged into the hall and thrown at the feet of councillor Aegyptius.

Aegyptius hears his story, then calls for Peisenor and Medon.

Peisenor and Medon listen to his tale, and send for Penelope.

By the time Penelope has done hearing it, the whole thing is laced with the tedium of repetition, and the colourful detail and justificatory dodges that had embellished his initial telling now have dissolved into dull statements of fact, as of time, place, manner and nothing else, not even speculation.

Aegyptius says: "We should tell King Orestes!" and everyone agrees that it is a good idea.

Orestes is summoned, and Elektra comes, followed a few steps behind by her brother and loyal men. "What is this?" she snaps, at the growing assemblage of the good, the potent and the merely curious. "What is this noise?"

Penelope regards her from behind the wall of learned councillors who now seek to speak for her, and thinks that for all of Clytemnestra's protests, there is a great deal of the mother in the daughter. How could there not be, when the father was so long from home?

"This man is a merchant from Corcyra," barks Peisenor, who always likes to get involved when royalty – even uncrowned would-be royalty – is in the room. "He plies the amber trade from the northern ports down to the Nile. Show his highness what you showed us!"

The sailor, whose name is Origen and who really deserves better than this, opens his palm to reveal the object of all the fuss. It is gold, heavy, sits neatly in the creases of his sun-beaten skin. Elektra leans down to take it, turning it slowly this way and that. The afternoon light through the windows of the hall is thick honey, drawing hard lines and hot spears through the still air. She feels the weight of the ring in her hand, examines its features, does not bother to show it to her brother.

"It is my mother's," she says at last, and there is a general, somewhat overdone gasping and drawing-in of breath. Penelope is a little late to the exhalation, having assumed it was obvious from all the fuss that everyone knows it was Elektra's mother's, but still, the overall effect is pleasing. "How did you come by it?" Elektra barks at the cowering man, and again, Penelope isn't going to be the one to say it, but there is much of Clytemnestra in the flash of Elektra's eye, the tilting of her chin. Who else was she to learn queening from anyway?

"A woman came to Hyrie," he replies, and a few tellings ago this would have been a grovelling babble, full of justification and pomp, but is now instead a somewhat calmer rendition given how many times he has already repeated it and not yet lost a limb. "Looking for passage to the north. She took ship with a merchant by the name of Sostrate, who had purchased a shipment of timber from me not two moons ago. She paid for her passage with this ring, which he gave to me in honour of the debt he owed. But when I tried to trade it for cargo to bring south, I was brought before the master of the town, who brought me before a Mycenaean who swore it was the ring of the traitor queen Clytemnestra. They then sent for men who brought me here, and here I am. To honour and serve," he adds hastily, now that royalty is in the room, "Loyally, as I am a servant."

Penelope listens with as much curiosity as do all the others in the hall, for this in truth is the first time she has heard this tale, and as she listens she wonders which pieces of it might bear Ourania's touch. Certainly the woman who first gave Sostrate the ring – she would be of Ourania's household, but she is gone now, smuggled away to some safe place from which she need not return for many moons. Who else, perhaps? Was Sostrate one of Ourania's too, or was he merely a useful piece to be played, a means to get the ring to Origen, and Origen to Penelope's court? (It is the latter. Sostrate does not know how he has been used, nor will Origen ever realise how predictable is his behaviour, or how easily manipulated his plans. The only risk Ourania took was when the port guard did not at once recognise the ring in Origen's hand, and the old spy had to send a girl to whisper in the man's ear that she had once seen such a thing in Mycenae. That girl is not remembered now.)

Elektra closes her fist around the ring as if she might bleed from it, knuckles white, wrist shaking. "Hyrie is within your domain, is it not?" she barks at Penelope. "Why are ships still sailing from it?"

Penelope has opened her mouth to answer – or rather, to apologise, to turn and say, "Good councillors, how could this terrible thing have happened?" – when Medon speaks.

"The messenger to the north was delayed by unfavourable winds. He has only just returned to us."

That is ... mildly true. The news sailed south first, to the ports of Zakynthos, and there the messenger was delayed by both unfavourable winds and favourable wine, it not perhaps having been imparted unto him quite how urgent were the words he carried. Such failures of communication are a common yet regrettable scourge upon an island kingdom.

Elektra scowls, scoffs, a circling lioness sniffing at a dry and bloody trail. "Where did this woman go?"

"I don't know," confesses Origen, tucking his head down into his chest like a frightened bird. "Sostrate trades in the north, with the pale barbarians. But he sailed a week ago; I had no idea that the ring was so important!"

"We can prepare the ships," offers the Mycenaean, Pylades, meagre in hope. "Perhaps sail on the evening tide ...?"

"We will speak of this in private," Elektra snaps, and then, aware that she has been perhaps a little too forceful in this dec- laration, adds, "My brother will issue his commands shortly."

She turns away with a nod, a minor act of courtesy given that the palace is not quite her own, and strides for her rooms, ring still gripped tight in her hand. Orestes follows, and his knuckles too are all bone and no blood where he clutches the sword at his side.

"How convenient," muses Medon into Penelope's ear, as the crowd, thwarted of some of its entertainment, disperses.

"What could you mean? It is a terrible shame, but hardly convenient."

"A shame, yes, but nothing we could have done. If only the messenger had gone to Hyrie before Zakynthos, perhaps your cousin would not have escaped."

"That is speculation; unhelpful speculation at that."

A patter of feet, and here he is, Telemachus, late as always to the party. "What happened?" he demands, unsure whether to direct his enquiry to Medon, Aegyptius or even, strangely, his mother, and ending up directing it to a point somewhere between Medon's shoulder and Penelope's nose.

"Clytemnestra has escaped," grunts Peisenor.

"Clytemnestra might have escaped," clarifies Medon, hands pressed over the curve of his belly.

"It's a disgrace!" barks Aegyptius. "We will have to make amends with Orestes!"

"A woman resembling my cousin was seen paying for passage to the furthest north," sighs Penelope. "The ring she used to purchase her journey is one known to be in possession of the fleeing queen."

"In Zeus's name," breathes Telemachus, paling beneath his sweaty flush. "So we have failed?"

"That is one way of looking at it," muses Medon.

The boy straightens. "I must go to Orestes. Apologise in person. This is my kingdom, and I must take responsibility." Penelope's eyebrows could have bridged that waterway that divides the east from the west, but she says nothing. "Did he seem ... angry?"

"Who knows what Orestes thinks." Medon is becoming

skilled in studying the ceiling as he speaks, as though he has only just noticed the weaving of a spider in the corner. "But his sister was less than amused."

"I must go to them." Telemachus no doubt sounds very kingly as he straightens and says these words. "I must try to undo some of the harm of this incompetence!"

He has a good stride, I'll give him that. He makes it all the way to Elektra's door without tripping over his feet or getting a bloody nose. The old men and women watch him depart, before finally Medon leans into Penelope's side and murmurs: "Should I . . . do something?"

"No," she sighs. "He can't do any harm, and maybe Elektra will enjoy a bit of abject grovelling from someone her own age. I have a headache, and must retire to my room to . . . " She looks for the words, fingers spinning on the air like the weaver on the ceiling.

". . . contemplate your womanly woes?" suggests Medon helpfully. "Quietly lie in the pain of your mournful suffering?"

"Yes. That. Thank you."

She turns to go, but as she does, Medon leans in close. "It will be full moon tomorrow."

"I know."

"You should speak to your son."

"I should?" A flush of panic, a moment of confusion. What has she missed now? What is it in the blind spot that is her child that she cannot see?

"Peisenor is preparing his militia to patrol the cliffs. If the raiders do return . . . "

"Ah – I see."

"He would be very unlucky indeed were he to encounter an enemy. And yet that is his purpose."

"What . . . what do you recommend I say?" There she is again, just for a moment, the girl Medon remembers, peeking through the queen. There is no jest in her voice, no sharp wit; she cannot meet the old man's eye.

"You could tell him you're proud of him? That he is very brave."

"Am I? Is that . . . is that what you would say?"

Medon pats his belly, as though such a gesture were itself almost a bow. "He's your son. I'm sure you'll work something out."

CHAPTER 28

>>

E lektra says:
     "My brother will set forth immediately with two ships
to Ilyrie, and seek information on our mother there. I will
remain in Ithaca."

"Of course, you are welcome to stay as long as you like –
however we can serve. I will have provisions sent to stock your
brother's ships and . . . "

"The gods are with us," Elektra snaps. "He will find her."

And if he does not, Menelaus sits in Sparta and rubs his hands,
yum yum yum, he thinks, look at Mycenae without a king, such
a tragedy, such terrible things to have befallen my brother's old
estates, yum yum yum.

"We are honoured to serve the king," Penelope says, and for
a moment almost forgets that she is too old and too queenly to
bow to Elektra and the silent boy by her side.

In the evening, she sends Eos to Semele's farm.

She herself stays indoors, weaving Laertes' funeral shroud. The
suitors sit in rows in the hall, beneath Elektra's whip-hot eye, and
do not roar in drunkenness, and are surprised to find that they

are more scared of this little creature dressed in ash than they were of her departed brother.

As Eos steps across the threshold of Semele's farm, Clytemnestra rises and snaps: "Where's Penelope? Where's my son?"

"The queen is in the palace, entertaining your daughter," replies Eos quietly, hands clasped before her. Clytemnestra snorts – very few people can entertain Elektra, and rarely in the manner they intended. "Your son has sailed north, after word reached him that you had been spotted departing Hyrie."

"Really? He believed that?"

"He has been shown a ring of yours. The ring you gave to Hyllas."

Clytemnestra has mighty eyebrows, most suited for arching. "Maybe the little duck isn't so stupid after all. So when do I sail?"

"There are still Mycenaeans watching the port. Fewer than there were now Orestes is gone, but the soldier Pylades stayed behind with Elektra."

"Why? Why did they stay?"

Eos's lips grow thin in her small, tight face, and she does not have an answer. This concerns her, but if her queen does not speak of it, neither will she. Thankfully, Clytemnestra's attention darts away before either woman can too particularly dwell upon this matter.

"Elektra can't watch everything. Everyone knows your little island is a haven for smugglers and wretched types."

"Tomorrow will be full moon. No one will sail then."

"Why not? It's surely the perfect time?"

"It's when the raiders come."

Clytemnestra leans forward, suddenly interested, studying the marble wall of Eos's unblinking visage. "Raiders? Your pretend Illyrians, you mean?"

"They attack at full moon."

"Ah – of course they do. But they should have sent an emissary

216

by now. Penelope should have paid them off. Why hasn't she?" Eos is silent. Eos learnt to be silent a long time ago. "Unless the price is too high?" breathes Clytemnestra. "Unless the price is the kingdom, no? Do you have a problem with one of your suitors? Has some big, strong man come up to Penelope's door and said, 'Marry me and I promise your troubles will go away'? He *has*, hasn't he? How delicious. You know, if I were queen in Ithaca, I'd lead him to my bedroom door, promise him his every earthly desire, then drive my dagger through his eye and feed his body to the sea. Terrible accident, everyone would say. I would pay the poets to say it."

Eos nods, considering this, playing it out before her eyes, before asking: "How is that working out for you?"

Clytemnestra draws back her hand to slap the maid, to send her spinning across the room, but Semele grabs her fist before she can let fly, and slowly shakes her head. She drops her hand and Clytemnestra drops with her, slumping back into her chair.

"Soon," says Eos. "When the moon is a little less bright." She stares down at the fallen queen a moment longer, then turns and walks away.

CHAPTER 29

>>

Dawn over Ithaca. The last dawn before a fat, full moon-kissed night.

There are no clouds in the sky, and this is unfortunate, for there will be nothing to mask the light of the full moon, a gift to guide sailors by. On the hill behind Eumaios's farm, Telemachus steps back from a swipe of Kenamon's sword, but the Egyptian presses his advantage. "If you go backwards, I will come forwards!" he barks. "I will keep coming until there is nowhere left for you to go backwards to! Only go backwards if you are setting a trap, now *move*!"

Afterwards, sticky and spent, Kenamon and Telemachus sit by the fresh water upstream of where Eumaios's pigs snuffle with wet snouts, and the Egyptian strips off his shirt and splashes his face and his armpits, dips his toes in the water and sighs, and after a moment, unsure of his skinny frame next to this man's whole one, Telemachus does the same, and there they sit a while.

Finally Kenamon says: "Full moon tonight."

Telemachus nods, but does not reply.

"Are you scared?" Telemachus shakes his head, and earns, to his amazement, a light punch in the shoulder. "Don't be ridiculous, boy! Of course you're scared. Do you think your father wasn't scared every time he went into battle? Scared is how you see the spear coming for your eye. Scared is how you choose where and when to strike. All this … " Kenamon gestures vaguely at the weapons strewn around them, "doesn't teach you how to use a sword or a shield. It teaches you how to focus, how to keep moving, when you are too frightened to think."

In the forest groves above the temple of Artemis, Teodora practises with the bow. She draws back the shot and thwack, thwack, thwack, until finally Priene stands beside her and says: "The tree has had enough."

Teodora draws back the bow again, lets out her breath, releases the arrow. Priene watches, and says no more. Priene has no home to defend. Her home was her people, and her people are dead. She is not sure if she likes the women she is training; she is absolutely certain that she will never like the queen she serves. But she remembers an idea that was home, and sees it in Teodora's eyes, and thinks for a moment she sees a kind of beauty, and finds the whole thing profoundly confusing.

Kenamon says: "Fight safely, boy," as Telemachus rises in a clatter of brass.

Telemachus nods, and the Egyptian's eyes do not leave the boy's back as he marches away.

Sunset, a golden mirror across the ocean, a fringe of blood on the western sky.

Peisenor sits with his fellow commanders of the militia: Aegyptius, Polybus, Eupheithes. "When they come … " Peisenor begins.

"If they're even coming!" Eupheithes objects.

" … we'll have to concentrate our forces."

"Well then the harbour, of course!" exclaims Polybus, in much the same breath as Eupheithes tuts: "Naturally the grain."

For a moment the two men glower at each other. Aegyptius

clears his throat, and adds: "There are villages unprotected to the north . . ."

"Without the harbour, Ithaca will starve," proclaims Polybus, emphasising every word with a stab of his finger into the air.

"Without grain, Ithaca will also starve!" retorts Eupheithes.

"The harbour has defenders and the silos are inland . . ." begins Aegyptius feebly. Many of the reasons why Odysseus did not take this councillor with him to war are becoming increasingly apparent.

"We cannot take risks," barks Polybus. "We have to protect the most important asset Ithaca has – and that's the harbour!"

"Even for Illyrians, both these targets are unlikely . . ."

"If you want my men to fight, you will protect the granaries."

Peisenor just about manages not to sigh. These words have been coming, of course, since the very first day he negotiated with these old men of the isles. He had not known how he would handle them then, and to his shame, he still does not know what to say to them now. Finally Aegyptius says: "Perhaps if we approach this . . . tactically." Aegyptius has never been in battle. "We set watches at the most northern and the most southern points, with fast horses and torches. If they see ships, they ride to alert the militia, who we can garrison at both the harbour and the granaries, as well as in places about the island, to muster and defend wherever it is we see the ships approaching."

The wise men of Ithaca contemplate this. Peisenor does not. He knows already that he has trained boys to die, and nothing else. He has known it for many weeks, and yet not known it, for he is a man rent in two – the sage who sees the truth of things, and the soldier who fears growing old, who saw death once on the field of battle but refused to look him in the eye. Athena, where are you now? Where is your warrior wisdom? It should shine down upon this broken man; it should shroud him in your grace. But you never cared for the broken ones, when all is said and done.

The commander who values his troops tries to say: "That will not do. Even if they can muster, it will take them too long. There will not be enough . . ." but the words just come out as a sigh.

"I want twenty men, at least, on the harbour!" barks Polybus.

"I want twenty on the granaries," retorts Eupheithes.

"That will not leave enough to defend the rest of the island . . ." Aegyptius begins.

"But as you say, once we get word from the watch, our men can join the others," Eupheithes replies. "They will meet the Illyrians at full force, and drive them back."

Aegyptius glances at Peisenor, waiting for the old man to say something, anything, that might change this situation. Peisenor does not. His head hangs low, and his lips are curled in as finally, to the expectant silence, he says: "I see no other way," for truly he does not.

As sunset fades to night, the militia marches out.

They make a bit of a show of it, all spears and shields and a motley array of armour of a dozen different types, strapped to boyish calf and skinny chest. Telemachus leads the line as best he can, which gets a few cheers. Both Eupheithes and Polybus thought of opposing this, spurred on by their indignant suitor sons − after all, it is not Telemachus's army that marches, but a militia of Ithacan men of whom he is merely one.

But then it occurs to them that they may well be seeing the son of Odysseus march off to die, and even if he does not, he is marching to defend their property, and the property that with a bit of luck their children might inherit. This revelation might humble other men, but the poison of ambition has sunk too deep into their veins, and instead they merely pull at their beards and meet no other's eye as the boys head out.

221

Amphinomous walks a few paces behind Telemachus, four men at his side. He is quiet, unusually so, and will not speak of any matter weightier than a comment on the breeze or a question about how best to cook a rabbit until the night's business is done. He is the only one of the suitors who joins the militia in their work. "No point being king of an isle if you aren't willing to fight for it," he opines, and is decidedly right, and everyone finds that very annoying indeed.

Kenamon stands at the side of the assembled people to watch Telemachus march, and smiles at the boy as he passes by, and the serious boy, not knowing why, smiles back.

Penelope does not wave her son off, and he pretends not to look for her in the crowd.

Later she will say it was because she did not want to distract him, but in truth, though she had meant to go, she was herself occupied with other affairs, and missed the drumbeat of the militia as they mustered, thinking it just another racket in her ears. This at least is the story she tells herself.

Here, join me as the full moon rises over Ithaca.

Let us, riding her light, shimmer into the halls of the palace, where Andraemon sits with Antinous and Eurymachus and laughs and says: "You call that a story? Let me tell *you* a story!"

Sometimes, very rarely, Andraemon's eyes glance to where Penelope sits weaving her shroud, and there is a look in his eye that seems to say: any time you've had enough, darling, any time, you just let me know.

She does not meet his gaze, but that does not mean his message goes unheard.

Leaneira serves food to the table, leaves of the vine and fishy broth, crimson wine staining lips purple. She lays a plate before Andraemon, who does not meet her eye nor thank her, nor does she spare him a word as she works.

Elektra sits and does not eat. "Orestes will return soon," she says, "with our mother's head." Pylades sits by her side, and does a good job of not patting her knee with every jaw-jutting proclamation she makes.

At the temple of Artemis, the women gather. There are no men here, and so the strangest of sounds is heard – that of women's voices, raised in notes other than the mourning dirge. Some sing songs of the forest and the deer, dancing round the great bonfire that the priestesses have made, and hear hopeful prayers in the beating of the drums. Others – those who have met in secret beneath the forest leaves at night – are more circumspect in their merriment. The oldest woman there is Semele's aunt, dragged unwilling from her nook by the northern shore to what she now proclaims to be "A miserable excuse for a party!" though she quite likes the food.

The youngest is a girl of three, fathered by a man from Elis who swore he would stay but was in fact passing through. She has no notion of pirates and angry seas, does not yet understand the full meaning of slavery, and eats so much honey from the hives of Penelope that she makes herself sick.

Some of the women – those of Priene's band – have brought little knives, or a few tools of the farm with them. "This old thing? Forgot I was carrying it," they say. They are not ready to fight, of course, but should any Illyrian dare to come to even this sacred land, they will not die unprepared.

Priene watches from the edge of the forest, and in a little while, Teodora joins her, bow at her side, and they do not speak as the moon rises.

CHAPTER 30

>>

In a quiet room at the top of the night-hushed palace, a door opens. Three figures flutter by in silence, hands clasped around the thin flames that guide them. They knock once on a heavy door, furtive, then descend cold stairs to a hollow cellar beneath the earth. Another door, guarded, knock knock, a heavy bolt drawn back, a wooden bar lifted. They enter a place that smells of damp earth and chalk. There are some skins hung upon a rack; on the floor are a few ingots of tin, and another of brass. There are two silver cups, a wedding gift from Icarius to his daughter perhaps, or Laertes to his son. There is the smell of dried fish, and a sack of precious salt. Mostly there is empty floor, still marked with the dusty outlines of places where perhaps once stood chests of glinting gold or stolen bronze, plundered timber or bottles of sweet perfume from the south. In the middle of this empty place stands Penelope, Eos at her side, a lamp between them.

The three come into this room stop, deep in shadow, then one steps forward, holds his light up higher to survey the scene.

"Andraemon," says Penelope.

"Queen," he replies.

"I hope you will forgive the lateness of the hour and the in-civility of our meeting place. I'm sure you can understand why

I would not wish the other suitors to know of our conversation, and why of course it would not be appropriate to have it in my quarters."

He nods once, briskly, glances to the women behind him. Leaneira makes to go, but Penelope raises her hand and, a little, her voice. "I would like Leaneira and Autonoe to stay, please. It is already unacceptable that I meet a man who is not my husband or my son alone. And I believe Leaneira has some interest in the outcome of our discourse, yes? She has been most insistent that I speak to you."

Andraemon glances to the Trojan maid, who turns her face to shadow.

"I have … been trying to catch a word in private, yes," he says. "But you have been evasive, my queen. I fear you have left things too late."

"My apologies. As you know, I cannot show particular favour to any suitor, lest the others take offence."

"One would think you were showing offence to us all by your attitude."

"I am sad that is the impression given. And yet it is better that I offend all than just one, is it not? For the sake of balance?" He scowls, casting the light of his lantern over the meagre offerings of the room, his eyes catching silver as the light moves past the wedding cups. "My treasury," Penelope explains simply. "As you can see, the times have not been favourable."

"Please." He scowls. "Everyone knows the queen of Ithaca hoards gold in some hidden cave. Your husband is a descendant of Hermes, your father-in-law sailed on the *Argo*, was blessed in his marriage with gifts from the trickster god himself."

"Gifts from a trickster? That doesn't sound like a sound basis for an economy."

To her surprise, Andraemon grins. "No. No it doesn't. But both your husband and his father were notorious raiders and thieves, before the war. Tin and amber flow through your ports; so don't try to convince me that Ithaca has no gold in its belly."

"And how do you think we paid for the war?" she sighs. "Do you think, all that time my husband sat on some Trojan beach, that the men of Greece could simply pluck everything they needed from the sand? Every ten moons messengers would return to Ithaca demanding I send more, more, more. Weapons to replace their broken spears. Wood to mend the chariots. Wool and hemp for their tents, sails, cloaks and shrouds. Gold for the changeable allies of Agamemnon. And of course, more men. Every boy child old enough to haul on rope or hold a soldier's helmet I sent to Troy, and not one has returned. So tell me, please, do tell me. How, with an island of women and goats, do you think I should fill my treasury?"

Andraemon paces, a little to the left, a little to the right, studying Penelope's face, the corners of the low, shadowed room. "You're a clever woman," he says at last. "Cunning at trade."

"Ah yes, trade. You are right that the western isles sit in a favourable position to conduct a great deal of business in these busy waters. But even if I could make any great profit from the enterprise – and truthfully I can barely make enough to keep my household in the poor state you see it now – you suitors have drained me dry. Deliberately, of course. The more you eat, the more you drink, the more you test to breaking point every sacred rule that stands between guest and host, the more desperate you make me. A desperate woman with an empty treasury must, surely, at some point yield. Must at some point choose a husband, to put an end to this slow bleed. I see your stratagem, and respect it. I cannot dishonour my house by not feeding you, and more importantly, I cannot attempt to rule alone and turn away the suitors altogether, especially not now that my cousin Clytemnestra has proven how disastrous such an attempt would be. There must be a king in Ithaca, but who? Eurymachus? Amphinomous? You?"

"I would be a good king." What may one hear in Andraemon's words? A promise? A threat? A truth? Something of all three, perhaps, depending on how one is inclined to listen.

"Perhaps you would," Penelope sighs. "But you would kill my son."

"No."

"Please. We are speaking honestly now, in the dark, as Leaneira wanted."

Leaneira studies the floor, her face burning like the lamp in her hand.

Andraemon hesitates, then a slow smile curls his lips. "Very well. It would be simpler to kill him, yes. But if you swear yourself to me this night, I will exile him instead. Send him to Nestor or Menelaus for education, opportunity. He will come to no harm by me."

"No harm?" she muses. "How long do you think it will take him to raise men and return to war against you? A year? Maybe two?"

"That would be his choice. Not mine."

"Let's not pretend he will make any other. No – you will exile him, and he will return and attempt to strike you down. If you, defending yourself, kill him, then I will have lost my son regardless. And if he, attacking you, kills you, he will then perhaps turn his blade on me for having dared to lie with a man not his father, and my life will be . . . precarious. We are all learning from Clytemnestra in that regard. Either way, exile is just death deferred. Antinous, of course, would simply send assassins after my boy. I do not impute you by saying this. I merely say it is a thing that some people would do."

"Some people," he snaps. "But I am a soldier, not some simpering farmer's son."

"Ah yes — a soldier. Strong, capable of defending me when war comes."

"I *would* defend you," he says. "Not just because you are queen. I would defend a woman."

"Thank you, that is good to know."

She falls silent, and the silence is strange to Andraemon. He is unfamiliar with being kept waiting for other people's thoughts, let alone the contemplation of a woman on whose answer his fate depends. Finally, "Well?" he snaps. "Do we have a bargain?"

"What will happen to Leaneira if you are king?" asks Penelope.

Leaneira's head rises fast, eyes narrow. Andraemon glances her way, surprised, as if he had forgotten she stood in the room. "What do you mean?"

"Will you keep her as your concubine?" He opens his mouth to bluster, to flap and flail, but no words come out. Penelope smiles. "If I said I would marry you, but that the price was Leaneira, would you pay it? I do not say I expect you to be faithful. No doubt as the years roll by — assuming we survive — you will want to pleasure yourself in younger, more fruitful pastures. But not with her."

Andraemon glances again to the maid, whose eyes now burn, bright embers raised from the floor to fix themselves upon Penelope's face. "What would you suggest?"

"Sell her. I don't care where. It is of no interest to me with whom my maids lie — only that they are loyal. The Trojan is loyal to you, not me, and thus I have no further use of her."

"If I say no?"

"Then you will never lie in my marriage bed," Penelope replies simply. "Amphinomous is good with a spear, and can raise men. I am not sure if he can beat you in an even fight, but then I would ensure any such fight would not be even. Come, come, don't be absurd, this is a small price I am asking you to

228

pay for Ithaca. Give up the maid, banish her to some farmstead and you can be king."

"I will set her free."

"No," Penelope replies, contemplating the tips of her fingers as if she had suddenly seen a blemish there. "You will not."

"I swore that I would."

"Then you will have to break that oath. I am sure that will not be too taxing for you. She is just a slave girl."

Here, Andraemon paces. A little to the left. A little to the right. Zeus used to pace in such a manner when contemplating matters of great import. He found that the action of movement, of striding this way and that, made it seem less dumb than when he simply stood, jaw drifting down, eyes up, lost in thought. A leader should look like their thought is a vibrant, potent thing, consuming all their body, all their might. For many, the performance of thinking oftentimes exceeds the actual energy being expended on the thought itself.

I'll say this for Athena – she is not afraid to simply stand and think.

Andraemon reaches a conclusion, and it is dramatic, and he stiffens his chin and puffs up his chest and does not look Leaneira in the eye. "Fine," he says. "For Ithaca – for the kingdom. We have a deal."

Leaneira does not gasp, does not double over in pain. This is not an extraordinary moment, this biting loss of hope. This is merely a resumption of life as she knew it was to be lived; an inevitable conclusion. A return to normality. Hope was the flickering illusion. Hope was the deceiver. She half closes her eyes, and in a whisper, lets it go.

Andraemon does not look her way as he steps towards Penelope, perhaps to grab her hand or even – outrage – seal the bargain with a kiss. She backs away, one hand raised. "There is one other thing," she says quickly, and he hisses between his teeth. "Illyrians have been attacking Ithaca's shores. They come every full moon. First Lefkada, now Phenera. They appear to have some knowledge of my kingdom, know where to strike, where will be most vulnerable. I hear rumours that they were guided into Phenera – that someone stood upon a cliff to show them the way. Of course, many merchants and traders pass through my ports who may have given them information, but I suspect – I believe – that they are getting it from a somewhat nearer source. And I ask myself, why would a raider attack without making demands? Even Illyrians know how the game is played – the profit is in buying protection, not in actually risking your life by setting out to sea. Where have been the overtures of safety, the offers of security for my people in exchange for what little wealth I have? And it strikes me that *you*, Andraemon, have been the most importunate of all the men in my palace to speak with me."

"I am not patient," he replies. "Ithaca must have a king."

"Not patient – yes, that sounds right. Patience. Such a difficult thing. The others are willing to eat me into poverty, to drink and whore until *my* patience cracks. But not you. What, I wonder, would you to do ... speed things along? You were at Troy. You know many warlike men – men who themselves might be feeling the nip of hungry greed now that the war is done. I imagine it would be easy to whisper in their ears that there is a profit to be made. Either the profit of easy plunder from successful raids, or the profit of protection gold that I must pay from some ... strange treasury everyone seems sure I have. Or perhaps the profit of a kingdom whole, now under the command of their old comrade and friend. Either way – easy pickings for hungry men."

Andraemon licks his lips. He is not as good at games of cunning as he thinks, for when he is choosing when to lie or when to speak the truth this is his obvious tell. Antinous, who is gifted

230

with dice, knows it, and it is one of the few secrets he has not spilled to his fellow gamblers in the palace hall.

"When I am king," he says at last, "I can promise you that no Illyrians will raid our shores."

"Yes," she murmured. "I thought you might. That was one of the other reasons I have been steering clear of you, of course. To avoid this reckoning. If I did not speak to you, then perhaps you could imagine that you might yet achieve all that you desire, and in that fantasy delay your assaults upon my people. But if we speak, as now we must, an answer must be given. Either I sell myself to you, or I do not. If I do, I risk my son, and beget a bloody war with Amphinomous, Antinous, Eurymachus and all the other suitors on the isle. If I do not, we will be at war anyway. You will send to your men and they will plunder my shores until there is nothing left, yes? These are the absolutes that arise from conversation, and so you see, to avoid the fall of the axe, I have avoided you."

"Not any more," he growls. "Not any more."

"No. But the full moon is rising, and tonight many men and boys could die. My son could die. So I am here to make my position clear. I know your crimes, your sins against my kingdom, and I will never forgive you. When Orestes returns with Clytemnestra's head, he will be my ally. I will petition Mycenae for aid, and he will grant it. Then I will dedicate myself to proving that you have violated every bond of hospitality that we hold dear. The other suitors will love the opportunity to destroy you; they will fight for the privilege to throw the first stone. This is what will happen when Orestes is king in Mycenae. But for tonight, to avoid bloodshed I am giving you a chance – call your men off. You have nothing to gain here. Your plan will not work, and if you continue down this path, I will destroy you."

Even a man who knows how to look good thinking is sometimes caught looking stupid. "You . . . just said . . ."

"I was curious as to what your terms would be. As to what manner of man you truly are. Now I know. Now we have talked. While you are my guest, I cannot harm you, so you are of course welcome here. You may have your friends attack my lands and there is nothing I can do to prevent it. But the more you do this – the more you seek to hold a knife against my throat – the worse it will be for you. It would be wise to end this folly now, for us both. That is what I wished to say to you. Call them off."

Andraemon stands dumb, mouth agape, and does not move. Penelope appears disappointed by this manner, for she raises a hand and flicks her fingers to the door.

"We are done. You will make your choice." And then, an afterthought: "You may go now."

Andraemon was once dismissed from Menelaus's presence in the same way, but Menelaus was a king. He teeters on the tips of his toes, swaying as if unsure whether to plunge forward and strike his foe or retreat. Penelope waits, fingers still turned towards the door, Autonoe at her side. Then he spins, and strides away.

The women stay behind.

Penelope turns to Leaneira.

There are many words in the air, and many ghosts who would utter them. Euracleia, were she not snoring upstairs, would scream: you slut, you harpy, you shameless baggage! We take you in and this is how you repay us, we feed you, clothe you, you little bitch!

Anticlea, dead with crimson on her lips, would have simply turned away and said: tomorrow you will be sent to market. Bid farewell to anyone who can bother to speak to you.

Anticlea, wife of Laertes, mother of Odysseus, was also the daughter of Autolycus, son of Hermes. She was raped the day before her wedding by Sisyphus over a matter of some stolen cattle – he found it the most convenient way to make his point.

She was sure the next day, while she was still bleeding, to entice her new husband to the marriage bed, that her blood might be mistaken for something other than pain, and her son be born to a worthy father. Penelope, when she first came to Ithaca, learnt a lot about what it was to be a queen from Anticlea. She learnt that when the south wind is dull and heavy, you do not sweat; nor when the north howls in the harshest of winters must you shiver. The storm may bend your back, but only you can straighten it again.

Leaneira and Penelope regard each other, and for an instant, I am not sure which one is the queen.

Death to all the Greeks, whispers the drumbeat of Leaneira's heart.

Then Penelope says: "There are good houses in Kephalonia, Hyrie. People I trust."

Leaneira glares, and is not entirely sure what she is glaring at, what these words portend.

Penelope steps a little closer to her, and animal-like Leaneira retreats, a snarl spreading in the corner of her mouth. Autonoe stands nearby, and simply watches her, curious.

"Ourania has need of women. I have need of women to tend my husband's land. There are estates, groves; in time you could find yourself a husband, find a . . . "

"I need no husband!" snarls Leaneira. "*I had a husband!*"

Penelope retreats a slight shuffle from her cry, while Autonoe glances to the closed door behind them, fearful perhaps that the woman's shriek might echo through the slumbering house, wake the suitors.

"Yes," Penelope says at last. "You did. And he is dead. Your home is gone. There is nothing for you. You will be used by men who know this. That is all you are now. You are someone to be used. Do you understand?"

Leaneira will not weep. Later – perhaps tomorrow, while dangling her fingers through the cold water of the running stream, or in the evening, when the smell of vines hits her senses like a lover's lips — she will weep uncontrollably, run howling to a place of darkness. But not now. Not now.

"You ordered me . . . you *told* me to . . . "

"I asked you to watch Andraemon. I could see he was interested in you. Enticed by you. But you chose his bed."

"Choice? What choice? *What choice?!*"

Troy burns, and Leaneira sometimes wonders why she did not have the courage to burn with it.

"Perhaps none," Penelope muses, voice like ashes over dust. "This is the world we live in. We are not heroes. We do not choose to be great; we have no power over our destinies. The scraps of freedom that we have are to pick between two poisons, to make the least bad decision we can, knowing that there is no outcome that will not leave us bruised, bloody on the floor. You have no choice. Your choices have been taken from you. I have taken them. I will use you as readily as any man. I will bend you to my will, I will hurt you, if it serves my purpose and my kingdom. And if I were offered mastery of all Ithaca in exchange for discarding you, I would do it in an instant. Andraemon and I are the same in that. The only difference is that he does not know it. He . . . thinks he is of the heroic sort. And he will never understand. Do you?"

Leaneira does not nod. Does not speak. She will not give a Greek the satisfaction.

"Andraemon is waiting outside these doors," Penelope breathes, soft as spider silk. "He will beg your forgiveness, swear he only said it because he loves you. He still has use of you. As do I."

When Penelope was sixteen, her would-be husband turned to her and said, "Will you have me?" and made it seem like there was a choice. He asked as if the bastard daughter of a naiad and a king could say no to the one suitor who saw in her something better than the daughters of Leda and Zeus, her cousins hatched from a swan's egg. As if she had any power at all. It was not, she felt, an entirely honest start to the relationship, but it was, if nothing else, well played.

Leaneira straightens her back.

Looks Penelope in the eye.

Says: "May I be excused, my queen?"

Penelope nods.

Leaneira turns away, struggles for a moment with the heavy door, steps into the dark. Autonoe raises an eyebrow, but Penelope shakes her head. "Let her go."

"She can hurt us. There are things she knows," murmurs Autonoe.

"Let her go," she repeats. "If she is to be any use to us, she must think she chooses it. And if she is not, then the damage is already done. We should not have let things go so far between her and Andraemon. We are to blame."

In the darkness of the night, Leaneira runs. She runs for the stream that flows behind the palace, a thin sliver of water down to the sea. She runs for its coolness and still quiet, for the hidden shadow of the heavy hanging trees that droop over it as if their leaves hunger for a sip. She thinks of throwing herself into the ocean, of crying out in a tongue none here can speak, of plucking a knife from the kitchen and driving it into Penelope, into Autonoe, into Euracleia, into Andraemon, into herself. She staggers up the cool mud steps to the stream and nearly screams when a hand grabs her arm, but turns the sound instead into a cat-like hiss as she scratches and claws at the face half pale in the growing light of the moon, ready to dig her fingers into eyes and nose and lips until something gives.

A snarl of pain, a curling-away, a curse, and she stops, frozen with teeth still bared as Andraemon clutches at his bleeding skin and exclaims: "Bitch!" He feels for his flesh, but the only thing oozing from the tracks of her nails is thin, clear liquid of shallow skin, rather than blood. Still: "Bitch!" he mutters again, before managing to turn the sound into a smile, into nearly a laugh. "You got me."

"What do you want?"

"You know what I want. To apologise." To beg forgiveness, perhaps. "What I said back there . . . I was trying to do the right thing, end this then and there. You heard what she said – she hates you."

"And you?" she snaps. "You weren't rushing to my honour."

"Your . . . honour?" He stumbles on the word, sounds for a moment like he might laugh, manages again to turn it instead into a smile, hands on her arms, holding her firm, upright, a grasp somewhere between the shaking of a brother and the embrace of a husband. "I didn't realise that anyone had any honour left to defend. Certainly I don't. You know as well as I that if I am to be king on Ithaca, I will have to possess the harlot queen. It is just how it is. You know this. But it's you I love. Only you."

"Are you sending the raiders?" Leaneira only half hears her own question. She is tired, feels the weight of every bone beneath her bending flesh as she stands in his grasp. "Do you send pirates to attack Ithaca?"

"Yes," he replies simply. "I do. I intended it as a provocation, to end this matter before more suitors could come and complicate things. Now I intend simply to take by force all the riches she will not give me by marriage. One way or another, I will have them."

"And me?" she asks.

"And you," he replies. "Whatever it takes, I will have you."

"Then we can leave tonight." She feels him stiffen, but pushes on, drunk on moonlight. "You heard her – she will never marry you. You will have to take what you want by force – you *are* taking it by force. She knows this about you. So why stay? We can leave tonight. She'll never find us, and you can still raid and plunder and we can be free."

"It's . . . not so simple."

"Why not? What could be simpler? You are not Paris, I am not Helen. What could be easier than this?"

"To be truly free, we need wealth. The raids take their share of slaves and goods, but I have to divide it amongst the crew, they have to have what I promised them. I may be their captain, I may direct them where to attack, but until we find her treasure, the real gold . . . "

"She doesn't have any! She lies and schemes and lies, but I know her – she spends her days trading goats and fish! There isn't any gold!" Leaneira half screams it, realises that she can no longer hold the tears back, no longer keep her shoulders from shaking.

Andraemon sighs, a patient father, and holds her close to his chest. His touch repels her, the patronising embrace of a thief, the source of her anguish, and yet she would never let him let go, and curls her fingers into the soft flesh of his back and holds a little tighter and weeps.

Death to all the Greeks.

"My love," he breathes, fingers caressing the scalp at the back of her head, tangling in her hair. "My beautiful one. You see how Penelope has lied to you?"

Leaneira has not cried since Troy, but tonight she closes her eyes and lets the tears flow like the river unto the sea, while Andraemon holds her tight in his arms.

Above, the moon is a perfect orb in the star-crossed sky, and beneath it, the pirates come.

CHAPTER 31

>>

I find Athena standing upon the beach, her bare toes curled into black sand as the waves wash against her ankles. She wears no disguise, and carries not a branch of olives, but her spear and shield. Her helmet is by her side, half washed in the waves. She is watching the sea, watching where three ships skim towards Ithaca, the wind at their back and the oars beating fast against the foam.

I have been putting this off far too long. Now men with blades and flames come to Ithaca; now there is no choice but to speak to the lady of war. Tonight our interests either align, or this business ends for good.

I slip off my golden sandals and approach her, shivering in pleasure at the cool touch of the ocean as it brushes through the cracks of my toes. As I draw level she says: "You have been meddling, old woman."

"You too, goddess of wisdom," I reply.

Her lips pucker in distaste, but still her eyes do not leave the form of the vessels as they angle their prows towards shore. I wonder if it's too late to have a word with my brother. "Wouldn't it be nice, dear one," I might say, "if a squall battered all the ports of Ithaca, or an unexpected tornado struck? That would really upset the people of Odysseus." Perhaps he'd fall for it, perhaps not. Athena will not do it, of course – she is waiting for the moment her father commands Poseidon to relinquish his grudge against the Ithacan king, and must play a long, slow game.

A torch burns bright upon the crest of a hill; someone else has seen the ships. It waves frantically towards the south, but the wind gutters it and no one sees its sign. I let my eye slip to the boy who lit it, who even now struggles to mount one of Ithaca's few fast horses to gallop to the granaries – or perhaps the docks – where the rest of the militia idle, too far, too few, a waste of time if ever there was one.

Athena says: "They're heading for shore."

And indeed they are, men starting to pull on armour now, to test the edges of their blades. Their destination is still unclear, the wind pushing against the side of the ships as they fold the sails and pull the oars.

"So," Athena muses, as we watch the ships draw near. "An army of women?"

"Wasn't my idea," I shrug.

"But you have hardly discouraged the venture."

"I am practical. The island does not have enough men of fighting age, and yet there are people here who would fight."

She purses her lips. Somewhere inland, a boy gallops for his friends, and cannot believe that his horse moves so slowly when death travels so fast across the sea.

Finally she says: "If Zeus finds out, he will be furious. It is all very well for the women of the eastern tribes to dress in trousers and ride horses, but not in his lands."

"I am relying on my husband not checking."

She nods. That is a good assumption to make. I glance her way and still she does not meet my eye. Will she tell? She and I have always despised each other, and yet for all that she is an illegitimate little cow, sprung from foul union with a Titan and a god, she is wise. She needs Odysseus to have a home to return to. Finally: "I do not like you meddling on Ithaca."

"I have barely meddled at all," I retort stiffly. "Merely kept a watchful eye – as you now do."

"Because Clytemnestra is here?" She scowls. "Your precious little murderess?" I sigh, do not grace her with an answer. Finally she barks: "Have you spoken to Artemis?"

"No. Why?"

Now she turns her head, and her look is withering contempt. "Women training with bow and arrow? Setting snares for men, learning how to fight in the forest around her temple? Festivals in her honour that happen to coincide with a raid on Ithaca's shores? Please. It is only her self-absorption that has kept her from howling through the forest already. It is not that she will disapprove – but she will disapprove of all this happening without her blessing, without her taking a share of the blood. You had better speak to her before she learns it any other way, otherwise she *will* go running straight to Father."

My lips curl in displeasure at the thought. "I don't suppose . . . "

"Absolutely not. Though I will not – yet – expose this little venture of yours, stepmother dear, I will not risk my name by tangling in it. Do your own work."

"I am saving Odysseus's land for Odysseus!" I snap.

"You are saving it for his wife," she replies primly. "As if anyone cares whether she survives to the end of his story."

I swallow down a bitter rebuke. Were we in any other place, I might send my palm ringing across her face for her disrespect, or call her a thousand names, each one a biting ant to burrow in her flesh. Yet here, this night, we are briefly allies, and I will need her to stay silent on Olympus if I am to be free to do my work. The truth of that wounds me, makes my stomach turn – Athena was wise when she swore never to be a wife, not that I was given much choice in that regard.

At last she says: "I will keep your secret, queen of secrets. I will let you do . . . whatever you think you are doing. But I have a price."

I bristle, I flare, I blaze a divine light – a little too divine, a flash of fire on the beach, best snuffed out before the sand at my feet turns to glass or a roaming celestial eye catches my fury. The cheek of the woman! Bartering with *me*!

She watches the ships without blinking, as if the radiance of my power were of no interest to her, and slowly, I diminish. I am briefly as mortal as the form I seem to wear, an old, tired woman who struggles to remember now what it was to be young. "What price?" I ask.

"Telemachus," she replies. "He is mine."

I have to hold back the urge to shrug. "That is a high price to pay," I lie, for good form's sake. "Giving you the son of Odysseus as well as the father to play with – the others might resent it if there are *two* heroes who sing your glories instead of one. They'll say you're greedy."

"They'll say nothing of the sort. Both father and son have a cunning that makes them mine by nature," she retorts briskly. "The gods are foolish and blind – they think the greatest poems are the ones of death in battle and the ravishing of queens. But the stories that will live for ever are of the lost ones, the fearful ones, who through bitter hardship and despair find hope, find strength – find their way home. Victory should always have a price. I want Telemachus. He is mine. I will not interfere with you if you do not interfere with him."

There will be consequences to this night, I fear, but she has left me no time to think on them. Tricksy Athena – her wisdom can be the crude, base stuff of the marketplace as well as the wit of the symposium. "Fine," I snap. "We have a bargain."

A burst of fire dances between us, invisible to the mortal eye; a writ sealed between goddesses, written upon our diamond bones. I shudder at its touch, but she seems unmoved by it, eyes turned out upon the waters, There is the beginning of a frown as she observes the approaching ships. I follow her gaze, see the vessels turning again, barely a hundred paces from shore, refining their destination and moving to avoid a plume of rocks half hidden beneath the swell. The rider in the dark is nearly thrown from his horse as it stumbles on the dirt track, calls out, "They're here! They're here!" but cannot push his voice through the night-time wind.

"Where are they going?" I muse, half to myself, as the raiders turn towards a little cove, a place of crabs and barefoot children. There is no plunder there, no hidden gold or slaves – only rocks and a difficult landing. A figure waits for them upon the shore, a torch briefly raised and answered by another on the ship. He is the same man who guided these men to Phenera, face shrouded in shadow. For a moment Athena doesn't seem to know, then her eyes widen.

"Laertes," she blurts.

I glance inland and see in a moment the same thing she has already divined: the rough path leading away from the water to an isolated farm where an old man snores like wet mud. Father to a king, unguarded save for a few boys and women, the old monarch of Ithaca, last of the Argonauts, sleeps.

"Surely they would not dare?!"

"They would dare," she replies briskly, picking up her helmet. There is acid in her mouth, vengeance on her lips. "They would attack his *father.*"

I put a hand on her arm before she can turn.

"What are you going to do?" I ask. "If you strike them down, Zeus will surely know, Poseidon will taste the blood in the water – and then what? I will be banished back to Olympus for meddling in the affairs of men, and you will never get Odysseus off Ogygia. They will say you have overstepped your boundaries;

everything we do is suspected – especially where it concerns the deeds of men."

Her lips curl, baring teeth, but she does not move, eyes flashing over the water. Then without a word she is gone, vanished into silver mist beneath my palm. I scowl and dissolve into the wind, a particularly bitter gust carried up and out across the isle, chasing her through the dark. She does not travel far; Ithaca is not a large island. Instead she settles like the memory of some disease in a thin pallor over Telemachus, where he waits in the shadow of one of Eupheithes' stables, set to guard the goods of his enemies with a gaggle of four or five men, and into his heart she hisses: *look!*

He stirs, a little slow, sluggish in the cool of night and the lateness of the hour. I grasp a sliver of moonlight, tangle it round my little finger, bid it skim across the sea to catch the shape of a ship. He gasps and straightens all at once, alert, hand going to his spear as Athena, nearly shaking him by the shoulders, hisses as loudly as she dares: *LOOK!*

Now he sees the ships upon the waves; now he hears the pounding of horses' hooves as the messenger comes, foam in the mouth of the beast he rides, white sweat lines tidally etched across its hide. "Raiders!" the boy screams out. "Raiders!"

"Get to Laertes," Athena whispers as I spin uneasy in the air about her. "Save him!"

CHAPTER 32

>>>

T wo battles are fought in Ithaca that night.
        Neither is sung by the poets.

The second battle is fought between a group of sixteen boys
and thirty-nine pirates. The other boys of the militia never heard
the cry, never came. They were watching Polybus's storehouses
or guarding the villa of Eupheithes. Amphinomous guards, with
five of his men, a village of fish and clay, though the women are
inland at some temple feast for Artemis, which no one bothered
to tell the militia about. No – the first that Amphinomous and
his ilk will hear of the battle that they should have fought is in
the morning, when the mourners' songs spread through the isle
like the first pollen of spring.

Here then, in this moonlight, are a mere sixteen boys of
Peisenor's militia rushing to their doom. Telemachus is there, of
course, roused by Athena to grab, without fear, spear and shield.
Three of the others are his friends, boys raised by mothers since
infancy, loyal to his cause. They struggle at first to find each
other, waving torches across low, curling valleys as they stumble
through the silver night, seeking to unite into a meagre force of
bronze and spear.

From the coast come the raiders. They still wear their Illyrian garb, for if the other kings of Greece were to learn how bitterly Penelope's faith as hostess is betrayed by one of her guests, all laws of hospitality would be ended and Andraemon would be pinned by the throat to the palace walls. So they are crudely disguised, but oh so crude, such a feeble mockery of deception. Make no mistake – these are veterans of Troy, mercenaries of the seas of Achaea, who know only how to fight, and how to take.

They beach their ships in rough sand, a sound like knives over bone, assemble together on the shore, where one man waits for them. He is hooded, shoulders broad, hands curled. We have seen him before – whispering in shadows, watching as Phenera burnt. He gestures – come, come, I know the way – come – and leads the would-be Illyrians up the narrow path away from the sea, without war cry or battle drum, a host of thieves and murderers in the dark.

"Where are they going, where are they going?" babbles one of the boys of the militia, and Athena again lays her hand on Telemachus's arm and whispers: *think, boy, think, where are they going, where are they going . . . ?*

She could just tell him, of course, but he is Odysseus's son and she has certain expectations of him that now he must fulfil. *Think, boy, think!*

It is hard for Telemachus to think with all these eyes upon him, but no other commander has come – no Aegyptius, no Peisenor – so he must prove himself now and make a judgement, and that judgement must be right.

You know every inch of this island, whispers Athena, *you have yearned to escape it, stood upon the rocks and dreamt of great battles in faraway places, but now you MUST use your knowledge! Think! You know where the raiders land, you know there is nothing for them there, so where is there something of value? Where will they go?*

She is on the verge of just shouting it at him – of shaking him by the shoulders and screaming, *in Olympus's name, boy, are you a total bloody idiot?!* – when he realises, eyes widening and breath rattling into his lungs.

"Grandfather," he breathes, and Athena rolls her eyes in muted satisfaction, *finally, boy, finally!* She was beginning to think you weren't worth her time after all. "Grandfather!" he repeats, a little more sure of himself, standing tall to command the presence of the boys about him. "They are going to Laertes' farm!"

The boys of the militia run through the dark. Athena runs beside them, a shadow that lends them breath, lends them strength, so they are for a moment free again, children playing in the field, unencumbered by armour, no thought of death in their hearts, merely of valour and stories – the stories of the poets, the ballads of the heroes that they will become. How strange it seems that to make men of these boys, Athena first makes them children, driving from their minds all thoughts of mortality, all notion of blood as they run, run, run for Laertes' farm.

I am there already, of course, rousing the household with chill winds, foul dreams, the bite of itching insects upon their hot flesh and a memory of the smell of smoke. Laertes is one of the last to wake, and rolls over beneath the thin wool cloth he calls a blanket – far less fine than the shroud his daughter-in-law pretends to weave – and grumbles and grouches, a little spit slithering in the corner of his mouth. I cannot strike him around the face nor dazzle him with my divine presence, for others will see, Zeus will stir in the heavens and wonder what exactly his wife is doing toying with the minds of men, so I grab instead one of the old women who attends upon him and make her bladder ache so that she whimpers and scurries quickly out into the dark, where in the moonlight she might look down towards the sea.

Look! I shriek at her. *Behold!*

I may have overdone the bladder business, because she is so focused on relieving herself that for the first minute I cannot get her to do anything other than sigh as she squats above the pit, but

246

when she is at last finished, I shake her again and snarl as close to audibly as I dare, *LOOK, YOU STUPID BLOODY WOMAN!*

She at last raises her head, and for a moment does not see, but I put a little something in her eye, and she looks again and catches at last the glint of moonlight on armour, the sound of metal carried on the wind. She does not understand, and then thinks she does and rushing into the house shrieks: "There are soldiers! There are soldiers coming! Odysseus has returned!"

The sound of my palm striking my forehead is enough to knock dust from the low ceiling, to send straw tumbling from the roof. Laertes, who is somewhat more circumspect in these things, sits up slowly, mouth working round his sorry pink gums as if he cannot speak until he has exercised them to warmth, and finally says: "Soldiers?"

"Heading this way!" shrills the woman. "Your son has returned!"

I do not know why Athena is so obsessed with Laertes' son, but I will say this for his father – he is sometimes not a total dolt. There is a reason he sailed with Jason on the *Argo*, and given that the rest of that crew contained bastard sons of Zeus with muscles like the lion and the brains of the moth, I can assure you Laertes was not valued for his steely strength. Rather, he brought a savage wit, a quiet cowardice that Jason could have done with heeding a little more intently when times were hard. So it is that he draws himself out of bed, does not bother to put on much more than a slip of cloth – already somewhat stained – to cover his most private parts, and hobbles to the door. He peers into the night, draws in his breath, listens to the sound of the darkness and proclaims: "We shall now run away and hide in a ditch."

The old woman gasps and I could hug the old man, squeeze him until he pops.

"But sir . . . " she begins.

"When my son returns, he will come alone, respectfully,

and with a proper explanation for where he's been the last eight years," tuts Laertes. "He will in short have some grovelling to do. Fetch my cloak! We will go and hide until this whole business is over."

She hurries to get his cloak, while I spin giddy in the air about him. Laertes half closes his eyes. He knows my presence, perhaps; remembers its touch from when he was a younger man, but now is not the time to dwell on things that were. Donning his tatty, faded grey cloak, he nods once and, with the dignity of the centaur, proudly runs away.

Some few minutes after he does so, the raiders reach his door. They break inside to find lamplight burning, blanket disturbed upon his low wooden bed. They call out for the old man, thinking perhaps that Laertes, being of noble blood, will answer when his name is called as though he were Hector or Achilles, and not in fact hiding in a ditch on the other side of a darkened field that smells of pig shit. King of Ithaca! they cry. Come out, old man! Come out!

Laertes does not come out, but lies with his back to the house and the tips of his fingers pinched together before his chest, as if he were trying to calculate the motion of the stars above, while his household cower in silence.

When it becomes clear that Laertes is nowhere to be seen and the riches of the house are meagre at best, one of the raiders with a bit of initiative seizes a burning log from the fireplace and throws it into the warmth of the king's disturbed bed, thus starting the blaze that will, before dawn, burn the farm of old Laertes to the ground.

This done, they turn away, without riches or ransom, and head back to their ship.

Thus ends the first battle of the night.

The second is fought some few minutes later as the raiders, returning from the rising pyre of Laertes' farm with empty hands and bitter faces, walk straight into the line of armed boys, shields locked and spears raised, that Telemachus has deployed along the path to block their escape. The first not-quite-Illyrian to see them stops so hard that his colleagues near walk into him, a piglet in his arms and a goat strung to his back, and then the march of men all slows, spreading into a little half-moon of somewhat confused pirates. They are confused for a number of reasons. Firstly, they had not expected resistance of any kind, and so the silent wall of armed might-be men before them is an unwelcome impediment to their ambitions. Secondly, what resistance they had expected would surely have been farmers armed with sticks, not armed, almost-nearly-perhaps trained men with spears and shields. But alas, any impression that these are the legendary soldiers of Ithaca, brave followers of Odysseus, wanes a little upon closer inspection, for lo, that boy's breastplate is too large for his frame, the edges pushing out his armpits uncomfortably and awkwardly to the side so his shoulders flare like a seagull. And lo, another's helmet barely sits upon his wobbling brow, and another's shield is already bent nearly beyond recognition, one side flattened against his arm. Truly, if this is the best soldiery that Ithaca can muster, then the age of heroes is dead indeed.

And then the pirates look, and look again a little more closely, and for the first time seem to discern that what the boys lack in military experience, good equipment and expertise, they also thoroughly, categorically lack in numbers.

"Well," I murmur in Athena's ear, as I slip by her side behind the line of Ithacans. "So much for that."

She glowers at me, but there is uncertainty in her brow. Oh, if she could fight with these boys, she alone would turn the tide of battle; the blade would sing such songs in her hand, such simplicity in her movement, the tiniest step, the easiest dance, an oration of blood. For glorious Ares every battle was a triumphant sweep of axe, a huge rolling of power, the roar of lungs and the thundering of weapon on shield. But I have seen Athena win a fight simply by slicing the hands of her enemies that held the blade, taking one finger at a time with the lightest twist of her wrist as though to say, come on then, let's be sensible about things.

She could, if she wished, do so now, step into the guise of just another boy of the isle and rip these pirates apart. But others would hear her music; eyes would turn from Olympus and the great gods would wonder just what it was that we women did upon Ithaca, *meddling*, always meddling. It's all very well for Athena to meddle with Odysseus, he is a hero and busy shagging a nymph anyway, but this? This smacks of something ... uncouth. This meddling whispers of power and freedom.

So instead Athena murmurs: "I have summoned another," and before I have a chance to ask her what she means, the pirates draw their blades. Not sicas – not the curved weapon of the Illyrian – but the short swords of the Greeks, weapons you might hold against a woman's throat as you explained in short words what her future would be. Weapons you might wield if you wanted a hand free to drag a child into your vessel, ready to turn a profit.

I will say this for Telemachus's boys – they do not flinch. Their thin little line, one boy deep, does not waver. It curves a little as the raiders begin to spread around them, straining to stay close yet still with room to move. The pirates give no warrior cries; there are no taunts, nor jeers, nor cries to surrender. The men of the seas are too experienced in their business to waste breath on anything but slicing, stabbing, the motion of battle, and the boys are now feeling the first touch of mortality nibbling at the edges of their courage, the first whisper of doubt and dread.

"Steady," murmurs Telemachus, as much to himself as the others. "Steady. Do as Peisenor taught. Stay behind the shield. Stay together."

Peisenor did teach this, but he had not yet covered what to do when you find yourself entirely surrounded by veterans who have no respect for your weaponry or your skill, who are beginning now to see the frightened pallor of youths before them, and in whose eyes is the place where fear has turned to thought, and a calm plan that leads only to your demise. As the circle tightens, I am startled to feel Athena grip my arm. She is pale, lips thin, her knuckles white where she holds her spear, and for a moment I do not know what to make of this. Then she whispers: "Whatever happens, save Telemachus."

In a battle of sword against spear, a well-used spear should have the advantage. Its reach will let a trained soldier cut the throat of his enemy long before a sword gets within range. Yet these boys are not yet well trained, and so, after a moment of the slightest consideration, one of the pirates – we might call him a leader – steps forward and with his bare hand reaches past the tip of the nearest spear that waggles in his face, catches it by the shaft, and pulls so hard that the boy who holds the other end tumbles face first into the mud. Someone chuckles, and in that moment of blackest despair, the pirates charge.

When the muses sing, they do not sing of skirmishes such of these. They do not sing of feet slipping and voices crying out and of sword beating through shield. They do not sing of boys with helmets pulled from their heads, of pirates who see that they can simply ignore the attacks of their enemies, that each blow is insignificant next to the killing strike they may land. They do not sing of massacres.

Oh, some of the boys of Ithaca fight back. Some are lucky, and drive a spear point home. Others change their weapons to shorter stabbing blades as the line collapses, meeting their attackers on their own terms, all advantage of reach and range lost. Athena whispers in their hearts, courage, courage, courage, but she does not stand beside them as they fall, howling in the dark. Nor does she take their pain away; that is not her gift. If they had been women, it might have been mine, but instead I circle, impotent, above the bloody scene.

Telemachus does poorly in the first few seconds – any battle of this kind is measured in seconds, not minutes – trying to keep behind his shield as Peisenor had taught, trying to thrust his spear forward and back. But two men work together to take him down, one drawing the point of his spear left while another steps into the right to grab the shaft of the weapon and haul it free from the young man's grasp. Telemachus considers holding on, but lets go a moment before he would be pulled to the ground and steps away instead, drawing his sword and driving his shield into the chest of the nearest man. This knocks him back, more successful than Telemachus had expected, and he follows it with a slicing blow towards the gut of the other pirate, who leaps away, dropping Telemachus's spear into the mud.

In his ditch some little distance off, Laertes can hear the sound of battle, and still lies on his back, studying the stars. One of his household quietly weeps, and he hisses: "None of that!" and the sound of sobbing is hastily muffled.

Around Telemachus, boys are falling, blood watering the earth. Athena dips down for just a moment to send wide a blade that slashes towards the back of his head, snipping at the tips of his hair; then she is gone again lest even that minor intervention be of note, leaving him to spin confused at the passage of air behind his skull. A pirate lands a blow that he catches badly on his shield, full power meeting his feeble block, and he staggers back. The next blow he handles slightly better, running in to meet it before it can gather its full speed, but even that resonates up his arm and sings into his spine with the thrumming of strength on strength. He knows his friends are dying, and that he will too, but tries a trick an Egyptian taught him, slashing low beneath the cover of his shield for a pirate's ankles. To his surprise, he connects, skimming through blood and flesh, but the momentum of his blow is slowed by the impact in a way it never was when training, so he loses a precious moment of recovery in which another man drives his blade hard towards his chest. He deflects the point, which skims down the circle of his shield to drive straight for his arm, but the boy doesn't notice the pain, the blood too high in his skull, the breath too meagre in his throat.

"Help him!" Athena cries, and there is genuine distress in her voice, a thing I had never thought I would hear. I look across at her and feel something, strange and coiled, that might almost be pity. She could help him if she chose, but at what price? How many more years of imprisonment might the father pay if Athena now steps in to save the son?

Another blow knocks Telemachus back, and he stumbles on the body of a boy who was once his friend, falls, tries to get up, hands encumbered with weaponry, legs kicking for purchase against blood and flesh.

"Help him!" she shrills, and again I look her way and wonder what it is she expects me to do. I am no creature of war; I punish those who forsake a battle with poison and bile, but their battles are still their own.

A pirate knocks the shield from Telemachus's grasp, and for a moment he is open, throat bare, chest bare, eyes wider than the full moon that illuminates them. Another draws his sword back for a killing blow, too angry to be efficient, too wild to make it quick, wanting his victim to see his end.

The javelin strikes through his chest at an angle from behind, the tip emerging out through his left shoulder as if he were a poorly constructed fence, and I realise with a slight start of indignation that it was not to me that Athena cried.

The pirate does not immediately fall, and when he does, it is in the same direction that the javelin flew, as if only it could now give him momentum. The next javelin flies wide, missing the pirate who turns to greet it, but Kenamon's strike, as he leaps from the darkness, is a thing that seems to twist in the air, a rising stab that appears to be for the belly then turns at the last to come in sideways for the neck. The pirate falls, Kenamon landing near on top of him, and in the spray of blood and crash of pain the Egyptian reaches out for the fallen boy and snarls, "Run, lad! Run!"

Telemachus takes the hand that is offered him, uses it to crawl to his feet, staring round at the bloody scene. Only a few militia still stand, the ground now seeded with the bodies of boys and men, and for a moment it seems that he would shake his head, refuse the rescue that has come his way.

Here, at least, I have a certain potency. I sweep down upon the boy before he can open his mouth to say something absurd, slip my breath through his lips and hiss into the very heart of him, *RUN!*

Athena would never say such a word; it is not in her vocabulary.

One day she might have the grace to be thankful that it is within mine.

Telemachus turns his back on his friends, and with Kenamon at his side, he runs into the dark.

CHAPTER 33

>>

D awn should be bloody after a battle, yet it so rarely is. Too many wars are fought beneath her shimmering gaze for her to turn crimson for any but the most spectacular of affairs. So then, a cool silver dawn, scented with flowers and salt.

On the beach beneath Laertes' farm, three jagged lines where three ships were beached, and where three ships have long since sailed.

On the path that leads from the sea to the hills, the idling boys of Peisenor's militia – those who did not come, those who did not make it to their deaths in time. They still stand in armour and holding their spears, some embarrassed by their failings in the night, most relieved. Those who have seen the bodies of the dead are grateful they were not there, for all that their honour is lessened. There are those who are beginning to realise that honour has nothing over a still-beating heart.

Laertes sits on a stool that was one of the few objects to be salvaged from the burnt ruin of his farm, arms folded, back turned to the ash. The surviving members of his household step through the charred remains, digging through scalding char for any trinkets or items of note. Medon has already spoken of rebuilding, of starting again, but Laertes says nothing, arms folded, looking straight through the old councillor as if he were not there.

A few paces down the hill from his farm, the mourners have come once again to count the bodies of the dead.

They must strip the armour from the dozen or so boys who lie in dirt, crows circling their remains, the ground moist with blood. They must lay it in careful piles to be washed clean and returned to the armoury, and then bind the bodies for burial, the shrouds tight to pull together the many gaping wounds across the boys' flesh. Of the five still living, one will die of his wounds tonight, calling out to Apollo, god of healers, who will not come. Two more will survive, in time, and one will recover fully, graced with pure luck, there being no divine intervention upon him.

There are no dead pirates. This is not because they did not die — six are indeed slain — but their bodies have been carried away to be thrown into the sea, lest anyone on Ithaca look too closely at the faces or weapons of the dead and say, "Hold on a moment, I thought they were Illyrian?"

The mourners come, as they always do, and kneel down around the bloody scrum of earth to wail and do the whole business with hair and ash that they're so good at. Anaitis comes from the temple of Artemis to watch without words; Aegyptius and Peisenor stand sombre as the bodies are carried away. Polybus and Eupheithes are nowhere to be found. Amphinomous leans upon his spear, and has not slept all night, and will not sleep in the night to come until at last the exhaustion is overwhelming, and he sleeps a fitful hour and wakes with muddy eyes and shame in his chest.

Kenamon stands further off. He has washed the blood from his face and his blade. Only if you look closely will you see the slightest speckling of crimson upon his garb, and when he finds it later today he will scrub it in cold water until nothing more remains.

Telemachus sits in a bloody heap near his grandfather's feet, while the old nursemaid Euracleia wails: "My poor boy! My darling boy! A wound – such a wound! My dear boy!"

He has indeed a minor scratch to his shoulder, where the point of a pirate's sword dug in. It is not as deep as it could have been, its speed slowed by the scraping across the shield it endured on its way to his flesh, but it will serve as a suitably manly scar to remind the world that he, Telemachus, has been blooded in battle. It would not be polite to ask how he survived with such limited injuries when all others are dead. He is the son of Odysseus, and lived; that is enough.

Penelope stands a few steps in front of him, pale as a cobweb. She did not run to him as Euracleia did. Rather, when word came to the palace with the first light of dawn – a battle, a fire at Laertes' farm! – she gathered herself careful and slow, bade Eos and Autonoe both arm themselves in secret, summoned every guard whose loyalty she could rely upon, and rode through the rising morn.

Did she think of her son?

Why yes, with every step. With every fall of the horse's hoof she thought of her son, and sometimes thought of kicking the beast into a gallop, and then did not. Why rush to see her boy dead? Why race towards that moment of destiny, to find the bloodied corpse that has been in her dreams every night since the first suitor came? No. A slow and steady journey, stately and regal, will suffice. Every minute in which she does not see him dead is another in which he may still live. It is another moment in which her son breathes, in her mind if not in reality, another second that she may cherish from all the many, many years she realises now she has not cherished enough.

Reaching the site of the fire, still hot as people ran from the stream to the house to throw water upon it, she looked through the half-light of rising day to try and see order, meaning, to get a number of the dead or a sense of the scale of this thing. She saw Laertes first, and approaching him knelt down at his feet and knew not what to ask or to say, but so it seemed neither did he, for he merely nodded, and she thought perhaps there was a kind of forgiveness in that, framed in firelight.

She did not at once see her son sitting wretched in the long grass, bloody sword at his side, but instead noted Kenamon some little way off, who simply nodded and gave the empty smile of one who has forgotten pleasure, and then, at the slight inclination of his head, she sees Telemachus.

She approaches on legs that she thinks might fail, and at a mis-step Eos darts forward to catch her by the arm, supporting her the last few paces until she stands before her son. "Telemachus," she breathes.

He looks up slowly, sees his mother's eyes, looks away.

There was once a boy who would run to his mother when he grazed his knee.

Once a child who laughed to be held by her.

Once a young man who asked her for advice, and valued her answer.

Now there is a bloody soldier sitting in the grass, who has seen his friends all die that night, and has no real interest in his mother.

There are things she should say. My son, my love, my beautiful boy. My Telemachus. You are everything to me. She should run to him and hold him in her arms. But he will be angry if she does. He will say: I am a man now. I do not hide behind women. I do not need to be known as the son of a woman!

And he will push her off, and spit at her feet, and never look her in the eye again.

But perhaps one day, he will remember that she was there, that she wept for him, that her love surpasses all others. Perhaps one day yet to come.

Penelope stands frozen, and does not speak, and does not move, thinks this is all her fault, and knows that she has lost her son in ways that transcend violence. She opens her mouth to speak, to blurt: Telemachus. My son.

She thinks she will tell him she is proud of him. She thinks she will tell him that his father would be proud of him. He will not hate her for that.

Then Euracleia is all "My darling boy!" and "What a wound!" and slathers wet kisses on his brow and holds him though he flinches while Penelope looks on. Telemachus does not seem to respond much to the ministrations of his old nurse-maid, but neither does he throw her off or resist as she tells him what a hero he is, what a man. Oh, but was it terrible, was it terrible, you must have killed so many, you saved your grandfather's life, you saved him, such a man, such a man, so terrible, *your wound!*

I have sometimes considered smiting Euracleia for being an insufferable pain in the backside, but when I look a little closer, I see something of myself in her that is a little too close for comfort, and so I withdraw my wrath, and find the whole thing uneasy in ways I choose not to dwell upon.

The breath leaves Penelope's lungs, and in years to come she is surprised to catch herself still breathing.

So here is our painted picture.

Telemachus, sitting upon the ground, while Euracleia fawns and squeaks and coos at him.

The women of Ithaca, carrying away the bodies of his friends.

Aegyptius and Peisenor, silent in their failure.

The burnt farm of the father of the king of Ithaca.

Laertes, silent on his stool as though it were Zeus's throne, back turned to the ashes of his old age.

Kenamon, standing further off.

Amphinomous, standing nearer by.

Penelope in the middle of it all, the wind pulling at her veil, hiding the tears in her eyes from the gaze of men.

In this manner all things could have remained, for I do not think either mother or nursemaid would have roused Telemachus or Laertes from their rest, save that finally on horseback another comes. Elektra, flanked by some of her Mycenaean men. She surveys the burning scene, smells the blood in the air, considers the song of the mourners, quickly counts the bodies of the bloody boys being loaded onto the back of the donkey cart, sees Telemachus, hesitates, then approaches.

She walks straight past Penelope, glowers at Euracleia until the old nursemaid curls and coils away from her stare, then kneels down directly in front of the silent, bleeding boy, and takes his hands in hers.

"Telemachus," she barks, without a jot of kindness, without a shimmer of sympathy in her voice. Slowly he raises his eyes to meet her own. She has drawn ashes down her face with two fingers, as if she might split her features in half. She wears it for her father, but today, perhaps, she wears it for Ithaca too. "Vengeance," she says.

He blinks, as if the word came from some unfamiliar tongue, and behind the princess, Penelope stiffens.

"Vengeance," Elektra repeats, squeezing his hands tight. And again: "Vengeance."

He nods once, rises slowly, flinching at the pain throughout his body as he does so. When he later removes his armour, he will find bruises across his ribs and all down his arms, the shock of metal deflecting metal beaten through his bones. She smiles a single flickering smile as he rises, and then in a sudden move, embraces him, holds him tight, lets him go. His blood flecks her milky skin, and she is satisfied.

"Vengeance," he breathes, and Elektra smiles as if he were her own.

CHAPTER 34

>>

They bring Laertes to the palace, back to his old room. He sniffs the air and says: "Someone has been sleeping here!"

"Orestes, prince of Mycenae," Penelope replies, head bowed as it always is before her father-in-law.

"Huh." He was ready to kick up such a fuss, so he was, he was ready to have a really good time making everyone's life a misery, as miserable as his own – but Orestes, son of Agamemnon . . . well, even Laertes must admit that's probably acceptable, just about. Times being what they are.

The suitors are assembled by the gates of the palace. They have come to show respect, ostensibly, but most of them are now wondering: will there be *more* mourning? More days without carousal and merriment, under the ash-coated eyes of Elektra and Penelope?

Andraemon stands at the back, and as Penelope passes upon her grey horse, he looks at her, eyebrow raised as though to say: had enough yet?

She does not return his gaze.

Elektra stands in the door of Penelope's room and blurts: "Pirates, Penelope?" She makes it sound like a moral fault, or some pestilence found in a brothel. There is something in her voice that suggests that if anyone had dared do a bit of pirating in *her* domain, she'd have eaten them for supper. The family of Atreus have always had a certain fondness for an hors d'oeuvre of human flesh.

"Pirates," Penelope replies, and that is all the answer she is willing to give.

As Telemachus, bloodied but walking, passes through the silent streets of the town, no one comes to cheer. Amphinomous approaches as they near the palace gates, tries to speak some words of comfort, words between warrior men: "Telemachus, I . . ."

. . . but the young man gives him such a look that even he recoils, and closes his mouth.

"You must be bathed, you must be oiled, my beautiful boy!" shrills Euracleia. "Hot water – fetch hot water!"

It takes eight maids the best part of an hour to fetch enough hot water to fill the tub that Euracleia has dragged across the stone floor, and every minute consists of her shrilling and shrieking at them that they are going too slow, too slow – you're all so useless!

Penelope descends as the last bucket is sloshed into the water, and says: "I will tend to my son myself."

Euracleia pouts, hands on hips, but has learnt enough not to argue with the lady of the house. Then Telemachus raises his head, and for the first time speaks. "No."

There is a fine splattering of blood across his face, like duck-egg spots. It came from the heart of the man Kenamon killed with that first javelin, but in the fuss and the dark, in the roaring in his head, Telemachus is not sure whose blood it is, or even if it is his own.

"Telemachus," Penelope begins. "You are hurt. Let me tend you."

He rises slowly from his perch on the edge of the steaming

tub, straightening and grimacing in pain, and snarls – nearly screams – "*I do not need my mother!*"

Penelope recoils, and for the first time she can remember in so many years, there is heat upon her cheeks, heat in her eyes, which even she cannot disguise. Even Euracleia has suddenly and spontaneously discovered the benefits of being tiny, grey and invisible. Telemachus sinks back down, head bowed. There is the faintest cough from the door. Elektra stands in it, her hair already pulled back from her face, her hands bare and fingers curled.

"I will help you with your armour, cousin," she says simply, and Telemachus stares at her for a moment, almost confused, before he gives a weary nod. Elektra approaches, runs her hand over the bloody bronze, tilts his chin this way and that as if seeking confirmation that there are no more injuries, smears a few loose beads of blood across her fingertips and down his throat. Glances to the older women standing in the door. "Thank you, ladies," she says. "I will send if I need assistance."

Euracleia is smart enough to vanish in an instant.

Penelope stands where she is, a tree struck by lightning, swaying in the cold breeze of the storm. If she blinks, she may displace foolish water from her eyes, so she does not blink, does not move. Elektra glances her way again, as if surprised to see her standing there. "Thank you," she repeats. "I will send for you."

I put my hand in Penelope's. *Come*, I whisper. *Come. Lean on me.*

She does not know it as she turns away, but it is I who carry her from the door, catch her before she can fall, brush the tears from her eyes, lest someone see in her a sentiment that is unbecoming for a queen.

No weakness, I breathe. *No tears. Only you can straighten your back.*

She staggers, hand to her belly, a gasp, a sucking-in of harsh breath.

Then she straightens, slow.

Breathes away foolishness.

Stands as the mountain does.

I squeeze her hand one last time in mine, then let go.

CHAPTER 35

>>

P enelope is not at the evening's feast.

Neither is Telemachus, or Elektra.

Instead, to everyone's surprise, Laertes descends slowly and sits in the very chair that is kept reserved for his son, body twisted to the right, legs sprawled out to the left as if he cannot find comfort in sitting straight. He glares at the assembled suitors, who have fallen silent at his approach, before finally barking: "Well? Aren't you going to eat, you dogs?" and snatches a bone from the plate of the nearest maid who is standing by. He chews with his mouth open, grinning as the red flesh is mulched to grey beneath his yellow teeth, and slowly, heads down, the suitors eat.

Andraemon is not amongst them, nor Amphinomous.

Antinous whispers: "I heard they didn't even put up a fight – I heard not a single Illyrian was killed!"

Eurymachus mutters: "Some of the ones who died are our friends, Antinous, servants of our fathers . . ."

Antinous snorts through his dish. "You think my father would send anyone he actually values to die in that sorry militia? The only people dead are cripples and imbeciles."

"Antinous!" Laertes' voice rings across the hall, silencing

265

them. "You look like you're saying something important! Why don't you share it with the room?"

In another life, Laertes would have made a truly terrifying tutor to the whelps of Ithaca. Antinous simpers, a smile that was meant to be friendly and comes out as a shimmer of loose lip and tongue, and raises his hands. "No, no, not at all! Just . . . honouring the heroic lives lost."

"Course you were," chuckles Laertes. "That's just like you."

Kenamon sits apart from the others, eyebrows knotted. His usual friendly curiosity is tonight replaced by a silence that no one dares penetrate.

The moon begins to wane, and beneath the blackened ashes of Laertes' farm, seven women meet in secret.

"They attacked my father-in-law! They attacked the king of Ithaca!"

Penelope has not raised her voice since . . . she cannot remember. It is not becoming for a queen to shout or stamp her foot or prowl up and down with smoke in her hair, but tonight there are only women to see her, and so she throws her hands to the sky and snarls: "They attacked Laertes! They killed the boys – boys! Children in metal clothes! My son . . . They could have . . . How dare they?! *How dare they?!*"

Athena watches too, from the edge of the wood. I see the flash of her spear, smell her smug, sanctified breath through the drifting ash of the dark. She is watching Penelope, and perhaps for the very first time sees something in the queen's eyes that interests her. A fire – a fury. A thing that speaks of war. Athena has not looked at the wife of Odysseus before. I am not sure whether I am pleased that she looks now.

The women of her council stand in polite silence as Penelope prowls and curses, swears damnation and prowls a little more, venting at last the heat of the day into the cool darkness of the

266

night. Priene stands armed, hand on the hilt of her sword, as if half expecting the raiders to come again, to crawl back from the seas right now, and wouldn't she love that? She watched them work from the darkness of the forest, and yes, oh but yes, she has the sense of them now. Their scent is in her nostrils, flaring.

Teodora stands beside her, a bow in hand, quiver at her hip. The blisters on her hands have burst, and now new flesh calluses over, warm and thick in the bent places of her fingers. Semele carries a hunting knife, an acceptable implement for a woman who works these hard lands, less of a weapon than a surprisingly sharp tool, depending on who you ask. The weapons that Eos and Ourania carry are both hidden, as is right for women of the palace. Only Anaitis is unarmed. Perhaps she thinks Artemis will defend her, when the moment comes.

The thought of Artemis runs through me like the gallop of the stag, an unwelcome beating upon my heart. I will have to do something about my stepdaughter soon, before the moon is dark. Damn her to Tartarus, but Athena is right on that point too.

"Of everything he could have done – of all the places – *this*! It violates every law, every writ of decency, he has *eaten my food*, he drinks my wine, he ... How *dare* he?!"

In front of the council of men, Penelope does not get to ask such questions. The answers are, of course, obvious, but she does not ask these things in ignorance. Rather she exclaims them as often the women do, trying to puzzle out an arrogance, a confidence, a blithe entitlement amongst the men of Ithaca's table that has been beaten so far from the women's comprehension that though they can see all the evidence before them saying look, lo, this is real, in their hearts they still struggle to believe it. I felt that way once, when Zeus held me down by the neck, having grown bored of my sisters, his former wives. I knew what he did to me, understood from the look in his eye that he was taking only what he felt he was owed, a logical and an apt thing, and

267

yet to this day there is a part of me that still cannot understand it. I see that look in his eye when he gazes down at women, and I realise that what makes him king amongst the gods is less the thunderbolt he wields, and simply that he believes himself set upon high.

"Interesting that they went for Laertes," Priene says at last, bored perhaps of Penelope's fury. "Bold." There is a note of admiration in her voice. This fight has now escalated, and she is pleased to know that when she slaughters pirates, she will be killing soldiers worth her attention, rather than mere Greek beasts. There is a notion of honour in that – a strange word she thought she had left behind but that now pricks again at the horizon of her recollection.

"Andraemon," snarls Penelope, the word a curse thrown upon the ground. "He tries to force my hand, to steal Odysseus's father! His father – the arrogance of it, the sheer . . . "

"And nearly succeeded too." Priene's voice drifts through, and I see a flicker of a smile on Athena's lips, a strategist watching another scheme. "Pure luck that Laertes woke and fled."

Oi! Luck? I'll show you luck, missy, I'll . . .

Anaitis clears her throat, and perhaps the priestess is good at her job, perhaps she can sense a little flicker of divine exasperation upon the wind. "Luck – or the blessings of the gods."

I settle down a little, resisting the urge to send insect bites to Priene's bare neck, swollen eggs of yellow beneath her skin.

"Is there nothing we can do against Andraemon?" asks Ourania thoughtfully. "There are . . . discreet means of removing him."

"You suggest I dispose of one of my own guests?" Penelope retorts, hackles still high, even at those she loves. Ourania curls her lips, a careful consideration of a blasphemous thought. Penelope scowls it away. "Even if I could rid myself of Andraemon, the others would never accept it. One of their number could walk off a cliff of his own volition, and they'd still blame me. Say I

was scheming. We have to deal with Andraemon another way –
prove to the world that he has violated every law of hospitality
so he can be righteously dispatched, in the eyes of all."

"Ah, only that then," sighs Ourania.

"Where is Leaneira?" Penelope asks, turning on Eos.

"Still at the palace. She does her duties and says nothing."

"Does she talk to Andraemon?"

"He spoke to her briefly last night, but if she has seen him
since, it has not been observed."

A brisk nod; a matter to be dealt with later. "When will the
women be ready?" Penelope turns to Priene, who stares up to
the moon as if seeking its answer.

"They are doing well," she says at last. "Better than I expected.
We will have to pick our battleground carefully. Last night your
boy-child militia was scattered in five different places across
Ithaca, utterly incapable of mustering to a fight, let alone winning it. Andraemon has controlled every battle thus far. I will
control the next one."

"And how do you propose doing that?"

"Obviously," she tuts, "we bait him into a trap."

There is an awkward silence in the field. Then Ourania murmurs: "Telemachus . . . "

"No." Penelope's voice is a lash, and though Ourania winces,
she tries again.

"Andraemon has proven himself interested in kidnapping –
or killing – the blood of Odysseus. If we could guarantee
Telemachus was in a certain place at a certain time . . . "

"We are not risking my son!"

"Does he know about this? About us?" Priene asks, casual as air.

"No."

"Should he?"

Penelope lets out a slow, jagged breath. "His friends are dead.
His vaunted militia routed. His valour . . . questioned. Which

of you intends to approach my son and tell him that a hidden assemblage of women is going to do that which he, the son of Odysseus, could not?" Priene makes to raise her hand, but it is pulled down by Teodora. Penelope glowers round the circle. "My son must be his own man. I know that. But until he can defend himself, I will defend him even if he hates me for it. Do you understand?"

There is nodding, a mumbled chorus of assent. Finally Ourania says: "Would Andraemon kidnap *you*?"

There is no malice in the question, just a polite enquiry on a strategic point. There is something almost relieving about the bluntness of it, a snapping of singing tension and a letting-out of breath. Penelope considers it a moment, then shakes his head. "No. If we learnt anything from my cousin Helen, it's that carrying off a queen with or without her consent causes nothing but trouble."

"What about Clytemnestra?" Semele asks. All eyes turn to her.

"It would be unwise to let Andraemon know we have the queen," mutters Ourania. "The sooner we can get her off Ithaca, the better."

"Now that Andraemon's raiders are gone — at least for now — the waters should be safe enough," replies Penelope. "Ourania, I will need you to arrange my cousin's passage."

"You're not giving her to Orestes?" Anaitis asks.

"No. It would be politically . . . it would be the wisest . . . but I find the idea of a child killing their mother on my soil to be particularly distasteful. Her sins were profound, but she was not without . . . provocation. I have no doubt my cousin will make a fuss somewhere else, draw attention to herself — she was never a modest one. But it will not be here, and it will not be my fault."

Beautiful queen, I murmur, stroking Penelope's cheek. You can be my beloved too. All my power will be yours, and you will be mine, favoured of the gods.

270

Finally Ourania says: "Well, if we can't use human bait to lure Andraemon, we will have to offer something else."

Penelope sighs. "I will work on it. In the meantime, Priene, I need you to find an acceptable place for a fight."

The warrior nods once, turns away, Teodora at her back. I see Athena watching the women depart, feel her tangling in their senses, mingling with their dreams. Then there is a sound like an itch in the small of my back, a fly buzzing that I cannot kill, a furriness on my teeth that will not wash away. I turn to the source of it and see, oh how displeasing, Anaitis offering a prayer to Artemis, hands clasped, eyes closed. It is the most sincere of prayers, more's the pity, and it grates and makes me grind my jaw.

On the edge of the field, the trees bend and the leaves billow. I look again for Athena, but she is gone, leaving me once again to do the dirty work. I shake my fist at her departure and the cold wind swirls at my displeasure, icy drizzle falling in a small yet pointed patch around Anaitis and the women gathered there.

CHAPTER 36

>>

D ays roll by in Ithaca.

Polybus storms into the council, trailed somewhat less dramatically by Eurymachus, his son.

"You can't just come in while we're ..." Aegyptius begins, but Polybus cuts him off.

"Why are the Mycenaeans still here?" he fumes. "Why are they still searching our ships?"

In the corner where she habitually sits, Penelope does not glance up from her contemplation of yarn. Autonoe strums a note on the lute. It is high, a little too bright to the ears, and the tune she seems to be seeking for is not resolved.

"Orestes has gone looking for his mother ..." Medon tries again, but once more Polybus is having none of it.

"Orestes might have left, but the men of his insane sister are still all over every ship that comes and goes from harbour, no matter where they sail from! I have had nothing but complaints, and this morning they refused passage for one of Nestor's men until they had searched the vessel prow to stern! I have spent my breath apologising abjectly for *your* mistakes, and I have had enough!"

Telemachus is not in council. He has barely been seen these

past five days, and if Autonoe had not spotted him shuffling towards Eumaios's farm, arm in a sling and sword at his side, even Penelope would not be entirely sure her son were not swallowed whole into the earth. His absence is perhaps something of a relief, for today it means no one raises their voice until Polybus has finished raising his.

Peisenor stands silent and grey as the old man shouts. Medon waits; Aegyptius fumes but gives no answer. Autonoe seeks another note, and it lands, by total chance it would appear, like strange punctuation every time Polybus seeks to draw a breath, until finally he rounds on her and barks: "Will you cease your picking?!"

In the silence, Autonoe raises an eyebrow but does not answer. Penelope, eyes down, focused wholly it seems on her woollen work, murmurs: "I find the sound of music soothing. As my husband's wife I must of course attend council in his name, but the matters are so weighty and of such complex stuff that I do need a little calming music to stop my head getting quite in a twist from all the important things my councillors say. For example, this business with the Mycenaeans sounds very difficult indeed. It seems that, short of ordering the children of Agamemnon to leave the island – an action that would doubtless result in you, and I, and all our kin being burnt alive when they returned – there isn't much these good men can do except wait and hope. But I am not sure about these things – perhaps there is something someone else can think of." Another note, the resolution of a chord perhaps; Autonoe smiles as though she has solved a great musical mystery. "Of course until then," Penelope muses, "I am extraordinarily grateful that you so nobly bear the brunt of their indignities. It seems to me that the whole isle owes you – and your son – a great thanks for your tact, forbearance and patience against the provocation of a power that could, if they were not our allies, crush us like a daisy."

Somewhere in the calmer recesses of Polybus's mind it occurs to him that he misses his wife more profoundly than he could ever have imagined. She died giving birth to a child who did not last the night, but whenever the urge to shout, rage and proclaim against injustice came upon him, he could vent to her, and being done, fall silent again and thus not rage against people who perhaps, if he is briefly honest with himself, were not fully deserving of his ire.

He is not fully honest with himself; the moment of rationality passes. Only grief sits now where there should have been the memory of the woman he loved, and grief is unacceptable. Sorrow unmans him. He will never look upon it, never wash it away with cool balm, nor name it, nor call it his own, and so instead inwards, inwards, inwards it curls like the weedy root that becomes a tree within the unwatched soil of his heart. So goes the spirit of a sometime-was-good man.

Instead he snarls: "Women and doddering fools! You could not rule sheep, let alone an island!" and spins on his heel, and storms away. Eurymachus follows. He has learnt from his father what it is to be a man, and is learning still. If his mother had lived, she would have grieved for the lessons he has taken.

In the quiet of the council chamber, Aegyptius is the first to speak. He is a little cowed since the night Laertes' farm burnt, but he is also nothing if not a man who gets on with things. Good fortune or great disasters, he will keep on shambling; it is his main appeal as a councillor. "Why are the Mycenaeans still searching our ships? Why is Elektra still here?"

It is Peisenor's turn to answer, to state the bloody obvious, as is his wont. Premonition bids all eyes turn to him, but he does not speak, still stares down at nothing much, lost in his own thoughts, and his shame. Those boys who survive in the militia have returned to training. There is more space in the yard, now that some are slain, and Peisenor has not come back to teach them, nor Telemachus to lead. Instead Amphinomous stands before them and coughs and says: "Well. Yes. So. Let's try ... javelin throws, shall we?"

It will not be acceptable for Amphinomous to do so for very much longer, and both Penelope and Peisenor know it. It would give him the appearance of being a responsible leader, a good man, a capable soldier – all qualities that suit a king. Better by far that he be a drunkard again, unremarked and unremarkable.

A few more days. Penelope will let her broken general have a few more days.

In the silence of the council, Medon clears his throat. "Well, if no one else ... Clearly we all think it ... clearly Elektra thinks it." Aegyptius says nothing, and for the briefest of moments, Autonoe stops in her tune. Medon looks one to the other, incredulity rising in his eyes before blurting: "She still thinks Clytemnestra is here! Why else would she have stayed behind when her brother sailed?"

"The ring – the evidence before her very eyes ... " begins Aegyptius, and Medon raises his hands.

"I know, I know. It seems folly. Clytemnestra is gone and fled. But they have to kill *someone*. Orestes cannot be king in Mycenae until his father is avenged."

Medon does not look at Penelope as he says this, but Aegyptius's eyes flicker her way. It would of course be best for Orestes to kill Clytemnestra, but failing that, would a cousin do, if that cousin might be said to have helped her escape?

Penelope half hums a counterpoint to Autonoe's tune, as if remembering a childhood song.

Then Aegyptius says: "We should discuss mercenaries," and for once, everyone in the room is grateful for the change of subject. "It's clear we need trained soldiers to defend the isles. The attack on Laertes' farm proved it."

"Who will pay for them?"

"Come now, come! Everyone knows Autolycus gave Odysseus treasure, that there is secret gold ... "

"'Secret gold', not you too, do you really think ... "

"How else does she keep paying for things? The feasts, the suitors – she said the armoury was empty, but Peisenor armed the militia ... "

"Fish, wool, oil, amber and tin." Penelope's voice is still half matched to the maid's music, a gentle breeze in the room. "We have very few surpluses, but we have plenty of fish, sheep and goats, and many olive trees. These are of course very common throughout Greece, but we add in a certain labour – not just raw wool, but refined thread that the women have spun into excellent yarn that may earn a slight premium when sold to certain merchants in Pylos. Not merely oil, but the finest oil we press, both light and fragrant, valued by a great many wealthy households in Colchis. The poorer threads and oils we keep for the domestic market here, Ithaca being more easily satisfied with simple produce than our inland cousins. And as for amber and tin – I sell at exorbitant prices the fermented fish and fresh water that the traders need for their journeys south, and buy at a rate that I can then mark up significantly the tin and amber they bring from the forests of the north. On their return trips I also occasionally purchase linen, gold, rare timbers, spice, copper and sweet fragrances that fetch an excellent price when shipped to Sparta or Argos, taking full advantage of the sea and eastern trade. Thus I keep the suitors fed. It is very simple, really."

The room is silent. If the poets will not sing about the sexual desires of women, let me assure you – not one chord has ever been struck in a noble hall on the topic of the price of fish. Oh most certainly all the councillors of Odysseus are *aware* of trade, but to speak about it in polite society? Absolutely not! It is something that their trusted slaves must do, or in the very worst case

276

their wives. The great men of Ithaca are far too busy doing more poetry-worthy stuff, such as losing battles or stealing other men's mistresses. Indeed, Penelope could not have expressed a notion more awkward in that minute than if she had stood up and proclaimed: "Also, I bleed from my private places every moon or so and giggled the first time I saw Odysseus's willy."

Aegyptius finally splutters, unable it seems to process this moment: "But . . . the treasure of Odysseus?"

"All gone, I'm afraid. All spent."

"How is that possible?" he wails. "Why would the suitors come if not for treasure?"

Penelope blinks twice, thrice, and for the first time seems to meet his gaze. "Did I not just say? Because I put an exorbitant price upon the goods I sell from the traders of the western sea. If people want to believe that I keep the suitors in meat through some . . . twenty-year gift of gold from a demigod with a penchant for stealing cows, then that's their choice. I have been, I feel, extremely clear about the importance of buying low and selling high."

Autonoe is not laughing. Autonoe has got a little better at muffling her mirth down the years. Finally Medon clears his throat. "Perhaps we should . . . adjourn," he muses. "I shall make a few further enquiries into the matter of the Mycenaeans, and perhaps Peisenor . . . perhaps Aegyptius can look into the question of mercenaries and precisely how little we can afford them. Yes? Yes. Thank you all."

Peisenor leaves only when Aegyptius touches his arm, bidding him move.

Aegyptius glances back over his shoulder as they go, but Medon remains planted before Penelope, a smile on his face and not in his eyes. He waits for the door to close before turning fully to his queen and saying: "Is Clytemnestra on Ithaca?"

The music falls from Autonoe's fingers. Penelope glances at

her maid, and nods once. Autonoe darts to the door, slipping through it to stand outside, guarding the corridor against all eyes, all ears that might dare intrude. Eos and Penelope remain, and neither pretends to give Medon anything less than her full attention.

"If she were," says Penelope at last, "she would have come here despite me."

Medon lets out a hiss of frustration, hands flying to his head. "She's *here*?!"

"I didn't say that . . ."

"Where is she? Do you have her? Tell me she isn't in the palace!"

"I can categorically state that my cousin is not in the palace."

"Does Elektra know? Blessed gods, if she finds out . . ."

"She clearly suspects. Clearly she does. If she had fully believed the business with the ring . . ."

"Of course that was you," he groans, grabbing onto the table as if sickness might overwhelm him. "All that stuff with messengers and Zakynthos and – of course it was you. What did you do?"

"I attempted to send my cousins to Hyrie," she sighs. "And from there, hopefully, home, empty-handed."

"You know they won't leave empty-handed! They must have a head!"

"I was trying to buy time."

"Time for Elektra to snoop around! Time for them to decide that *we're* the enemy? In Zeus's name, what were you thinking?!"

"I was thinking Elektra would fall for it," she snaps, voice rising as she does, then dragged back down hastily to a teeth-pushing snarl as Eos's eyes dart instinctively to the door. "I was thinking they'd be gone and Clytemnestra would be gone and we could go back to being uniquely distressed in a local, Ithacan way!"

Medon shakes his head, grips the table a little tighter,

straightens, opens his mouth, cannot find the words, sags again. "We're all going to die terrible, terrible deaths," he concludes.

"Thank you, councillor, for your sage advice."

"What are you going to do now?"

"I'm not sure. I didn't predict that Elektra would stay so long, or that her men would be so ... enthusiastic in their duties. I'll think of something. She cannot stay here for ever."

Medon nods without agreeing, the dumb gesture of a man who has seen inevitability and acknowledges it without pleasure. "And the mercenaries?"

"Mercenaries." Penelope scowls. "They exist to be paid, not to fight. We may as well pay Andraemon directly and be done with it."

Medon bolts up again as if struck by lightning. "Andraemon?"

"What? Oh, yes, you weren't ... "

"The raiders are Andraemon's men? You are sure of it?"

"Yes. I'm sure."

"That ... that *vulture* eats at Odysseus's table, drinks Odysseus's wine, and his men tried to kidnap Odysseus's father?"

"That's about the extent of it."

"Do you have proof? If you can prove it, we can have him executed right now."

"I do not, unfortunately, have proof. As matters currently stand, it is his word against mine."

What little strength has been bestowed upon him leaves Medon again. He looks pale, almost ill, as grey as Peisenor and with similar cause. "Marry him."

"I beg your pardon?"

"Marry him. It's the only way. It's clearly what he wants and we are in no position to refuse."

Penelope's lips thin. She glances at Eos, whose face gives no reply, but Medon sees the look fly and, with one final effort, mutters: "What? What else don't I know?"

"You know that of all men I trust you ..."

"The last time you said that, you were twenty-one years old and had stolen your mother-in-law's bangle to lay in surety against a shipment of oil."

"Which investment proved most profitable, did it not?"

Medon has known Penelope longer than her father did, and if we are honest, was more glad to know her than perhaps her father was. "What have you done?" he breathes, and does not know of all the feelings within his breast – sorrow, fear, pride, resentment, love – which now is the strongest.

She lets out a long, slow breath. "I did not tell you because it may be seen as ... politically unsound, should word get out ... and perhaps, depending on your view of things ... a little bit sacrilegious."

He throws his hands up. "Of course! Sacrilege! What more could this day bring?"

"There are, as you know, women in the east who fight with the men ... "

When his jaw drops, he can hear the weight of it popping in his ears. "*You didn't.*"

"Penthesilea, for example, fought against Achilles himself ... "

"And died!"

"Against *Achilles* – everyone died against Achilles, it was his predominant characteristic."

"If the kings of Greece find out that you are thinking of raising an army – women – *an army of women!* – if the suitors find out ... "

"They will not. No one will."

"How do you hide an army?"

"Medon," Penelope tuts, "what a foolish question. You hide them in precisely the same way you hide your success as a merchant, your skill with agriculture, your wisdom at politics and your innate cutting wit. You hide them as women."

Medon opens his mouth to object with the noise and volume of the clattering seagulls that circle rotting fish, and finds that the words have left him. Defeated, he near buckles onto the table at his back, while Eos rises, gathering wool into her arms and gliding at Penelope's nod towards the door.

"Terrible, terrible deaths," Medon offers feebly, his final word.

Penelope rests a hand gently on his arm. "Matters are coming to a head," she declares, without malice or delight. "There are things upon which I will still need your help."

CHAPTER 37

>>

L eaneira.
She's still here.

Euracleia sees her as she stokes the fire in the kitchen for another endless feast, and scowls: "Trojan slut!"

The words barely pass over Leaneira as she hears them. Euracleia used to be better at insulting her, used to have a gift for cruelty that sliced straight through to the most tender heart of a maid. But her words are running down with her power and the strength of her limbs, and now Leaneira barely hears her speak.

Melantho leans in close, arms weighted with timber stacked so high she has to balance the topmost log with the tip of her chin, and murmurs: "Are you ... all right?"

Leaneira doesn't answer, and watches the flames catch at wood.

Gutting fish in the afternoon sun, a knife through the belly, snip, snack, splat, intestines into the bucket at her feet, Phiobe approaches Leaneira as she works and says: "I heard something happened between you and the queen! Tell me tell me oh tell me *pleeeaaasssse* ... "

Leaneira picks up the next fish, splat, slice, snick ...

"Oh please tell me go on go on please I just ... "

Turns to Phiobe, the knife clutched in her hand, and shouts, roars, roars as the fires roared through Troy: "Go away! Go away go away go away *go away!*"

Putting out plates for the evening feast.

Eos, who learnt to be ice from the queen she loves, sees her and says: "No, not those. The others. They were drunk again last night, and smashed three of our better bowls."

Leaneira glances Eos's way, her face drawn as though to shriek, to scream, to sigh: what does it matter? They break everything in the end anyway.

But Eos has already floated on by, no room for conversation, so Leaneira undoes her work, and obeys.

Leaneira serves meat at the evening feast. The mood is rising again now the smoke has settled over Ithaca. Laertes spends most of his days presiding over the ashes of his farm, rebuilding, he says, better, bigger, and with sharp spikes hidden in dubious places too, and a nice high wall around the villa. He is rarely at the feast. Elektra keeps to her rooms – praying, they say – and Telemachus has not been seen for days. This leaves only Penelope and her maids, maybe sometimes an ashen councillor or two, and so the volume and merriment of the men once again waxes.

"Leaneira," chuckles Antinous as she passes him by, "I hear you're looking for a man to warm your bed now Andraemon won't have you. I can take pity on you if you're getting dry."

The others around the table laugh, Eurymachus wiping his greasy lips with the back of his hand, not sure if this is an appropriate joke but laughing because the others do. Leaneira moves by them without a word, and a hand lashes out for her backside, squeezes, and the laughter grows all the greater as she drags herself away.

Andraemon is back at the feast, and he does not look at

Leaneira once, but stares at Penelope as if he could glower her into submission, hand wrapped tight around the little stone ornament at his neck. The others have spotted this and gather round him, drum their fists on the table and chant his name. "Andraemon is going to strike Penelope down with his eyes!" shrills Nisas. "He's going to undress her with his glare!"

Penelope sits at her loom, weaving Laertes' shroud, and does not raise her gaze. The men stamp their feet and chant: "And-rae-mon, And-rae-mon, And-rae-mon!" and when his gaze doesn't falter and she doesn't raise her head or spontaneously undress, they break out into a roar, a flood of merriment, before bored returning to their seats again.

Kenamon sits apart, and when Autonoe passes her whispers: "Is Telemachus here?"

The question surprises the maid, who pauses long enough to actually consider her answer. "He returned from his . . . rest this afternoon, and is at his prayers."

Telemachus, upstairs in his room, gazes to the sea and is very much not at his prayers. He watches a ship speed out across the waters, wind and the strength of the rowers carrying it fast as an eagle, and there is a certain something in the way he draws his breath that displeases me. I look a little closer, and then catch in the corner of my eye that fucking owl. It sits upon the wall outside, and as I draw near to Telemachus, it opens its beak and goes: hoot bloody hoot. Hoot *I see you* hoot.

For a moment I lock eyes with Athena, daring her to hoot at me one more time – but I feel the touch of our bargain within my bones, burning gentle upon my soul. Her eyes are fixed upon Odysseus's son as if she would drink him whole, and with a shudder I turn away.

CHAPTER 38

>>>

I have put some business off too long.

With a shimmer of distaste, I dress in my least favourite gown and least loved golden sandals, and catch the wind that bends the tops of the forest trees.

There – there below. There is a grove where Artemis bathes.

There are many groves where Artemis bathes, but this one has a special appeal for her, combining soft banks of grass that catch the warm western sun with smooth stones in the water where one may pose, legs draped into the cool running stream. There is a waterfall and hollow pool beneath, behind which caves of sapphire crystal glint and glimmer, and nearby the den of a bear and her cubs, who will maul anything that comes near, be it man or beast – something that Artemis finds disquietingly funny. "Look!" she will shrill. "Look how squishy their inside parts are!"

I drift down upon a cloud to avoid the worst of the ursine natives, and approaching over the dewy grass hear the slow pull of a bow as one of her guardian ladies draws back the arrow in the string.

"Shove it," I snap at her, and for a moment she merely blinks at me, seemingly unafraid of the queen of the gods, before slowly lowering her weapon. As I draw nearer the pool, others of Artemis's women eye me up, well over a dozen in all, some armed with bows, others with knives at their sides and bloody meat in their teeth. Yet for all that they are a hideous crowd, my daughter-in-law also has a taste, it must be said, for women of the fairer sort, hair fabulously washed and braided, oil rubbed into their extremely bare and muscled flesh.

Rounding a mossy stone upon the water's edge, I look down and there is the goddess of the hunt herself, reclining backwards upon the surface of the pool while next to her a maid ... let us say she is combing Artemis's hair, for decency's sake.

"Could you be any louder?" proclaims my stepdaughter as I stand upon the water's edge. "I heard you coming a league off."

"I didn't want to startle you," I retort. "Given how badly you take to being startled." She sighs luxuriously, eyes closed, hair the colour of autumn leaves drifting loosely around her head. I try to keep my gaze on her face as much as feasible, but the distracting processes of the moment quickly overwhelm me and I blurt: "Could you put some clothes on? I mean, it's all very ... but how do your women keep from getting cold?"

"They run naked through the winter snow," muses Artemis. "They run until their cheeks are red and their hearts roar in their heads, then they fall into each other's arms around the fire, flesh of their flesh embraced in a ... "

"Yes, thank you, I think I get the picture."

She puffs, waving away the maid who had been otherwise so occupied, and opens her eyes. For a moment she seems almost surprised to see me, before blurting: "Gracious, are you that old?"

I take in a deep breath. "It has been a long time since you graced us with your presence in Olympus, stepdaughter. Your father misses you."

She rises slowly from the water, making no effort whatsoever to cover her nudity, gesturing at her maids to move off a little that we might converse in private. "No he doesn't. He misses my brother. They share similar tastes in . . . many things."

"All right. He doesn't miss you."

"And you certainly don't," she adds.

"I . . . Things are never quite as simple as you seem to think, stepdaughter. I admit we haven't always agreed on things . . . "

A snort of derision as she pauses to wring out her hair, streams of water tumbling down the curve of her back and into the shadow of her buttocks. Artemis has never resembled the fashionable notion of womanhood. Her skin is too dark from days in sunlight; her legs too strong, thighs too broad, breasts too small and shoulders too thick. She can disguise herself, when she wants to, as a boy and go heckle her brother Apollo's ceremonies, or cheer the men who run at the summer games without fear of anyone calling her a woman, and yet there is undeniably a beauty in her strength and a grace to her motion that even Aphrodite can envy.

". . . yet we are both goddesses," I continue through gritted teeth. "We share . . . certain bonds, do we not?"

"Do we?" Artemis chimes. "I hadn't noticed."

I glance to the heavens. The skies are clear, but even Zeus hesitates before peering down at Artemis's sacred groves. She could not challenge him in her wrath, of course, but my word the girl is a biter. She makes men pay for where their eyes roam. So in a bare whisper I dare it and breathe: "We both despise the rule of men, do we not?"

She glances my way and this time sees perhaps more than my face, my hands, my discomfort as I stand upon the edge of the water. She straightens, coiling her hair around the back of her thick neck, a band of triangular muscle running from it to the tops of her arms. "What do you want, old queen?"

I let out a slow, careful breath.

"I have a project that may be of interest to you."

287

A wave of her hand, a bending of the wrist flicking away the notion. "I'm not interested in your schemes. Whatever it is, I am certain it'll bore me."

"There are men who have been attacking a certain island. They come every full moon. One night they tried to kidnap the father of that island's king. They are doing it not for gold or ransom, but to force a woman to marry a man she does not want."

"So? She should just kill the man and be done with it."

"The man is a guest under her roof."

Artemis huffs. She understands the sacred laws of hospitality, and even she will not violate them, but like so many of the laws of gods and men, they bore her. They are stupid and dull and she has no time for either. "So? I don't see how this concerns me."

"The lady has come up with a somewhat novel solution."

Artemis blinks, dull as wood. She can stand still and pretend to be stupid for a very long time if she wants – stillness is a hunter's gift. I feel the urge to chide her, to tell her off for acting like a child, but this is her grove and I need her. Pity me, ye skies, but I need her.

"In a grove near your temple, she has a warrior of the east teaching her women how to fight."

Again Artemis blinks, but now I think perhaps her mind is elsewhere, though her body remains, flitting through the hollows of her temples like the smell of pine. Then her eyes widen and slowly she says: "Is this Ithaca?" I feel the urge to swallow, but keep it in check – my cheeks will not flush nor my eyelids flicker unless I will it. Artemis straightens a little more, shoulders drawing back. "Is this Ithaca?" she repeats, indignation rising in her voice. "There was a feast in my honour at full moon, all the women gathered, the dancing was terrible – but I did enjoy the food. The priestess has been praying for strength with spear and bow, and in the forest in the night I have heard the sound of arrows flying, yet they have not hit any of the creatures of the hunt. What have you been doing in *my* forest, woman?"

For a moment she grows taller, broader, and there she is, the bloody archer, crimson on her tongue, blood in her eyes. I consider matching her height for height, letting the full radiance of my power shine out upon this place – but no. I must be, sickening though it is, meek, the schemer not the queen, so quiet I remain, poised beneath her gaze, and reply simply: "Yes. This is Ithaca."

"Women with bows? In my forest? Without offering blood to *me*?!"

By now, mortal men would have turned to base creatures of the wood beneath her fury, to a hare or a whimpering squirrel. I face the full force of her anger, and though it is a little hot around the edges, I let it wash through me like the water of the river. "Would you have come when they called?" I enquire politely. "Or are you too busy ... washing your hair?" For a moment I think I've gone too far, and her fury will stir even the lazy oafs on Olympus. So I add: "Look, it's very simple. There are women armed with bow and spear who are perfectly prepared to kill in your name. But if they are to survive, if they are to flourish, they will need your blessing. Not mine. Not Athena's. Yours. They need the huntress."

Slowly the crimson fire goes out in Artemis's eyes. She withdraws a little, seems to shrink, becomes again a woman, pulling at her hair as if nothing in the world had disturbed her. "Killing men, you say?" she asks, as light as a songbird.

"Yes."

"Pirates?"

"Yes. Veterans of Troy come to plunder Ithaca's shores."

"To try and force that queen – what's her name?"

"Penelope."

"Oh yes. The one the ducks like. To try and force her into marriage?"

"That's about right."

Artemis's lips thin. I wait. If there is one thing the huntress dislikes more than not getting her share of a kill, it is weddings. "And you are proposing the women kill them? Drive arrows through their eyes, rip out their hearts and flay their skin from their still-bleeding flesh and so on?"

"I hadn't quite got to the flaying, but in principle, yes."

She pauses again to blink at me, and there is a look in her eye that, were I not a restrained goddess, I might have read as a cry of: *but dearest stepmother, that is surely the best bit?*

"What does Athena think of all this?" she asks at last, losing interest in her braid and easing down onto the grass beside me, knees up, arms across her shins, as comfortable socialising as a bear in a symposium.

"She is aware, but remains aloof. Her main interest is getting Odysseus home. If Poseidon finds out she is also helping Penelope and Telemachus, he will claim that she has overstepped her bounds, and he will never let Odysseus off Calypso's island. She has to be diplomatic in her dealings, and suggested that I talk to you."

"I bet that's put the wasps in her helmet," chuckles Artemis. "Having to come to *me* for help. Did you know she once tried to pat me on the head? Her thumb tasted of fennel."

"She knows that you are powerful, a great protector ..." I begin, but Artemis dismisses my words with a wave of her hand.

"I don't like talking. But I do like Athena looking stupid. And you? Why do you care?"

"That's my business." She makes an obscene sound between her lips, and I bristle, thinking again on thunder and retribution, but she is utterly unperturbed, all the power in the world at her fingertips and she knows it. Weary, I let out a breath. "There are three queens in Greece. I do not think there will be any queens spoken of after them."

Artemis's eyebrows furrow, and then rise again. For a moment I think there is almost pity in her eyes, and we are sisters again, rebelling against the tyranny of Zeus. "Oh queen of the gods," she breathes. "I remember you. You were mighty once. Before the poems were rewritten at Zeus's command, before the past was all … made-up human things … I remember. You rode with Tabiti and Inanna of the east and the world quivered beneath you. The mortals looked up from their caves with hands painted in ochre and blood and called Mother, Mother, Mother. You tore down the sky upon your enemies, and bade the seas part for the ones you loved. But you trusted Zeus. You swore your brother would never betray you. And look at you now, skulking from the eye of heaven lest he see the footprints you leave upon the earth."

My shame is a pain being driven up into my belly, the weight of my brother as he pressed me down, the burn marks the tears left scarred on my face. I choose when to straighten my spine, but it grows hard, so, so hard. "I … " I stumble, fumbling for words. "I … No man must live. None of them must leave Ithaca alive. If it is said that the women of Ithaca defended their own, there will be nothing left to defend. Will you … will you help me?"

She thinks about it a moment, then nods, once, and rises from the riverbank.

My shame is a world without friendship, a life without trust. I will never trust again. I will never love any creature that is not my own. Yet now, my stepdaughter, whom I loathe, takes my hand in both of hers, and smiles, and it occurs to me that the hunter knows something of the quality of mercy when they aim to take the cleanest, simplest shot.

"And will you put on some clothes?" I add, into the silence between us.

Artemis puffs her cheeks, sticks out her tongue, and I know that she will fight when the moon rises again over Ithaca.

CHAPTER 39

>>

Here: let us examine the turning seas.

In the north, Orestes sits sullen at the stern of his ship as his men prowl the western isles. They have been at this game for days, months, weeks, chasing his mother. He does not think they will find her. He cannot imagine that he will be king. This notion does not disquiet him as much as it disquiets everyone else around him, and being a man who likes to please, he keeps his mouth shut.

In the east, Menelaus sits with his feet up on the serving table, a cup of water and wine clasped in a hand like a cleaver, and says: "Who else will support my claim – if I am forced to make it, that is?" Then he smiles. Menelaus has not smiled at very much, for a very long time.

In the south, Calypso says: "I will make you a god," and for a moment – for more than a moment – Odysseus considers it. Then he shakes his head. What kind of a god would he be if a woman made him one?

And in the west, Leaneira moves through the hall of the palace of the kings of Ithaca, removes the empty cup from before Andraemon, and he does not blink, does not acknowledge her, does not look her way.

Autonoe sighs and says: "What a mess, we'll have to scrub, we'll have to . . . "

Leaneira hauls buckets of water from the well beneath the midnight stars.

Euracleia mutters: "Little sluts."

Leaneira holds the ram still as Eos runs the knife across its throat.

Antinous calls: "How is Laertes' shroud? I trust you're better beneath the sheets than making them?"

Leaneira carries Penelope's loom to her room, Melantho by her side. She clears away the slobber and spittle of drunken men, brushes their hands from her thighs, throws dried timber onto the fire, cleans the ashes about the stove, washes tunics in the stream, chases a rat, stirs the pot, scrapes scales from the fish, turns over the soil above the pissing pits. She throws the bones of meat and the greasy bread with which the suitors held their meals to the pigs and the dogs and the gulls and the crows that feast behind the palace gates.

Outside the palace walls, Eurymachus sings: ". . . and soooooooo the towers felllllll old Iliuuuummm . . .!"

By the palace gates, Antinous leans over to Amphinomous and proclaims: "No one's impressed by your pretend soldiering, soldier. No one's impressed at all."

In a small room in the most turned-around corner of the palace, Kenamon raises his eyes to heaven and wonders if his gods can hear him in this alien land. They could, if they bothered to listen, though his voice would be faint and of little interest.

Leaneira sits by the thin stream that flows down to the sea as the midnight insects sing their song, and washes her feet, and washes her hands, and cannot wash the smoke away.

She reaches a decision, and blows out her lamp.

In darkness, fingers on the wall, moving by memory, she

slips through the palace of Odysseus. Where does she go? To a knife, perhaps? To a weapon to kill her pain, or end the pain-giving of another?

I follow her, curious, but she does not stop to arm herself as Clytemnestra would, but proceeds into that most sacrilegious of places – the rooms where the men slumber. Only a few of the suitors sleep within the palace walls; the most honoured, those who do not have a place to go that will keep them, or those who lack for family and friends in Ithaca. Andraemon is none of the above, but he won his bed within the walls in a game of dice from a man from Same, who now sleeps in the town in the grubby house that was Andraemon's rest.

She knows his door by the old cracked wood, by the way it scrapes across stone when it's opened, by the smell of him in the room. He is sleeping, and then at the touch of her presence in the room he is wide awake, hand reaching for the knife beside his head. And then he blinks and sees the occlusion that her form makes upon the darkness, and hears her say his name.

"Andraemon," she breathes, settling herself down upon him. "I choose you."

He hesitates a moment, hand still on the knife. Then lets go. Runs his hand across her chest, up her neck, around her lips, into her hair. He grabs tight, pulls her head down to his, tastes her mouth with his own, pushes her away, fingers still twined tight. "I don't believe you," he says.

She does not flinch at his touch. Her right hand rests upon his heart, her left closes around the stone he still wears about his neck, his little piece of Troy. "I know where Penelope hides her treasure. The gold given to Odysseus by his grandfather; the spoils of plunder and the goods she hoards, I know . . ."

His grip tightens, and even she cannot hide the grimace

of pain tugging at the corner of her lips. He raises his head a little closer, near enough to bite. *"I don't believe you."*

She catches his arm by the wrist, holds it until his grip loosens just a little, then says: "Let me prove it."

CHAPTER 40

>>

In the darkness, Penelope knocks on Elektra's door. It is answered by one of Elektra's maids, her face daubed in ash, who sees Penelope and says simply: "Wait."

It is outrageous that a queen should be forced to wait in her own palace, and for a moment Penelope catches her breath. But then she lets it go, slow, exhale, calm, and half closes her eyes and waits a little longer until the door opens again.

"Good queen." Elektra sits facing the window, her back half turned to her visitor. For a moment Penelope sees Anticlea there, sitting in precisely the same manner as this Mycenaean princess, halfway to drowning her sorrow, her heart already submerged in the crimson deep. "I am sorry to have kept you waiting. I was praying."

She was not praying.

"Of course," murmurs Penelope, with a little nod. "And I am sorry to have disturbed you at this hour, but I feared I was neglecting you, the most important of all my guests."

A little wave of the hand, a dismissal of an idea. "You have been as gracious a host as we had come to expect."

Penelope glances at the waiting maids, and seeing her look,

Elektra dismisses them with a tilt of her chin, but though they leave, she does not invite Penelope to sit. "Has there been any word from your brother?" Penelope asks at last.

Elektra shakes his head. "I expect to hear good news from him soon."

"Of course. And you are ... keeping well?"

Another dismissal; the question is too trivial to bother with. Penelope feels herself about to sigh, to let out a pent-up breath, and catches herself. Instead, she muses: "I have heard of your man – Pylades, I think it is? – still searching by the docks. My councillors say that your men patrol Ithaca."

"There are those who will have helped my mother escape," Elektra replies, light as summer. "Others who must be punished."

"It had not even occurred to me that that might be the case – but of course, you are wise."

Elektra's eyes flash, just like her mother's, and she turns a little in her chair to stare more particularly at the older queen. "Am I? That means a lot, coming from you, cousin."

The ghost of Anticlea still haunts this room, berating young Penelope, caught weeping when her husband sailed away. Child! Do not blink. Do not flinch. Do not catch your breath. Stand up straight. You are a queen, not a girl!

There is a challenge in Elektra's stare, and an opportunity too. Penelope sees it, knows it, and for a moment considers taking it. But no – not yet. Not quite yet. She half nods, not quite a bow, murmurs: "Well, if you have all you need ... "

A flicker of almost disappointment behind Elektra's eyes, and then she turns away. Dismisses Penelope with the back of her hand, the cheek of it, the gall, I don't know if I'm impressed or outraged – but then neither does Penelope. "Yes, yes, thank you." Even in her arrogance, Elektra catches herself before adding, "You may go," but Penelope feels the ghost of

Anticlea on her left, the brush of my presence on her right, and so, like the winter mist, lets herself out into the dark.

Three nights later, Orestes returns.

He arrives at sunset, sailing from the north, and Elektra runs to the docks and throws himself at his feet and proclaims: "My brother! My king!"

There are no beating drums, no proud trumpets. Orestes does not hold the severed head of his mother up for the crowds to see. Instead, he turns to the waiting councillors of Ithaca as his sister weeps at his feet and says simply: "We did not find trace of her on Hyrie."

The old men shift uneasily. Even Polybus and Eupheithes, standing slightly behind, have the wits to turn pale.

Elektra gives a scream, an animal howl of fury and rage, a little too loud, a little too dramatic for my taste, but it gets the job done. She sobs and pounds her fists against the earth until finally her brother kneels down and wordlessly picks her up, supporting her by one arm as if she were a broken feather fallen from heaven as they return, silently, to the palace of Odysseus.

"Well," Medon says, as he and Penelope watch Orestes' men disembark their battered ships. He tries to think of what words might follow that best encapsulate the complexity of feeling now swirling in his heart, and settles at last for the most concise. "Terrible, terrible death."

Penelope glowers at him through her veil, then follows her cousins to the palace.

Orestes stands in the council room, Elektra behind him.

Opposite stand Telemachus, Medon, Peisenor and Aegyptius.

Penelope sits in her corner with her maids, but just this once, Autonoe does not play.

Orestes speaks as he looks to some other place, in some other voice that is barely meant for human consumption. "We sailed for many days. We asked many questions in Hyrie but had no reply. We sailed west, and those ships we saw we investigated. But there was no sign. We sailed north. But there was no sign. We were running low on water and food, and then a storm blew up and drove us south, back towards Ithaca. Of my mother there is no sign."

I glance to the skies, and briefly wonder: does my brother send Orestes back to this miserable little island? Are the storms his? But no, no. Poseidon is so busy blasting Ogygia with impenetrable waves, his hatred focused on Odysseus and Odysseus alone. I do not think he would have the wits to make Odysseus's wife's life a misery by driving back the children of Agamemnon. Sometimes a storm is just a storm. Still, one to keep an eye on . . .

Aegyptius says: "It is a tragedy, a terrible tragedy, but of course all of Ithaca is at your command — whatever it takes . . . "

Medon interposes: "We don't have much, of course, Ithaca is not rich, but yes, to echo my colleague's sentiment, if we can help we . . . "

Telemachus blurts: "We will find the witch. We will destroy her. This to you I swear."

There is a slightly awkward silence. What Athena sees in the boy I do not know.

Orestes simply replies: "Thank you." And then, because everyone is looking at him, expecting him to say something more, give a little speech perhaps, he adds: "Thank you."

People are still staring, and suddenly he is just a twenty-two-year-old would-be man who was sent far from home to be raised by other men's fathers, to be separated from his mother's grief and guilt and rage. He was five when Iphigenia died, and his father bade him go to Athens with a cry of: "I'll not have him raised by women!" In Athens they beat him and told him it was what his father would want, and if his father wanted it, then of course

Orestes deserved to be beaten. And yet in some strange way, in some peculiar twist of the loom that make the Fates cackle in their mischief, the suspicion is growing upon me that Orestes longs to be a good man. This will surely be his undoing.

Now all eyes are fixed upon him, and just this once, in just this moment, he cannot bear it. He cannot bear what he sees in their faces, he cannot bear his failings or who it is he is meant to become. He turns and nearly runs, nearly flees into the dusty cool of the palace, Elektra a mere moment behind.

As the room empties of Mycenaeans, the Ithacans are left, a little embarrassed. Medon half turns to Penelope and his lips shape the unspoken words: *terrible death*.

She sighs, opens her mouth to speak, but to her surprise, Telemachus gets in there first. "We must search Ithaca again," he proclaims. "We must search all the isles."

"Um, but we've already . . . "

He slams his fist into the table loud enough to make Medon jump. "We are dishonoured! We are deceived! We have failed Orestes and all of Greece! Am I the only one who sees what will happen if Clytemnestra is not slain? Orestes will fall. Elektra will be . . . and Menelaus will seize Mycenae! He will seize the kingdoms of the north, he will appoint himself king of all the Greeks and no one will stand in his way! Or if he does not, and it transpires that someone . . . " he does not look at his mother, how much he does not look at his mother, "has protected the *whore* queen of Greece, then Ithaca will burn! My father's kingdom will burn and it will be justice for the sins we have committed!"

The room is quiet. There is, it must be said, some astuteness to Telemachus's political analysis, but it is so hard to unpick from the tyranny of youthful stupidity that frames it that it is barely noticed by the listeners. Then Penelope says: "May I speak to my son alone?"

The councillors, relieved, quickly nod and move towards the

door, but Telemachus stops them. "Anything my mother says she can say here, before you all."

"Telemachus . . ."

"She can speak before you all!" he repeats. "I am not some child to be schooled in private, Mother, not some boy you can talk to as if I know nothing. I am the son of Odysseus. I am the heir to this kingdom, I have shed my blood for it. And I will be addressed as the son of a king."

How much of this, I wonder, is Athena's influence on the whelp? She is, for all her innumerable faults, not particularly prone to pouting or great displays of pomp. Perhaps all this sudden snarling from the lion's cub is to demonstrate teeth that are entirely his own.

Penelope is as pale as her gown. She takes each word at a time, shaping the sound tongue-to-teeth, lest she flounder in speech. "You are the son of a king," she grinds out at last. "But I am still your mother."

"You birthed me," he replies, "but I am a man now. Men owe duty to their mothers. They owe love and consideration and care. I will do my duty as your son. But they do not hide behind their mothers. Men do what is needful, and what is right."

"And do not men take counsel?"

"They do. From those who are wise."

"Mothers are not wise?"

"Was Helen wise when she abandoned her children? Was Clytemnestra wise when she murdered her husband? Were you wise, Mother, when you let the suitors into the palace, and smiled and simpered at them and said, 'oh yes, sir' and 'oh no, sir' and 'let me give you wine, sir'."

"I did nothing of the sort, you know I did nothing of the sort, I . . ."

"And now?" he snarls. "My grandfather's home attacked! My cousins dishonoured! My friends dead, slaughtered, their

301

blood ... and you ... you stand here, all of you, stand here and talk. You are weak! You are cowards. You are not fit to raise men."

Someone has to storm from the room in a huff at this point, and in fairness to all of Telemachus's posturing, he is still the youngest of the assembly, and least experienced at holding his ground, so it is he who leaves.

The councillors look anywhere except Penelope's face.

She hesitates a moment – too long, my sweet, too long – then follows him, calling his name. He does not look back, but as she charges after him, another steps forward, one of the great skulkers of the palace, Andraemon, there he is, smiling bright, eyes lit up like the moon, and Penelope stops so fast that she nearly trips over her own feet. Andraemon follows her gaze after her retreating son, then smiles, and bows low, and goes about his business.

Thus passed the last chance Penelope had to hold her son close to her heart, for many a year to come.

CHAPTER 41

>>>

Kenamon waits for Telemachus behind Eumaios's farm, but Telemachus does not come.

Kenamon seeks Telemachus in the halls of the palace, but Phiobe says: "Sorry, sir, the young prince is busy."

Kenamon thinks he sees Telemachus talking urgent and low with Elektra.

Thinks he sees him sitting silent and sombre with Orestes, but as he approaches the Mycenaean, another, Pylades, steps between him and the son of Odysseus and says: "The princes are talking. Thank you."

He is not sure if "thank you" translates clearly between this tongue and his own, for it seems to express nothing so much as "push off, you nosy foreigner" rather than any meaningful expression of gratitude or appreciation. But it is not wise to delve too deeply into these things, he is finding, so he pushes off as commanded.

It is not until the moon is a thin nail, waning in the evening sky, that he catches Telemachus alone, standing in the empty courtyard where during the day the ragtag remnants of the militia have tried to train. He is hefting a shield with his injured arm, hoicking it up, thrusting it forward, testing its weight, wincing at the pain of it. He carries on a little while, unseen, until at last Kenamon clears his throat and steps forward.

Telemachus whirls, ready to fight, tooth and glare and fire and snarl, and then relents a little, seeing the Egyptian, and looks away, as if ashamed.

"How are you healing?" Kenamon asks.

Telemachus doesn't answer.

"You should take it slowly. It is good to practise, but too much, too soon, you will only injure yourself further."

Telemachus bashes forward with the shield towards an unseen enemy, a foolish move, and his face crinkles in pain, sweat bright and bold on his brow. Kenamon watches, without judgement or condemnation, and it is perhaps the strangeness of this, the unfamiliarity of kindness, that makes Telemachus lower his weapons, and at last set them down.

He sits on the dusty floor, back against the wall, knees pulled to his chest. He does not invite Kenamon to join him, but after a while, the Egyptian does, companionably, mimicking the folded stance of the younger man.

"Do you want to talk?" Kenamon asks at last.

Telemachus shakes his head.

"Have you prayed?"

Telemachus hesitates, then shakes his head again.

"If you cannot talk to men, you should at least talk to the gods," tuts Kenamon. "Not that they will listen – but it is good to talk."

"And say what?"

"I don't know. Whatever you need to say. Whatever you don't think you can say to anyone else. Whatever you can't say to me."

Telemachus thinks about this statement for a while, face flushing even as the sweat slowly dries in a salty crust.

He wants to say: damn you, damn you, damn you all.

He wants to say: forgive me, forgive me, forgive me.

He wants to say: I wish I'd died.

He wants to say: I am so grateful I lived.

He wants to say: it was nothing like I imagined, and I am not a hero. Not a hero. Not a hero. Not a hero.

He wants to say ...

... well, he barely knows what he wants to say. He barely knows anything any more; from so many years of not saying anything, the words in his heart have tumbled together into a terrible sorry mess, a tempest of unspoken things so jumbled that now he cannot tell the difference between sea and sky.

But then he does say one thing, which is important and true, and that is, times being what they are, unusual. He looks Kenamon in the eye and says simply: "Thank you."

Kenamon nods, opens his mouth to say *it was nothing*, or perhaps *you did your best*, or maybe even *I am proud of you*, but he doesn't get his chance, for having said the true thing, the vulnerable thing, the thing that he dare not say to anyone else out loud, Telemachus rises and walks away, lest he break apart and let the lightning of his soul out upon a man who might, impossibly, be his friend.

In the night, in the secret place away from the eyes of men, Clytemnestra fumes.

"What do you mean, another delay? Why another delay?"

Semele has grown used to Clytemnestra's tempers. She has in fact grown so used to them that she barely even notices another is happening, as the Mycenaean queen prowls and paces and throws her arms into the air.

Penelope stands in the moonlit doorway, Eos at her back, both cloaked and veiled against the watchful night.

"Orestes is back," sighs Penelope. "Between his ships and Pylades on the docks, we will have to find another opportunity to get you out."

"Orestes? He's back? How is he?"

Penelope takes a moment to process the words, uncertain what to make of the sudden fluttering in Clytemnestra's voice, the breathy eagerness of her speech. "He's . . . fine. As fine as he ever is."

"He wasn't hurt on his voyage? There weren't any storms?"

"He's currently in the palace, as silent and moping as ever."

"Not moping – he doesn't mope! He is heartbroken, of course, but he's brave. He's a very brave boy."

Clytemnestra has seen her son on eleven occasions since he was sent away to Athens. Eight of those times he came to visit her, and dutifully stood before her and recited all that he had learnt, and demonstrated some of the skills he had been taught. Twice she went to visit him, and proudly stood behind the window watching him train in the arts of war. Once he charged down the path towards the lodge where she and Aegisthus were hiding, a band of men at his back, and threw the spear that killed her lover, driving his sword through Aegisthus's spine just to be sure of the thing before turning his attention to his mother. But she was on the horse Aegisthus had bade her ride, galloping away into the night, the beast's head turned forward, hers turned back to witness the manliness of her warrior son.

She has not, therefore, had to explain to her son any of the following matters, such as: what it means for a boy's voice and testes to drop, why he has grown hair in unexpected places, how to talk to girls, how to repair a tear in a tunic, how to cook, how to adjudicate in matters of law where the precedent is unclear, and what his father was like. Others covered some of these thorny matters, although in the case of the last one, she might be surprised to hear that Orestes actually has a fairly good sense of what Agamemnon was like as both a man and a king.

She has not had to listen to him, aged thirteen, pout and stamp his feet and proclaim that everything in the world is just so unfair, the most unfair it could possibly be, and no one understands him.

She has not had to put up him with him refusing to eat foods he does not like, nor calling her stupid and old, nor refusing to do his work and insulting his teachers. Orestes, whenever he saw his mother, was on his very best behaviour, and so gave the very best of all impressions, as indeed did she. It was Elektra who lived close to Clytemnestra in the years in which she ruled, and say what you will for Elektra, she has a sulk that even I admire.

Penelope, of course, has seen all of this and more in her own son, and it is perhaps nearness to one's kin that leaves the Ithacan so confused when Clytemnestra demands to know of the child who would kill her: "Has he been eating well? And regularly scrubbing his teeth with char – it's so important to look after your teeth."

"I have no idea as to his dentistry," Penelope replies. "But I have seen Elektra putting the food in his mouth when he refuses to eat, which, while a little . . . unusual, does mean he is not yet wasting away."

Clytemnestra nods, once, sharp. "At least that girl is good for something. And his friends? Does he keep good company?"

"Amongst his men, he has Iason and Pylades, both of whom seem . . . very loyal."

"Pylades is a good man, he'll make sure my son is all right. Does he speak of me much?"

"He speaks of almost nothing else."

Clytemnestra clasps her hands, for lo, her son speaks of her! He is not much of a conversationalist, but at least she is on his mind. Then, a more serious thought: "If Orestes is back, does Elektra search the island for me?"

"Officially, no. Officially they accept that you have fled."

"Officially is for fools who lack imagination."

"Unofficially," concedes Penelope, "Pylades and his men

307

ride across Ithaca every day on 'hunting parties'. They are bringing back meat as a 'gift' to my table to thank me for my hospitality. In the process of doing so, they are visiting every house, every nook and every forest lodge on the island. Iason has taken men to Kephalonia too, where they go 'fishing' in every cove, cave and harbour. They have not, as far as I know, caught any fish."

"They know I'm here."

"Elektra suspects, of that I'm certain."

"How? You're supposed to be clever, little duck. Aren't you clever enough?"

"Perhaps," murmurs Penelope, "Rumours of my cleverness have done me a bad turn. Perhaps your daughter thinks I'm clever too."

"Well then, I can't stay here," blurts Clytemnestra, with an imperious sweep of her hand around the little room. "You'll have to move me somewhere safer."

"You are safe enough with Semele for now. My women watch the road; if there is any sign of trouble you will be moved."

"Why can't I go to back to the temple? It was even more pathetic than this lodging, but at least I was safe in sanctuary!"

"Elektra has offered reward to certain women of the island to keep watch on the temples. Naturally they obeyed, rather than be seen as traitors."

Clytemnestra's smile is the slow grin of the crocodile. "But they told you. Of course. I wonder what my son would say if he suspected what the widows of Ithaca really do in the dark."

"Based on his conversation thus far, very little," Penelope retorts. "He seems quite the dolt."

Clytemnestra lunges, fingernails first. Semele sticks a foot out, casual as anything, tripping the queen as she passes by. Penelope recoils as Clytemnestra stumbles, then lets her fall. Clytemnestra hits the floor with her left hand first, then flops breathless, scratching the impudent earth, a hiss like the wounded adder passing from her lips.

Penelope nods to Semele in thanks. "You want for anything, my friend?" Semele shrugs. "Then I will take my leave. Thank you, as always, for your hospitality."

She turns, leaving Clytemnestra snarling on the floor.

CHAPTER 42

>>>

T he moon is shrouded dark when all Hades breaks loose.
It began with a whisper.

Leaneira breathed her secret in Andraemon's ear. "I'll prove it to you," she gasped, as he curled his fingers into her skin. "I'll prove that I love you. Listen. Listen."

Andraemon heard the truth of it and nibbled her neck and hissed, "If you're lying . . . "

"I'm not lying. I love you. I choose you."

They rocked together in darkness, and the next night he watched when she bade her, and then watched again, and on the third night was sure of the truth of it and held her tight and breathed: "When I am king, you will be raised up above all other women, and Penelope will serve *you*."

She turned her face from his, so he could not see the look in her eye as he said it.

Andraemon then whispered in the ear of Eurymachus. Better, he felt, that this thing come from another of the suitors; better that he not play his hand too far.

Eurymachus has never been able to keep a secret in his life, so he blurted it into the ear of Antinous, saying he had it from Melantho, who loved him, because of what a great lover he was.

Antinous ignored the latter part of that sentiment, but whispered the rest to his father, and Eupheithes exploded in fury and demanded that Antinous watch a little longer to confirm the claim, and when Antinous did, Eupheithes roared: "THAT HARPY LITTLE BITCH!" so loud that the neighbours poked their heads through half-open doors and asked his slaves what all the fuss was about.

Finally, when the moon is hiding her face, Eupheithes and Antinous march into the evening hall where the feast is unfolding and roar: "WHERE IS THIS QUEEN?!"

The room falls silent. Telemachus, Orestes and Elektra sit furthest from the door, and the latter freezes as if the queen might be the one that interests her, the only one that counts – before remembering with a little sigh that another queen sits behind her, Penelope, weaving patiently on her loom as the suitors dine.

"WHERE IS THIS SO-CALLED QUEEN OF ITHACA?!" Eupheithes adds, just to clear up any confusion, and with that the last of the suitors falls silent. Amphinomous stirs uneasily; Kenamon stiff and grey, any mirth he may have felt upon coming to Ithaca lost now in nights of noisy isolation, ashes and blood.

Eyes turn to Penelope, and she, at last, stands, hands folded in front of her, small and, it seems, meek, until she speaks. Then her voice is a lash, spinning out across the room. "How dare you disturb the sacred bounds of this feast?"

Eos scurries away from the shadows of Penelope's back, into the corridors of the palace, fetches more maids, loyal men, muster muster, they will all stand with ears pressed to doors, where is Ourania, prepare the boat, find Priene – go!

Eupheithes does not notice the maid leave. No one ever does. Leaneira pushes herself back into a corner, hands clasping a jug of wine. Autonoe eyes the room from the kitchen doors, a chopping knife tucked discreetly behind her back. She knows that if a fight comes, the maids will die – but she will make them bleed for it.

The old man strides through the hall towards Penelope, until he stands a few paces from her, ignoring the children of Agamemnon, the son of Odysseus. The hot fires of anger now are a simmering char in his heart; he will use it, and not be used by it, this wily man of Ithaca. "Liar," he spits at her feet. "Traitor. You dare invoke the laws of hospitality when *you* break them every day and every night, when *you* sully your husband's name, and the honour of his throne?"

The room stirs, eyes dancing from one man to another. They are unarmed, but oh, oh, they think, perhaps now it'll be out, perhaps now we'll learn that she has slept with *this* suitor or maybe *that*, that she has already chosen a man who would be king, and then we'll be for it, then we'll have a ruckus on our hands. A few of the wiser men start eyeing up their surroundings, looking for tools they can improvise into weapons, furniture they can throw. A few of the wisest eye up the door. Best to get out and come back later with spears; the survivors can tell the poets what to sing, after all.

"You accuse me of treachery?" snarls Penelope. "You come into my home and sully my honour in front of my guests? By all the gods, if I were a man I would strike you down, whoever you were. It is only my womanly modesty that restrains me."

Elektra approves of this speech. Telemachus is a little shocked by it. Orestes, if he hears it at all, shows no sign on that face of his. But Penelope, for all that there is fire in her voice, speaks careful and slow. She too has prepared her words – not necessarily for this moment, since she does not fully know what this moment is, but for a thousand moments like it, a thousand twists of the thread upon which her life might hang, plans within plans, waiting for disaster.

Eupheithes grins. It is the grin that disturbs her the most. Then he spreads his arms and turns slowly to the suitors, to the hall, taking everything in. "You all know me," he proclaims. "And you all know my son, the most honourable, most honest man amongst you."

Eurymachus nearly honks his disagreement, but is kicked beneath the table by Amphinomous before he can let his contempt sound.

"Every man here wants the same thing – for there to be a king in Ithaca. For Ithaca to be strong again, for all Greece to know our might. For a worthy man to sit upon the throne that she . . . " a finger stabbed towards Penelope's face, though he does not deign to turn now to look on her, "claims to protect. To serve. Good people of Ithaca" – Eupheithes does not consider it likely that men from beyond Ithaca can be good – "you are deceived. You are betrayed. This Spartan harlot, this shrew . . . "

Telemachus rises. He too is unarmed, and not quite intelligent enough to look for an improvised weapon, but he'll learn. Kenamon shakes his head a little at the boy, sit down, sit down, but if Telemachus sees the Egyptian, he does not acknowledge it. "Eupheithes, were my father here he would feed you to the dogs!"

"But he isn't here, is he?" snarls Eupheithes, warming to his theme, chest pumping to meet the action of Telemachus's swelling bosom. "Not alive nor dead, merely missing! But we all know – poor boy, you must know it too – we all know that Odysseus *is* dead. Dead and gone, and *she* . . . " a stab of finger towards Penelope again, "strings us along! Weaves us, you might say, into some pattern, weaves us like a shroud no less, and while we're here, Penelope, how is that fine shroud that you weave for good King Laertes?"

She does not speak, nor move, but like the thin branch of the silver birch when the storm sweeps through, seems to shudder from root to top, fingers closing once, then releasing. That she does not immediately speak is her first mistake, for when she finally snaps: "What nonsense is this? You talk of treason and shrouds, insult my name, my husband's ..." the room has already seen the flicker of doubt within her. Amphinomous rises, and because Amphinomous does, so does Eurymachus. A few others follow, and then there is a general motion up, because if one man is going to blink in this hall, everyone else must blink too or be struck blind.

Eupheithes beams like the sun, blasting away the last fog of night. "What was it you said? Let me weave a funeral shroud for good Laertes, and when it's done, I will choose a husband? A fair condition. The loyal and thoughtful act of a dedicated daughter-in-law. But how long it has taken! How slow the work, how agonising the labour. Each knot takes a day, and yet here you sit with your precious loom, and for what?"

He takes a step towards her, and instinctively she steps back. Telemachus plants himself between the two, and is for a moment a soldier, a man almost, bigger and stronger than Eupheithes. Antinous should perhaps take this moment to interpose too, to measure up man to man, but it doesn't occur to him. He is either very smart or remarkably dense, that one.

Again Eupheithes spreads his arms to the room, as though to say look, look – the mother is struck dumb, the son postures as if he would be king! What liars and tyrants would this family of Odysseus be. Then, in a lower voice: "Have we not all wondered why it goes so slow? Have we not all wondered what could take this woman so long?"

They have. It is written on their faces, and those who have not wondered before are doing some hasty work to catch up and do the wondering now. Kenamon watches Telemachus, Antinous, calculating perhaps the fastest way to strike, the easiest target to disable, the quickest way to escape. I look for Athena, but do not sense her presence, wonder whether to call her name, to cry

314

out for her wisdom. I'm not sure I could stomach it. Perhaps time to bring out those coincidental cobras again, or a strategic infestation of spiders? Yet even as I wonder what intervention might be most effective without arousing too great a suspicion, my eyes fall on Elektra's and for a moment I think she sees me.

She sees me.

The daughter of Clytemnestra stares right at me, and though I am shrouded in that place that the mortal mind cannot perceive, lest it burn at the very sight of me, she looks and I would swear upon my own divinity that she sees *me*. And in her eye there is the crimson touch of the Furies, the spark of a divinity, a profanity, that is older than even the Titans themselves. She will be a queen, that one – how strange that it took me this long to understand it, to see it in her eyes! But in that moment she sees me, and I see her, and she will be a queen in Greece, beloved unto me. When the others are dead and gone, when Clytemnestra's body is burnt and Penelope has breathed her last, only Elektra will remain, the last woman to carry my fire. But not yet – not yet.

Eupheithes levels his arm at Penelope, draws back his smile like the archer preparing his bow, and proclaims: "It has been brought to me that every night this lying queen retires to her chambers, she does not pray, she does not sleep. Rather she takes her needle and, by the thin light of the lamp, unpicks the work we have seen her do by day. For every ten lines we see her weave by day, at night she unpicks nine."

The reaction to this is not as immediate or as profound as Eupheithes might have hoped. Nearly all the men in the hall for whom this was news had imagined, to one degree or another, terrible sexual acts or vile deeds up to and including incest, for why not? The deeds of Clytemnestra had made fashionable the exploits of dread queens – dread *sexual* queens, no less, queens of a dread sexuality that every man absolutely abhorred and would be entirely fascinated to meet – so the revelation of a bit of loom-liberty does not at once sit easy upon them. Here at least Antinous is a little more helpful, for seeing the room not immediately erupt into condemnation, he roars: "Liar! Traitor queen!" and a few of his friends, and a few more who sense which way the wind is blowing, join in, until at last, with the independent thought of a cucumber, the whole room is shouting, roaring, only Kenamon and Amphinomous standing a little awkward aside, quiet.

In the corridors behind closed doors, the maids are running, mustering Penelope's few loyal men, arm yourself, arm, a rider is already on her horse and galloping towards the temple of Artemis, another running down to Ourania's house. The women in the forest may not make it to the palace in time to do anything, but at least they can avenge the slaughter.

"You have no proof – you have no proof!" Penelope hollers, and the crowd roars, for that is not a denial. "Bring me proof, show me your evidence . . . " she tries again, and then is silenced, for Telemachus is turning to stare at her too, and in his eyes is understanding, fury, betrayal. He stands nearest to her of all in that room, and as she tries to mumble something, some semblance of an excuse, an apology, an explanation, he sees the truth of it in her eyes, sees the lies crumbling away. Oh Athena, if you are not already here, you should behold this, you should see what happens when a boy who would be a man realises he has been a boy all along.

"A liar! A tricksy child of the river and the sea, a temptress who never says yes and never says no, a would-be *whore* . . . " roars Eupheithes, and perhaps what the hall does not know, cannot see, are the men he has waiting outside, ready to step in and stamp down on any who disagree with his point of view. Tonight will be a night for reckoning, tonight will be the kind of night from which kings are made. "A whore of Ithaca!" he enthuses, raising his hands as if the gods might applaud his rather crude theatrics. I prepare an infection of intestinal worms for him, a dose of gout, pestilence unlike any he has ever dreamt of . . .

And Elektra rises.

Somehow that mere act is enough to almost knock Eupheithes back, as if her motion had sent a shockwave stronger than the hurricane through the room. This little woman, this child in ash, takes one step forward, and that too is enough to push Eupheithes away, send him staggering a few paces from this royal cluster. Glorious lady, hateful daughter, will-be queen! I salute you, and all that you will become. Her brother does not move, but watches his sister as if he has only just seen her for the very first time, is curious to know what her voice sounds like when propelled into the air.

"Men of Ithaca," she proclaims, and she says "men" as her mother sometimes did, as though to proclaim "you who call yourself male, behold how unmanly this title suits you". "Men of Ithaca. People of Odysseus. How ashamed your king would be of you now."

There is a sound through the hall that may best be described as much shuffling of sandal.

"When my father went to war, he sent ambassadors to summon the western isles to his side – not because they were many, or rich in gold and arms, but because no man stood stronger before the storm than the men of Ithaca. Not for them the lute or the pleasures of greed or wine, but solid brotherhood and honest guile. How far you have fallen. How swollen and fat you have become."

Penelope is older and a little taller than Elektra, and yet now she is but the kitten curling behind its mother as Elektra steps further into the hall. Men part around her, as once they did for Clytemnestra, while Orestes sits behind, one leg folded over the other, silent as a throne.

"You have been indulged too long. Grown fat on your queen's meat. You have forgotten what honour means. You are the drunken Trojans come to my uncle's feast, who think it perhaps funny to steal another man's wife, to seduce and bawd your way into a royal woman's bed. And like the Trojans, all of Greece will rise up and destroy you for your impudence. This is not a threat. This is what Troy shows us. This is what my father, king of the Greeks, taught me. This is what my brother knows."

Eyes dance to Orestes, and his face is cold as winter dusk, eyes seeming to see nothing, everything, nothing at all.

Now Elektra turns on Eupheithes. "You. Old man. Do you have evidence?"

"I have the evidence of my eyes – we all have the evidence of our eyes!" An attempt to muster, to rally people in another cry, a shout of defiance, but no man meets Elektra's gaze who is not at once silenced.

"The eyes of drunkards and fools. Would-be petty princes who would stab their neighbour in the back for a taste of power. The little, little power of these western islands – it must seem so big to you. I take it then you have no evidence. No witness willing to stand in proof and say yes, yes, I saw Penelope unpick the shroud, I saw her do it, with my eyes. No one?"

There is one, cowering in the corner, who could speak if called – but what is the voice of a slave against the testament of a queen?

Eupheithes flushes crimson, but Antinous has backed away from his father's side. Eurymachus is suddenly small, anonymous, a funny little fellow profoundly interested in his wine rather than these unfolding events. Andraemon is nowhere to be seen.

The daughter of Agamemnon pushes air through her teeth as if she would spit, then rounds on the rest of the room. "And what if she did unpick the work?" she barks. "You would marry a queen whose devotion to her husband is any less? You would take a whore who opens her legs to any man who comes, not a wife who fights with her last breath to honour her departed lord? You disgrace the word marriage. You disgrace the idea of husband. In Hera's name" – I shudder with strange delight and curious disgust to hear myself invoked upon her lips – "if my brother were not so kind and temperate, so mild-mannered and just in all his dealings, I think he would have set the fleets of Mycenae against you all, taken these little islands under his protection to end this strife – strife that *you* have created! Strife of which *you* are the fathers, not some . . . some woman! Seeing this – seeing you now – I can only pray that his mercy lasts. That his love for our cousin, noble Penelope, and her many great imprecations to him to show charity to the gluttonous, foul peoples of her island, outlast the sorry welcome you suitors have given him."

All silent. All dumb. Elektra holds the room between her finger and thumb. If she but squeezes, they will be squished. I drift a little closer to her, heart swelling with admiration, bend to whisper in her ear; but she turns away from me and squares off at once to Antinous, son of quaking Eupheithes, who visibly flinches before her gaze. "Sir," she says. "You are a guest here, as well as your father's son. I bid you – sit down."

Antinous looks desperately at his father's back, but receives no guidance from it. The old man shakes from crown to toe, but cannot speak, seems to be half choked with the pestilences I have not yet visited upon him. Antinous looks again at Elektra, and then slowly, fumbling for a place, sits.

Amphinomous follows, then Eurymachus and the rest. Soon only Elektra and Eupheithes stand. She does not bother to turn to him; does not bid him stay, nor go, nor sit, but merely returns to her place of honour beside her brother, and lowers herself into her chair like Agamemnon into Priam's throne.

A little while longer, Eupheithes shakes.

Men stare.

Then men start to murmur.

They talk amongst themselves, whisper as if there were nothing to see here at all, nothing to discuss.

Someone strikes the sound of music.

Leaneira detaches herself from the wall to pour a cup of wine.

Antinous does not look at his father.

Telemachus does not look at his mother.

Then Eupheithes turns and storms away.

In the moments that follow, Telemachus lingers, quivering too. He turns to Elektra, to try and find something to say, and thinks that she is perhaps the ugliest woman he has ever seen, and wonders what her tongue would taste like against his own, and feels nauseous and doesn't know how to speak. So instead he turns to his cousin Orestes, and blurts: "Are you ..." and cannot find the words. Orestes' head turns slow, so slow, as if he were being spun by some other force than nature, and slack and patient the young Mycenaean waits. Telemachus shakes his head, tries to find an apology, cannot grasp it, tries again.

Elektra, who gazes down at the hall as if surveying her father's funeral feast, says: "My brother and I are tired. We will retire. Thank you, as always, for your hospitality."

There is a shudder through the room as she rises, a lapse in conversation. It does not resume until she has left.

After a little while, Penelope follows behind, and Telemachus last of all.

In the settled night, when the suitors are snoring drunken in their sodden heaps, the maids come and clear away the loom, and it will neither be seen nor spoken of again.

CHAPTER 43

᚛᚛᚛᚛᚛᚛᚛᚛᚛᚛᚛᚛᚛᚛᚛᚛᚛᚛᚛᚛᚛᚛᚛᚛᚛᚛᚛᚛᚛᚛᚛᚛᚛᚛

In the morning dark, that dull place between midnight and dawn when all things grow honest and cruel, Penelope comes to Elektra's door.

Again, she waits, shuddering, shivering from top to toe.

Again, at last, the maids let her in, and as they do so it seems that something transforms in the Ithacan queen, her heart stopped, her breath frozen; she will not shake before their eyes.

Elektra sits in her usual spot by the window, and Orestes sleeps in Elektra's bed. Penelope stops, startled at this sight, but Elektra presses a finger to her lips and whispers: "He does not sleep well some nights. He has dreams. I let him come in here sometimes, and stroke his head, and sing him to sleep. He will not wake now for a little while. Let us go outside and talk."

Elektra has washed away the ashes from her face, and combed her hair. Her voice is soft, almost kind, as she speaks of her brother in this sacred hour, and for a moment she is just a woman, a sister, far from home.

Penelope nods once, and together they walk by the little light of Autonoe's lamp, down to the cool stream where Leaneira sometimes bathes her feet away from the eyes of men. Here Penelope takes the lamp from Autonoe, bids her stand a little further off, sets it down upon a mossy stone and eases herself into a half-crouch on the edge of the water, as if she might wash the taste of the day from her mouth. Elektra sits beside her, legs out straight, ankles bare and tiny toes wiggling in the cool night, back arched and head turned towards the sky. For a while she closes her eyes, and listens to the faint sound of the sea as it beats against the shore below, and the song of the insects and the rush of water over stone.

Penelope makes to speak, but before she can, Elektra cuts in, eyes still closed, arms straight by her sides. "Tell me about your mother," she says.

Penelope is surprised by the question, and should not be. "My ... mother was kind. Strict, but only in matters that she felt were important for a child to thrive. She believed that every woman of Sparta must be as strong as a man, stronger perhaps. How could there be strong men if the women were not able to bear healthy children, nor raise those children to be clever, learned, good with a sword and faithful to their king? These things, she believed, came from the mothers. Therefore a mother must also be clever, learned and faithful."

"And good with a sword?"

"Good enough to recognise when someone was bad with a sword, at least."

"I heard your mother was a naiad," Elektra muses. "A daughter of the river and the stream."

Penelope stiffens, but has spent enough time with her divine bastardy to know how to catch her breath before it passes sharply between her lips. "Perhaps she was," she replies at last to the shadow of Elektra's eyes. "But Polycaste raised me though I was not from her womb, and picked me up when I fell and cut my knee, and told me what to do when as a girl I started to bleed. She is my mother."

"And your father?"

"He was ... not very good around children. But he knew it was his duty to love, and he did his best to fulfil it."

Elektra half turns her head, amazement breaking across her features. "He ... had a duty to love?"

"As he saw it, yes."

"Why?"

"Because he was our father."

"But he was a king."

"Yes. He attempted, in his way, to be both. He was only human, after all."

Elektra gapes, as if she has never heard such a thing. A king who is a father? A father who is a man? Perhaps in the rarest form one might be two of the three – a king who spends time fathering his heir, perhaps, or a father who is sometimes frail in his failings. But to be all three? It seems to her an impossible lunacy, and she nearly barks in merriment at the notion, before shaking her head and returning to her contemplation of the sky. "I was raised by nursemaids," she says at last. "My mother had a kingdom to run, and my father had a war to win. It was needful that I be raised to be a princess, suitable for marriage to a man whose lands might be incorporated into my father's own. Not too great a man – my father needed it always to be known that anyone who married his children did so at his indulgence. The kind of man who would bow and grovel and scrape at my father's throne and say how lucky he was to have me and know that if he dishonoured me I could cut his throat and no one would question it. A weak kind of man. That was my destiny."

"And now?"

"Now? Now either my brother takes the throne, or my uncle will take it for himself and I will be sold to some half-cut merchant for a sack of grain and a vat of wine. Someone wealthy but without name, who through the prestige of the match may be able to sit at a fine table and say 'Well, my wife is a queen!'

to all his fishmonger friends. My uncle has enough children of his own, you see, that he need not over-think what he does with me." Again Penelope tries to speak, and again Elektra cuts through her. "I want you to understand this. I want it to be clear. I will not be sold. I will not be some bartered wife. To avoid this, I need my brother to be king in Mycenae. Not just for me – all of Greece needs my brother to be king. There must be a division in power between the sons of Atreus, else Menelaus's strength will grow overwhelming and none will resist him. He will pick up your little islands without a thought, marry you to one of his sons, send Telemachus on some quest from which he will never return, bleed your people dry, without even noticing what he does. Have you seen Helen? Have you seen her since she was dragged back from Troy? I have. Neither of us wants to be a wife of a child of Menelaus."

In a far-off place, Helen stares at her face in a pool of still water, and does not breathe, does not exhale, for fear of disturbing its silvered surface. Yet the less it ripples, the more she cannot hide the truth of the wrinkles just below the almonds of her eyes, and she puts her fist in her mouth and bites so that she will not scream. So it is with the last of our three Grecian queens.

Penelope says at last: "What you did tonight . . . "

Elektra dismisses it, as her mother might. "It was a reckless power play by a foolish old man. If he had thought it through, he would have realised that nothing good could come of it, save tyranny, war and blood. The arrogance of his actions displeased me, that is all."

"Nevertheless, that war and blood would likely have been mine, and that of my child."

"Ah yes, Telemachus. He's a mess, isn't he?"

Of all the many things that people on Ithaca might say to Penelope – including a great many honest friends, bosom-sworn to their queen – this is something that none save perhaps the daughter of Agamemnon dare pronounce, as if she were commenting on a caterpillar. Penelope feels the rage draw into her lips at once, the denial, the guilty fury. Then she exhales, and it is gone with the beating of a butterfly's wing, and in its place, relief, horror, amazement, tinged with tears, and then, strangest of all, laughter. There are no words, but Elektra watches her, curious, as if trying to puzzle out the wet-eyed hysteria of this otherwise icy queen, until at last the laughter passes and the two women sit together by the little stream as if there were nothing between them but this moment, and the darkened moon.

In the forest above the temple, Priene says: "The raiders will come here, into this cove. We must let them land, let them get a little way from their ships. None can survive."

In his house on the edge of town, Eupheithes strikes Antinous across the mouth, as if he were a woman, and his son falls mute to the floor, clutching his bleeding lip.

In his room, Telemachus stares down to the sea, and there is a little whisper in his ear, a fly that will not leave him, that hums in the voice of Athena.

In the bed of Andraemon, Leaneira cries out, and he puts his hand over her mouth lest someone hear her. Only she will know if her cry was ecstasy or agony as he drives into her flesh. "My love, my love, my love," he breathes. "When I am king, when I am king ..."

By the running water beneath the shrouded sky, Elektra says: "I know you understand that Orestes must be king. I also want you to understand that it is not about my mother. I do not despise her, whatever she might think. I do not forgive her. I do not ... feel anything for her, I think. I have spent much time trying to feel something – hatred, rage, disgust – but the more I think about it, the less there is inside of me. I don't care if she lives or dies. I don't care if you help her escape or not. I only care that my brother is king, and for that, my mother has to die."

In the silence that follows, Penelope dips her fingers into the stream. Sometimes she thinks it responds to her touch, twines a little around her skin like the soft embrace of the curious octopus, recognising maybe a little something of her mother's blood – of the mother who birthed and left her – in her human flesh.

"There was a man," Elektra continues, "called Hyllas."

Penelope is the stream, and if she closes her mind, she thinks perhaps she can flow with it out into the ocean. She often thinks it might be nice to be an ocean. She might find her husband's body at the bottom of it, and she'll wrap it tight and bring it to the surface, what little remains, and say look, look, here it is. It is done. You lot get on with things, and I'll just go back to being the endless wave beating upon your bloody shores.

But now Elektra is speaking, and for all her dreams, Penelope cannot escape. "This Hyllas was a smuggler in the western isles – you may know him? It was he who helped my mother escape after Aegisthus died. He took her to Ithaca, but while here, she made some mistake, some error of judgement, that revealed her identity to him. She gave him two rings – one to get her to Ithaca, one to carry her beyond. When he realised who his passenger was, he sent his slave with one of the rings to a certain agent of Mycenae who resides on Zakynthos, as proof of who he carried. By then Orestes and myself were already closing on our mother's trail, so it was not difficult when we received word to divert our course to Ithaca."

Penelope nods at nothing much, and hears again a trick on her cousin's tongue, a lilt of language she should perhaps have paid more attention to.

You gave him jewellery, gold, stamped with the seal of Agamemnon. A ring – a unique piece.

You found them?

Not one ring, but two.

"By the time we reached Ithaca, this Hyllas was dead.

Probably by my mother's hand. But if he was dead, she could not have fled the island. When then the other of my mother's rings appeared from Hyrie, I was honestly shocked – as you can imagine. Genuinely angry, surprised at her cunning. Orestes of course had to follow the trail – too many people knew that was where the road led, and if there was any danger at all that he was not going to catch her, he had at least to have been *seen* to have fought the gods themselves in his efforts to succeed. He could not sit and wait for her to show her face on Ithaca again – patience is not the quality of a hero. But I could. For a few days perhaps I even believed your ruse, but then I thought: Penelope, wife of Odysseus. The cleverest man in Greece – that's what my father said. And how well Odysseus chose his wife. My mother's cousin. She may have been cruel to you when you were young – she was a daughter of Zeus. But she always said you were clever. Clever Penelope-duck. Clever little duck. Tell me – is it hard to be a queen in this place?"

"Very," Penelope agrees, as the water dances around her fingertips.

"Very hard, yes. I would like to be a queen one day, but not like my mother was. She let everyone see that she was a queen. She liked it when people bowed, enjoyed watching great men having their spirits torn down. How she could destroy a man, when she put her mind to it! Vengeance for all those years of a thousand petty hurts, she unleashed her fury and it was . . . I suppose . . . magnificent. She didn't even bother to hide Aegisthus, she grew so bold. She and he would . . . Sometimes he pinched my cheeks. He promised he would love me. I don't know what those words meant when he said them. I don't know. I will not be a queen like that. When I undo a man, he will not know to curse my name on his way to Hades."

Penelope purses her lips, but says nothing. Neither she nor I are convinced that Elektra will quite achieve this ambition, though perhaps – perhaps – in time, even I will learn to live with her aspirations, to accept that the last queens of Greece will be queen only in secret, their fires bright, blazing, and hidden behind their downcast eyes. It hurts, it hurts, it hurts, I did not know my heart had any blood left to bleed, my queens, my daughters, my soul. Be with me, I cry, be with me, be my light, my vengeance, my prayer, my queens!

They do not hear me. I learnt a long time ago to keep my voice to a whisper.

"I admire you, cousin, I really do," muses Elektra. "You have played a very difficult game. Your handling of the suitors is a point of education I shall be sure to take with me, even the business with the loom. I feel I have learnt a great deal observing you. But enough. We are out of time. As of tonight, your security depends no longer on your wits, but on my mercy. Only the goodwill of my brother will keep your little kingdom from descending into chaos, your son from being slaughtered by these hungry men. If we withdraw it – if we make it known that Ithaca no longer stands within Mycenae's protection – you will not last another moon. If the suitors don't take you, Menelaus will. I hope that has been made clear tonight."

"Very clear, cousin," Penelope replies, without rancour. "And delivered with a clarity that I must also thank you for."

"It is refreshing, is it not, to speak this way? This is how queens should speak," muses Elektra. "Perhaps this is how my father spoke to your husband, yes?"

It is certainly how Agamemnon might think he spoke to Odysseus. He might even think Odysseus spoke honestly in his reply. That was one of the many, many failings of Agamemnon.

"So." Elektra sits up, then folds down a little over her crooked knees, arms wrapping round her shins. "Everyone has played their games. You sent my brother on a bit of a chase, and I indulged it, let you save face and he serve honour, create a story

328

worthy of the poets, until the time was right for this matter to conclude. That time is now, and there an end to it. Are we agreed?"

Penelope sometimes dreams she is an ocean, and her heart has currents within it that can move sunken cities, that turn in silence and do not feel the great tumult of the storm overhead. "Agreed?" she muses. "I did not hear a negotiation."

"No," Elektra concedes. "No, you didn't. I hope in future years that this does not cloud our relationship. I would very much like us – one day – to be friends."

Elektra has no friends. Her mother grew jealous of real love, whenever it bloomed around her strange, scowling child. Now that her mother is dead, Elektra has sworn to find a friend no matter what, and does not know quite what friendship means, or how to twine it to her heart. *My queens, my queens*, I whisper, *let us keep each other company, bonded in secrecy and shadows, my beautiful queens*. "I . . . I wanted to ask. A thing that . . . You protect your kingdom, but to protect her . . . it does not seem like something a queen should do."

"You want to know why? Why I sent your brother off to Hyrie, risked it all to protect your mother?"

Elektra nods, swallowing hard.

Penelope considers it, trying to tease apart a mess of thoughts, pluck truth from uncertainty. When she does, her words are stones set upon my breaking heart. "When she dies, there will be no more queens in Greece. I know that I . . . but it is not given to me to be *seen* to rule. Helen is . . . and I know that you . . . but if you marry even the wisest, the gentlest man in all the isles, his servants will be men, his councillors will be men, the voices that tell him what it is to be a man will come from men who themselves were told by their fathers and their fathers before them that to be a man is to rule. That to be a man is to be set above, to possess those qualities of mastery that a woman can

329

never have. You will never be a queen, Elektra. Not like your mother was. No matter what you do. We have raised too many sons who will never understand. Clytemnestra is the last of us. She does not deserve to die."

Elektra considers this, frozen as if brushed by some chill wind. Then shakes her head, casting off a thing that she cannot, will not, has no choice but to understand. And that moment is gone, as if these words were never spoken, truth never pronounced in the dark, and my tears are moonlight and frozen dew. "I know it will be hard to be my friend," she blurts. "If I succeed, I will be very powerful. You will need to say nice things to me. I know I can be difficult. I will try. I will learn to try, you see?"

Sometimes, when she was properly grieving for her husband, a young bride stamping her foot and making a big show of her grief, Penelope declared that she didn't have any friends in the world at all, and Anticlea would look at her with a sideways glare as though to say, "So? Your point?" Then she grew a little older, and she stamped her foot a little less, and Ourania would tell her filthy stories of a man she knew who knew a fellow who knew a thief who'd stolen old Nestor's prize jewels from under the pillow where the king sat snoring. And Eos would sing the songs of her childhood, and even old Medon – had he ever not been old? – would sit with her after council and explain some detail of the state that the others didn't think she needed to trouble her little head with. "Pick your fights," he would say. "You only have so many arrows."

These friendships came so slowly upon her, not as the poets proclaim in a flash of fire and the brotherhood of arms, but sneaking into her window with the lightness of Hermes' step until she barely noticed how many friends she had, and how the loss of them would strike her dumb more even than the loss of Ithaca.

Penelope rises, and Elektra follows, and for a moment the

two study each other in the low light of the lamp and the thin dazzle of starlight. Then Penelope says: "Mycenae and Ithaca have always been friends. I do not know if you and I shall be. I do not know who you are, daughter of Clytemnestra. You catch me ... at a challenging stage in my queenship. As I perhaps am seeing you at yours. Friends should find each other in gentler times, when there is a mutual space to learn of each other's hearts without danger or threat to unite them. I do not know when there will next be gentle times, but for what little it's worth ... I hope one day to meet you there."

To both women's surprise, Elektra smiles and bows a little to the Ithacan queen. "I would like that," she says, and so the deal is sealed.

CHAPTER 44

>>>

In the blackened night, I blaze across the surface of the earth, baleful comet, and beneath me the seas rock and Poseidon is wise enough to make no remark, and above me the heavens crack and my husband tuts and says "one of her moods again", and on Ithaca Clytemnestra sleeps, she sleeps, she sleeps, my truest queen, my beautiful one, my lady of the blade, my love. Three daughters of Sparta became three queens in Greece, and I love them, power in their voices and fire in their eyes, even Penelope, even the one who smiles and says she does it for her husband, I love her, I love her. But no one ever said the gods did not have favourites, and it is Clytemnestra I love best, my queen above all, the one who would be free.

I rend apart the clouds, split the blackened rock, blast the leaves from the bending forest trees, because for all that I love Clytemnestra above them all, I am still the queen of queens, and there are certain things a queen must do.

Athena watches from the shore.

Artemis prowls in the forest.

And in the belly of the earth, the Furies are stirring.

They snuffle at the little crack of air that runs between

332

heaven and the guts of this world, catching perhaps a sniff of damnation, murder, chaos, blood. Even us gods, who bend the sky and rend the sea, turn away when we hear their wings unfurl.

Beware that child who would spill his mother's blood. Though the gods themselves may turn away, the Furies will not.

Athena whispers in Telemachus's ear at night, and by day he prowls the docks, looking at the ships with sails furled and oars stowed.

Artemis steps from the darkness, curiosity overwhelming apathy, and as Teodora raises her bow again, the huntress catches her by the hand, steadies the shot, whispers to the women of the woods: the greatest hunter kills with a single arrow. Her eyes glisten scarlet in the reflected fires that line the grove where the women train, and where she walks, the earth churns.

The loom upon which Laertes' shroud was woven sits dusty and ignored in some corner workshop. Someone else can finish the job that Penelope began, when the time is right. They'll do it faster and better anyway, and no one need ever know.

Laertes paces around the ashes of his farm. "Big walls!" he exclaims. "Big walls with sharp things all around the top!"

And in the quiet places of the palace where only the women go, Penelope sits in silence before Leaneira. The maid stands. They are both more than capable of an hour of quiet, an hour of furious nothing. Then finally Penelope says: "Well. It is done. Indeed yes. It is done."

Leaneira is the mountain, who does not change by the brush of the sea.

"The suitors say it was Melantho who told them of the loom. She has been instructed to say nothing on this matter. You will stay in the house of Ourania until this is done," adds the queen. "Then you will be sent for."

Leaneira is the great gulf beneath the ocean, where fire and darkness meet.

She gives a single sharp nod, and walks away.

And in the darkness, I burn my grief across the stars and blot out the moon, which does not cease in her turning.

CHAPTER 45

>>>

In the morning, Kenamon sits upon the hill where sometimes he sat with Telemachus, but Telemachus does not come.

Instead, Penelope climbs, slow and steady, her veil beating in the high wind. Kenamon rises as she approaches. Eos waits below, studying white flowers flecked with dazzling purple, as if she might educate herself in the secret witchery of herbs.

"My lady, I did not . . ." Kenamon blurts as soon as Penelope is within the sound of his voice.

"Don't be ridiculous," she tuts. "My maids have seen you come up here every morning for weeks. Ever since you met my son here, yes?"

The Egyptian flushes a little, but at her gesture sits back down upon the hard, stubbled earth. "You . . . know about the slight education I have been giving him? You do not disapprove, I hope?"

"Disapprove? Why should I? From what I hear, you have saved his life. Perhaps twice."

"I didn't think that . . ."

She waves away the sentence before he can finish it. "I cannot say anything to you in the palace, or show you gratitude. You understand this."

"Of course. Favouritism only makes me a target."

"You should be lucky if it were favouritism," she chides. "This is merely . . . a mother's courtesy. A mother's thanks. Thank you."

"It was my pleasure to teach your son."

"But you don't teach him any more."

"No. He has been . . . distant since the night of the attack. More so since that unfortunate business with the loom. Strange customs you have – strange indeed."

"Has he said anything to you? Anything at all?"

"Has he not spoken to you?"

"No. He tells me nothing. I had thought perhaps . . . given that he trained with you . . . he might see you as being more . . ." Her voice trails off, plucked away by the wind.

Kenamon shakes his head. "No. I had hoped perhaps too. But no."

"I am very, very frightened for him," she says simply, staring down to the sea.

"He is . . . brave. And he can be clever."

"I know. And he is also still a child."

"He is growing up. Right now, before you. He is growing up."

Penelope turns to Kenamon, and manages to smile, and the veil hides the tears in her eyes. "Will you take my advice? Not as . . . as a queen. As someone who owes you a debt. As a mother whose son is . . . Will you take my advice? Leave Ithaca. Save your life."

So saying, she stands, and he watches her climb down the hill towards the palace.

In the dark, Penelope visits Clytemnestra, and sits with her by the fire, and for a while both women are silent. Finally Penelope says: "There is a ship. It leaves in a few days' time from Same."

"Where for?"

"Phaeacia."

Clytemnestra's face curls in displeasure. "How boring. Have you met Alcinous and that wife of his? Dull dull dull."

"It will only be temporary. Another vessel will carry you south from there."

Clytemnestra puffs her cheeks. "Fine. Tedious. But fine."

And again they sit in silence.

What does Clytemnestra hear in that quiet?

Does she hear the thundering of Penelope's heart? The cry of Aegisthus as he died? The last gurgle of Agamemnon beneath her blade? The distant beating of the Furies' wings as they rouse from their slumber? So much to do, so much blood and damnation upon which they might feast.

The sound of a goddess gently weeping at the end that has to come?

Just this once, I do not intrude upon Clytemnestra's thoughts. They are a thing uniquely hers, precious and sacred, for this night alone.

A few hours before dawn, the end comes.

The last dawn, my love, dress up well. Semele is a terrible hostess, a crude farmer woman, but Eos comes, with a comb and some fresh honey and wax. The styles she knows are old-fashioned nonsense, but what more can you expect from this backwards island of piddling country folk? It is good to have another woman's fingers arrange your gown; it is most pleasing when her fingers accidentally brush the back of your neck, exposed now to the coolness of night.

Clytemnestra, my beautiful queen, stand tall, stand straight. There is very little in the way of make-up in Ithaca; no sticks of finely sharpened charcoal coated in wax to line your eyes, no pastes of white lead to coax a little pallor into your skin. But you smell of oil and the thick pollen of the fat yellow flowers the bees imbibe when they make their nectar, and when you face the door, you are a queen. In the flash of your eye and the set of your mouth, in the steadiness of your step and the straightening of your back, you are a queen. My queen. I had never thought I would love one of Zeus's bastards so much as I love you, glorious Clytemnestra.

I walk with you to the little circle of women who await: Teodora armed with bow and blade, Autonoe who helps you mount a meagre waiting bay – and how much less meagre you make it seem with you upon its back. Anaitis too has come from the forest, but you barely recognise her, the priestess who gave you sanctuary. She is of little note to royalty such as yourself. Ourania, and one of her men – it is quite the send-off they are giving you, a noble escort to the sea.

I ride beside you, and breathe a little of myself into your blood, taking away doubt and fear. The moon is waxing, a thin sliver of light, and beneath its subtle illumination I give you the gift of memory. As you travel towards the sea, I return you again to your first entry to Mycenae, to the beating of drums and the blowing of horns, to the people lining the streets to cry out where, where – there! There she is, the daughter of Zeus! There she is, the great queen, a child of Olympus, the most magnificent, praise her name!

And as you turn down an empty path away from the town below, I give you again the bowing of Agamemnon's men as they fell before your might and your wisdom, begged your indulgence, grovelled for their sins. You did not punish them for the joy of punishment; you were not a tyrant, you were not cruel. You took away the illusions that they had wrapped themselves in, showed them that their strength was arrogance, their intellect was foolery. You were the queen of honest revelation and levelheaded merit, and the great men of Mycenae loathed you for it, loathed you for striking down their pretensions, and I loved you, I love you, I love you.

Lights are burning on a beach below; a cluster of shadows around a little boat, the slim vessel that will carry you to Kephalonia. You think you see something familiar in the shape of a man who stands in the flickering half-light of a torch, but I turn your head to the skies, where your brothers shine for ever in their immortality, sprinkled across the stars. Perhaps, you think, when you die, your soul will be cut out of your body and thrown up to heaven like a scattering of milk, a spilling of starlight to join your immortal kin. I bless this fantasy and let it boil a little while in your mind, let you taste the sweet tang of infinity before at last your eyes return to this blackened earth.

And as you descend the winding path towards the bay, I give you the laughter of your children, back when they loved you, back when you knew what it was to love. Iphigenia does not scream as the men pull her to the altar. Elektra does not stand in the doorway and proclaim: "Father loves me more than you!" Orestes is not gone to Athens, and when your children look to you, you know exactly what to say to each in turn. You hold each in your arms and whisper: *Mummy is only scary because Mummy wants to teach you how to be strong. But Mummy will also teach you how to be sad, and be afraid, because sometimes you will be sad, and you will be frightened, and that will be all right too.*

These are my gifts to you, Clytemnestra. Walk without fear; I am with you.

Above, the Olympians are gathering: Hermes spins in the clouds, Poseidon sends black-eyed crabs spilling round the edge of the water, Hades breathes soft mist upon the land. Even Artemis has come, slinking barefoot from the forest, huddled on her haunches, arms wrapped around herself as if she would be a stone. I glance about and do not see Athena, and am surprised, but this is no time to wonder at the absence of my stepdaughter.

Clytemnestra descends into the bay, and long before she slows her horse to a stop and dismounts, she has seen the figures who await her by the little boat. The oars are stowed, the sail is down; this vessel is not for the oceans tonight. Instead, caught in the fat firelight of the torches that are held aloft, stand her children.

Orestes has a sword at his hip. Elektra stands a little behind, Pylades by her side. Penelope is behind all three, ashamed, perhaps, her eyes focused on the thin edge of the water where it laps Ithaca's shores.

Clytemnestra sees all this, glances to where the little ring of riders that led her to this place are dismounting, forming a half-circle at her back, a wall she cannot pass. Turns again to her children, shows no reaction to Elektra's frown, ignores Penelope entirely and settles her gaze at last on Orestes.

"Darling boy," she says, holding out her arms to him. He does not move to meet her embrace, shows no reaction, his brows buried like a mine. She lowers her arms, steps towards him anyway. "You look ... well."

No one speaks. Behind the children of Clytemnestra, it occurs to Penelope that perhaps she should have warned Elektra that this was how the conversation might go. When she struck her thrice-damned bargain with the princess, she perhaps should have paused in the working-out of the details – how and when their mother would be presented to the slaughter – to add: "She is very concerned about the dietary habits of her son."

But she did not. Instead, the guilt and the shame of her deeds sticking in her throat, she was a coward, and bid Ourania speak to Elektra instead, another woman carrying the mantle of Penelope's treachery upon her own cousin. Did Penelope ever truly mean to let Clytemnestra go? I look into her heart and the answer is occluded from herself, so tangled in doubt and grief that even I, whose gaze turns blood to rubies, do not know. There is a woman still living inside Penelope full of hope and fear and dreams and despair. But she has been a queen far longer than she was ever anything else, and the queens of Greece are not given many choices that are their own.

Everyone except Penelope is surprised when, to the slow quiet of the sloshing beach, Clytemnestra adds with another half-step towards Orestes: "You have good people you can trust in Mycenae, yes? You didn't leave the gates unguarded? You've had to come all this way – all this way. I know that you never really got on with all your father's pomp, but it is so important people *see* you. It really does pay to make an effort."

Another half-step, and it is such a strange, jerking movement, as if her body might tumble forward over flapping feet, that Elektra draws in a sharp breath, not knowing how to perceive her mother's stumbling. Clytemnestra sees this, and straightens up, smooths down her gown, checks that not a single stray lock of hair has fallen out of place. "Well," she says at last, a little quieter, voice pulled at by the sea. "Well. You look very fine. Very fine. A very fine showing."

Beneath the earth I think I hear the scuttle of talons upon black basalt, the unfolding of leather wings. The Furies are peeking up through cracks in the stone, bleeding eyes peering upwards, watching, waiting. When did a son last kill his mother? What bloody meat these times bring.

It seems that Clytemnestra is out of words. *That's all right,* I breathe, squeezing her hand in mine. *For some silence is weakness; for a great queen it is a weapon. You are most great, most great, my love, most great above them all.*

Orestes opens his mouth and tries to speak. His mouth shapes a sound, his knuckles are white where he holds his blade, and as he sways in the sea breeze Elektra reaches forward and puts a hand upon his arm, as if she might steady him. Clytemnestra's eyes flash towards her daughter, but she does not grace her with speech.

For a moment they stay like this, and I am about to crack,

spit venom in Orestes' ear, when I feel another presence alight upon the cliff above me. Athena has come at last, her helmet on, face obscured save for the fire of her eyes, spear held tight and shield slung across her arm. She is dressed for war, for endings, for the ending of all these things, and at her side, guided by her unseen hand

is Telemachus.

She has brought Telemachus here.

I do not know by what stumbling trickeries or little deceits she has pulled the son of Odysseus from his bed, but she has done it, and he now stands, swathed in darkness that my gaze parts like spider silk, staring down at this scene. I turn to Penelope, but she has not seen her son, and for a moment I am tempted to nudge her, to whisper look up, look up, see! But Athena stands so close to Telemachus's back she might pluck him from his feet and fly, whispers in his ear, and I feel the eyes of Hermes and Poseidon, Hades and Zeus himself upon this moment, upon this beach, and before their gazes I shrink. I shrivel. I diminish. I pull my hand free from Clytemnestra's, a final touch, and at my departure she catches her breath as if seeing the sword at her son's side for the very first time, as if feeling the taste of mortality spill within her. She is briefly just a woman, alone, afraid, and I blink back the golden liquor from my eyes to see her heart crack. *Be strong, my love*, I breathe. *Be a queen.*

My husband grumbles far-off thunder, urging on the end of this night's business. Has he come to witness the death of Agamemnon's killer? Or has he come to see the last great queen of Greece fall by her own son's hand? I am not sure in that moment what enthrals him more – the death of kings or the death of queens. I doubt he has the subtlety to appreciate both.

Elektra opens her mouth as if she would speak, but does not. She has doubtless prepared some speech, some list of her mother's sins, some great exhortation to blood and retribution to spur her brother on. Now, upon this shore, it fails. The words flee from her like breath, and she reaches out to hold her man Pylades' arm, as if she had never before needed the warmth of human flesh upon her icy skin.

Clytemnestra sees this, smiles, nods. She is still greater than her daughter then – that is good. She is glad of it. Her eyes run past Elektra to Penelope, and again, a smile, sadder now, another nod. "Little duck," she breathes. "Learnt to be a queen after all."

Penelope glances away, but she has sworn in this hour that she will give her cousin the gift of her respect, the company of her eyes until the last, so forces herself to look back up, and thinks for a moment she sees another upon the cliff – her son perhaps, and with him a woman all in white – but blinks and sees it not.

Again my husband thunders across the sea, a little closer now, and the waves bounce impatient upon the shore. The gods will not give Clytemnestra the honour of rain; they will not wash away her blood or hide her tears with falling water, they will not rend the heavens in her name.

Orestes' hand is upon his blade, but he still hasn't drawn it.

Clytemnestra's lips twitch in disapproval, in hope, in an expression she hides at last from us all. Elektra leans towards her brother as if she might whisper in his ear, go on, go on, do it, go on, but she does not manage to say it. Instead she detaches herself from Pylades, steps to Orestes' side, puts her hand upon his hand where he holds the hilt of the blade, and together, they draw it. She wraps both her little fingers around his fist and helps him turn the blade towards their mother. She steps forward, and with her body propels him a staggered half-pace towards the waiting queen. Then another. They stop, the tip of the blade a hand's palm from Clytemnestra's chest, and there again they remain.

Clytemnestra does not flinch, nor beg for mercy, nor cry out. There are tears on her face, her breath is fast and thin, but her lips do not shake, her back does not bend, her eyes do not leave those

343

of her son. Instinctively I reach for her again, but feel at once the slap of Zeus's will upon my hand, batting it away. I rage and spit black shadows at the indignity of it, but he will have none, all the eyes of heaven fixed now upon this moment. The Furies cackle beneath the earth, a rattling of claw and bone. Athena holds Telemachus fast, hands on his shoulders, that he might not blink and miss a drop of this ending.

Mercy. I try to say the word, to cry out to my kin. Will someone not stay Orestes' hand? Will someone not bid the Furies flee? Will someone not cry out, mercy, mercy, mercy? There is a boat, there are ways to end this that do not spill a mother's blood, set her free, set her free, mercy! Where is your mercy, you sons of Olympus? Where is your mercy, you murderous fucking bastards?!

Still they stand frozen, the family of Agamemnon. Elektra's whole body shakes as if in her own private earthquake. Orestes' eyes are brimming red, and in that moment I see at last the boy I had not deigned to look on, and realise with a jolt of horror what it is that has struck the son of Agamemnon so dumb. For why, look, and look again, and you may see that despite his blood, despite the destiny wrought upon him, Orestes loves his mother. He loves his mother, and his sister, and his people. He seeks to perform his duty, to be a loving son, a noble king, and one day perhaps to be a generous husband and a father who dotes upon his offspring. He has sworn that he will lift his children to the sun and cry, "Your father loves you! Yes he does, yes he *does* ..." and he will speak honestly to his wife of his fears and his doubts, and confess when he is ignorant, and listen to her desires, and do honour by his people and his kin. He will break the curse of the house of Atreus, he will wash away their sin by deeds of goodness, by deeds of justice and peace, and of all of us who stand upon the shore, he is perhaps the only one for whom "mercy" may be uttered, for whom the word is familiar as the taste of water, the kiss of sun. Mercy, say his eyes, and mercy, beats his heart, and mercy is written in every part of him, and yet he knows – he knows he knows he knows – that for there ever to be peace in Mycenae, his mother must die.

Mercy, cry his eyes, and why does no god hear him? Why are we numb to his prayers? I feel them blasted away in Poseidon's wind before they can even form, drowned out by the hammering of the approaching storm that thunders for blood.

Mercy, the tip of his tongue presses against his teeth, for he knows too that if he does this, he will never have children. If he slays his mother, the blood of Atreus will have proven itself stronger than any kindness, and he would rather that the curse die with him than carry on to blight another generation.

Mercy, beats his heart, and perhaps finally Clytemnestra sees it too. Perhaps she looks into his face and sees not a prince of Greece, not even her son, but the man Orestes wants to be. For she smiles upon him, and reaches up to stroke his cheek, and breathes: "Be brave, my king."

Elektra's fingers tighten around Orestes' own.

She steps forward, pulling the blade with her. Orestes staggers at the motion, and at the last moment Elektra's hands let go, but the speed is already there, unstoppable now, and he gasps as his own weight drives the sword down, through, cutting through his mother's gown and his mother's breast, twisting past bone and deep into flesh. The Furies howl in delight and the earth shudders at their unleashed joy. The seas roll and hiss a kind of celebration, the storm flickers sheet lightning overhead, Hermes spins on feet of gold, Artemis shakes her head in disapproval at the messiness of the kill, and Athena stands with her hand upon Telemachus's back and whispers, *watch. Watch and learn, my boy.* Her eyes are huge and damp, swollen with a kind of ecstasy. Her body shakes with the thrill of it, as Clytemnestra falls.

I catch her as she tumbles, lest her fall be ungraceful, a messy rending of gut and bone. The others do not object. The business of the night is done, and they will not stop Hera crooning over the body of one of her own. I ease her to the ground lightly, put her head in my lap, stroke her brow, whisper sweet sounds without form to her. Orestes staggers back, pulling the blade free, and stares at it as if he has never held a sword before. Elektra catches him quickly by the shoulder, turns him away so he does not have to look upon his mother as she dies. Pylades steadies the young man as he tries to take a step and staggers, nearly falls. Elektra glances back at Clytemnestra, and for a moment I think she will run to her mother now, wrap herself about her neck, spill salt tears upon her brow, and for a moment perhaps Elektra even considers it. But then she turns and slips her arm around Orestes' back, eases the bloodied blade from his fingers, helps him take a step, another, and another, away from fallen Clytemnestra.

My queen, greatest of all the queens in Greece, stares up at the sky, and does not see her brothers in it. Her son and her daughter stumble away, away, not looking back. Poseidon sighs back into the deeps; Zeus releases his thunder and his gaze. Telemachus turns from the cliff, guided by the gentle touch of Athena. Artemis tuts and slips back into the roots of the earth. Hermes spins no more in the busy clouds above. All eyes of gods and men depart, save I.

Another kneels down beside me. Penelope takes Clytemnestra by the hand, and holds it soft, bending over her cousin's fallen form. The women of Ithaca gather round as the waves lap at the hems of their gowns, and together they sing, quiet as dusk, the mourning songs of their island. They do not raise their voices in the wails of the women dressed in ash, nor rend their hair or tear their gowns. Instead they sing the songs of the sailors' wives, who mourn a lover lost to the sea, their final resting place forever unknown.

I dabble my fingers in Clytemnestra's brow, banish her pain, banish her fear. I bid the blood seeping from her grow thin, the breath slow. I will not let her linger long, but as her eyes close, I add my voice to the singing of the women, that she might be carried upon celestial music to her story's end.

CHAPTER 46

>>

The women bear Clytemnestra's body to the town.

Some say they should dishonour it, rip her head from her shoulders and carry it aloft for all to see. Elektra purses her lips and considers the potential benefits and disadvantages of this, but Orestes simply says: "No. She was a queen."

These are the last words anyone will hear Orestes say for a very long while.

So instead they bind her body in a shroud, her face exposed so that all men might see the face of Agamemnon's wife, killer of kings, and the messengers are sent far and wide to inform all of Greece that the work is done. Orestes, son of the king of kings, greatest of all the Greeks, has slain his mother, and will return to his home, a warrior and a man, to be crowned.

A few people attempt celebrations, cries of "The whore is dead!" but are shushed at once by the assembled crowds.

Penelope bestows upon her cousins fresh water and jugs of fermented fish for their safe voyage home.

Orestes prays at the temple of Athena, there being no structure more suitably imposing to kneel before.

Elektra busies herself with organising the ships, the sailors, bids the sail bearing the golden face of her father be unfurled and hung to replace the drab sheets of faded black under which they had sailed to Ithaca. She washes the ashes from her brow, eats a little, smiles once upon Penelope, forgets to smile upon Telemachus except a little late, a little slow, a politeness to now be relearnt. No matter. He does not smile upon her.

"Vengeance," he says.

Elektra looks at Telemachus, and for the first time seems to see the man he might become. He stands in her door, hand upon the sword at his hip, back straight, eyes hard. "Vengeance," he repeats.

She approaches him, slow. Lays two fingers upon his lips. Runs them down the line of his throat. He does not move. Does not blink. Her fingers pause in the soft notch where neck meets chest, the curve of pale silken skin that sinks into the join. She considers pushing them in, driving them into his neck to see what happens. She has wondered about this several times, contemplated summoning a man to her room, a slave, laying him out naked on the sheets and exploring every part of his body to see what is soft, what is hard, where ecstasy arises and which parts of a man are most tender, most easy to cut and sever so that even the strongest, greatest warrior may die.

She considers pressing her lips to his. She hopes that when Telemachus takes her, he will do so violently, hard, like she imagined her father when he first threw her mother to the ground. She hopes he will thrust her against the wall and gasp in ecstasy as he pins her in place, his eyes nowhere near her own as he does his business, skin scarlet and breath panting. This is how she understands what it is for a man to be a hero, for male to possess female, as it must always be.

For a moment she looks at him, and thinks she sees that there. Sees the could-be hero of Greece, the king who knows what it is to take, to command, to be stronger than the rest. That is what a man must be, after all. And Elektra, for all that she will be a queen, cannot imagine ever being without a man.

Then his eyes flicker to her, and for a moment, a terrible, disappointing moment, she sees something else. She sees – just for a moment – the faintest flickering of a frightened boy, who will ask her if she is well, be tender, express concern for her well-being, seek – how nauseating this notion is to her – to understand her pleasure.

And Telemachus?

What does Telemachus see?

As Elektra pulls her fingers from his throat, turns her back to him, he sees something of her father living even in her – even in a woman. He sees the pride of Agamemnon, the power of his house. He does not see any piece of Elektra's mother, dead and wrapped in her bloody shroud, nor of the woman Elektra might one day be. He barely even sees the woman who stands before him now, who turns away, and who simply says: "It is done."

He will not speak again with Elektra for several years to come.

And so, in but a few days' time, all things are settled and the Mycenaean ships depart.

Penelope stands upon the dock, and does not wave. There are no drums or horns to celebrate the departure of Greece's new king and the body of his mother, but people turn out from across the town to see them go, and make a hubbub of noise that could be interpreted any way an eager ear might wish it.

Elektra is the last to board, standing before Penelope on the quay. She thinks of saying thank you, goodbye, well met. None of these words seem satisfactory, so instead she clasps Penelope's hands in her own, as if they might pray together, and bobs her head, the nearest a queen of Mycenae will ever come to a bow, and scurries away before things can get more awkward than they already are.

It seems to the Ithacan queen that this is an unceremoniously swift ending to their affairs.

It seems that there is a great deal that has been left unsaid, and that unsaid things, in her experience, often grow upon a silent tongue into a deluge of words that should have been screamed.

It seems to Penelope implausible, improbable indeed, that this business should be over. If she half closes her eyes, she thinks she hears the sound of talon on stone, the laughter of the deeps, feels the chill touch of winter upon her skin, though the sun still shines strong.

This is not over, she thinks, with a clarity and forcefulness that shocks her, that feels divine in its conviction. Medon stands beside Penelope as the ships set sail.

"Well," he says at last. "That's one terrible death averted."

"Is it? I suppose it is."

"Absolutely. Orestes king in Mycenae, our sworn ally, indebted no less to the people of Ithaca for helping him catch his murderous mother – all very good stuff. Very good stuff indeed. You've practically bought yourself a breather."

"Have I?"

"I know she was your cousin. Clytemnestra. You must be . . . I imagine you have . . . " Medon gestures vaguely in the air, hoping the motion of his waggling fingers will encapsulate the concept of feminine sentiment without having to handle the inconvenience of such sentiment being expressed.

"She was a woman as flawed and intelligent as any man," sighs Penelope. "She always said I quacked like a duck."

Medon has a feeling that there is something more being expressed here than the purely ornithological, but again, he is not sure he wishes to probe too deeply, so instead moves on to more certain territory. "Of course, we are still scheduled for another terrible death. If you recall."

"What? Oh, yes. Andraemon's pirates. Vengeance and blood and all that." She sounds so tired. She sounds as thin as the veil that smothers her face from the view of men.

351

"Are you ... do you have a plan?"

"Hum? Yes, a plan. Yes, I have a plan. I just ... I see no end. I see no end to it. To any of it at all."

Medon is not sure what to make of this. If she were his daughter – his real daughter – he might put an arm around her and say, it'll be all right. Don't you worry. It'll be all right.

Instead he nods his head at nothing much, turns his gaze towards the sea to watch the retreating ships of Orestes and Elektra, clicks his tongue in the roof of his mouth and says: "Well. Looks like rain later!"

Later, it rains.

CHAPTER 47

> >

S ome things, it seems, will never end.

"Melantho, come here, you big-bosomed, gorgeous little . . ."

"More wine! Phiobe, more wine!"

"Where's Leaneira? Haven't seen her for a while . . ."

The feast flows in meat and wine, in fish and green herbs plucked from the summer fields. There is no loom now in the corner, but rather Penelope sits behind the shield of Autonoe and two of her more musical maids, a wall of plucking to separate her from the feast. Andraemon does not look upon her, does not threaten her with his gaze, does not scowl or posture or preen, but keeps quiet in a corner, and does not ask for Leaneira, nor wonder where the maid has gone.

In the courtyard where the boys of Peisenor's militia barely bother to train, Telemachus hefts his shield, thrusts his spear into the air, steps, turns, guts an unseen enemy, drives another through the heart. Kenamon approaches, mumbles: "Your footwork is better," but Telemachus does not speak, does not seem to see the Egyptian, does not make reply, so after a little while the stranger hangs his head, and returns to sit alone upon his hill, gazing weary across the sea.

In the forest above the temple of Artemis, where the clash of sword and the thunk of arrow has torn through the night for near these last two moons, a pause! An interruption as a figure comes late into the circle of firelight, a woven basket in her hands, an irregular splat of stickiness upon its surface. Semele exclaims: "I brought cake!" and all the women, the warrior women of Ithaca, the last line of defence of this last line of Greece, descend upon her with cries of mine, mine, I want that bit!

Priene throws her hands up in the air. "We are still training!" she calls to the turned backs of the women, but Teodora puts a hand upon her shoulder.

"Sometimes," she says, "even soldiers crave honey."

In that moment, it occurs to Priene that she has forgotten to hate the Greeks, and she is briefly very annoyed with herself at this lapse of judgement, until Anaitis approaches, fingers sticky with golden goo, and says meekly: "Would you like some?"

The moon is three days from being full, and the women are afraid. Their fear is caught in the flickering shadows thrown by the torchlight; it breathes in every archer's exhalation, it sighs in the swish of blade cutting air. Yet their skill has grown; lately even the weakest of the archers seems able to shoot the fluttering bird from the branch.

Priene takes the food that is offered her, and will admit, as she bites down, that it is significantly better than fish.

Penelope finds her son in the morning. He is dressed in his battered armour, helmet on, blade out, spinning, spinning round the yard behind Eumaios's farm. She watches a little while, and when he does not slow she blurts: "Telemachus, I . . ." His blade lifts, a thing that could have been a sideways slice that turns now to an uppercut, coming in for the unguarded chin of an unwitting enemy. "I heard you sometimes come here and I . . ."

He drops sudden and fast, a targeted shot to a thigh. If he can angle the slice just right, then as he swings through he will sever an artery, and rich pulsing life will gush forth from his enemy's limb, killing them as sure as a spear through the skull.

"I wanted to talk to you about ... about some of the things that have been happening. About some of the things that will happen. I wanted to explain about ... to apologise for ... I know I have been very distracted recently. More than recently. For some years, I have been ... Well, it's been ..."

An unseen enemy behind him; Telemachus senses the strike and with an effortless grace turns to block, then moves through the block itself, passing his enemy's blade to the side and ramming his shield, shoulder-driven, into his opponent's invisible chest.

"Can we talk?" blurts Penelope. "Can we ... There are things ..."

He stops as sharp as an arrow's point, turns, sword by his side, shield loose in his grasp. He is learning to stand like a soldier, like Priene or Andraemon, utterly loose and easy when he is not in the fit of the fight. His eyes are two narrow points within the framework of his helmet, his lips pink and tight through the little slit of bronze. He stares at her, waits, and when she stumbles for words, shrugs, impatient, waiting again.

"I ... I wondered if we could talk," she stammers. "If we could perhaps ... I didn't mean to disturb you, but it has been so hard to ... Would you eat with me this evening? Away from the suitors. I'll ask Medon to look after them tonight, we could just eat, you and I, it could be ..."

Her words stumble out. She is so good with words usually, but not here. Not with her son. He waits a moment longer, is disappointed in her silence, turns away to resume his imaginary battles. "Not tonight," he replies, gaze already fixed on an invisible enemy dressed in blood. "I'm busy."

"Busy? With what?" she blurts.

He doesn't deign to reply, and she, oh weakness, does not have the spirit to push further.

CHAPTER 48

>>>

And so the moon turns.

But who is this?

It is two nights before full moon, and from the house of Ourania, a woman slips into the dark. She is cloaked and hooded, wrapped tight in a ragged shawl, but she cannot hide her face from me. Leaneira, I cackle, Leaneira – is that you sneaking out of your hidden corner?

She should be in Lefkada by now, or Elis – she should have been banished from Ithaca for her betrayal – and yet no, she is still on the island, and Ourania's watch has grown thin.

She leads two men from the palace of Odysseus into the slumbering dark. She has led them both on this path before, but now that the moon is rising, its silver light bathing the blasted isle in cool contentment, she shows them the way one more time, that they might know it by heart. She leads them along tracks well trod by the people of Ithaca, to paths that are only sometimes known by hunters. She leads them along little wiggles of dust half obscured by the high grey thorns that cling to the island's stones, beneath an overhanging of high rock and down a causeway of carved steps hacked from the land itself, barely wide enough for a child's foot to balance upon. The stars spin as they travel, and the journey is hard and slow, but at last they reach their destination, a hollow mouth of a blackened cave beside a grubby stream where sometimes startled deer take their rest, high above the salty growl of the sea. The cave itself should be unremarkable, save for this – that it is guarded.

There are two soldiers dressed in bronze who keep watch over this place. Both of them are known to Leaneira and at least one of her companions – faithful servants of Penelope, two of the small handful of guards she keeps about her palace. What brings them here, to this blasted place?

The three intruders hunker down into the blackened night to watch, wait, observe.

"Are you sure?" whispers Andraemon into Leaneira's ear at last, when the two guards do not move from their rest.

"Certain," she replies, before pressing her fingers to her lips.

The second man we know too. His name is Minta, and we have seen him before, on the beach at Phenera guiding the Illyrian ships into port; in the cove beneath Laertes' farm the night the pirates came. We have seen him whispering in corners with Andraemon, his trusted servant, his most beloved and loyal friend. He owes his life to Andraemon, and it is a debt he is enjoying repaying.

A light moves within the cave; a torch rising from the deep. The two guards straighten; the three intruders huddle, as with a torch in one hand and a rough woven cloak across her back, Autonoe emerges from the dark. She nods at the men who guard this place, then climbs up by another path away from the stream, confident and sure of her step. The bag on her back is lumpen, weighs her down, clonks sometimes with a metal that is more dense than tin.

The three watchers have seen enough, and together they withdraw into the night.

*

Andraemon does not make love to Leaneira that night.

Oh, he takes her to his bed in the small room in town that Minta has vacated for their lovers' meeting. He pulls the gown from her breast and presses his thumb into her lips, but finds that he is too preoccupied for more. Mind spinning, he tosses and turns, and no efforts on her part will distract or soothe him.

He says: "When I am king, people will know this is a proper island. A proper island that deserves respect. When I am king . . ."

Leaneira says, her hand wrapped tight around the hollow stone he wears about his neck: "Sleep, my love, please, you have to sleep."

He waves her away. "When I am king, the queen will be punished for how she has treated you. She will stay in her room, and eat when she is told to, and speak when she is spoken to, and wear what I bid her, and shave her head."

Leaneira folds her body away from his, knees pulled to her chin, arms clasped tight into her chest, while Andraemon stares into the golden fantasy of the night.

And the moon turns.

She grows fat, the silver moon, and three ships glide across Poseidon's waters towards Ithaca.

I find Artemis pacing the water's edge, bow in hand, a belt of arrows the only adornment upon her body. "Don't you *ever* get dressed?" I splutter.

She stops in her prowling, blinks at me in confusion, stares down at herself, does not appear to understand the question. "I am wearing my quiver," she replies, each word a slow drop, lest I am too old and stupid to be redeemed. I roll my eyes, but turn to follow her gaze across the sea. "They're coming," she blurts, and nearly giggles. "Men in ships, men of war, they're coming!"

Her fingers run up and down the taut timber of her bow, and

she raises it fast, takes aim, sends an imaginary arrow flying, hops delighted on the spot, then turns and paces again. "Why can't they get here faster?" she wails. "I'm so bored!"

Artemis once slew her dearest friend with an arrow shot to the furthest point on the horizon. Her brother tricked her into making the kill, having grown jealous that Artemis might enjoy even the platonic friendship of a man. Since then she has been a little – if only a little – more circumspect about how she aims her bow.

"You could . . . hunt? To keep yourself occupied?" I suggest.

She shakes her head. "A good huntress knows how to wait patiently for her prey."

"You just said you're bored."

"Usually my prey is prowling the land! Majestically slipping from shadow and shade, nostrils flared, sensing the presence of the divine upon the wind! The thrill of the pursuit, the battle of wits, the tricks of perception, strength of body and will – proper waiting! None of this . . . *waiting for a boat*." She hops again foot to foot, before finally blurting, "Humans are terrible! How does anyone get anything done?!"

And at last, beneath the full-bellied moon in a scudding sky, I find Athena upon the hill where sometimes Kenamon sits, gazing across the isle as if she were Zeus himself. I descend beside her, light as starlight, and for a moment feel almost contented by her side. She lets me stay a while, and says: "I will, of course, fight." I glance her way, eyebrow raised. "Discreetly," she sighs at my expression. "I will disguise myself as a mortal and kill no more than my fair share. No one will notice."

"Well, so long as you're killing no more than your fair share . . ."

"It is fit and proper," she intones, "That Odysseus have a kingdom to return to. I . . . questioned your presence when first I caught you skulking round my domain. But I perceive now that there is some utility to your actions. That there is some merit in there being one who watches over queens."

"Stepdaughter, one day you will learn how to give me thanks."

"I doubt that very much, old mother. But from a tactical point of view, I will concede that your disposition for secrecy, manipulation and guile does in this particular case serve my cause too. It is a lesson that I have noted."

"There was a time when we could have been friends," I muse.

"Friends? Friendship will not stop the battle. Friendship does not unite the kingdom. Friendship is as much subject to the great sweep of politics, to the richness of the harvest and the motion of the skies, as any fluttering butterfly. Mortals create friendship to give themselves the illusion of safety and a sense of self-worth. We are gods. We should be above such trivialities."

I sigh, and let my breath spin the wind about us, rippling the grass that brushes our knees, the dancing pollen on the breeze. "Well then. I suppose we're stuck being family."

"What an unpleasant notion," she replies, without rancour or regret.

"Quite."

"A bond that is, if anything, even more irrational than friendship."

"I couldn't agree more."

"And yet somehow we give it sanctity."

"Indeed."

Athena's brow furrows, her helmet hanging loosely in her hand. "I have sometimes wondered upon what it truly is to be wise. Naturally I am the wisest of all the gods, my intellect vastly superior to yours; yet the world turns despite my counsel. Every immortal and mortal may say 'yes, let us be wise' and yet turn their faces away when the best course is set before them. It is . . . troubling. How is it that we can know the most intelligent way to act, yet choose not to do it?" She lapses into silence, and when I do not speak, turns at last to gaze upon me. "Well?" she demands. "What have you to say?"

I shrug. "You're the goddess of wisdom," I reply. "Lightning blast me if I know."

She sighs, but is perhaps at least briefly contented to know that none other has come close to unravelling the mystery her vaulted genius cannot pick apart. Then she says: "Odysseus will return home. It will be soon."

"Are you sure?"

"I have refined my strategy, and worked most carefully upon my father. He is not quite resolved, but the conclusion of the business is inevitable."

"Odysseus's conclusion may be inevitable," I mutter. "Ithaca's is not."

"I am surprised you care so much for Penelope, given that she betrayed your beloved queen."

"She made a decision that queens must," I reply, the words slipping sorrowful between my teeth. "She made the only decision a queen could. Of the three queens of Greece, Helen betrayed her throne by choosing instead to love as a woman might. Clytemnestra, who chose to be a woman, a mother, a lover and a queen, burnt the brightest and could not live long being so many things at once, too beautiful and great for this earth. But Penelope — Penelope is the one who sacrifices all, to be a queen and nothing more. This too, though it wounds me, though I wish it were any other way . . . this too I can love."

Athena nods, once, a sharp jerk of her chin down and up again. Then: "There will be blood. Menelaus will not accept his nephew on Mycenae's throne as easily as perhaps you think. He has had fifty years to learn to resent his brother, and all his brother's kin. Troy only sharpened the whetstone of his appetite."

"Will you oppose him if he seeks to rule in Mycenae?" I ask, but she immediately shakes her head.

"I cannot afford to spread my influence too thin – not while Odysseus is still on Calypso's isle. Besides, Ares has long stood at Menelaus's back, and it is not wise that two gods of war come into such stark opposition. When consequences come for young Orestes – and they shall – you must be prepared."

I scowl, but do not answer. My brother sends word from the underworld – *the Furies, the Furies, I hear their wings*, he cries – but not yet. I cannot deal with that quite yet.

I feel a movement in the corner of my eye, sense the air change, thicken, a drawing-in of power and potency as if the earth were suddenly holding its breath. Athena puts on her helmet, and as she does, her aspect shifts, her shoulders pulling back and arms growing strong as she hefts her spear and cracks her neck side to side. She points with the tip of her weapon across the water, and the air hums and bends away from its touch. I follow it to where three ships glide upon the horizon, Illyrian-plumed and sailed by Greeks, heading beneath the moon's silver light to Ithaca.

CHAPTER 49

≫≫≫

Beneath the full moon, the pirates come.

They already have some sense of where they are going, alerted by messengers who lay in their way at the ports down the eastern coast, but they follow as they have always followed before the torch that Minta lights for them up on the cliff. He waves his fiery brand towards the sea, and after a little while, the ships answer, turning their prows towards the darkened shore.

In the palace of Odysseus, the suitors roar, the wine flows, great dreams and paltry goods are gambled, won and lost; Melantho dodges the grasping hand of a man who reaches for her gown, Autonoe strums upon her lyre, Penelope gazes at nothing at all, as though lost to a dream. Andraemon sits a little apart, watching, the smile he cannot hide playing upon the corners of his lips.

The temple of Artemis is silent, the doors shut up. There will be no libations cast in this sacred place tonight.

The forest that shrouds it is empty, and no fires blaze. The trees are pocked and cracked from a hundred arrow shafts. The ground is rippled from feet moving in a deadly dance. The animals fled in the night from the passage of so many women, but now the air is still, and the little creatures of the dark return, snuffling through the strange smells the humans left behind.

The house of Semele is empty. There is no sign it ever held a guest.

In the ashes of Phenera, the crows have grown bored of their pickings.

And beneath the full moon, the pirates come, sailing fast towards Minta's light, weapons bright in the starlight.

They land without note.

A clump of goats scuttle away as the ships drive up the beachhead.

A seagull bickers at its neighbour who tries to steal the good perch from beneath its feet, beaks snapping and feathers beating dull upon the wind.

There are few farms in this place, few enough settlements, none burning light. Only Minta's torch shines on the beach.

The raiders – warriors who sometime fought in Troy and now know no other way than bloodshed – hop from their ships into the beating foam, climb onto dry land. A few embrace Minta, call him brother, friend. More are unloading rope and boxes, empty, ready to load up their treasure. Thus far, this raid is less of a warriors' feast than greedy merchants come to steal a poor man's wares. Minta gestures towards the darkness of the inland isle. The men form up behind him, a dozen or so remaining to guard the ships, and follow.

The owl hoots as they climb though the brambles and rough darkness of Ithaca.

They try not to strike too many lights, to spread the glow of Minta's torch too far along the thin band of spread-out soldiers, but the path is thick, uneven, and one man thinks he steps on a snake that spits and hisses and darts away; and another thinks he hears the howling of wolves. Thorns catch at bare legs or scrape against shin guards. Rough holes twist the ankles of the men stumbling in the column behind. Sometimes I think I see the shape of Artemis as she darts through shadow beside them, the land rising at her touch. In the moonlight, naked and in her element, she is beautiful. No one runs the hunter's path with such grace; no one dances through the midnight shadows with the same star-kissed ease. Her strength is written in every part of her, irrefutably hers, unsullied by the touch of any creature, immortal or man, an innocence painted in the savagery of her smile.

Then she is gone again, a flicker in the corner of a man's eye, a startling and a shuffling in the line of men – did you see something? Did you hear something move?

No, no, nothing – I heard the owl call and the leaves bend in the trees. That is all.

Hoot hoot, adds Athena, circling overhead. Hoot hoot hoot.

The line of men draws a little tighter, not perhaps noticing what they do. They have slept together, shoulder to shoulder on the rough deck of the sea. They have lain together before the walls of Troy, and some, who were sworn brothers true, have laid sweet kisses upon the scarred flesh of their neighbour warrior, drunk in the blood and salt that rimmed their skin, sworn they will live and die as one, no greater bond than the brotherhood they share. Now they feel a darkness pressing upon them that should be no heavier than the sullen watches spent guarding the ships before Troy, and yet – and yet – there is that in this night that speaks of secrets and hollow discord, of the women's tricks that are *my* domain.

They reach the brambled path down to the cave before the moon has turned too far towards the horizon, and peer down, blades drawn, spears ready. A single torch burns in the mouth of the cave from which Autonoe had been seen to emerge with such heavy goods upon her back – but of the guards who should keep watch, there is no sign. A few glances are exchanged, enquiring as to this absence – but what of it? The guards were only two, and these are the men who slaughtered the so-called militia of Ithaca, the boys in men's garb, without any challenge. The treasure of the island is for their taking; so let them take it.

They approach, cautious and slow. They have survived battles and so know, even when things look easy, that their lives are worth a little safety. Seeing no sign of danger, most go inside, with chests carried between them to load with treasure. Eight remain outside. Among those eight are the first to die.

The arrows that strike them do not all fly direct to target. Though the women have trained with the bow more than any other weapon, this is their first time using them on men, and in the excitement of the moment, many of the hidden huntresses, faces daubed in mud and backs aching from their hunched crouches in the shadow, send their shots wide or high. Three men fall immediately, stuck through with four shafts apiece. One goes down a few moments later, when a slightly slower, more considered shot from Teodora's bow buries itself in his thigh. Of the others, two are merely lucky, throwing themselves into the nearby dark, and two are saved by their armour, which is of sterner stuff than the half-concocted medley of hide and metal the others wear. They run to the cave, calling out brothers, brothers, we are attacked! Alas, though they wear bronze, one has not put his helmet on, so his skull is split in two just before he reaches the mouth of that darkened pit by a shaft released from the darkness of the night.

So it is that three men make it to the mouth of the cave, and one falls bleeding, an arrow through his calf just as he reaches safety, their voices ringing out hollow into the echoing dark.

The others grab their wounded colleague and drag him further inside, feet slipping on wet rock. As they slither and crawl deeper into the bowels of the earth, the women emerge from the night behind them, their bodies dressed in clay and dirt, grass woven through their hair and girdles, leaves into their quivers and mud into their hair. They are not females of any species that

367

the fleeing men might recognise, should they bother to glance back at their attackers, but rather monsters of the fetid night, sprung from the earth itself.

"We're attacked!" roars a man, as they emerge into the main chamber of the cave. "Attacked!"

The rest of the soldiers, pillagers of Ithaca's goods, are assembled here, but there are only men. They look about them in confusion, for were they not promised chests of gold? Piles of stolen treasure, the riches of Odysseus? Leaneira led Minta and Andraemon here not five nights since; they saw Autonoe, trusted maid of Penelope herself, burdened with the weight of hidden treasure as she scurried from this place! Gold and silver, plundered riches that every man in Greece knows are hidden on Penelope's isle – this is where they must be! And yet there are none, only amphorae of sticky oil, piled all around the room and spilling across the floor, glooping against their feet.

The men who fled the arrows slow, pause, lay down their bleeding colleague. Minta steps towards them, and in that moment, perhaps, their leader understands.

Alas, a little late. It is Mirene, daughter of Semele, who throws the burning torch into the cave, as she has a good throwing arm and can put on a surprising turn of speed when it comes to running away. Two men half glimpse her muddy face in the firelight as she hurls the brand, and then it hits, catches the first slick of spilt oil, and after a moment, ignites.

Men scream as the trap closes and the flames billow across the cavern. In the night beyond, Artemis raises her mouth to the sky and howls, howls like the wolf. Athena prowls upon the ridge above, her spear blazing unseen fire. I stand behind the women at the mouth of the cave, bows drawn, waiting, tallying the extinguishing of life as each man staggers through the smoke and pain of the inferno.

Two die quickly, their bodies soaked in fire. The rest turn

and scramble, arm over arm, feet slipping on their colleagues' bending flesh, the way they came. Those who had not seen the archers run ahead, too fast, and four of them die in the pricking of arrows that greet them as they reach the mouth of the cave. The rest recoil as their comrades fall, caught now between arrow and flame. Minta roars: "Form up, form up!" and hopping on burnt legs, choking and spluttering black smoke and sticky saliva, the men draw together, shoulder to shoulder, blades drawn, and on his command, with the heat singeing the flesh from their backs, charge for the mouth of the cave.

"Scatter!" Priene commands, as the men barrel towards the open air, propelling by the sheer strength of their bodies a cloud of smoke before them. The women split apart, scurrying for the night, pulling themselves hand over hand by protruding branch and familiar rock up into the dark. Artemis catches the foot of one who slips, pushes her up again, breathes air into the panting lungs of another who stumbles and nearly falls behind, shrilling with delight, *run, run, my beauties, run, my huntresses, run, my women of the night!*

A few men try to follow, but a new flourish of arrows descends from above, where Priene has reassembled with a dozen or more women, half framed against the moonlight, Athena silent at their backs.

"Stay together!" roars Minta, and the men form up again, framed in black silhouette against the blazing mouth of the cave behind them. "Move together!" he adds, and as one, they start back along the path, a thrusting hedgehog of blade and blood, holding each other up, muttering encouragement in their neighbour's ear. There is, I think briefly, something magnificent in them, a unity of purpose, a courage and a brotherhood that the poets would yearn to see. Athena sees it too, for as the men move, she raises her shield as if she would salute them, and I think I see their eyes flash her way, and grow wide as finally, finally, some glimpse the goddess who stands above them, and perhaps begin to understand. Their comprehension lasts only a moment, for then Athena is gone, vanished into the mortal ranks of women who scatter before the soldiers. They will not know to name her when they come to Hades' gates; their comprehension will be as fleeting as their mortal lives.

The women do not try to fight the men as they climb; they rush into the darkness far from the touch of spear and the baring of teeth. For a little moment perhaps, Minta and his comrades think the worst is done, that with burnt flesh and arrow shaft they will escape this cursed place. But alas, the path that leads back to their ship is long and narrow, and they cannot move down it save in a thin, scuttling line.

That was one of the reasons Priene chose this place for her battle, for as the men stretch out, the arrows come again, and now the path that was clear when they approached is laid with snares of thorn dragged between the stubborn trunks of the trees to catch and pierce their legs as they stumble by in the dark. Figures move in the shadows around them, but never linger long enough for them to say there – there! There is the enemy, or perhaps no – there! There I saw a creature move!

Four more fall to arrows, and a fifth falls behind, bleeding slow, face ashen. His friends, his brothers, his heart's-kin try to carry him, but the load slows them down to a crawl, and from the darkness behind a heavier weapon flies, a javelin, flung from Semele's hand, that passes through the heart of he who would carry his friend to safety, knocking them both to the ground.

Artemis spins in joy, breathes fury into the bows of the women who scuttle, beetle-like, through the dark. Two more men fall; another who grew too slow hears a sound behind him and turns to only briefly see the dagger that cuts his throat. Voices cry out in pain, but Minta tries to keep them together, keep moving, run if you must, get to the boats, go!

370

All pretence of order is left behind as the men make for the sea, arrows snapping around them. By the time they hear the water's edge, they are nauseous from their pounding, and nauseous too from the slither of sickness I twist into their bellies, and looking around, they see that of all who went to Ithaca's cave of treasure, only now eight remain.

Only eight.

They glance down to the beach below and see a dozen figures waiting by the ships, ignorant, it might appear, of the disaster that has befallen them. They scramble down – they will barely have the men to row a single vessel out into the night, the others they will have to abandon, burn perhaps to hide their shame. As they descend to the shore below, figures swathed in forest grey emerge along the cliff behind them, bows ready, javelins at their sides, but they do not attack, do not charge, merely watch and wait for the injured, breathless crew of men to stumble towards the ships.

A man called Timaios is the first to see the bodies of his kin. He was a soldier once of Nestor's troop, a man of honour and dignity; but honour and dignity did not feed his wife and three children while he was at war, and when he returned, they belonged to another man and he could not sell his decency. So he turned pirate, and found in that trade at least another kind of honour, amongst his fellow sailors and friends. Now he sees the first of the men who guarded the ships, face-up in the foam beneath the prow of his vessel, eyes bloody and sightless. He opens his mouth to cry out, but too late. The dozen or so figures who stood guard over the pirates' ships step forward, draw their blades and, in the sullen darkness, cut down those staggering, bloodied warriors who approach. Athena moves amongst them, an easy efficiency to her murder, no more than one thrust if one thrust is all that is needed to pass by a warrior's guard; no block that is not a journey into another attack, no target chosen that will not either inflict the most pain or end the life of her

371

adversary entirely. She has none of Artemis's wild delight, and yet her eyes glisten bright, reflecting crimson.

Priene fights beside her, and though a mortal's weaponry will never match a goddess, she too has nothing about her of flair or performance, no baring of teeth or cries of war. Her purpose is death, nothing more and nothing less; the death of her enemies is the most effective means by which she shall live, and thus all her purposes are fulfilled.

Soon Minta is the last man left alive. The last of all his brothers. The last of the noble warriors, men who gave their all for honour, Greece and Troy. He stares at his fallen comrades, at the breathless, bloody women who now surround him. A lesser man might throw down his blade and close his eyes so that he does not see the end, but Minta is a warrior still. He singles out Priene by her easy movement, the relaxation of the blade within her hand, sees in her an enemy that is perhaps familiar – at last, a familiar enemy – and charges for her.

Priene has not taught the women of Ithaca to fight with honour. With only two moons to train them, there was no time for nuance. Minta dies before he can get within sword's reach of the eastern woman, a hunting knife in his back.

When he falls, Priene steps round his body, kicks his blade away, pulls his head up by the hair, and cuts his throat, just to be safe.

CHAPTER 50

>>>

I n the morning, the people of Ithaca wake to the circling of
crows and the smell of decaying flesh.

The first to find the bodies cries out heaven help us, blessed
Hera, sacred Zeus! I am pleased to hear my name invoked before
the rest in her list of appropriate deities.

She runs to find others, who fetch more, who summon
the great men of the island, who in time remember to
inform Penelope.

So they assemble in the bay before the raiders' ships and behold
the grisly scene.

Arrayed upon the decks of the ships are the corpses of the men
who would have plundered Ithaca. Their eyes have been closed,
but that has not deterred the most enthusiastic of the gulls and
crows that sweep in for the feast. The blood has not been washed
from their faces, and the flies buzz in black delight around their
swelling flesh. Many still have their weapons – double-edged
straight blades of Greece, laid out next to their Illyrian plumes.
Many do not. Lighter javelins, the fastest swords and daggers,
the smallest armour and most useful shoes have all been stripped
from the bodies, vanished into the secret places of the houses
of Ithaca.

One, in full armour, his spear propped up against his body like a walking stick, has been lashed to the prow of the nearest vessel, limbs slipping heavy in strange angles through the ropes that bind him. His throat is an open grin, and his eyes have been left open, rolled up towards the sky. Some think they know him, murmur his name. Is that not Minta, the friend of one of the suitors? Yes, yes, Minta it is — a friend of Andraemon. What does he do here?

Of the great men of Ithaca who have assembled, it is Peisenor who approaches the corpse. The old man has a glint in the corner of his eye, as if the stench of blood has roused him from his month-long stupor, and now he reaches up to a certain item slung round Minta's lacerated neck, and with a little tug, pulls it free.

The others gather in, Aegyptius and Medon bending down to see it. Penelope stands far off, lest the smell of blood and sight of gore disturb her ladylike delicacies; but her eyes are locked on the huddle of men.

It is a stone, little bigger than a man's thumb, with a hole bored into the top through which a leather thong might be strung.

This little stone, murmurs one, this stone — I have seen it before. A strange trinket.

It is a stone from the ruins of Troy, Medon replies, cold as winter's dark. It is the same token that Andraemon wears about his neck.

As the crows pick at the bodies laid out across the ships, the women of Ithaca gather on the edge of the shore, and no songs are sung.

It is past midday by the time the wise men of Ithaca return in a little procession to the palace of Odysseus. The suitors are gathered, summoned by word of another massacre, another battle, waiting to hear who was taken, what place burnt. But then a different word has come, a strange whisper on the wind – the attackers are slaughtered, their bodies laid out upon the ships, it is a miracle, a terrible, profane miracle.

Telemachus strides down to meet the approaching convoy of dignitaries and their somewhat confused accomplices. "What happened?" he barks. "Who is slain?"

"The pirates are dead," Aegyptius replies, as one in a daze. "They are all dead."

"How? How did they die?"

Aegyptius simply shakes his head, for he has no answer. Telemachus turns his gaze to Peisenor, who also shakes his head. Medon pushes past, no time now for questions of the sacred or the sacrilegious.

Behind the men comes the body of Minta. It is hauled on the back of a donkey-dragged cart, wrapped crudely in a strip of bloody sail. They set it down in the courtyard before the great hall of Odysseus, and slowly the suitors gather, and their fathers too, and all who can fit into this place, until at last every soul who can is pressed in from wall to gate to witness this matter. Penelope stands politely in a knot of her maids, veil upon her face, head bowed, hands clasped. Her child stands on the opposite side of the crowd, a sword upon his hip, eyes fixed in the glower of the desert sun.

Medon pulls back the limp tangle of cloth that covers Minta's face, and is rewarded with a little gasp and a slight chittering amongst the suitors who behold it. "The raiders are dead," he barks, enjoying for once an audience that seems willing to hear him. "This man was found amongst them. Many of you know him. He is sworn blood-brother to Andraemon."

Medon has taken his moment to seek Andraemon out of the crowd before he speaks, so he can do a nice impressive flourish of his arm towards the suitor. I am tempted to clap, but it might be a little tasteless, a little too soon.

Andraemon steps forward from the crowd. I think he is about to bluster. To throw defiance, spit in the faces of all around him, mock Medon's accusation. Instead he kneels. He kneels beside Minta and holds his bloody face in his hands, thoughtless of his gaping throat. He whispers words in the dead man's ears, words that only Hades can hear, and cradles him tight a moment longer, before rising, blood on his hands, on his face.

Then he speaks. "My brother is dead," he snaps. "I demand vengeance," and his eyes blaze towards Penelope. Yet she is meek. She is humble. Clearly there are events afoot far beyond her wits to comprehend.

"Your friend was found amongst the bodies of pirates, slain by the gods themselves," Medon retorts.

"If he was found with pirates, it is because he defended *you*! You sheep of Ithaca, he was a warrior who fought!"

"No one who saw the body, the manner of it, could doubt that he was anything other than a villain, allied to these plunderers," barks Medon. "Or would you question the wits of all these wise servants of Odysseus?" He gestures expansively to the councillors of Ithaca, enjoying the performance, his other hand clutched tight against his chest.

Andraemon hesitates, glances down again to the body of Minta, stinking on the stony ground. His heart breathes an apology – I had not known he had such a thing within him – but he still has work to do. Minta would understand. "If this man was a friend to the enemies of Ithaca, then he was a traitor to me."

"A traitor who wore your precious mark?" Medon opens his fist, and there is the little stone on its leather knot, bloody, grasped within it. Instinctively Andraemon's hand moves towards his neck, but there is nothing there. Where was he last when he knew he wore this token? When did he last feel its comforting weight? Why, as he was lying beside Leaneira in sticky sheets, when her hand closed round the totem on his chest and she breathed: "Sleep, my love. Sleep."

Now – only now – does Andraemon begin to understand.

Leaneira stands in the crowd, Ourania at her side.

Why was she not banished from Ithaca?

Why did she still share his bed?

The old woman should have kept watch on her treacherous prisoner, and yet, and yet, here Leaneira stands, watching Andraemon from the crowd, without fear, without flinching. She lost any sense of where her body was, how it felt to wear it, a long time ago. But her eyes, and the things she sees with them – they are still her own.

Death to all the Greeks.

Once, on the battlefield, Andraemon fought for what he considered the best part of an hour with a soldier of Troy. The actual battle was approximately ninety seconds, but by the standards of a martial encounter, that is very long indeed. When Andraemon finally saw his chance, and drove his blade home, his opponent saw it too, saw the flash of weakness in his own armour a moment before Andraemon took the chance presented, and smiled. He was not happy to die. He was not impressed or pleased by Andraemon's cunning.

Death to all the Greeks.

That Trojan as he died perhaps recognised a thing that had been coming a long, long time, and acknowledged it through his fury as a father might greet the recalcitrant child that from years of being lost finally returns home.

So smiles Andraemon now upon Leaneira, and at last he understands.

He understands.

She does not smile back. What little power she has, she has taken. It tastes nothing like freedom.

"You painted cowards," Andraemon snaps, turning, turning,

catching with his arm all those assembled there. "You would-be petty kings. You fishmongers. You sailor's rats."

"Andraemon, you have broken every sacred code ... "

"You think you will be kings? *She* will slaughter you! The meat she feeds you will be human flesh, she will have you eat each other, just like the children of Atreus, just like Clytemnestra! You will never be safe from her. You will never live to be kings in Ithaca."

"... every sacred rule of hospitality, you have assaulted our lands, you have violated our trust, you have ... "

The blade Andraemon draws is small, a thing for slicing meat, not killing men. But it will serve to kill a woman, and for a moment he is torn as to which woman he will kill in what little time he has left. His eyes turn to Leaneira again, but his arm reaches out for Penelope, and as if his feet were drawn by the will of Eris herself, he turns on the queen and charges for her.

Eos steps forward.

She does not make any large moves, or scream, or in any way show a sign of fear. Nor does she put herself directly in Andraemon's path, or offer up her chest in the place of her mistress. Instead she stands a little to the side, so that Andraemon might barge her with his shoulder as he attacks, and indeed, he barely notices her presence, so set is he upon his murderous intent.

He also barely notices the knife go into his ribs as he slams past her, but he does notice it come out, for the weight of his momentum against the passage of the blade slows and turns him, and he spins a little with the motion of it, his knife hand flapping wild. Someone grabs it as he staggers, another knocking the knees out from beneath him. Eos steps away, the blade she wielded already vanished into her gown, a streak of crimson across her robes.

"He ran onto his knife," she explains, and when this doesn't seem to produce an apt response, Penelope puts one hand to her brow, gives a profound and ringing sigh of womanly desperation, and helpfully collapses in a hysterical pile to the floor.

CHAPTER 51

>>>

L ate summer turns to early autumn in Ithaca.
        The copper leaves crinkle and crack beneath the crooked
trees, the sunset turning burnished gold, the scarlet of fresh blood
and the cracked grey of old leather. The hot thunderstorms of
summer break to rolling wet blasts and the women trample olives
barefooted in the greasy vats.

This change of season might, you think, bring about a change
in the beating hearts of men, but no. They have grown used
to the departure of Demeter's daughter, and so in the hall of
Odysseus ...

"Autonoe! Do you call that music? Give us a good bawdy song!"

"I'm not sure, Antinous, that seems like a rather big wager ..."

"Come on, Eurymachus, don't be such a woman's child!"

"Kenamon, sit with me. You have been too long slouching
in your corner."

"I am not good company, Amphinomous."

"You have to be better company than this sorry lot — come,
come, sit with me! Tell me stories of your homeland."

In the kitchens:

"You call that cooking? I would be ashamed to call
that cooking!"

"But you are not the cook, are you, Euracleia?"

"Disgrace, the lot of you! Absolute disgrace!"

In the house of Polybus, father of Eurymachus:

"With Andraemon dead and gone there is an opportunity – a good opportunity – to advance Eurymachus's cause ... "

In the house of Eupheithes, father of Antinous:

"Eurymachus will be trying to find an opening now, but we'll catch him before he can make his play, Antinous will yet be king ... "

In the farm of Laertes, who once sailed upon the *Argo* and will now forever be remembered as merely the father of Odysseus, greatest of Ithaca's missing kings:

"Don't you know how to dig a latrine? Do I have to do everything myself? Ye gods!"

In the council of the wise men of Ithaca:

"But it's absurd!"

"But useful. No one is going to raid our shores for quite some time now."

"But *absurd*! Andraemon's men weren't just ... smitten by some Olympian power! They were killed by men! How are you so calm at this? How are you not terrified by the idea of unseen armed men upon Ithaca?"

"Perhaps they were killed by Odysseus? Perhaps he has returned and is moving secretly amongst us?"

"Not now, Telemachus!"

And so the moon rises and the moon sets, and though things are much the same, some things are most definitely different.

In the temple of Artemis, Anaitis sprinkles wine upon the altar and is, all things considered, feeling very pleased with herself. The attendance at her shrine and the gifts being bestowed upon it are of a finer and more luxurious quality than any the huntress of these isles has received before.

"I heard that Artemis herself slew the pirates," whispers one supplicant, copper bangle upon her wrist. "I heard that the western islands stand under her dread protection!"

Anaitis considers this. On the one hand, it is mildly disrespectful to the midnight shadows who still dart through firelight in the forest above her temple, to the women with sharpened forks and skinning knives at their hips, to give full credit to a goddess alone. On the other hand, it's not like credit can go anywhere else, and Artemis *is* a great and powerful protector, so all things considered . . .

"The huntress loves those who love her," she exclaims brightly, receiving the proffered metal and putting it into the rather full basket at her feet. "The lady's blessing be upon you!"

In the forests above the temple, Priene says: "That was one battle. What we need now is a broader defensive strategy. We need pockets of resistance in Hyrie, in Zakynthos, in Kephalonia, women who can hold the line until word has reached the other islands that reinforcements are required. We must think about supply lines and . . ."

Teodora, the last living daughter of Phenera, says: "So you're staying?"

Priene freezes. "What?"

"Given that you hate the Greeks . . ."

"I do. I absolutely hate the Greeks."

"But you *are* staying? On Ithaca?"

Priene considers this a moment, battling with questions of herself that she has never dared ask, thoughts and sentiments she has never permitted herself to feel. She looks around at her women, waiting expectantly beneath the wooded grove. Semele leans upon an axe for chopping wood; Teodora stands arms folded, bow by her side. There are nearly ninety of them now, waiting in silence upon her word. She has a terrible feeling that these women expect her to express ... notions that are profoundly uncomfortable to her. That there is a word – *home*, perhaps, or maybe even *family* – that they are waiting for their leader, their captain, to say.

Then a thought strikes her that brightens all other things and lets her banish away, for now, any petty, piddling questions of who she is, where she belongs, or what her purpose is in life. "Menelaus is clearly the greatest threat to the western isles!" she exclaims. "We must think how best to slaughter him!"

A little knocking on the door in the dead of night.

Penelope calls out to her son – Telemachus? Telemachus, are you there?

He is, but he does not answer.

Telemachus. Talk to me.

Talk to me.

Just ...

... talk to me. I am your mother! I am ... please, Telemachus. I know that we haven't spoken properly, that things have happened, Andraemon, the raiders, your ... but please. Talk to me. I'll tell you everything you want to know. Telemachus. Telemachus!

She pounds her fist upon the door, but he has pressed a chest against it so it will not budge. Now he sits upon it as she rattles at his back, and sharpens his sword, and barely hears her speak, if he ever heard her at all. There are things that are happening on Ithaca – things he does not understand. His enemy is dead, and he did not kill him. The pirates who threatened his shore are dead, and he did not slay them. He does not know quite how they died, but he knows this: that no prince ever became a hero-king by listening to his mother.

*

Later, by the cool stream that flows behind the palace, Leaneira washes her feet, washes her hands, washes her face, washes every part of her flesh that may be blessed, until at last Penelope sits behind her, and the woman grows still.

Finally Penelope says: "Thank you. The things you did ... the part you played in this. I know I asked a great deal, and you gave ... much. You have given much. Whatever place you desire in this house is yours, if you wish to stay."

Leaneira stares into the broken reflection of her face in the running water, and says at last: "And if I wish to be free?"

"Where would you go?"

She closes her eyes, and has no answer. "I hate." She feels she should specify precisely what it is that she hates, but finds that it would take too long, that the shorter list would be merely of those rare things she does not despise. So instead she tries: "Andraemon was never going to set me free."

"No. But he gave you hope. That is ... not insignificant."

"Hope is for fools and children."

"And yet you still live, Leaneira. We live."

Leaneira shrugs, throws cool water down her back, sticking to the fabric of her gown. Penelope sits a little while longer beside her, as the day turns towards night.

In the halls of Mycenae, Orestes tries not to knock the diadem that sits upon his brow. It is a little too big, isn't quite balanced right, but he has to at least get through this whole absurd ceremony without anyone making a fuss. His uncle, Menelaus, has come all the way from Sparta, with Helen and their kin. His presence fills the hall like flame. The last standing hero of Troy, brother of slaughtered Agamemnon, he is not taller than any other man, nor are his shoulders broader than an ox, and yet he need but nod once, chin to chest, or turn his head a little to the side, or draw in his lips as if he might be displeased with a thing he is too polite to name, and every man and woman, warrior and slave in the hall cowers.

He says he is happy with his kingdom in Sparta. Me and the missus, together at last, he proclaims, and slaps Helen on the thigh. Nothing like staying home and watching the kids grow up, is there? Happy to leave it to you young things. Happy to let the next generation have its chance. Of course I'll always be here if you need me, don't you worry about that. Uncle Menelaus is always here for you.

Elektra stands beside her brother, skin painted in lead, but when he closes his eyes all he can see is his mother's frown, and all he can hear are the wings of the bats and the cackling of sharp-toothed women.

I look along the lines of assembled kings and great men of Greece and see the gods amongst them too: Hermes picking at the finger-food, Ares scowling with his back to the wall, Athena stiff as her spear, even Hestia half ossified with boredom in a corner. But we all hear them when their claws scratch upon the palace doors; we all smell their rotten breath upon the air. The Furies, jaws of the shark and eyes of blood. I shudder and let myself fade away, a discreet departure from the sweating hall. Hermes is already gone, startled into flight at the first squeak of the bat. Ares postures a moment more, but even he will not stand between the Furies and their prey.

After all, Orestes has killed his mother.

Menelaus grins as Orestes adjusts the heavy diadem on his head, and that grin follows me into the night.

On Ogygia, Calypso sits beside Odysseus on his favourite rock, and for a while they are companionable in the beating of the sea below. Then all of a sudden, he seizes her by the neck, presses his lips against hers, his tongue into her mouth as if he would break her apart, rolling her down beneath his weight, eyes closed.

In the sacred place of the hidden wood, Artemis says: "What? Oh yes, killing men. That was nice. Anyway, doing other things now, other things to do, you know."

I do my best not to stare down at the reclined form of my stepdaughter as her women very much comb her hair, and for a brief moment envy her capacity to live neither in tomorrow nor yesterday, but simply here, in this moonlit grove.

At last, reluctant, I seek Athena. There are things we should discuss discreetly, now that the moon has spun across the sky.

She is not on Olympus.

Nor is she peeping down at Calypso's bed, ear cocked to the moans that rise from that scented place.

I peer down at her sacred shrines, ride the edge of her most earnest prayers, and finding her not, descend to Ithaca.

She is not hooting in some blasted tree, nor slithering into the dreams of the palace. She is not inhaling the sweet imprecations of those who bow before her altar, nor prowling some foam-washed shore. I narrow my godly vision, rip through the souls of women and men, my passage bringing to their lips the taste of metal and the memory of foul deeds, until at last, finally, I behold her, wrapped in a thick disguise of mortal rags, before a vessel that waits in harbour upon the turning of the tide.

The ship is not one I have seen before, with a sail of faded grey, touched, I suspect, by a blessed hand. It is fully stocked with fresh water and dry meat, and at the oars sit those few of the friends Telemachus has yet living, and a few more besides from Peisenor's militia who have, for some reason that may not be entirely their own, chosen now a sojourn on the sea. The captain is a man touched by Poseidon, white in his hair and salt in his skin, a trusty hand who perhaps does not know what he has gotten himself into, and standing upon the dock in earnest talk with the disguised figure of Athena is Telemachus.

He stands in his armour and cloak, a bag at his feet, a sword on his belt. He nods and listens carefully to whatever Athena says, then hefts his belongings and starts to march down the quay towards the boat.

I swoop down at once, opening my mouth to cry out: Telemachus, what in the name of all the gods do you think you're doing, you idiot boy, get back here right now or I'll . . .

But Athena's gaze flashes up and nearly knocks the breath from me, spins me like a sparrow in the storm. *He is mine*, she snarls, in the voice of the turning tide. *He is mine.*

I stagger back, struggling briefly to control my fall, blazing indignation. Telemachus is setting foot on the boat, Athena smiling and waving at him from her filthy mortal guise, bidding him on, on, go on! I spit and curse for a moment, impotent in the skies above, then dart towards the palace, soar through Penelope's open window, scratch at her face and shriek, "WAKE UP RIGHT NOW YOU SLEEPING IDIOT!" Darkness flutters and tears at my fury; she starts awake with a shudder and a gasp of breath, hand flying to the knife beside her bed, looks through me like a nightmare, then catches herself, heaves in air, slows the pounding of her heart. She goes to the window to draw down the cold calm of night, and as she does, I bid her eyes raise and see the ship in the harbour below, the sail unfurling to catch the wind. She frowns, as surprised by its presence as any sensible queen should be, but turns away from it, skin prickling now in the midnight air.

Tonight Autonoe sleeps outside Penelope's door, but the queen does not wake her as she eases her way into the silent palace. She will walk until her nerves are steady again, until she feels the sweet gift of slumber drag down her eyelids. She will sit in the little yard where sometimes the maids hang out their tunics to dry, and smell the dampness of their labours upon the air, and catch her breath and be at peace. A little peace – that is all she wants. Just a little peace.

She does not find it. Instead, she hears a sob, an old woman's cry, amplified by my fingertips to scrabble across the wall. It comes from the direction of Anticlea's room, the room that so recently Elektra kept for her own. Penelope hesitates, surprised, and I nudge her towards it, push her in the small of the back, so the first few steps she takes are hardly her own. Then her natural curiosity kicks in, and following the sound, she eases back the crooked door to see an old woman huddled by a low burning lamp.

"Euracleia?" she asks.

The nursemaid's head spins round, a little too fast – she'll have cramp in the morning. She scrambles to rise, clutching the flame near her as if it were her only friend. "I told him not to!" she whimpers. "I begged him not to do it!"

"Told who? Begged who?"

The dull realisation dawns behind the dumb woman's eyes that she may already have said too much, but there is no getting away from it now. Penelope strides towards her, both hands snapping hard around the nursemaid's shoulders. "Told who?" she snarls.

"Telemachus," Euracleia whimpers. "I told him not to do it."

"Where is he? Where is Telemachus?"

The answer comes in little dribs and drabs, a stumbling stutter that finally, with a shake of her shoulders, spurts out into: "The docks! He's going to find his father!"

This is not Penelope's heart breaking.

She has woven so much rope around her heart, tied it and tied it and tied it shut, that though it shatters, yet it cannot fall apart. Not yet. This is not the sound of her world falling apart, for every morning she stands upon Ithaca's soil and says to herself, I am here, and I will do what is done. The world does not tumble away from you when you have spent so much time learning to walk upon it.

Rather, this is the sound of bare feet running on dirt, of "Let me by!" as she tears through the gates still in her nightgown, plain tunic and no veil, of panting breath, of wind in her ears, hair falling loose about her skull, of blazing fire upon her mind, of a heart

of such a heart

that cracks and cracks and cracks, and yet, like an ancient heirloom peeled together with wet clay, she will not let it break though it be already torn out of all order.

This is the sound of her running onto the dock, nearly out of all air, out of all sense, of her howling: "Telemachus!" while at her back, late and sleepy and confused, stagger her maids and her guards, wondering just what madness has overcome their queen.

"Telemachus!" she cries, but his ship is already sailing out the harbour mouth, the oars beating steady and slow against the waves, and he stands at the prow and does not hear her. Athena watches from the skies above, and shakes her head, and turns away.

"Telemachus!" screams Penelope, and at this cry at last the strength falls from her limbs and she sinks to the ground, and finally, wrapped in the arms of her maids, as her son sails into the night, Penelope, wife of Odysseus, queen of Ithaca, weeps.

I turn my gaze to Olympus, look to my brothers and sisters, wonder which of them will answer this wretched woman's cry, for in this moment all illusions are broken, all charms shattered. She lied, she lied all this time — Penelope was a mother after all, was a woman with a beating heart, see how she tricked you all into thinking she was just a queen? But the gods are slumbering, or drunk, or dallying elsewhere. Athena flies with eagle wings above the departing shadow of Telemachus; Artemis bathes in moonlight. My husband sleeps in a drunken stupor, arms draped across the backside of some wretched nymph. Ares peeks round doors at forbidden Aphrodite oiling her skin, Apollo strums his lyre, Poseidon beats fruitless against Ogygia's shores. Only Hades rouses himself a little at Penelope's cry, creaks one eye open to see what mortal despair disturbs him, but finding it of little note, drifts back to darkness again.

Yet her voice is not quite unnoticed amongst the beings immortal and divine that soar above the earth.

Three hags of ancient fire, who even now circle sleeping Orestes' bed, hear her shriek upon the wind, writhe in ecstasy at her impotence and rage, chuckle at her despair and lick their lips to taste the salt of her tears carried upon their tongues.

Telemachus! giggles one.

And *Telemachus!* mimics another.

My sweet son, whispers a third, licking blood from beneath her taloned toes. *We come, we come.*

Then they see me.

Then they look up.

Even I, queen of the gods, will not challenge them, for they are nearly as old as the Fates themselves, their will set in fire upon the turning earth.

The Furies spread their wings across the sea and across the isles; they spin their tapestries in the blood of mothers and the cries of maids, they drink deep of heart broken and brother slain, they laugh, they sing, they spit boiling rain. Oh wonderful freedom, they cry! Released at last by a mother's blood spilt upon the earth! Summoned forth by vengeance and madness and cruel despair! The seas will be crimson with the gore of women and heroes alike before they are done.

In Mycenae, Orestes cries out in sudden fear from his

slumbers, clutching at the golden place where the diadem should bind his head.

In Sparta, Menelaus slumbers with crimson wine upon his lips and something redder still about his tongue, swagged in the stolen robes of a dead Trojan king.

Elektra thinks she hears her mother singing through the shadowed halls of the palace, a song from another time that billows away to dust when she tries to reach it. Odysseus gazes across the silver-kissed seas; Clytemnestra runs her fingers through the forgetful waters of the rivers of the damned.

And on Ithaca, Penelope weeps upon the edge of the sea, hands raised after the ship on which her son now sails away. Telemachus stands at the prow of his vessel, eyes set on a far-off horizon, while high above, clad in midnight and shadow, the Furies come.